D0046477

Edited by

Robert Silverberg

ARBOR HOUSE
NEW YORK

S

THE NEBULA ...

 Published in the United States of America by Arbor House Publishing Company and in Canada by Fitzhenry & Whiteside, Ltd.

ISBN: 0-87795-521-2

Manufactured in the United States of America
10 9 8 7 6 5 4 3 2 1

This book is printed on acid free paper. The paper in this book meets the guidelines for permanence and durability of the Committee on Production Guidelines for Book Longevity of the Council on Library Resources.

Acknowledgments

"Souls," by Joanna Russ. Copyright ©1981 by Mercury Press, Inc. Reprinted by permission of the author.

"No Enemy But Time," (chapter one), by Michael Bishop. Copyright ©1982 by Michael Bishop. Reprinted by permission of Timescape Books, a Pocket Book division of Simon & Schuster, Inc.

"The Pope of the Chimps," by Robert Silverberg. Copyright ©1982 by Agberg, Ltd. Reprinted by permission of Agberg, Ltd.

"Burning Chrome," by William Gibson. Copyright ©1982 by Omni Publications International, Ltd. Reprinted by permission of the author.

"Fire Watch," by Connie Willis. Copyright ©1982 by Davis Publications, Inc. Reprinted by permission of the author.

"Corridors," by Barry N. Malzberg. Copyright ©1982 by Barry N. Malzberg. Reprinted by permission of the author.

"Another Orphan," by John Kessler. Copyright ©1982 by Mercury Press, Inc.

"A Letter from the Clearys," by Connie Willis. Copyright © 1982 by Davis Publications, Inc. Reprinted by permission of the author.

"Swarm," by Bruce Sterling. Copyright ©1982 by Mercury Press, Inc. Reprinted by permission of the author.

Contents

Introduction

THE Science Fiction Writers of America (SFWA)—the first organization of professional science fiction writers that lasted much longer than the cocktail party at which it was proposed—was founded in 1965 at the instigation of the well-known editor and writer Damon Knight, then of Milford, Pennsylvania. A small circle of other writers provided the initial support—such people as Lloyd Biggle of Michigan, who was the first secretary-treasurer, James Blish, Harlan Ellison, Terry Carr, Alan E. Nourse and—yes, Robert Silverberg. But primarily it was a one-man show at the beginning: Damon drew up the bylaws, Damon solicited memberships, Damon published the organization's magazine, Damon harassed publishers who were treating writers unfairly, and so on and so on. Gradually he drew others into more active participation—myself included. I well remember the night in Milford when he talked me into taking over for him as SFWA's second president, and I also remember well my relief at handing the job on in 1968 to my successor, Alan Nourse.

One of SFWA's earliest projects was the inauguration of an awards program. Not that the science fiction world really *needed* a new set of awards, because the Hugos—for better or for worse—had been instituted in 1953 and had since 1955 been an annual event. But SFWA had no income (the dues, originally, were $3 a year, I think) and Secretary-Treasurer Biggle proposed raising money by establishing some sort of annual SFWA anthology, a slice of the earnings of which the organization could keep. That suggestion led inevitably to the notion of filling the anthology by polling the membership on the year's best science fiction stories—the theory being that the Hugo winners are chosen by vote of the sf readership, while the Nebulas, as the new awards were dubbed, would represent the considered choice of *professionals*. It turned out to be an interesting experiment: over the years there have been some striking differences between the stories that have won Hugos and those that have won Nebulas in the same year, although there has also been, of course, considerable overlap between the two awards.

The first Nebulas were designed by Judith Ann Lawrence, then James Blish's wife, from a sketch by Kate Wilhelm (Mrs. Damon Knight). With some modifications they are essentially the same today: a spiral nebula made of metallic glitter and a specimen of rock crystal, both embedded in a block of clear Lucite. They are strikingly handsome objects, and quite expensive to produce—costing rather more, in fact, than the organization has ever been able to recover out of its shares of the proceeds of the annual anthology.

On March 11, 1966, the initial Nebula awards ceremony was held simultaneously at the Overseas Press Club in New York and at a restaurant in Los Angeles called McHenry's Tail O'the Cock. Of the first four award winners, Frank Herbert and Harlan Ellison attended the Los Angeles ceremony, Roger Zelazny and Brian Aldiss (who made the trip from England for the occasion) were present in New York. The following year, President Knight proposed holding the event in a small restaurant in Matamoras, Pennsylvania, which happened to be just up the road from his home. This led to the railroading through of a hasty bylaw requiring the organization to hold its awards ceremony in New York City, and that has been the site of most of them since, although for the past decade it has been held in alternate years in California—generally San Francisco or Los Angeles—because such a preponderance of science fiction writers live on the West Coast.

The Nebula winners over the years have included just about every important practitioner of science fiction, though there are a few conspicuous and startling omissions, chiefly writers whose ill luck it was to do most of their best work before the Nebulas were established—Bradbury and Heinlein, for example—or to have run into extraordinary competition in the years of their best work. There have also been some occasions when the award has gone to a virtually unknown writer—this year being a good example of that, since such people as Connie Willis and John Kessel are not yet household names in the science fiction world, and even Michael Bishop, widely respected though he is, does not have at this moment the sort of name-recognition value of, say, Isaac Asimov, Arthur C. Clarke, Ursula K. Le Guin or Frank Herbert. And on a few occasions—the law of averages being what it is—certain of the winning stories have, to experienced observers, seemed to be absolutely off-the-wall choices, explicable only by stochastic analysis. By and large, though, the record is a commendable one, as a glance at the list of previous winners at the end of this volume indicates.

The Nebula awards anthologies have had four publishers over the years—shifting for various reasons from Doubleday, the original one, to Harper & Row, then to Holt, Rinehart & Winston, and now, beginning with this year's volume, number eighteen, to Arbor House. Traditionally there are two criteria for choosing the editor of each year's volume: he or she should have worked on SFWA's behalf over the years, and should also be a writer of some prominence and accomplishment. Past editors have included such folk as Poul Anderson, Frank Herbert, Isaac Asimov, Jerry Pournelle, Ursula K. Le Guin, Samuel R. Delany, Frederik Pohl, Clifford D. Simak and founding fathers Knight and Biggle. Now it is my turn, since I am a past president and have held various other offices over the years. I think it is a pleasant coincidence that I should have been asked to edit the first volume in the Arbor House series of Nebula anthologies, since Arbor House is my very own well-cherished publisher.

I am involved in a second coincidence of this year's volume. The stories included in a Nebula anthology are, of course, the winners in the three short-fiction categories—short story, novelette, novella—plus an extract from the award-winning novel and a selection of outstanding runners-up; it happened this year that a story of my own was among the runners-up. Mindful of the propriety of the situation—no previous editor, so far as I have been able to determine, has been faced having to choose whether or not to publish one of his own stories—I asked various of the Secret Masters of SFWA what they thought I ought to do about the conflict of interest. When I co-edited a book called *The Arbor House Treasury of Science Fiction Masterpieces* and one of my own stories turned up on the contents page, I could at least turn to the fact that it was my co-editor's doing, and he in fact signed his initials to the introductory note for that story. But I have no co-editors to hide behind here, and it worried me. The Secret Masters gave heartening counsel. "Heck," said they with one accord, "go ahead and run the story. It's a good one, isn't it?" Faced with such unanimity of opinion, I yielded as gracefully as possible. In a field whose members are famed for their modesty and humility (cf. Messrs. Asimov, Clarke, Ellison) I have been studying at the feet of masters for decades: and I have included my "The Pope of the Chimps" in the book. Not an apology, just an explanation.

—Robert Silverberg

Souls

by Joanna Russ

Joanna Russ has been in the forefront of modern American science fiction since the late 1960s, when she established a firm following with the vigorously feminist sword-and-sorcery novel Picnic on Paradise *and the haunting and astonishingly vivid novel of extrasensory powers* And Chaos Died. *Her short story, "When It Changed," was a Nebula winner for 1972.*

The brilliant novella reprinted here, which may at first seem to be historical fiction but which gradually reveals its emphatic science fiction content, first appeared in The Magazine of Fantasy and Science Fiction.

Deprived of other Banquet
I entertained myself—
—Emily Dickinson

THIS is the tale of the Abbess Radegunde and what happened when the Norsemen came. I tell it not as it was told to me but as I saw it, for I was a child then and the Abbess had made a pet and errand boy of me, although the stern old Wardress, Cunigunt, who had outlived the previous Abbess, said I was more in the Abbey than out of it and a scandal. But the Abbess would only say mildly, "Dear Cunigunt, a scandal at the age of seven?" which was turning it off with a joke, for she knew how harsh and disliking my new stepmother was to me and my father did not care and I with no sisters or brothers. You must understand that joking and calling people "dear" and "my dear" was only her manner; she was in every way an unusual woman. The previous Abbess, Herrade, had found that Radegunde, who had been given to her to be fostered, had great gifts and so sent the child south to be taught, and that has never happened here before. The story has it that the Abbess Herrade found Radegunde seeming to read the great illuminated book in the Abbess's study; the child had somehow pulled it off its stand and was sitting on the floor with the volume in her lap, sucking her thumb, and turning the pages with her other hand just as if she were reading.

"Little two-years," said the Abbess Herrade, who was a kind woman, "what are you doing?" She thought it amusing, I suppose, that Radegunde should pretend to read this great book, the largest and finest in the Abbey, which had many, many books more than any other nunnery or monastery I have ever heard of: a full forty then, as I remember. And then little Radegunde was doing the book no harm.

"Reading, Mother," said the little girl.

"Oh, reading?" said the Abbess, smiling. "Then tell me what you are reading," and she pointed to the page.

"This," said Radegunde, "is a great *D* with flowers and other beautiful things about it, which is to show that *Dominus,* our Lord God, is the greatest thing and the most beautiful and makes everything to grow and be beautiful, and then it goes on to say *Domine nobis pacem,* which means *Give peace to us, O Lord."*

Then the Abbess began to be frightened but she said only, "Who showed you this?" thinking that Radegunde had heard someone read and tell the words or had been pestering the nuns on the sly.

"No one," said the child. "Shall I go on?" and she read page after page of the Latin, in each case telling what the words meant.

There is more to the story, but I will say only that after many prayers the Abbess Herrade sent her foster daughter far southwards, even to Poitiers, where Saint Radegunde had ruled an Abbey before, and some say even to Rome, and in these places Radegunde was taught all learning, for all learning there is in the world remains in these places. Radegunde came back a grown woman and nursed the Abbess through her last illness and then became Abbess in her turn. They say that the great folk of the Church down there in the south wanted to keep her because she was such a prodigy of female piety and learning, there where life is safe and comfortable and less rude than it is here, but she said that the gray skies and flooding winters of her birthplace called to her very soul. She often told me the story when I was a child: how headstrong she had been and how defiant, and how she had sickened so desperately for her native land that they had sent her back, deciding that a rude life in the mud of a northern village would be a good cure for such a rebellious soul as hers.

"And so it was," she would say, patting my cheek or tweaking my ear. "See how humble I am now?" for you understand, all this about her rebellious girlhood, twenty years' back, was a kind of joke between us. "Don't you do it," she would tell me and we would laugh together, I so heartily at the very idea of my being a pious monk full of learning that I would hold my sides and be unable to speak.

She was kind to everyone. She knew all the languages, not only ours, but the Irish too and the tongues folk speak to the north and south, and Latin and Greek also, and all the other languages in the world, both to read and write. She knew how to cure sickness, both the old women's way with herbs or leeches and out of books also. And never was there a more pious woman! Some speak ill of her now she's gone and say she was too merry to be a good Abbess, but she would say, "Merriment is God's flowers," and when the winter wind blew her headdress awry and showed the gray hair—which happened once; I was there and saw the shocked faces of the Sisters with her—she merely tapped the band back into place, smiling and saying, "Impudent wind! Thou showest thou hast power which is more than our silly human power, for it is from God"—and this quite satisfied the girls with her.

No one ever saw her angry. She was impatient sometimes, but in a kindly way, as if her mind were elsewhere. It was in Heaven, I used to think, for I have seen her pray for hours or sink to her knees—right in the marsh!—to see the wild duck fly south, her hands clasped and a kind of wild joy on her face, only to rise a moment later, looking at the mud on her habit and crying half-ruefully, half in laughter, "Oh, what will Sister Laundress say to me? I am hopeless! Dear child, tell no one; I will say I fell," and then she would clap her hand to her mouth, turning red and laughing even harder, saying, "I *am* hopeless, telling lies!"

The town thought her a saint, of course. We were all happy then, or so it seems to me now, and all lucky and well, with this happiness of having her amongst us burning and blooming in our midst like a great fire around which we could all warm ourselves, even those who didn't know why life seemed so good. There was less illness; the food was better; the very weather stayed mild; and people did not quarrel as they had before her time and do again now. Nor do I think, considering what happened at the end, that all this was nothing but the fancy of a boy who's found his mother, for that's what she was to me; I brought her all the gossip and ran errands when I could, and she called me Boy News in Latin; I was happier than I have ever been.

And then one day those terrible, beaked prows appeared in our river.

I was with her when the warning came, in the main room of the Abbey tower just after the first fire of the year had been lit in the great hearth; we thought ourselves safe, for they had never been seen so far south and it was too late in the year for any sensible shipman to be in our waters. The Abbey was host to three Irish priests who turned pale when young Sister Sibihd burst in with the news, crying and wringing her hands; one of the brothers exclaimed a thing in Latin which means "God protect us!" for they had been telling us stories of the terrible sack of the monastery of Saint Columbanus and how everyone had run away with the precious manuscripts or had hidden in the woods, and that was how Father Cairbre and the two others had decided to go "walk the world," for this (the Abbess had been telling it all to me, for I had no Latin) is what the Irish say when they leave their native land to travel elsewhere.

"God protects our souls, not our bodies," said the Abbess Radegunde briskly. She had been talking with the priests in their own language or in the Latin, but this she said in ours so even the women workers from the village would understand. Then she said, "Father Cairbre, take your friends and the younger Sisters to the underground passage; Sister Diemud, open the gates to the villagers; half of them will be trying to get behind the Abbey walls and the others will be fleeing to the marsh. You, Boy News, down to the cellars with the girls." But I did not go and she never saw it; she was up and looking out one of the window slits instantly. So was I. I had always thought the Norsemen's big ships came right up on land—on legs, I supposed—and was disappointed to see that after they came up our river they stayed in the water like other ships and the men were coming ashore in little boats, which they were busy pulling up on shore through the sand and mud. Then the Abbess repeated her order—"Quickly! Quickly!"—and before anyone knew what had happened, she was gone from the room. I watched from the tower window; in the turmoil nobody bothered about me. Below, the Abbey grounds and gardens were packed with folk, all stepping on the herb plots and the Abbess's paestum roses, and great logs were being dragged to bar the door set in the stone walls round the Abbey, not high walls, to tell truth, and Radegunde was going quickly through the crowd, crying: Do this! Do that! Stay, thou! Go, thou! and like things.

Then she reached the door and motioned Sister Oddha, the doorkeeper, aside—the old Sister actually fell to her knees in entreaty—and all this, you must understand, was wonderfully pleasant to me. I had no more idea of danger than a puppy. There was some tumult by the door—I think the men with the logs were trying to get in her way—and Abbess Radegunde took out from the neck of her habit her silver crucifix, brought all the way from Rome, and shook it impatiently at those who would keep her in. So of course they let her through at once.

I settled into my corner of the window, waiting for the Abbess's crucifix to bring down God's lightning on those tall, fair men who defied Our Savior and the law and were supposed to wear animal horns on their heads, though these did not (and I found out later that's just a story; that is not what the Norse do). I did hope that the Abbess, or Our Lord, would wait just a little while before destroying them, for I wanted to get a good look at them before they all died, you understand. I was somewhat disappointed as they seemed to be wearing breeches with leggings under them and tunics on top, like ordinary folk, and cloaks also, though some did carry swords and axes and there were round shields piled on the beach at one place. But the long hair they had was fine, and the bright colors of their clothes, and the monsters growing out of the heads of the ships were splendid and very frightening, even though one could see that they were only painted, like the pictures in the Abbess's books.

I decided that God had provided me with enough edification and could now strike down the impious strangers.

But He did not.

Instead the Abbess walked alone towards these fierce men, over the stony river bank, as calmly as if she were on a picnic with her girls. She was singing a little song, a pretty tune that I repeated many years later, and a well-traveled man said it was a Norse cradle-song. I didn't know that then, but only that the terrible, fair men, who had looked up in surprise at seeing one lone woman come out of the Abbey (which was barred behind her; I could see that), now began a sort of whispering astonishment among themselves. I saw the Abbess's gaze go quickly from one to the other—we often said that she could tell what was hidden in the soul from one look at the face—and then she picked the skirt of her habit up with one hand and daintily went among the rocks to one of the men, one older than the others, as it proved later, though I could not see so well at the time—and said to him, in his own language:

"Welcome, Thorvald Einarsson, and what do you, good farmer, so far from your own place, with the harvest ripe and the great autumn storms coming on over the sea?" (You may wonder how I knew what she said when I had no Norse; the truth is that Father Cairbre, who had not gone to the cellars after all, was looking out the top of the window while I was barely able to peep out the bottom, and he repeated everything that was said for the folk in the room, who all kept very quiet.)

Now you could see that the pirates were dumfounded to hear her speak their own language and even more so that she called one by his name; some stepped backwards and made strange signs in the air and others unsheathed axes or swords and came running towards the Abbess. But this Thorvald Einarsson put up his hand for them to stop and laughed heartily.

"Think!" he said. There's no magic here, only cleverness—what pair of ears could miss my name with the lot of you bawling out 'Thorvald Einarsson, help me with this oar;' 'Thorvald Einarsson, my leggings are wet to the knees;'

'Thorvald Einarsson, this stream is as cold as a Fimbul-winter!"

The Abbess Radegunde nodded and smiled. Then she sat down plump on the river bank. She scratched behind one ear, as I had often seen her do when she was deep in thought. Then she said (and I am sure that this talk was carried on in a loud voice so that we in the Abbey could hear it):

"Good friend Thorvald, you are as clever as the tale I heard of you from your sister's son, Ranulf, from whom I learnt the Norse when I was in Rome, and to show you it was he, he always swore by his gray horse, Lamefoot, and he had a difficulty in his speech; he could not say the sounds as we do and so spoke of you always as 'Torvald.' Is not that so?"

I did not realize it then, being only a child, but the Abbess was—by this speech—claiming hospitality from the man and had also picked by chance or inspiration the cleverest among these thieves, for his next words were:

"I am not the leader. There are no leaders here."

He was warning her that they were not his men to control, you see. So she scratched behind her ear again and got up. Then she began to wander, as if she did not know what to do, from one to the other of these uneasy folk—for some backed off and made signs at her still, and some took out their knives—singing her little tune again and walking slowly, more bent over and older and infirm-looking than we had ever seen her, one helpless little woman in black before all those fierce men. One wild young pirate snatched the headdress from her as she passed, leaving her short gray hair bare to the wind; the others laughed and he that had done it cried out:

"Grandmother, are you not ashamed?"

"Why, good friend, of what?" said she mildly.

"Thou art married to thy Christ," he said, holding the head-covering behind his back, "but this bridgegroom of thine cannot even defend thee against the shame of having thy head uncovered! Now if thou wert married to me—"

There was much laughter. The Abbess Radegunde waited until it was over. Then she scratched her bare head and made as if to turn away, but suddenly she turned back upon him with the age and infirmity dropping from her as if they had been a cloak, seeming taller and very grand, as if lit from within by some great fire. She looked directly into his face. This thing she did was something we had all seen, of course, but they had not, nor had they heard that great, grand voice with which she sometimes read the Scriptures to us or talked with us of the wrath of God. I think the young man was frightened, for all his daring. And I know now what I did not then: that the Norse admire courage above all things and that—to be blunt—everyone likes a good story, especially if it happens right in front of your eyes.

"Grandson!"—and her voice tolled like the great bell of God; I think folk must have heard her all the way to the marsh!—"Little grandchild, thinkest thou that the Creator of the World who made the stars and the moon and the sun and our bodies, too and the change of the seasons and the very earth we stand on—yea, even unto the shit in thy belly!—thinkest thou that such a being has a big house in the sky where he keeps his wives and goes in to fuck them as thou wouldst thyself or like the King of Turkey? Do not dishonor the wit of the mother who bore thee! We are the servants of God, not his wives, and if we tell our silly girls they are married to the Christus, it is to make them understand that they must not run off and marry Otto Farmer or Ekkehard Blacksmith, but stick to their work, as they promised. If I told them they were married to an Idea, they would not understand me, and neither dost thou."

(Here Father Cairbre, above me in the window, muttered in a protesting way about something.)

Then the Abbess snatched the silver cross from around

her neck and put it into the boy's hand, saying: "Give this to thy mother with my pity. She must pull out her hair over such a child."

But he let it fall to the ground. He was red in the face and breathing hard.

"Take it up," she said more kindly, "take it up, boy; it will not hurt thee and there's no magic in it. It's only pure silver and good workmanship; it will make thee rich." When she saw that he would not—his hand went to his knife—she *tched* to herself in a motherly way (or I believe she did, for she waved one hand back and forth as she always did when she made that sound) and got down on her knees—with more difficulty than was truth, I think—saying loudly, "I will stoop, then; I will stoop," and got up, holding it out to him, saying, "Take. Two sticks tied with a cord would serve me as well."

The boy cried, his voice breaking, "My mother is dead and thou art a witch!" and in an instant he had one arm around the Abbess's neck and with the other his knife at her throat. The man Thorvald Einarsson roared "Thorfinn!" but the Abbess only said clearly, "Let him be. I have shamed this man but did not mean to. He is right to be angry."

The boy released her and turned his back. I remember wondering if these strangers could weep. Later I heard—and I swear that the Abbess must have somehow known this or felt it, for although she was no witch, she could probe a man until she found the sore places in him and that very quickly—that this boy's mother had been known for an adulteress and that no man would own him as a son. It is one thing among those people for a man to have what the Abbess called a concubine and they do not hold the children of such in scorn as we do, but it is a different thing when a married woman has more than one man. Such was Thorfinn's case; I suppose that was what had sent him *viking*. But all this came later; what I saw then—with my nose barely above the window slit—was that the

Abbess slipped her crucifix over the hilt of the boy's sword—she really wished him to have it, you see—and then walked to a place near the walls of the Abbey but far from the Norsemen. I think she meant them to come to her. I saw her pick up her skirts like a peasant woman, sit down with legs crossed, and say in a loud voice:

"Come! Who will bargain with me?"

A few strolled over, laughing, and sat down with her.

"All!" she said, gesturing them closer.

"And why should we all come?" said one who was farthest away.

"Because you will miss a bargain," said the Abbess.

"Why should we bargain when we can take?" said another.

"Because you will only get half," said the Abbess. "The rest you will not find."

"We will ransack the Abbey," said a third.

"Half the treasure is not in the Abbey," said she.

"And where is it then?"

She tapped her forehead. They were drifting over by twos and threes. I have heard since that the Norse love riddles and this was a sort of riddle; she was giving them good fun.

"If it is in your head," said the man Thorvald, who was standing behind the others, arms crossed, "we can get it out, can we not?" And he tapped the hilt of his knife.

"If you frighten me, I shall become confused and remember nothing," said the Abbess calmly. "Besides, do you wish to play that old game? You saw how well it worked the last time. I am surprised at you, Ranulf mother's-brother."

"I will bargain then," said the man Thorvald, smiling.

"And the rest of you?" said Radegunde. "It must be all or none; decide for yourselves whether you wish to save yourselves trouble and danger and be rich," and she deliberately turned her back on them. The men moved down to the river's edge and began to talk among themselves, dropping their voices so that we could not hear them any more. Father Cairbre, who was old and short-sighted, cried, "I cannot hear them. What are they doing?" and I cleverly said, "I have good eyes, Father Cairbre," and he held me up to see. So it was just at the time that the Abbess Radegunde was facing the Abbey tower that I appeared in the window. She clapped one hand across her mouth. Then she walked to the gate and called (in a voice I had learned not to disregard; it had often got me a smacked bottom), "Boy News, down! Come down to me here *at once!* And bring Father Cairbre with you."

I was overjoyed. I had no idea that she might want to protect me if anything went wrong. My only thought was that I was going to see it all from wonderfully close by. So I wormed my way, half-suffocated, through the folk in the tower room, stepping on feet and skirts, and having to say every few seconds, "But I *have* to! The Abbess wants me," and meanwhile she was calling outside like an Empress, "Let that boy through! Make a place for that boy! Let the Irish priest through!" until I crept and pushed and complained my way to the very wall itself—no one was going to open the gate for us, of course—and there was a great fuss and finally someone brought a ladder. I was over at once, but the old priest took a longer time, although it was a low wall, as I've said, the builders having been somewhat of two minds about making the Abbey into a true fortress.

Once outside it was lovely, away from all that crowd, and I ran, gloriously pleased, to the Abbess, who said only, "Stay by me, whatever happens," and immediately turned her attention away from me. It had taken so long to get Father Cairbre outside the walls that the tall, foreign men had finished their talking and were coming back—all twenty or thirty of them—towards the Abbey and the Abbess Radegunde, and most especially of all, me. I could see Father Cairbre tremble. They did look grim, close by, with their long, wild hair and the brightness of their strange clothes. I remember that they smelled different from us, but cannot remember how after all these years. Then the Abbess spoke to them in that outlandish language of theirs, so strangely light and lilting to hear from their bearded lips, and then she said something in Latin to Father Cairbre, and he said, with a shake in his voice:

"This is the priest, Father Cairbre, who will say our bargains aloud in our own tongue so that my people may hear. I cannot deal behind their backs. And this is my foster baby, who is very dear to me and who is now having his curiosity rather too much satisfied, I think." (I was trying to stand tall like a man but had one hand secretly holding onto her skirt; so that was what the foreign men had chuckled at!) The talk went on, but I will tell it as if I had understood the Norse, for to repeat everything twice would be tedious.

The Abbess Radegunde said, "Will you bargain?"

There was a general nodding of heads, with a look of: After all, why not?

"And who will speak for you?" said she.

A man stepped forward; I recognized Thorvald Einarsson.

"Ah, yes," said the Abbess dryly. "The company that has no leaders. Is this leaderless company agreed? Will it abide by its word? I want no treachery-planners, no Breakwords here!"

There was a general mutter at this. The Thorvald man (he *was* big, close up!) said mildly, "I sail with none such. Let's begin."

We all sat down.

"Now," said Thorvald Einarsson, raising his eyebrows, "according to my knowledge of this thing, you begin. And according to my knowledge, you will begin by saying that you are very poor."

"But, no," said the Abbess, "we are rich." Father Cairbre groaned. A groan answered him from behind the Abbey walls. Only the Abbess and Thorvald Einarsson seemed unmoved; it was as if these two were joking in some way that no one else understood. The Abbess went on, saying, "We are very rich. Within is much silver, much gold, many pearls, and much embroidered cloth, much fine-woven cloth, much carved and painted wood, and many books with gold upon their pages and jewels set into their covers. All this is yours. But we have more and better: herbs and medicines, ways to keep food from spoiling, the knowledge of how to cure the sick; all this is yours. And we have more and better even than this: we have the knowledge of Christ and the perfect understanding of the soul, which is yours too, any time you wish; you have only to accept it."

Thorvald Einarsson held up his hand. "We will stop with the first," he said, "and perhaps a little of the second. That is more practical."

"And foolish," said the Abbess politely, "in the usual way." And again I had the odd feeling that these two were sharing a joke no one else even saw. She added, "There is one thing you may not have, and that is the most precious of all."

Thorvald Einarsson looked inquiring.

"*My people.* Their safety is dearer to me than myself. They are not to be touched, not a hair on their heads, not for any reason. Think: you can fight your way into the Abbey easily enough, but the folk in there are very frightened of you, and some of the men are armed. Even a good fighter is cumbered in a crowd. You will slip and fall upon each other without meaning to or knowing that you do so. Heed my counsel. Why play butcher when you can have treasure poured into your laps like kings, without work? And after that there will be as much again, when I lead you to the hidden place. An earl's mountain of treasure. Think of it! And to give all this up for slaves, half of whom will get sick and die before you get them home—and will need to be fed if they are to be any good. Shame on you for bad advice-takers! Imagine what you will say to your wives and families: Here are a few miserable bolts of cloth with blood spots that won't come out, here are some pearls and jewels smashed to powder in the fighting, here is a torn piece of embroidery which was whole until someone stepped on it in the battle, and I had slaves but they died of illness and I fucked a pretty young nun and meant to bring her back, but she leapt into the sea. And, oh, yes, there was twice as much again and all of it whole but we decided not to take that. Too much trouble, you see."

This was a lively story and the Norsemen enjoyed it. Radegunde held up her hand.

"People!" she called in German, adding, "Sea-rovers, hear what I say: I will repeat it for you in your tongue." (And so she did.) "*People, if the Norsemen fight us, do not defend yourselves but smash everything! Wives, take your cooking knives and shred the valuable cloth to pieces! Men, with your axes and hammers hew the altars and the carved wood to fragments! All, grind the pearls and smash the jewels against the stone floors! Break the bottles of wine! Pound the gold and silver to shapelessness! Tear to pieces the illuminated books! Tear down the hangings and burn them!*

"But" (she added, her voice suddenly mild) "if these wise men will accept our gifts, let us heap untouched and spotless at their feet all that we have and hold nothing back, so that their kinsfolk will marvel and wonder at the shining and glistering of the wealth they bring back, though it leave us nothing but our bare stone walls."

If anyone had ever doubted that the Abbess Radegunde was inspired by God, their doubts must have vanished away, for who could resist the fiery vigor of her first speech or the beneficent unction of her second? The Norsemen sat there with their mouths open. I saw tears on Father Cairbre's cheeks. Then Thorvald said, "Abbess—"

He stopped. He tried again but again stopped. Then he shook himself, as a man who has been under a spell, and said:

"Abbess, my men have been without women for a long time."

Radegunde looked surprised. She looked as if she could

not believe what she had heard. She looked the pirate up and down, as if puzzled, and then walked around him as if taking his measure. She did this several times, looking at every part of his big body as if she were summing him up while he got redder and redder. Then she backed off and surveyed him again, and with her arms akimbo like a peasant, announced very loudly in both Norse and German:

"What! Have they lost the use of their hands?"

It was irresistible, in its way. The Norse laughed. Our people laughed. Even Thorvald laughed. I did too, though I was not sure what everyone was laughing about. The laughter would die down and then begin again behind the Abbey walls, helplessly, and again die down and again begin. The Abbess waited until the Norsemen had stopped laughing and then called for silence in German until there were only a few snickers here and there. She then said:

"These good men—Father Cairbre, tell the people—these good men will forgive my silly joke. I meant no scandal, truly, and no harm, but laughter is good: it settles the body's waters, as the physicians say. And my people know that I am not always as solemn and good as I ought to be. Indeed I am a very great sinner and scandal-maker. Thorvald Einarsson, do we do business?"

The big man—who had not been so pleased as the others, I can tell you!—looked at his men and seemed to see what he needed to know. He said, "I go in with five men to see what you have. Then we let the poor folk on the grounds go, but not those inside the Abbey. Then we search again. The gates will be locked and guarded by the rest of us; if there's any treachery, the bargain's off."

"Then I will go with you," said Radegunde. "That is very just and my presence will calm the people. To see us together will assure them that no harm is meant. You are a good man, Torvald—forgive me; I call you as your nephew did so often. Come, Boy News, hold on to me."

"Open the gates!" she called then. "All is safe!" and with the five men (one of whom was that young Thorfinn who had hated her so) we waited while the great logs were pulled back. There was little space within, but the people shrank back at the sight of those fierce warriors and opened a place for us.

I looked back and the Norsemen had come in and were standing just inside the walls, on either side the gate, with their swords out and their shields up. The crowd parted for us more slowly as we reached the main tower, with the Abbess repeating constantly, "Be calm, people, be calm. All is well," and deftly speaking by name to this one or that. It was much harder when the people gasped upon hearing the big logs pushed shut with a noise like thunder, and it was very close on the stairs; I heard her say something like an apology in the queer foreign tongue. Something that probably meant, "I'm sorry that we must wait." It seemed an age until the stairs were even partly clear and I saw what the Abbess had meant by the cumbering of a crowd; a man might swing a weapon in the press of people, but not very far, and it was more likely he would simply fall over someone and crack his head. We gained the great room with the big crucifix of painted wood and the little one of pearls and gold, and the scarlet hangings worked in gold thread that I had played robbers behind so often before I learned what real robbers were: these tall, frightening men whose eyes glistened with greed at what I had fancied every village had. Most of the Sisters had stayed in the great room, but somehow it was not so crowded, as the folk had huddled back against the walls when the Norsemen came in. The youngest girls were all in a corner, terrified—one could smell it, as one can in people—and when that young Thorfinn went for the little gold-and-pearl cross, Sister Sibihd cried in a high, cracked voice, "It is the body of our Christ!" and leapt up, snatching it from the wall before he could get to it.

"Sibihd!" exclaimed the Abbess, in as sharp a voice as I had ever heard her use. "Put that back or you will feel the weight of my hand, I tell you!"

Now it is odd, is it not, that a young woman desperate enough not to care about death at the hands of a Norse pirate should nonetheless be frightened away at the threat of getting a few slaps from her Abbess? But folk are like that. Sister Sibihd returned the cross to its place (from whence young Thorfinn took it) and fell back among the nuns, sobbing, "He desecrates our Lord God!"

"Foolish girl!" snapped the Abbess. "God only can consecrate or desecrate; man cannot. That is a piece of metal."

Thorvald said something sharp to Thorfinn, who slowly put the cross back on its hook with a sulky look which said, plainer than words: Nobody gives me what I want. Nothing else went wrong in the big room or the Abbess's study or the storerooms, or out in the kitchens. The Norsemen were silent and kept their hands on their swords, but the Abbess kept talking in a calm way in both tongues; to our folk she said, "See? It is all right but everyone must keep still. God will protect us." Her face was steady and clear, and I believed her a saint, for she had saved Sister Sibihd and the rest of us.

But this peacefulness did not last, of course. Something had to go wrong in all that press of people; to this day I do not know what. We were in a corner of the long refectory, which is the place where the Sisters or Brothers eat in an Abbey, when something pushed me into the wall and I fell, almost suffocated by the Abbess's lying on top of me. My head was ringing and on all sides there was a terrible roaring sound with curses and screams, a dreadful tumult as if the walls had come apart and were falling on everyone. I could hear the Abbess whispering something in Latin over and over in my ear. There were dull, ripe sounds, worse than the rest, which I know now to have been the noise steel makes when it is thrust into bodies. This all seemed to go on forever and then it seemed to me that the floor was wet. Then all became quiet. I felt the Abbess Radegune get off me. She said:

"So this is how you wash your floors up North." When I lifted my head from the rushes and saw what she meant, I was very sick into the corner. Then she picked me up in her arms and held my face against her bosom so that I would not see, but it was no use; I had already seen: all the people lying sprawled on the floor with their bellies coming out, like heaps of dead fish, old Walafrid with an axe handle standing out of his chest—he was sitting up with his eyes shut in a press of bodies that gave him no room to lie down—and the young beekeeper, Uta, from the village, who had been so merry, lying on her back with her long braids and her gown all dabbed in red dye and a great stain of it on her belly. She was breathing fast and her eyes were wide open. As we passed her, the noise of her breathing ceased.

The Abbess said mildly, "Thy people are thorough housekeepers, Earl Split-gut."

Thorvald Einarsson roared something at us, and the Abbess replied softly, "Forgive me, good friend. You protected me and the boy and I am grateful. But nothing betrays a man's knowledge of the German like a word that bites, is it not so? And I had to be sure."

It came to me then that she had called him "Torvald" and reminded him of his sister's son so that he would feel he must protect us if anything went wrong. But now she would make him angry, I thought, and I shut my eyes tight. Instead he laughed and said in odd, light German, "I did no housekeeping but to stand over you and your pet. Are you not grateful?"

"Oh, very, thank you," said the Abbess with such warmth as she might show to a Sister who had brought her a rose from the garden, or another who copied her work well, or when I told her news, or if Ita the cook made a good soup. But he did not know that the warmth was for everyone and so seemed satisfied. By now we were in the garden and the air was less foul; she put me down, although my limbs were shaking, and I clung to her gown, crumpled, stiff, and blood-reeking though it was. She said, "Oh my God, what a deal of washing hast Thou given us!" She started to walk towards the gate, and Thorvald Einarsson took a step towards her. She said, without turning round: "Do not insist, Thorvald, there is no reason to lock me up. I am forty years old and not likely to be running away into the swamp, what with my rheumatism and the pain in my knees and the folk needing me as they do."

There was a moment's silence. I could see something odd come into the big man's face. He said quietly:

"I did not speak, Abbess."

She turned, surprised. "But you did. I heard you."

He said strangely, "I did not."

Children can guess sometimes what is wrong and what to do about it without knowing how; I remember saying, very quickly, "Oh, she does that sometimes. My stepmother says old age has addled her wits," and then, "Abbess, may I go to my stepmother and my father?"

"Yes, of course," she said, "run along, Boy News—" and then stopped, looking into the air as if seeing in it something we could not. Then she said very gently, "No, my dear, you had better stay here with me," and I knew, as surely as if I had seen it with my own eyes, that I was not to go to my stepmother or my father because both were dead.

She did things like that, too, sometimes.

For a while it seemed that everyone was dead. I did not feel grieved or frightened in the least, but I think I must have been, for I had only one idea in my head: that if I let the Abbess out of my sight, I would die. So I followed her everywhere. She was let to move about and comfort people, especially the mad Sibihd, who would do nothing but rock and wail, but towards nightfall, when the Abbey had been stripped of its treasures, Thorvald Einarsson put her and me in her study, now bare of its grand furniture, on a straw pallet on the floor, and bolted the door on the outside. She said:

"Boy News, would you like to go to Constantinople, where the Turkish Sultan is, and the domes of gold and all the splendid pagans? For that is where this man will take me to sell me."

"Oh, yes!" said I, and then: "But will he take me, too?"

"Of course," said the Abbess, and so it was settled. Then in came Thorvald Einarsson, saying:

"Thorfinn is asking for you." I found out later that they were waiting for him to die; none other of the Norse had been wounded, but a farmer had crushed Thorfinn's chest with an axe, and he was expected to die before morning. The Abbess said:

"Is that a good reason to go?" She added, "I mean that he hates me; will not his anger at my presence make him worse?"

Thorvald said slowly, "The folk here say you can sit by the sick and heal them. Can you do that?"

"To my own knowledge, not at all," said the Abbess Radegunde, "but if they believe so, perhaps that calms them and makes them better. Christians are quite as foolish as other people, you know. I will come if you want," and though I saw that she was pale with tiredness, she got to her feet. I should say that she was in a plain, brown gown taken from one of the peasant women because her own was being washed clean, but to me she had the same majesty as always. And for him too, I think.

Thorvald said, "Will you pray for him or damn him?"

She said, "I do not pray, Thorvald, and I never damn anybody; I merely sit." She added, "Oh, let him: he'll scream your ears off if you don't," and this meant me, for I was ready to yell for my life if they tried to keep me from her.

They had put Thorfinn in the chapel, a little stone room with nothing left in it now but a plain wooden cross, not worth carrying off. He was lying, his eyes closed, on the stone altar with furs under him, and his face was gray. Every time he breathed, there was a bubbling sound, a little thin, reedy sound; and as I crept closer, I saw why, for in the young man's chest was a great red hole with sharp pink things sticking out of it, all crushed, and in the hole one could see something jump and fall, jump and fall, over and over again. It was his heart beating. Blood kept coming from his lips in a froth. I do not know, of course, what either said, for they spoke in the Norse, but I saw what they did and heard much of it talked of between the Abbess and Thorvald Einarsson later. So I will tell it as if I knew.

The first thing the Abbess did was to stop suddenly on the threshold and raise both hands to her mouth as if in horror. Then she cried furiously to the two guards:

"Do you wish to kill your comrade with the cold and damp? Is this how you treat one another? Get fire in here and some woollen cloth to put over him! No, not more skins, you idiots, *wool* to mold to his body and take up the wet. Run now!"

One said sullenly, "We don't take orders from you, Grandma."

"Oh, no?" said she. "Then I shall strip this wool dress from my old body and put it over that boy and then sit here all night in my flabby, naked skin! What will this child's soul say when it enters the Valhall? That his friends would not give up a little of their booty so that he might fight for life? Is this your fellowship? Do it, or I will strip myself and shame you both for the rest of your lives!"

"Well, take it from his share," said the one in a low voice, and the other ran out. Soon there was a fire on the hearth and russet-colored woollen cloth—"From my own share," said one of them loudly, though it was a color the least costly, not like blue or red—and the Abbess laid it loosely over the boy, carefully putting it close to his sides but not moving him. He did not look to be in any pain, but his color got no better. But then he opened his eyes and said in such a little voice as a ghost might have, a whisper as thin and reedy and bubbling as his breath:

"You... old witch. But I beat you... in the end."

"Did you, my dear?" said the Abbess. "How?"

"Treasure," he said, "for my kinfolk. And I lived as a man at last. Fought... and had a woman... the one here with the big breasts, Sibihd.... Whether she liked it or not. That was good."

"Yes, Sibihd," said the Abbess mildly. "Sibihd has gone mad. She hears no one and speaks to no one. She only sits and rocks and moans and soils herself and will not feed herself, although if one puts food in her mouth with a spoon, she will swallow."

The boy tried to frown. "Stupid," he said at last. "Stupid nuns. The beasts do it."

"Do they?" said the Abbess, as if this were a new idea to her. "Now that is very odd. For never yet heard I of a gander that blacked the goose's eye or hit her over the head with a stone or stuck a knife in her entrails when he was through. When God puts it into their hearts to desire one another, she squats and he comes running. And a bitch in heat will jump through the window if you lock the door. Poor fools! Why didn't you camp three hours' down-river and wait? In a week half the young married women in the village would have been slipping away at night to see what the foreigners were like. Yes, and some unmarried ones, and some of my own girls, too. But you couldn't wait, could you?"

"No," said the boy, with the ghost of a brag. "Better... this way."

"*This* way," said she. "Oh, yes, my dear, old Granny knows about *this* way! Pleasure for the count of three or four, and the rest of it as much joy as rolling a stone uphill."

He smiled a ghostly smile. "You're a whore, Grandma."

She began to stroke his forehead. "No, Grandbaby," she said, "but all Latin is not the Church Fathers, you know, great as they are. One can find a great deal in those strange books written by the ones who died centuries before our Lord was born. Listen," and she leaned closer to him and said quietly:

"Syrian dancing girl, how subtly you sway those sensuous limbs,
"Half-drunk in the smoky tavern, lascivious and wanton,
"Your long hair bound back in the Greek way, clashing the castanets in your hands—"

The boy was too weak to do anything but look astonished. Then she said this:

"I love you so that anyone permitted to sit near you and talk to you seems to me like a god; when I am near you my spirit is broken, my heart shakes, my voice dies, and I can't even speak. Under my skin I flame up all over and I can't see; there's thunder in my ears and I break out in a sweat, as if from fever; I turn paler than cut grass and feel that I am utterly changed; I feel that Death has come near me."

He said, as if frightened, "Nobody feels like that."

"They do," she said.

He said, in feeble alarm, "You're trying to kill me!"

She said, "No, my dear. I simply don't want you to die a virgin."

It was odd, his saying those things and yet holding on to her hand where he had got at it through the woollen cloth; she stroked his head and he whispered, "Save me, old witch."

"I'll do my best," she said. "You shall do your best by not talking and I by not tormenting you any more, and we'll both try to sleep."

"Pray," said the boy.

"Very well," said she, "but I'll need a chair," and the guards—seeing I suppose, that he was holding her hand—brought in one of the great wooden chairs from the Abbey, which were too plain and heavy to carry off, I think. Then the Abbess Radegunde sat in the chair and closed her eyes.

Thorfinn seemed to fall asleep. I crept nearer her on the floor and must have fallen asleep myself almost at once, for the next thing I knew a gray light filled the chapel, the fire had gone out, and someone was shaking Radegunde, who still slept in her chair, her head leaning to one side. It was Thorvald Einarsson and he was shouting with excitement in his strange German, "Woman, how did you do it! How did you do it!"

"Do what?" said the Abbess thickly. "Is he dead?"

"Dead?" exclaimed the Norseman. "He is healed! Healed! The lung is whole and all is closed up about the heart and the shattered pieces of the ribs are grown together! Even the muscles of the chest are beginning to heal!"

"That's good," said the Abbess, still half asleep. "Let me be."

Thorvald shook her again. She said again, "Oh, let me sleep." This time he hauled her to her feet and she shrieked, "My back, my back! Oh, the saints, my rheumatism!" and at the same time a sick voice from under the blue woollens—a sick voice but a man's voice, not a ghost's—said something in Norse.

"Yes, I hear you," said the Abbess. "You must become a follower of the White Christ right away, this very minute. But *Dominus noster,* please do You put it into these brawny heads that I must have a tub of hot water with pennyroyal in it? I am too old to sleep all night in a chair, and I am one ache from head to foot."

Thorfinn got louder.

"Tell him," said the Abbess Radegunde to Thorvald in German, "that I will not baptize him and I will not shrive him until he is a different man. All that child wants is someone more powerful than your Odin god or your Thor god to pull him out of the next scrape he gets into. Ask him: Will he adopt Sibihd as his sister? Will he clean her when she soils herself and feed her and sit with his arm about her, talking to her gently and lovingly until she is well again? The Christ does not wipe out our sins only to have us commit them all over again, and that is what he wants and what you all want, a God that gives and gives and gives, but God does not give; He takes and takes and takes. He takes away everything that is not God until there is nothing left but God, and none of you will understand that! There is no remission of sins; there is only change, and Thorfinn must change before God will have him."

"Abbess, you are eloquent," said Thorvald, smiling, "but why do you not tell him all this yourself?"

"Because I ache so!" said Radegunde; "Oh, do get me into some hot water!" and Thorvald half led and half supported her as she hobbled out. That morning, after she had had her soak—when I cried, they let me stay just outside the door—she undertook to cure Sibihd, first by rocking her in her arms and talking to her, telling her she was safe now, and promising that the Northmen would go soon, and then when Sibihd became quieter, leading her out into the woods with Thorvald as a bodyguard to see that we did not run away, and little, dark Sister Hedwic, who had stayed with Sibihd and cared for her. The Abbess would walk for a while in the mild autumn sunshine, and then she would direct Sibihd's face upwards by touching her gently under the chin and say, "See? There is God's sky still," and then, "Look, there are God's trees; they have not changed," and tell her that the world was just the same and God still kindly to folk, only a few more souls had joined the Blessed and were happier waiting for us in Heaven than we could ever be, or even imagine being, on the poor earth. Sister Hedwic kept hold of Sibihd's hand. No one paid more attention to me than if I had been a dog, but every time poor Sister Sibihd saw Thorvald she would shrink away, and you could see that Hedwic could not bear to look at him at all; every time he came in her sight she turned her face aside, shut her eyes hard, and bit her lower lip. It was a quiet, almost warm day, as autumn can be sometimes, and the Abbess found a few little blue late flowers growing in a sheltered place against a log and put them into Sibihd's hand, speaking of how beautifully and cunningly God had made all things. Sister Sibihd had enough wit to hold on to the flowers, but her eyes stared and she would have stumbled and fallen if Hedwic had not led her.

Sister Hedwic said timidly, "Perhaps she suffers because she has been defiled, Abbess," and then looked ashamed. For a moment the Abbess looked shrewdly at young Sister Hedwic and then at the mad Sibihd. Then she said:

"Dear daughter Sibihd and dear daughter Hedwic, I am now going to tell you something about myself that I have never told to a single living soul but my confessor. Do you know that as a young woman I studied at Avignon and from there was sent to Rome, so that I might gather much learning? Well, in Avignon I read mightily our Christian Fathers but also in the pagan poets, for as it has been said by Ermenrich of Ellwangen: As dung spread upon a field enriches it to good harvest, thus one cannot produce divine eloquence without the filthy writings of the pagan poets. This is true but perilous, only I thought not so, for I was very proud and fancied that if the pagan poems of love left me unmoved, that was because I had the gift of chastity right from God Himself, and I scorned sensual pleasures and those tempted by them. I had forgotten, you see, that chastity is not given once and for all like a wedding ring that is put on never to be taken off, but is a garden which each day must be weeded, watered, and trimmed anew, or soon there will be only brambles and wilderness.

"As I have said, the words of the poets did not tempt me, for words are only marks on the page with no life save what we give them. But in Rome there were not only the old books, daughters, but something much worse.

"There were statues. Now you must understand that these are not such as you can imagine from our books, like Saint John or the Virgin; the ancients wrought so cunningly in stone that it is like magic; one stands before the marble holding one's breath, waiting for it to move and speak. They are not statues at all but beautiful, naked men and women. It is a city of seagods pouring water, daughter Sibihd and daughter Hedwic, of athletes about to throw the discus, and runners and wrestlers and young emperors, and the favorites of kings; but they do not walk the streets like real men, for they are all of stone.

"There was one Apollo, all naked, which I knew I should not look on but which I always made some excuse to my companions to pass by, and this statue, although three miles distant from my dwelling, drew me as if by magic. Oh, he was fair to look on! Fairer than any youth alive now in Germany, or in the world, I think. And then all the old loves of the pagan poets came back to me: Dido and Aeneas, the taking of Venus and Mars, the love of the moon, Diana, for the shepherd boy—and I thought that if my statue could only come to life, he would utter honeyed love-words from the old poets and would be wise and brave, too, and what woman could resist him?"

Here she stopped and looked at Sister Sibihd but Sibihd only stared on, holding the little blue flowers. It was Sister Hedwic who cried, one hand pressed to her heart:

"Did you pray, Abbess?"

"I did," said Radegunde solemnly, "and yet my prayers kept becoming something else. I would pray to be delivered from the temptation that was in the statue, and then, of course, I would have to think of the statue itself, and then I would tell myself that I must run, like the nymph Daphne, to be armored and sheltered within a laurel tree, but my feet seemed to be already rooted to the ground, and then at the last minute I would flee and be back at my prayers again. But it grew harder each time, and at last the day came when I did not flee."

"Abbess, *you?*" cried Hedwic, with a gasp. Thorvald, keeping his watch a little way from us, looked surprised. I was very pleased—I loved to see the Abbess astonish people; it was one of her gifts—and at seven I had no knowledge of lust except that my little thing felt good sometimes when I handled it to make water, and what had that to do with statues coming to life or women turning into laurel trees? I was more interested in mad Sibihd, the way children are; I did not know what she might do, or if I should be afraid of her, or if I should go mad myself, what it would be like. But the Abbess was laughing gently at Hedwic's amazement.

"Why not me?" said the Abbess. "I was young and healthy and had no special grace from God any more than the hens or the cows do! Indeed, I burned so with desire for that handsome young hero—for so I had made him in my mind, as a woman might do with a man she has seen a few times on the street—that thoughts of him tormented me waking and sleeping. It seemed to me that because of my vows I could not give myself to this Apollo of my own free will. So I would dream that he took me against my will, and, oh, what an exquisite pleasure that was!"

Here Hedwic's blood came all to her face and covered it with her hands. I could see Thorvald grinning, back where he watched us.

"And then," said the Abbess, as if she had not seen either of them, "a terrible fear came to my heart that God might punish me by sending a ravisher who would use me unlawfully, as I had dreamed my Apollo did, and that I would not even wish to resist him and would feel the pleasures of a base lust and would know myself a whore and a false nun forever after. This fear both tormented and drew me. I began to steal looks at young men in the streets, not letting the other Sisters see me do it, thinking: Will it be he? Or he? Or he?

"And then it happened. I had lingered behind the others at a melon seller's thinking of no Apollos or handsome heroes but only of the convent's dinner, when I saw my companions disappearing round a corner. I hastened to catch up with them—and made a wrong turning—and was suddenly lost in a narrow street—and at that very moment a young fellow took hold of my habit and threw me to the ground! You may wonder why he should do such a mad thing, but as I found out afterwards, there are prostitutes in Rome who affect our way of dress to please the appetites of certain men who are depraved enough to—well, really, I do not know how to say it! Seeing me alone, he had thought I was one of them and would be glad of a customer and a bit of play. So there was a reason for it.

"Well, there I was on my back with this young fellow, sent as a vengeance by God, as I thought, trying to do exactly what I had dreamed, night after night, that my statue should do. And do you know, it was nothing in the least like my dream! The stones at my back hurt me, for one thing. And instead of melting with delight, I was screaming my head off in terror and kicking at him as he tried to pull up my skirts, and praying to God that this insane man might not break any of my bones in his rage!

"My screams brought a crowd of people and he went running. So I got off with nothing worse than a bruised back and a sprained knee. But the strangest thing of all was that while I was cured forever of lusting after my Apollo, instead I began to be tormented by a new fear—that I had lusted after *him,* that foolish young man with the foul breath and the one tooth missing!—and I felt strange creepings and crawlings over my body that were half like desire and half like fear and half like disgust and shame with all sorts of other things mixed in—I know that is too many halves but it is how I felt—and nothing at all like the burning desire I had felt for my Apollo. I went to see the statue once more before I left Rome, and it seemed to look at me sadly, as if to say: Don't blame me, poor girl; I'm only a piece of stone. And that was the last time I was so proud as to believe that God had singled me out for a special gift, like chastity—or a special sin, either—or that being thrown down on the ground and hurt had anything to do with any sin of mine, no matter how I mixed the two together in my mind. I dare say you did not find it a great pleasure yesterday, did you?"

Hedwic shook her head. She was crying quietly. She said, "Thank you, Abbess," and the Abbess embraced her. They both seemed happier, but then all of a sudden Sibihd muttered something, so low that one could not hear her.

"The—" she whispered and then she brought it out but still in a whisper: "The blood."

"What, dear, your blood?" said Radegunde.

"No, mother," said Sibihd, beginning to tremble. "The blood. All over us. Walafrid and—and Uta—and Sister Hildegarde—and everyone broken and spilled out like a dish! And none of us had done anything but I could smell it all over me and the children screaming because they were being trampled down, and those demons come up from Hell though we had done nothing and—and—I understand, mother, about the rest, but I will never, ever forget it, oh Christus, it is all round me now, oh, mother, the *blood!*"

Then Sister Sibihd dropped to her knees on the fallen leaves and began to scream, not covering her face as Sister Hedwic had done, but staring ahead with her wide eyes as if she were blind or could see something we could not. The Abbess knelt down and embraced her, rocking her back and forth, saying, "Yes, yes, dear, but we are here; we are here now; that is gone now," but Sibihd continued to scream, covering her ears as if the scream were someone else's and she could hide herself from it.

Thorvald said, looking, I thought, a little uncomfortable, "Cannot your Christ cure this?"

"No," said the Abbess. "Only by undoing the past. And that is the one thing He never does, it seems. She is in Hell now and must go back there many times before she can forget."

"She would make a bad slave," said the Norseman, with a glance at Sister Sibihd, who had fallen silent and was staring ahead of her again. "You need not fear that anyone will want her."

"God," said the Abbess Radegunde calmly, "is merciful."

Thorvald Einarsson said, "Abbess, I am not a bad man."

"For a good man," said the Abbess Radegunde, "you keep surprisingly bad company."

He said angrily, "I did not choose my shipmates. I have had bad luck!"

"Ours has," said the Abbess, "been worse, I think."

"Luck is luck," said Thorvald, clenching his fists. "It comes to some folk and not to others."

"As you came to us," said the Abbess mildly. "Yes, yes, I see, Thorvald Einarsson; one may say that luck is Thor's doing or Odin's doing, but you must know that our bad luck is your own doing and not some god's. You are our back luck, Thorvald Einarsson. It's true that you're not as wicked as your friends, for they kill for pleasure and you do it without feeling, as a business, the way one hews down grain. Perhaps you have seen today some of the grain you have cut. If you had a man's soul, you would not have gone *viking*, luck or no luck, and if your soul were bigger still, you would have tried to stop your shipmates, just as I talk honestly to you now, despite your anger, and just as Christus himself told the truth and was nailed on the cross. If you were a beast you could not break God's law, and if you were a man you would not, but you are neither, and that makes you a kind of monster that spoils everything it touches and never knows the reason, and that is why I will never forgive you until you become a man, a true man with a true soul. As for your friends—"

Here Thorvald Einarsson struck the Abbess on the face with his open hand and knocked her down. I heard Sister Hedwic gasp in horror and behind us Sister Sibihd began to moan. But the Abbess only sat there, rubbing her jaw and smiling a little. Then she said:

"Oh, dear, have I been at it again? I am ashamed of myself. You are quite right to be angry, Torvald; no one can stand me when I go on in that way, least of all myself; it is such a bore. Still, I cannot seem to stop it; I am too used to being the Abbess Radegunde, that is clear. I promise never to torment you again, but you, Thorvald, must never strike me again, because you will be very sorry if you do."

He took a step forward.

"No, no, my dear man," the Abbess said merrily, "I mean no threat—how could I threaten you?—I mean only that I will never tell you any jokes, my spirits will droop, and I will become as dull as any other woman. Confess it now: I am the most interesting thing that has happened to you in years and I have entertained you better, sharp tongue and all, than all the *skalds* at the Court of Norway. And I know more tales and stories than they do—more than anyone in the whole world—for I make new ones when the old ones wear out.

"Shall I tell you a story now?"

"About your Christ?" said he, the anger still in his face.

"No," said she, "about living men and women. Tell me, Torvald, what do you men want from us women?"

"To be talked to death," said he, and I could see there was some anger in him still, but he was turning it to play also.

The Abbess laughed in delight. "Very witty!" she said, springing to her feet and brushing the leaves off her skirt. "You are a very clever man, Torvald. I beg your pardon, Thorvald. I keep forgetting. But as to what men want from women, if you asked the young men, they would only wink and dig one another in the ribs, but that is only how they deceive themselves. That is only body calling to body. They want something quite different and they want it so much that it frightens them. So they pretend it is anything and everything else: pleasure, comfort, a servant in the home. Do you know what it is that they want?"

"What?" said Thorvald.

"The mother," said Radegunde, "as women do, too; we

all want the mother. When I walked before you on the riverbank yesterday, I was playing the mother. Now you did nothing, for you are no young fool, but I knew that sooner or later one of you, so tormented by his longing that he would hate me for it, would reveal himself. And so he did: Thorfinn, with his thoughts all mixed up between witches and grannies and what not. I knew I could frighten him, and through him, most of you. That was the beginning of my bargaining. You Norse have too much of the father in your country and not enough mother; that is why you die so well and kill other folk so well—and live so very, very badly."

"You are doing it again," said Thorvald, but I think he wanted to listen all the same.

"Your pardon, friend," said the Abbess. "You are brave men; I don't deny it. But I know your *sagas* and they are all about fighting and dying and afterwards not Heavenly happiness but the end of the world: everything, even the gods, eaten by the Fenris Wolf and the Midgaard snake! What a pity, to die bravely only because life is not worth living! The Irish know better. The pagan Irish were heroes, with their Queens leading them to battle as often as not, and Father Cairbre, God rest his soul, was complaining only two days ago that the common Irish folk were blasphemously making a goddess out of God's mother, for do they build shrines to Christ or Our Lord or pray to them? No! It is Our Lady of the Rocks and Our Lady of the Sea and Our Lady of the Grove and Our Lady of this or that from one end of the land to the other. And even here it is only the Abbey folk who speak of God the Father and of Christ. In the village if one is sick or another in trouble it is: Holy Mother, save me! and: *Miriam Virginem,* intercede for me, and: Blessed Virgin, blind my husband's eyes! and: Our Lady, preserve my crops, and so on, men and women both. We all need the mother."

"You, too?"

"More than most," said the Abbess.

"And I?"

"Oh, no," said the Abbess, stopping suddenly, for we had all been walking back towards the village as she spoke. "No, and that is what drew me to you at once. I saw it in you and knew you were the leader. It is followers who make leaders, you know, and your shipmates have made you leader, whether you know it or not. What you want is—how shall I say it? You are a clever man, Thorvald, perhaps the cleverest man I have ever met, more even than the scholars I knew in my youth. But your cleverness has had no food. It is a cleverness of the world and not of books. You want to travel and know about folk and their customs, and what strange places are like, and what has happened to men and women in the past. If you take me to Constantinople, it will not be to get a price for me but merely to go there; you went seafaring because this longing itched at you until you could bear it not a year more; I know that."

"Then you are a witch," said he, and he was not smiling.

"No, I only saw what was in your face when you spoke of that city," said she. "Also there is gossip that you spent much time in Göteborg as a young man, idling and marveling at the ships and markets when you should have been at your farm."

She said, "Thorvald, I can feed that cleverness. I am the wisest woman in the world. I know everything—everything! I know more than my teachers; I make it up or it comes to me, I don't know how, but it is real—real!—and I know more than anyone. Take me from here, as your slave if you wish but as your friend also, and let us go to Constantinople and see the domes of gold, and the walls all inlaid with gold, and the people so wealthy you cannot imagine it, and the whole city so gilded it seems to be on fire, pictures as high as a wall, set right in the wall and all made of jewels so there is nothing else like them, redder than the reddest rose, greener than the grass, and with a blue that makes the sky pale!"

"You are indeed a witch," said he, "and not the Abbess Radegunde."

She said slowly, "I think I am forgetting how to be the Abbess Radegunde."

"Then you will not care about them any more," said he, and pointed to Sister Hedwic, who was still leading the stumbling Sister Sibihd.

The Abbess's face was still and mild. She said, "I care. Do not strike me, Thorvald, not ever again, and I will be a good friend to you. Try to control the worst of your men and leave as many of my people free as you can—I know them and will tell you which can be taken away with the least hurt to themselves or others—and I will feed that curiosity and cleverness of yours until you will not recognize this old world any more for the sheer wonder and awe of it; I swear this on my life."

"Done," said he, adding, "but with my luck, your life is somewhere else, locked in a box on top of a mountain, like the troll's in the story, or you will die of old age while we are still at sea."

"Nonsense," she said, "I am a healthy, mortal woman with all my teeth, and I mean to gather many wrinkles yet."

He put his hand out and she took it; then he said, shaking his head in wonder, "If I sold you in Constantinople, within a year you would become Queen of the place!"

The Abbess laughed merrily and I cried in fear, "Me, too! Take me too!" and she said "Oh, yes, we must not forget little Boy News," and lifted me into her arms.

The frightening, tall man, with his face close to mine, said in his strange, sing-song German:

"Boy, would you like to see the whales leaping in the open sea and the seals barking on the rocks? And cliffs so high that a giant could stretch his arms up and not reach their tops? And the sun shining at midnight?"

"Yes!" said I.

"But you will be a slave," he said, "and may be ill-treated

and will always have to do as you are bid. Would you like that?"

"No!" I cried lustily, from the safety of the Abbess's arms, "I'll fight!"

He laughed a mighty, roaring laugh and tousled my head—rather too hard, I thought—and said, "I will not be a bad master, for I am named for Thor Red-beard and he is strong and quick to fight but good-natured, too, and so am I," and the Abbess put me down, and so we walked back to the village, Thorvald and the Abbess Radegunde talking of the glories of this world and Sister Hedwic saying softly, "She is a saint, our Abbess, a saint, to sacrifice herself for the good of the people," and all the time behind us, like a memory, came the low, witless sobbing of Sister Sibihd, who was in Hell.

When we got back we found that Thorfinn was better and the Norsemen were to leave in the morning. Thorvald had a second pallet brought into the Abbess's study and slept on the floor with us that night. You might think his men would laugh at this, for the Abbess was an old woman, but I think he had been with one of the young ones before he came to us. He had that look about him. There was no bedding for the Abbess but an old brown cloak with holes in it, and she and I were wrapped in it when he came in and threw himself down, whistling, on the other pallet. Then he said:

"Tomorrow, before we sail, you will show me the old Abbess's treasure."

"No," said she. "That agreement was broken."

He had been playing with his knife and now ran his thumb along the edge of it. "I can make you do it."

"No," said she patiently, "and now I am going to sleep."

"So you make light of death?" he said. "Good! That is what a brave woman should do, as the *skalds* sing, and not move, even when the keen sword cuts off her eyelashes.

But what if I put this knife here not to your throat but to your little boy's? You would tell me then quick enough!"

The Abbess turned away from him, yawning and saying, "No, Thorvald, because you would not. And if you did, I would despise you for a cowardly oath-breaker and not tell you for that reason. Good night."

He laughed and whistled again for a bit. Then he said: "Was all that true?"

"All what?" said the Abbess, "Oh, about the statue. Yes, but there was no ravisher. I put him in the tale for poor Sister Hedwic."

Thorvald snorted, as if in disappointment. "Tale? You tell lies, Abbess!"

The Abbess drew the old brown cloak over her head and closed her eyes. "It helped her."

Then there was a silence, but the big Norseman did not seem able to lie still. He shifted his body again as if the straw bothered him, and again turned over. He finally burst out, "But what happened!"

She sat up. Then she shut her eyes. She said, "Maybe it does not come into your man's thoughts that an old woman gets tired and that the work of dealing with folk is hard work, or even that it is work at all. Well!

"Nothing 'happened,' Thorvald. Must something happen only if this one fucks that one or one bangs in another's head? I desired my statue to the point of such foolishness that I determined to find a real, human lover, but when I raised my eyes from my fancies to the real, human men of Rome and unstopped my ears to listen to their talk, I realized that the thing was completely and eternally impossible. Oh, those younger sons with their skulking, jealous hatred of the rich, and the rich ones with their noses in the air because they thought themselves of such great consequence because of their silly money, and the timidity of the priests to their superiors, and their superiors' pride, and the artisans' hatred of the peasants, and the peasants being worked like animals from morning until night, and half the men I saw beating their wives and the other half out to cheat some poor girl of her money or her virginity or both—this was enough to put out any fire! And the women doing less harm only because they had less power to do harm, or so it seemed to me then. So I put all away, as one does with any disappointment. Men are not such bad folk when one stops expecting them to be gods, but they are not for me. If that state is chastity, then a weak stomach is temperance, I think. But whatever it is, I have it, and that's the end of the matter."

"*All* men?" said Thorvald Einarsson with his head to one side, and it came to me that he had been drinking, though he seemed sober.

"Thorvald," said the Abbess, "what you want with this middle-aged wreck of a body I cannot imagine, but if you lust after my wrinkles and flabby breasts and lean, withered flanks, do whatever you want quickly and then, for Heaven's sake, let me sleep. I am tired to death."

He said in a low voice, "I need to have power over you."

She spread her hands in a helpless gesture. "Oh, Thorvald, Thorvald, I am a weak little woman over forty years old! Where is the power? All I can do is talk!"

He said, "That's it. That's how you do it. You talk and talk and talk and everyone does just as you please; I have seen it!"

The Abbess said, looking sharply at him, "Very well. If you must. *But if I were you, Norseman, I would as soon bed my own mother.* Remember that as you pull my skirts up."

That stopped him. He swore under his breath, turning over on his side, away from us. Then he thrust his knife into the edge of his pallet, time after time. Then he put the knife under the rolled-up cloth he was using as a pillow. We had no pillow and so I tried to make mine out of the edge of the cloak and failed. Then I thought that the Norseman was afraid of God working in Radegunde, and then I thought of Sister Hedwic's changing color and wondered why. And then I thought of the leaping whales and the seals, which must be like great dogs because of the barking, and then the seals jumped on land and ran to my pallet and lapped at me with great, icy tongues of water so that I shivered and jumped, and then I woke up.

The Abbess Radegunde had left the pallet—it was her warmth I had missed—and was walking about the room. She would step and pause, her skirts making a small noise as she did so. She was careful not to touch the sleeping Thorvald. There was a dim light in the room from the embers that still glowed under the ashes in the hearth, but no light came from between the shutters of the study window, now shut against the cold. I saw the Abbess kneel under the plain wooden cross which hung on the study wall and heard her say a few words in Latin; I thought she was praying. But then she said in a low voice:

"'Do not call upon Apollo and the Muses, for they are deaf things and vain.' But so are you, Pierced Man, deaf and vain."

Then she got up and began to pace again. Thinking of it now frightens me, for it was the middle of the night and no one to hear her—except me, but she thought I was asleep—and yet she went on and on in that low, even voice as if it were broad day and she were explaining something to someone, as if things that had been in her thoughts for years must finally come out. But I did not find anything alarming in it then, for I thought that perhaps all Abbesses had to do such things, and besides she did not seem angry or hurried or afraid; she sounded as calm as if she were discussing the profits from the Abbey's bee-keeping—which I had heard her do—or the accounts for the wine cellars—which I had also heard—and there was nothing alarming in that. So I listened as she continued walking about the room in the dark. She said:

"Talk, talk, talk, and always to myself. But one can't abandon the kittens and puppies; that would be cruel. And being the Abbess Radegunde at least gives one something to do. But I am so sick of the good Abbess Radegunde; I have put on Radegunde every morning of my life as easily as I put on my smock, and then I have had to hear the stupid creature praised all day!—sainted Radegunde, just Radegunde who is never angry or greedy or jealous, kindly Radegunde who sacrifices herself for others, and always the talk, talk, talk, bubbling and boiling in my head with no one to hear or understand, and no one to answer. No, not even in the south, only a line here or a line there, and all written by the dead. Did they feel as I do? That the world is a giant nursery full of squabbles over toys and the babes thinking me some kind of goddess because I'm not greedy for their dolls or bits of straw or their horses made of tied-together sticks?

"Poor people, if only they knew! It's so easy to be temperate when one enjoys nothing, so easy to be kind when one loves nothing, so easy to be fearless when one's life is no better than one's death. And so easy to scheme when the success doesn't matter.

"Would they be surprised, I wonder, to find out what my real thoughts were when Thorfinn's knife was at my throat? Curiosity! But he would not do it, of course; he does everything for show. And they would think I was twice holy, not to care about death.

"Then why not kill yourself, impious Sister Radegunde? Is it your religion which stops you? Oh, you mean the holy wells and the holy trees, and the blessed saints with their blessed relics, and the stupidity that shamed Sister Hedwic, and the promises of safety that drove poor Sibihd mad when the blessed body of her Lord did not protect her and the blessed love of the blessed Mary turned away the sharp point of not one knife? Trash! Idle leaves and sticks, reeds and rushes, filth we sweep off our floors when it grows too thick. As if holiness had anything to do with all of that. As if every place were not as holy as every other and every thing as holy as every other, from the shit in Thorfinn's bowels to the rocks on the ground. As if all places and things were not clouds placed in front of our weak eyes, to keep us from being blinded by that glory, that eternal shining, that blazing all about us, the torrent of light that is everything and is in everything! That is what keeps me from the river, but it never speaks to me or tells me what to do, and to it good and evil are the same—no, it is something else than good or evil; it *is*, only—so it is not God. That I know.

"So, people, is your Radegunde a witch or a demon? Is she full of pride or is Radegunde abject? Perhaps she is a witch. Once, long ago, I confessed to old Gerbertus that I could see things that were far away merely by closing my eyes, and I proved it to him, too, and he wept over me and gave me much penance, crying, "If it come of itself it may be a gift of God, daughter, but it is more likely the work of a demon, so do not do it!" And then we prayed and I told him the power had left me, to make the poor old puppy less troubled in its mind, but that was not true, of course. I could still see Turkey as easily as I could see him, and places far beyond: the squat, wild men of the plains on their ponies, and the strange, tall people beyond that with their great cities and odd eyes, as if one pulled one's eyelid up on a slant, and then the seas with the great, wild lands and the cities more full of gold than Constantinople, and water again until one comes back home, for the world's a ball, as the ancients said.

"But I did stop somehow, over the years. Radegunde never had time, I suppose. Besides, when I opened that door it was only pictures, as in a book, and all to no purpose, and after a while I had seen them all and no longer cared for them. It is the other door that draws me, when it opens itself but a crack and strange things peep through, like Ranulf sister's son and the name of his horse. That door is good but very heavy; it always swings back after a little. I shall have to be on my deathbed to open it all the way, I think.

"The fox is asleep. He is the cleverest yet; there is something in him so that at times one can almost talk to him. But still a fox, for the most part. Perhaps in time....

"But let me see; yes, he is asleep. And the Sibihd puppy is asleep, though it will be having a bad dream soon, I think, and the Thorfinn kitten is asleep, as full of fright as when it wakes, with its claws going in and out, in and out, lest something strangle it in its sleep."

Then the Abbess fell silent and moved to the shuttered window as if she were looking out, so I thought that she was indeed looking out—but not with her eyes—at all the sleeping folk, and this was something she had done every night of her life to see if they were safe and sound. But would she not know that *I* was awake? Should I not try very hard to get to sleep before she caught me? Then it seemed to me that she smiled in the dark, although I could not see it. She said in that same low, even voice: "Sleep or wake, Boy News; it is all one to me. Thou hast heard nothing of any importance, only the silly Abbess talking to herself, only Radegunde saying good-bye to Radegunde, only Radegunde going away—don't cry, Boy News; I am still here—but there: Radegunde has gone. This Norseman and I are alike in one way: our minds are like great houses with many of the rooms locked shut. We crowd in a miserable, huddled few, like poor folk, when we might move freely among them all, as gracious as princes. It is fate that locked away so much of the Norseman—see, Boy News, I do not say his name, not even softly, for that wakes folks—but I wonder if the one who bolted me in was not Radegunde herself, she and old Gerbertus—whom I partly believed—they and the years and years of having to be Radegunde and do the things Radegunde did and pretend to have the thoughts Radegunde had and the endless, endless lies Radegunde must tell everyone, and Radegunde's utter and unbearable loneliness."

She fell silent again. I wondered at the Abbess's talk this time: saying she was not there when she was, and about living locked up in small rooms—for surely the Abbey was the most splendid house in all the world, and the biggest—and how could she be lonely when all the folk loved her? But then she said in a voice so low that I could hardly hear it:

"Poor Radegunde! So weary of the lies she tells and the fooling of men and women with the collars round their necks and bribes of food for good behavior and a careful twitch of the leash that they do not even see or feel. And with the Norseman it will be all the same: lies and flattery and all of it work that never ends and no one ever even sees, so that finally Radegunde will lie down like an ape in a cage, weak and sick from hunger, and will never get up.

"Let her die now. There: Radegunde is dead. Radegunde is gone. Perhaps the door was heavy only because she was on the other side of it, pushing against me. Perhaps it will open all the way now. I have looked in all directions: to the east, to the north and south, and to the west, but there is one place I have never looked and now I will: away from the ball, straight out. Let us see—"

She stopped speaking all of a sudden. I had been falling asleep but this silence woke me. Then I heard the Abbess gasp terribly, like one mortally stricken, and then she said in a whisper so keen and thrilling that it made the hair stand up on my head: *Where art thou?* The next moment she had torn the shutters open and was crying out with all her voice: *Help me! Find me! Oh, come, come, come, or I die!*

This waked Thorvald. With some Norse oath he stumbled up and flung on his sword belt and then put his hand to his dagger; I had noticed this thing with the dagger was a thing Norsemen liked to do. The Abbess was silent. He let out his breath in an oof! and went to light the tallow dip at the live embers under the hearth ashes; when the dip had smoked up, he put it on its shelf on the wall.

He said in German, "What the devil, woman! What has happened?"

She turned round. She looked as if she could not see us, as if she had been dazed by a joy too big to hold, like one who has looked into the sun and is still dazzled by it so that everything seems changed, and the world seems all God's and everything in it like Heaven. She said softly, with her arms around herself, hugging herself: "My people. The real people."

"What are you talking of!" said he.

She seemed to see him then, but only as Sibihd had beheld us; I do not mean in horror as Sibihd had, but beholding through something else, like someone who comes from a vision of bliss which still lingers about her. She said in the same soft voice, "They are coming for me, Thorvald. Is it not wonderful? I knew all this year that something would happen, but I did not know it would be the one thing I wanted in all the world."

He grasped his hair. "*Who* is coming?"

"My people," she said, laughing softly. "Do you not feel them? I do. We must wait three days for they come from very far away. But then—oh, you will see!"

He said, "You've been dreaming. We sail tomorrow."

"Oh, no," said the Abbess simply. "You cannot do that for it would not be right. They told me to wait; they said if I went away, they might not find me."

He said slowly, "You've gone mad. Or it's a trick."

"Oh, no, Thorvald," said she. "How could I trick you? I am your friend. And you will wait these three days, will you not, because you are my friend also."

"You're mad," he said, and started for the door of the study, but she stepped in front of him and threw herself on her knees. All her cunning seemed to have deserted her, or perhaps it was Radegunde who had been the cunning one. This one was like a child. She clasped her hands and tears came out of her eyes; she begged him, saying:

"Such a little thing, Thorvald, only three days! And if they do not come, why then we will go anywhere you like, but if they do come you will not regret it, I promise you;

they are not like the folk here and that place is like nothing here. It is what the soul craves, Thorvald!"

He said, "Get up, woman for God's sake!"

She said, smiling in a sly, frightened way through her blubbered face, "If you let me stay, I will show you the old Abbess's buried treasure, Thorvald."

He stepped back, the anger clear in him. "So this is the brave old witch who cares nothing for death!" he said. Then he made for the door, but she was up again, as quick as a snake, and had flung herself across it.

She said, still with that strange innocence, "Do not strike me. Do not push me. I am your friend!"

He said, "You mean that you lead me by a string around the neck, like a goose. Well, I am tired of that!"

"But I cannot do that any more," said the Abbess breathlessly, "not since the door opened. I am not able now." He raised his arm to strike her and she cowered, wailing, "Do not strike me! Do not push me! Do not, Thorvald!"

He said, "Out of my way then, old witch!"

She began to cry in sobs and gulps. She said, "One is here but another will come! One is buried but another will rise! She will come, Thorvald!" and then in a low, quick voice, "Do not push open this last door. There is one behind it who is evil and I am afraid—" but one could see that he was angry and disappointed and would not listen. He struck her for the second time and again she fell, but with a desperate cry, covering her face with her hands. He unbolted the door and stepped over her and I heard his footsteps go down the corridor. I could see the Abbess clearly—at that time I did not wonder how this could be, with the shadows from the tallow dip half hiding everything in their drunken dance—but I saw every line in her face as if it had been full day, and in that light I saw Radegunde go away from us at last.

Have you ever been at some great king's court or some earl's and heard the storytellers? There are those so skilled in the art that they not only speak for you what the person in the tale said and did, but they also make an action with their faces and bodies as if they truly were that man or woman, so that it is a great surprise to you when the tale ceases, for you almost believe that you have seen the tale happen in front of your very eyes, and it is as if a real man or woman had suddenly ceased to exist, for you forget that all this was only a teller and a tale.

So it was with the woman who had been Radegunde. She did not change; it was still Radegunde's gray hairs and wrinkled face and old body in the peasant woman's brown dress, and yet at the same time it was a stranger who stepped out of the Abbess Radegunde as out of a gown dropped to the floor. This stranger was without feeling, though Radegunde's tears still stood on her cheeks, and there was no kindness or joy in her. She got up without taking care of her dress where the dirty rushes stuck to it; it was as if the dress were an accident and did not concern her. She said in a voice I had never heard before, one with no feeling in it, as if I did not concern her, or Thorvald Einarsson either, as if neither of us were worth a second glance:

"Thorvald, turn around."

Far up in the hall something stirred.

"Now come back. This way."

There were footsteps, coming closer. Then the big Norseman walked clumsily into the room—jerk! jerk! jerk! at every step as if he were being pulled by a rope. Sweat beaded his face. He said, "You—how?"

"By my nature," she said. "Put up your right arm, fox. Now the left. Now both down. Good."

"You—troll!" he said.

"That is so," she said. "Now listen to me, you. There's a man inside you but he's not worth getting at; I tried moments ago when I was new-hatched and he's buried too deep, but now I have grown beak and claws and care nothing for him. It's almost dawn and your boys are stirring; you will go out and tell them that we must stay here another three days. You are weather-wise; make up some story they will believe. And don't try to tell anyone what happened here tonight; you will find that you cannot."

"Folk—come," said he, trying to turn his head, but the effort only made him sweat.

She raised her eyebrows. "Why should they? No one has heard anything. Nothing has happened. You will go out and be as you always are and I will play Radegunde. For three days only. Then you are free."

He did not move. One could see that to remain still was very hard for him; the sweat poured and he strained until every muscle stood out. She said:

"Fox, don't hurt yourself. And don't push me; I am not fond of you. My hand is light upon you only because you still seem to me a little less unhuman than the rest; do not force me to make it heavier. To be plain: I have just broken Thorfinn's neck, for I find that the change improves him. Do not make me do the same to you."

"No worse—than death," Thorvald brought out.

"Ah, no?" said she, and in a moment he was screaming and clawing at his eyes. She said, "Open them, open them; your sight is back," and then, "I do not wish to bother myself thinking up worse things, like worms in your guts. Or do you wish dead sons and a dead wife? Now go.

"*As you always do,*" she added sharply, and the big man turned and walked out. One could not have told from looking at him that anything was wrong.

I had not been sorry to see such a bad man punished, one whose friends had killed our folk and would have taken for slaves—and yet I was sorry, too, in a way, because of the seals barking and the whales—and he *was* splendid, after a fashion—and yet truly I forgot all about that the moment he was gone, for I was terrified of this strange person or demon or whatever it was, for I knew that whoever was in the room with me was not the Abbess Radegunde. I knew also that it could tell where I was and what I was doing, even if I made no sound, and was in a terrible riddle as to what I ought to do when soft fingers touched my face. It was the demon, reaching swiftly and silently behind her.

And do you know, all of a sudden everything was all right! I don't mean that she was the Abbess again—I still had very serious suspicions about that—but all at once I felt light as air and nothing seemed to matter very much because my stomach was full of bubbles of happiness, just as if I had been drunk, only nicer. If the Abbess Radegunde were really a demon, what a joke that was on her people! And she did not, now that I came to think of it, seem a bad sort of demon, more the frightening kind than the killing kind, except for Thorfinn, of course, but then Thorfinn had been a very wicked man. And did not the angels of the Lord smite down the wicked? So perhaps the Abbess was an angel of the Lord and not a demon, but if she were truly an angel, why had she not smitten the Norsemen down when they first came and so saved all our folk? And then I thought that whether angel or demon, she was no longer the Abbess and would love me no longer, and if I had not been so full of the silly happiness which kept tickling about inside me, this thought would have made me weep.

I said, "Will the bad Thorvald get free, demon?"

"No," she said. "Not even if I sleep."

I thought: *But she does not love me.*

"I love thee," said the strange voice, but it was not the Abbess Radegunde's and so was without meaning, but again those soft fingers touched me and there was some kindness in them, even if it was a stranger's kindness.

Sleep, they said.

So I did.

The next three days I had much secret mirth to see the folk bow down to the demon and kiss its hands and weep over it because it had sold itself to ransom them. That is what Sister Hedwic told them. Young Thorfinn had gone out in the night to piss and had fallen over a stone in the dark and broken his neck, which secretly rejoiced our folk, but his comrades did not seem to mind much either, save for one young fellow who had been Thorfinn's friend, I think, and so went about with a long face. Thorvald locked me up in the Abbess's study with the demon every night and went out—or so folk said—to one of the young women, but on those nights the demon was silent, and I lay there with the secret tickle of merriment in my stomach, caring about nothing.

On the third morning I woke sober. The demon—or the Abbess—for in the day she was so like the Abbess Radegunde that I wondered—took my hand and walked us up to Thorvald, who was out picking the people to go aboard the Norseman's boats at the riverbank to be slaves. Folk were standing about weeping and wringing their hands; I thought this strange because of the Abbess's promise to pick those whose going would hurt least, but I know now that least is not none. The weather was bad, cold rain out of mist, and some of Thorvald's companions were speaking sourly to him in the Norse, but he talked them down—bluff and hearty—as if making light of the weather. The demon stood by him and said, in German, in a low voice so that none might hear: "You will say we go to find the Abbess's treasure and then you will go with us into the woods."

He spoke to his fellows in Norse and they frowned, but the end of it was that two must come with us, for the demon said it was such a treasure as three might carry. The demon had the voice and manner of the Abbess Radegunde, all smiles, so they were fooled. Thus we started out into the trees behind the village, with the rain worse and the ground beginning to soften underfoot. As soon as the village was out of sight, the two Norsemen fell behind, but Thorvald did not seem to notice this; I looked back and saw the first man standing in the mud with one foot up, like a goose, and the second with his head lifted and his mouth open so that the rain fell in it. We walked on, the earth sucking at our shoes and all of us getting wet: Thorvald's hair stuck fast against his face, and the demon's old brown cloak clinging to its body. Then suddenly the demon began to breathe harshly and it put its hand to its side with a cry. Its cloak fell off and it stumbled before us between the wet trees, not weeping but breathing hard. Then I saw, ahead of us through the pelting rain, a kind of shining among the bare tree trunks, and as we came nearer the shining became more clear until it was very plain to see, not a blazing thing like a fire at night but a mild and even brightness as though the sunlight were coming through the clouds pleasantly but without strength, as it often does at the beginning of the year.

And then there were folk inside the brightness, both men and women, all dressed in white, and they held out their arms to us, and the demon ran to them, crying out loudly and weeping but paying no mind to the tree branches which struck it across the face and body. Sometimes it fell but it quickly got up again. When it reached the strange folk they embraced it, and I thought that the filth and mud of its gown would stain their white clothing, but the foulness dropped off and would not cling to those clean garments. None of the strange folk spoke a word, nor did the Abbess—I knew then that she was no demon, whatever she was—but I felt them talk to one another, as if in my mind, although I know not how this could be nor the sense of what they said. An odd thing was that as I came closer I could see they were not standing on the ground, as in the way of nature, but higher up, inside the shining, and that their white robes were nothing at all like ours, for they clung to the body so that one might see the people's legs all the way up to the place where the legs joined, even the women's. And some of the folk were like us, but most had a darker color, and some looked as if they had been smeared with soot—there are such persons in the far parts of the world, you know, as I found out later; it is their own natural color—and there were some with the odd eyes the Abbess had spoken of—but the oddest thing of all I will not tell you now. When the Abbess had embraced and kissed them all and all had wept, she turned and looked down upon us: Thorvald standing there as if held by a rope and I, who had lost my fear and had crept close in pure awe, for there was such a joy about these people, like the light about them, mild as spring light and yet as strong as in a spring where the winter has gone forever.

"Come to me, Thorvald," said the Abbess, and one could not see from her face if she loved or hated him. He moved closer—jerk! jerk!—and she reached down and touched his forehead with her fingertips, at which one side of his lip lifted, as a dog's does when it snarls.

"As thou knowest," said the Abbess quietly, "I hate thee and would be revenged upon thee. Thus I swore to myself three days ago, and such vows are not lightly broken."

I saw him snarl again and he turned his eyes from her.

"I must go soon," said the Abbess, unmoved, "for I could stay here long years only as Radegunde, and Radegunde is no more; none of us can remain here long as our proper selves or even in our true bodies, for if we do we go mad like Sibihd or walk into the river and drown or stop our own hearts, so miserable, wicked, and brutish does your world seem to us. Nor may we come in large companies, for we are few and our strength is not great and we have much to learn and study of thy folk so that we may teach and help without marring all in our ignorance. And ignorant or wise, we can do naught except thy folk aid us.

"Here is my revenge," said the Abbess, and he seemed to writhe under the touch of her fingers, for all they were so light. "Henceforth be not Thorvald Farmer nor yet Thorvald Seafarer but Thorvald Peacemaker, Thorvald War-hater, put into anguish by bloodshed and agonized at cruelty. I cannot make long thy life—that gift is beyond me—but I give thee this: to the end of thy days, long or short, thou wilt know the Presence about thee always, as I do, and thou wilt know that it is neither good nor evil, as I do, and this knowing will trouble and frighten thee always, as it does me, and so about this one thing, as about many another, Thorvald Peacemaker will never have peace.

"Now, Thorvald, go back to the village and tell thy comrades I was assumed into the company of the saints, straight up to Heaven. Thou mayst believe it, if thou will. That is all my revenge."

Then she took away her hand, and he turned and walked from us like a man in a dream, holding out his hands as if to feel the rain and stumbling now and again, as one who wakes from a vision.

Then I began to grieve, for I knew she would be going away with the strange people, and it was to me as if all the love and care and light in the world were leaving me. I crept close to her, meaning to spring secretly onto the shining place and so go away with them, but she spied me and said, "Silly Radulphus, you cannot," and that *you* hurt me more than anything else so that I began to bawl.

"Child," said the Abbess, "come to me," and loudly weeping I leaned against her knees. I felt the shining around me, all bright and good and warm, that wiped away all grief, and then the Abbess's touch on my hair.

She said, "Remember me. And be... content."

I nodded, wishing I dared to look up at her face, but when I did, she had already gone with her friends. Not up into the sky, you understand, but as if they moved very swiftly backwards among the trees—although the trees were still behind them somehow—and as they moved, the shining and the people faded away into the rain until there was nothing left.

Then there was no rain. I do not mean that the clouds parted or the sun came out; I mean that one moment it was raining and cold and the next the sky was clear blue from side to side, and it was splendid, sunny, breezy, bright, sailing weather. I had the oddest thought that the strange folk were not agreed about doing such a big miracle—and it was hard for them, too—but they had decided that no one would believe this more than all the other miracles folk speak of, I suppose. And it would surely make Thorvald's lot easier when he came back with wild words about saints and Heaven, as indeed it did, later.

Well, that is the tale, really. She said to me "Be content" and so I am; they call me Radulf the Happy now. I have had my share of trouble and sickness, but always somewhere in me there is a little spot of warmth and joy to make it all easier, like a traveler's fire burning out in the wilderness on a cold night. When I am in real sorrow or distress, I remember her fingers touching my hair and that takes part of the pain away, somehow. So perhaps I got the best gift, after all. And she said also, "Remember me," and thus I have, every little thing, although it all happened when I was the age my own grandson is now, and that is how I can tell you this tale today.

And the rest? Three days after the Norseman left, Sibihd got back her wits and no one knew how, though I think I do! And as for Thorvald Einarsson, I have heard that after his wife died in Norway he went to England and ended his days there as a monk but whether this story be true or not I do not know.

I know this: they may call me Happy Radulf all they like, but there is much that troubles me. Was the Abbess Radegunde a demon, as the new priest says? I cannot believe this, although he called her sayings nonsense and the other half blasphemy when I asked him. Father Cairbre, before the Norse killed him, told us stories about the Sidhe, that is, the Irish fairy people, who leave changelings in human cradles; and for a while it seemed to me that Radegunde must be a woman of the Sidhe when I remembered that she could read Latin at the age of two and was such a marvel of learning when so young, for the changelings the fairies leave are not their own children, you understand, but one of the fairy folk themselves, who are hundreds upon hundreds of years old, and the other fairy folk always come back for their own in the end. And yet this could not have been, for Father Cairbre said also that the Sidhe are wanton and cruel and without souls, and neither the Abbess Radegunde nor the people who came for her were one blessed bit like that, although she did break Thorfinn's neck—but then it may be that Thorfinn broke his own neck by chance, just as we all thought at the time, and she told this to Thorvald afterwards, as if she had done it herself, only to frighten him. She had more of a soul with a soul's griefs and joys than most of us, no matter what the new priest says. He never saw her or felt her sorrow and lonesomeness, or heard her talk of the blazing light all around us—and what can that be but God Himself? Even though she did call the crucifix a deaf thing and vain, she must have meant not Christ, you see, but only the piece of wood itself, for she was always telling the Sisters that Christ was in Heaven and not on the wall. And if she said the light was not good or evil, well, there is a traveling Irish scholar who told me of a holy Christian monk named Augustinus who tells us that all which is, is good, and evil is only a lack of the good, like an empty place not filled up. And if the Abbess truly said there was no God, I say it was the sin of despair, and even saints may sin, if only they repent, which I believe she did at the end.

So I tell myself, and yet I know the Abbess Radegunde was no saint, for are the saints few and weak, as she said? Surely not! And then there is a thing I held back in my telling, a small thing, and it will make you laugh and perhaps means nothing one way or the other, but it is this:

Are the saints bald?

These folk in white had young faces but they were like eggs; there was not a stitch of hair on their domes! Well, God may shave His saints if He pleases, I suppose.

But I know she was no saint. And then I believe that she did kill Thorfinn and the light was not God and she not even a Christian or maybe even human, and I remember how Radegunde was to her only a gown to step out of at will, and how she truly hated and scorned Thorvald until she was happy and safe with her own people. Or perhaps it was like her talk about living in a house with the rooms shut up; when she stopped being Radegunde, first one part of her came back and then the other—the joyful part that could not lie or plan and then the angry part—and then they were all together when she was back among her own folk. And then I give up trying to weigh this matter and go back to warm my soul at the little fire she lit in me, that one warm, bright place in the wide and windy dark.

But something troubles me even there and will not be put to rest by the memory of the Abbess's touch on my hair. As I grow older it troubles me more and more. It was the very last thing she said to me, which I have not told you but will now. When she had given me the gift of contentment, I became so happy that I said, "Abbess, you said you would be revenged on Thorvald, but all you did was change him into a good man. That is no revenge!"

What this saying did to her astonished me, for all the color went out of her face and left it gray. She looked suddenly old, like a death's-head, even standing there among her own true folk with love and joy coming from them so strongly that I myself might feel it. She said, "I did not change him. I lent him my eyes, that is all." Then she looked beyond me, as if at our village, at the Norsemen loading their boats with weeping slaves, at all the villages of Germany and England and France where the poor folk sweat from dawn to dark so that the great lords may do battle with one another, at castles under siege with the starving folk within eating mice and rats and sometimes each other, at the women carried off or raped or beaten, at the mothers wailing for their little ones, and beyond this at the great wide world itself with all its battles which I had used to think so grand, and the misery and greediness and fear and jealousy and hatred of folk one for the other, save—perhaps—for a few small bands of savages, but they were so far from us that one could scarcely see them. She said: *No revenge? Thinkest thou so, boy?* And then she said as one who believes absolutely, as one who has seen all the folk at their living and dying, not for one year but for many, not in one place but in all places, as one who knows it all over the whole wide earth:

Think again....

EXCERPT FROM

No Enemy But Time

by Michael Bishop

Michael Bishop, born in Nebraska but for some years a resident of Georgia, is generally recognized as one of the finest writers to enter the science fiction world during the 1970s. A long list of Hugo and Nebula award nominations and a growing shelf of the awards themselves testify to the high regard in which he is held by readers and writers alike. His novelette, The Quickening, *won a Nebula for* 1981.

No Enemy But Time, *the opening chapter of which is presented here, has been widely acclaimed for its dual portrayals, equally penetrating, of Pleistocene Africa and of the world of the late twentieth century.*

FOR nearly eight months Joshua lived in a remote portion of Zarakal's Lolitabu National Park, where an old man of the Wanderobo tribe taught him how to survive without tap water, telephones, or cans of imported tuna. Although hunting was illegal in the country's national parks, President Tharaka granted a special dispensation, for the success of the White Sphinx Project would depend to an

Winner, Nebula for Best Novel of 1982.

alarming extent on Joshua's ability to take care of himself in the Early Pleistocene.

Despite having lived his entire life among the agricultural Kikembu people (Zarakal's largest single ethnic group), Thomas Babington Mubia had never given up the hunting arts of the Wanderobo. In 1934 he had taught a callow Alistair Patrick Blair (today a world-renowned paleoanthropologist) how to catch a duiker barehanded and to dress out its carcass with stone tools chipped into existence on the spot. Now, over half a century later, Blair wanted his old teacher to communicate these same skills to Joshua—for, although considerably slower and not quite so sharp-eyed, Babington had lost none of his basic skills as stalker, slayer, and flint-knapper.

Babington—as everyone who knew him well called him—was tall, sinewy, and grizzled. In polite company he wore khaki shorts, sandals, and any one of a number of different loud sports shirts that Blair had given him, but in the bush he frequently opted for near or total nudity. Welts, scars, wheals, and tubercules pebbled his flesh, in spite of which he appeared in excellent health for a man belonging to *rika ria Ramsay,* an age-grade group that had undergone circumcision during the ascension of Ramsay MacDonald's coalition cabinet in England. For Joshua the old man's incidental bumps and cuts were less troubling than a deliberate vestige of that long-ago circumcision rite.

Ngwati, the Kikembu called it. This was a piece of frayed-looking skin that hung beneath Babington's penis like the pull tab on a Band-Aid wrapper. It hurt Joshua to look at this "small skin." He tried not to let his eyes shift to Babington's crotch, and, for reasons other than Western modesty, he did his darnedest not to shed his shorts or make water within the old man's sight. He was half afraid that to be looked upon naked by Babington would be to acquire *Ngwati* himself.

Until his circumcision Joshua's mentor had attended a mission school run by Blair's Protestant Episcopal parents, and he knew by heart a score of psalms, several of Shakespeare's soliloquies, and most of the poems of Edgar Allan Poe, a great favorite of the old Wanderobo's. Sometimes, in fact, he disconcerted Joshua by standing naked in the night and booming out in a refined British accent whichever of these memory-fixed passages most suited his mood. In July, their first month in the bush, Babington most frequently declaimed the lesser known of two pieces by Poe entitled "To Helen":

> *"But now, at length, dear Dian sank from sight*
> *Into a western couch of thunder-cloud;*
> *And thou, a ghost, amid the entombing trees*
> *Didst glide away.* Only thine eyes remained.
> *They* would not *go—they never yet have gone.*
> *Lighting my lonely pathway home that night,*
> They *have not left me (as my hopes have) since."*

Sitting in the tall acacia in which he and Babington had built a tree house with a stout door, Joshua looked down and asked his mentor if he had ever been married.

"Oh, yes. Four times all at once, but the loveliest and best was Helen Mithaga."

"What happened?"

"During the war, the second one, I walked to Bravanumbi from Makoleni, my home village, and enlisted for service against the evil minions of Hitler in North Africa. I was accepted into a special unit and fought with it for two years. When I returned to Makoleni, three of my wives had divorced me by returning to their families. I was Wanderobo; they were Kikembu. Although Helen was also Kikembu, she had waited.

"We loved each other very much. Later, a year after the war, she was poisoned by a sorcerer who envied me the medals I had won and also my Helen's Elysian beauty. I lost her to the world of spirits, which we call *ngoma.* On nights like this one, dry and clear, I know that she has fixed the eyes of her soul upon me. Therefore, I speak to her everlasting world with another man's poignant words."

This story touched Joshua. He could not regard Babington as a ridiculous figure even when, during the arid month of August, he stood one-footed in the dark and recited,

> *"Hear the sledges with the bells—*
> *Silver bells!*
> *What a world of merriment their melody foretells!*
> *How they tinkle, tinkle, tinkle,*
> *In the icy air of night! . . ."*

Nights were never icy in Lolitabu, which was tucked away in Zarakal's southwestern corner. Instead of bells-on-bobtails you heard elephants trumpeting, hyenas laughing, and maybe even poachers whispering to one another. Babington took pains to insure that Joshua and he never ran afoul of these men, for although some were woebegone amateurs, trying to earn enough money to eat, others were ruthless predators who would kill to avoid detection.

The big cats in the park worried Joshua far more than the poachers did. They did not worry Babington. He would walk the savannah as nonchalantly as a man crossing an empty parking lot. His goal was not to discomfit Joshua, but to school him in the differences among several species of gazelle and antelope, some of which had probably not even evolved by Early Pleistocene times. Joshua tried to listen, but found himself warily eying the lions sprawled under trees on the veldt.

"We do not have an appetizing smell in their nostrils," Babington told Joshua. "The fetor of human beings is repugnant to lions."

"So they will not attack us unless we provoke them?"

Babington pushed a partial plate out of his mouth with his tongue, then drew it back in. "A toothless lion or one gradually losing its sense of smell might be tempted to attack. Who knows?"

"Then why do we come out here without weapons and walk the grasslands like two-legged gods?"

Said Babington pointedly, "That is not how I am walking."

During this extended period in the Zarakali wilderness Joshua dreamed about the distant past no more than once or twice a month, and these dreams were similar in a hazy way to his daily tutorials with Babington. Why had his spirit-traveling episodes given way to more conventional dreaming? Well, in a sense, his survival training with Babington was a waking version of the dreamfaring he had done by himself his entire life. With his eyes wide open, he was isolated between the long-ago landscape of his dreams and the dreams themselves. He stood in the darkness separating the two realities.

One day Babington came upon Joshua urinating into a clump of grass not far from their tree house. Joshua was powerless to halt the process and too nonplused to direct it away from his mentor's gaze. At last, the pressure fully discharged, he shook his cock dry, eased it back into his jockey shorts, buttoned up, and turned to go back to the tree house.

"You are not yet a man," the Wanderobo informed him.

Joshua's embarrassment mutated into anger. "It's not the Eighth Wonder of the World, but it gets me by!"

"You have not been bitten by the knife."

It struck Joshua that Babington was talking about circumcision. A young African man who had not undergone this rite was officially still a boy, whatever his age might be.

"But I'm an American, Babington."

"In this enterprise you are an honorary Zarakali, and you are too old to live any longer in the *nyuba*."

The *nyuba*, Joshua knew, was the circular Kikembu house in which women and young children lived.

"Babington!"

But Babington was adamant. It was unthinkable that any adult male representing all the peoples of Zarakal should proceed with a mission of this consequence—the visiting of the *ngoma* of the spirit world—without first experiencing *irua,* the traditional rite of passage consecrating his arrival at manhood. If Joshua chose not to submit to the knife (which Babington himself would be happy to wield), then Babington would go home to Makoleni and White Sphinx would have to carry on without his blessing.

On a visit to the park in early September, Blair learned of this ultimatum and of Joshua's decision to accede to it—so long as Joshua could impose a condition of his own.

"I don't want a Band-Aid string like Babington's," he told the Great Man. "I think I can put up with the pain and the embarrassment, but you've got to spare me that goddamn little casing pull."

Although less than six feet tall and possessed of a pair of watery blue eyes whose vision had recently begun to deteriorate (a circumstance insufficient to make him wear glasses), Blair was still an imposing figure. His white mustachios and the sun-baked dome of his forehead and pate gave him the appearance of a walrus that had somehow blustered into the tropics and then peremptorily decided to make the region its home. He seemed to be swaggering even when sitting on the sticky upholstery of a Land Rover's front seat, and his voice had the mellow resonance of a bassoon. In the past ten years his appealing ugly-uncle mug had graced the covers of a dozen news magazines and popular scientific journals, and for a thirteen-week period three years ago he had been the host of a PBS program about human evolution entitled *Beginnings,* an effort that had rekindled the old controversy between paleoanthropologists and the so-called scientific creationists and that had incidentally served to make Blair's name a household word in even the smallest hamlets in the United States. By now, though, Joshua was used to dealing with the Great

Man, and he had no qualms about voicing his complaints about Babington's plans for the circumcision rite.

Blair assured Joshua that educated Kikembu, especially Christians, also regarded *Ngwati* with distaste, and that Babington would not try to make him keep the "small skin" if Joshua were vigorously opposed to it.

"I am," said Joshua, but he neatly parried the Great Man's many well-meaning proposals for sidestepping the circumcision rite altogether. He felt he owed Babington, and he wanted to earn the old man's respect.

Apprised of Joshua's intentions, Babington declared that the ceremony would take place two days hence, in the very grove where he and his protégé had their tree house. Blair then informed Joshua that in order to prove himself he must not show any fear prior to the cutting or cry out in pain during it. Such behavior would result in disgrace for himself and his sponsors. Moreover, to lend the rite legitimacy, Babington had sent messages to several village leaders and asked Blair to invite some of the Kikembu from the outpost village of Nyarati as onlookers. Once the knife glinted, they would applaud Joshua's steadfastness or, if he did not bear up, ridicule his public cowardice.

"Onlookers!"

"It's traditional, I'm afraid. Of what point are the strength and beauty of a leopard if no one ever sees them?"

"Of considerable point, if you're the leopard. Besides, we're not talking about leopards. We're talking about my one and only reproductive organ. Onlookers be damned!"

"They're for purposes of verification, Joshua."

"Maybe Babington ought to circumcise a leopard, Dr. Blair. I'd love to see them verify *that.*"

"Now, now," said Alistair Patrick Blair. "Tsk-tsk."

Joshua spent the night before his *irua* at the park's sprawling Edwardian guest lodge with Blair. At dawn he bathed himself in a tub mounted on cast-iron lion's paws, donned a white linen robe, and, in company with the paleo-anthropologist, set off for his rendezvous with Babington aboard a Land Rover driven by a uniformed park attendant.

They arrived in the acacia grove shortly after eight o'clock and found it teeming with young people from Nyarati, both men and women. The women were singing spiritedly, and the boisterous gaiety of the entire crowd seemed out of proportion to its cause, the trimming of an innocent foreskin. Blair pulled off Joshua's robe and pointed him to the spot where the old Wanderobo would perform the surgery.

"You're not to look at Babington, Joshua. Don't try to watch the cutting, either."

"I thought that would be part of proving my manhood."

"No. Rather than being required, it's prohibited."

"Thanks be to Ngai for small mercies."

Naked and shivering, he entered the clearing beneath the tree house, sat down on the matted grass, and averted his face from the ladder that Babington would soon be descending. Blair, his aide, could offer him no physical assitance until the rite was concluded.

The songs of the Kikembu women, the bawdy masculine repartee at his back, and the anxious hiccuping of his heart isolated him from the reality of what was happening. This was not happening to him. Only, of course, it was.

Then Babington was there, kneeling before him with a knife, and Joshua put both fists to the right side of his neck, placed his chin on one fist, and stared out into the savannah. The cutting began. Joshua clenched his teeth and tightened his fists. Doggedly refusing to yip or whimper, he caught sight of a pair of tourist minibuses rolling over the steppe from the vicinity of the guest lodge. That morning while boarding the Land Rover, he recalled, he had seen them parked inside a courtyard next to the lodge. Somehow the tour guide had learned of the approaching ceremony. When the minibuses pulled abreast of the acacia grove, clouds of dust drifting away behind them, Joshua wanted to scream.

The faces in the windows of the two grimy vehicles belonged primarily to astonished Caucasians, many of them elderly women in multicolored head scarves, out-of-fashion pillbox hats, or luxuriant wigs much too youthful for their wearers. The cutting momentarily ceased. Passengers from both vans dismounted at the outher picket of trees and filtered inward to stand behind the swaying and ululating Kikembu women.

"Jesus," Joshua murmured.

"Hush," cautioned Babington. "Or I will deprive you of much future pleasure and many descendants."

A portly, middle-aged tour guide with a florid complexion used a megaphone to make himself heard over the singing and hand-clapping Africans.

The cutting had begun again. Joshua shut out the man's spiel to concentrate on the waves of pain radiating through him from the focus of the knife.

The eyes of the female tourist nearest the guide, Joshua noticed, had grown huge behind her thick-lensed glasses. She was a stout ruin of a woman whose magenta head scarf resembled a babushka. Her body appeared to sway in time with those of the svelte, graceful Africans. Her swaying and the guide's ceaseless patter distracted Joshua from the pain of the circumcision rite.

"Finished," Babington announced.

"Don't leave *Ngwati,*" Blair countered. "Remove it, please."

Babington snorted his contempt for this command, but swiftly removed the offending string of flesh.

In celebration of the successful *irua,* a chorus of voices echoed through the grove and across the steppe. Now Joshua could look down. He saw blood flowing from him into the grass like water from a spigot. Blair steadied him from behind and wrapped the immaculate white robe around his shoulders.

Now people were dancing as well as singing, extolling the initiate's courage as they wove in and out among the trees in a sinuous daisy chain of bodies. Some of the tourists had joined the conga line, and the two groups, Africans and foreigners, were suddenly beginning to blend. The Kikembu waved their arms in encouragement, and more tourists—sheepish old white people—snaked their way into the celebration.

Joshua, afraid he would faint, held the front of his robe away from his groin to keep from staining the garment. The woman with the magenta scarf approached him from the edge of the grove and addressed him in the flat, Alf Landon accents of a native Kansan.

"I'll give you twenty dollars for that robe."

Joshua gaped.

"Tell him twenty dollars for the robe," the old woman commanded Blair. "Another five if he'll let me take a Polaroid. Our tour guide said to ask before I took a Polaroid."

"Mrs. Givens!" Joshua exclaimed. "Kit Givens from Van Luna, Kansas!" He had last seen the old woman at his grandfather's funeral fourteen years ago, piously occupying a rear pew in the stained-glass, apricot-and-umber ambiance of the First Methodist Church. She was seventy-two if she was a minute. Her withered cheeks and chin were tinted all the iridescent colors of a mandrill's mask.

"I've never seen him before," Mrs. Givens told Blair, as if sharing a confidence. "I don't know how he could know my name."

"You pulled my hair in my grandfather's grocery when I was a baby."

The old woman rallied. "You're an impudent little nigger. I wouldn't pay you five dollars to mow my yard."

Defiant despite his weakness, Joshua doffed his robe and handed it to Mrs. Givens. "Here. I want you to have this. Take it back to Van Luna—the sooner the better."

Mrs. Givens took the robe from the bleeding man, backed away from him clutching it, and turned again to the paleoanthropologist. "You'll walk me back to the tour bus, please. I've never met this man in my life."

"Of course, Mrs. Givens."

As Blair directed the old woman through the rowdy throng to the bus, Babington helped Joshua climb the ladder into the tree house. Many of the Kikembu from Nyarati had brought banana leaves to the ceremony, and the old Wanderobo had already arranged the leaves into a pallet upon which Joshua could rest without fear of exacerbating his wounds. His penis would not stick to the banana leaves as to linen or other sorts of bedding, and the wounds would therefore heal more readily.

Lying on this pallet, Joshua saw Babington's creased face staring down at him. A face that seemed to have been created in the same way that wind sculpts sand dunes or rain erodes channels into the hardest rock.

"Everyone wants a piece of the sacred," Joshua whispered. "Even if it isn't sacred. Dreaming makes it so, and the dreaming goes on and on until it's a habit."

"Go to sleep, Joshua," the old man said.

Three weeks passed before Joshua felt strong enough to resume his survival training. For two nights, despite the antibiotics that Blair had brought to Lolitabu from the hospital at Russell-Tharaka Air Force Base, he was delirious. In his delirium he was visited by the lacerated ghost of his adoptive father, as well as a gnomish Spanish woman who opened her blouse and let him nurse like a baby, a young black infantryman with no head, and the robed figure of Mutesa David Christian Ghazali Tharaka, President of Zarakal. This last visitor, Joshua learned from Babington, had actually been there.

"Why was he here? What did he say?"

Babington handed Joshua an autographed picture of the President. "He said he was very proud of you. You are bridging a chasm between Zarakal's pluralistic tribal beginnings and its modern aspirations. That you, an American black man, submitted to the knife bespeaks the fullness of your commitment to our dream."

"What else did he say?"

"He gave me a photograph, too." Babington pointed at the wall of the tree house, where he had hung another copy of the same photograph. This one bore an inscription to the Wanderobo. Joshua could not see it from where he lay, but he could tell that it had made Babington very happy.

At first it disturbed Joshua that he was taking so long to heal, but Babington explained that he himself had suffered intense pain and then a throbbing tenderness for well over a month after his *irua*. By mid-October, just as his mentor had predicted, they were stalking game again, digging tubers, picking fruit, and diving ever deeper into wilderness lore. Joshua's glans was no longer so sensitive that simply to urinate was to conduct electricity. He was himself again.

Joshua paid attention to Babington's lessons. He learned how to alter his upright silhouette by tying foliage about his waist, how to move on a wily diagonal while stalking game, how to club a stick or wounded animal to death without exhausting himself or making an ugly mess of his kill, and how to eat raw meat, bird's eggs, and insects without nausea or qualm. The time in Lolitabu passed quickly.

The night before Joshua was to return to Russell-Tharaka for additional study—textbook and simulator work, with reviews of the paleontological information he had digested last spring and summer—he awoke and went to the door of the tree house. Babington, silhouetted on the edge of the grove, was reciting from Poe:

"Yet if hope has flown away
In a night, or in a day,
In a vision, or in none,
Is it therefore the less gone?
All *that we see or seem*
Is but a dream within a dream."

The Pope of the Chimps

by Robert Silverberg

A look at contemporary chimpanzee intelligence studies carried just a short way into the future—with some thoughts about how chimp-human interactions may inadvertently bring about the evolution of religious beliefs among our primate cousins—in this story from Alan Ryan's anthology Perpetual Light. *Robert Silverberg and Samuel R. Delany are the only writers who have won four Nebula awards: Silverberg's award-winning stories are "Passengers" (1969), "Good News from the Vatican" (1971),* A Time of Changes *(1971), and "Born with the Dead" (1974).*

EARLY last month Vendelmans and I were alone with the chimps in the compound when suddenly he said, "I'm going to faint." It was a sizzling May morning, but Vendelmans had never shown any sign of noticing unusual heat, let alone suffering from it. I was busy talking to Leo and Mimsy and Mimsy's daughter Muffin and I registered Vendelmans' remark without doing anything about it. When you're intensely into talking by sign language, as we are in the project, you sometimes tend not to pay a lot of attention to spoken words.

But then Leo began to sign the trouble sign at me and I turned around and saw Vendelmans down on his knees in the grass, white-faced, gasping, covered with sweat. A few of the chimpanzees who aren't as sensitive to humans as Leo is thought it was a game and began to pantomime him, knuckles to the ground and bodies going limp. "Sick—" Vendelmans said. "Feel—terrible—"

I called for help and Gonzo took his left arm and Kong took his right and somehow, big as he was, we managed to get him out of the compound and up the hill to headquarters. By then he was complaining about sharp pains in his back and under his arms, and I realized that it wasn't just heat prostration. Within a week the diagnosis was in. Leukemia.

They put him on chemotherapy and hormones and after ten days he was back with the project, looking cocky. "They've stabilized it," he told everyone. "It's in remission and I might have ten or twenty years left, or even more. I'm going to carry on with my work."

But he was gaunt and pale, with a tremor in his hands, and it was a frightful thing to have him among us. He might have been fooling himself, though I doubted it, but he wasn't fooling any of us: to us he was a *memento mori,* a walking death's-head-and-crossbones. That laymen think scientists are any more casual about such things than anyone else is something I blame Hollywood for. It is not easy to go about your daily work with a dying man at your side—or a dying man's wife, for Judy Vendelmans showed in her frightened eyes all the grief that Hal Vendelmans himself was repressing. She was going to lose a beloved husband unexpectedly soon and she hadn't had time to adjust to it, and her pain was impossible to ignore. Besides, the nature of Vendelmans' dyingness was particularly unsettling, because he had been so big and robust and outgoing, a true Rabelaisian figure, and somehow between one moment and the next he was transformed into a wraith. "The finger of God," Dave Yost said. "A quick flick of Zeus' pinkie and Hal shrivels like cellophane in a fireplace." Vendelmans was not yet forty.

The chimps suspected something too.

Some of them, such as Leo and Ramona, are fifth-generation signers, bred for alpha intelligence, and they pick up subtleties and nuances very well. "Almost human," visitors like to say of them. We dislike that tag, because the important thing about chimpanzees is that they *aren't* human, that they are an alien intelligent species; but yet I know what people mean. The brightest of the chimps saw right away that something was amiss with Vendelmans, and started making odd remarks. "Big one rotten banana," said Ramona to Mimsy while I was nearby. "He getting empty," Leo said to me as Vendelmans stumbled past us. Chimp metaphors never cease to amaze me. And Gonzo asked him outright: "You go away soon?"

"Go away" is not the chimp euphemism for death. So far as our animals know, no human being has ever died. Chimps die. Human beings "go away." We have kept things on that basis from the beginning, not intentionally at first, but such arrangements have a way of institutionalizing themselves. The first member of the group to die was Roger Nixon, in an automobile accident in the early years of the project, long before my time here, and apparently no one wanted to confuse or disturb the animals by explaining what had happened to him, so no explanations were offered. My second or third year here Tim Lippinger was killed in a ski-lift failure, and again it seemed easier not to go into details with them. And by the time of Will Bechstein's death in that helicopter crackup four years ago the policy was explicit: we chose not to regard his disappearance from the group as death, but mere "going away," as if he had only retired. The chimps do understand death, of course. They may even equate it with "going away," as Gonzo's question suggests. But if they do, they surely see human death as something quite different from chimpanzee death—a translation to another state of being, an ascent on a chariot of fire. Yost believes that they have no comprehension of human death at all, that they think we are immortal, that they think we are gods.

Vendelmans now no longer pretends that he isn't dying. The leukemia is plainly acute and he deteriorates physically from day to day. His original this-isn't-actually-happening attitude has been replaced by a kind of sullen angry acceptance. It is only the fourth week since the onset of the ailment and soon he'll have to enter the hospital.

And he wants to tell the chimps that he's going to die.

"They don't know that human beings can die," Yost said.

"Then it's time they found out," Vendelmans snapped. "Why perpetuate a load of mythological bullshit about us? Why let them think we're gods? Tell them outright that I'm going to die, the way old Egbert died and Salami and Mortimer."

"But they all died naturally," Jan Morton said.

"And I'm not dying naturally?"

She became terribly flustered. "Of old age, I mean. Their life-cycles clearly and understandably came to an end, and they died, and the chimps understood it. Whereas you—" She faltered.

"—am dying a monstrous and terrible death midway through my life," Vendelmans said, and started to break down, and recovered with a fierce effort, and Jan began to cry, and it was generally a bad scene, from which Vendelmans saved us by going on, "It should be of philosophical importance to the project to discover how the chimps react to a revaluation of the human metaphysic. We've ducked every chance we've had to help them understand the nature of mortality. Now I propose we use me to teach them that humans are subject to the same laws they are. That we are not gods."

"And that gods exist," said Yost, "who are capricious and unfathomable, and to whom we ourselves are as less than chimps."

Vendelmans shrugged. "They don't need to hear all that now. But it's time they understood what we are. Or rather, it's time that we learned how much they already understand. Use my death as a way of finding out. It's the first time they've been in the presence of a human who's actually in the process of dying. The other times one of us has died, it's always been in some sort of accident."

Burt Christensen said, "Hal, have you already told them anything about—"

"No," Vendelmans said. "Of course not. Not a word. But I see them talking to each other. They know."

We discussed it far into the night. The question needed careful examination because of the far-reaching consequences of any change we might make in the metaphysical givens of our animals. These chimps have lived in a closed environment here for decades, and the culture they have evolved is a product of what we have chosen to teach them, compounded by their own innate chimpness plus whatever we have unknowingly transmitted to them about ourselves or them. Any radical conceptual material we offer them must be weighed thoughtfully, because its effects will be irreversible, and those who succeed us in this community will be unforgiving if we do anything stupidly premature. If the plan is to observe a community of intelligent primates over a period of many human generations, studying the changes in their intellectual capacity as their linguistic skills increase, then we must at all times take care to let them find things out for themselves, rather than skewing our data by giving the chimps more than their current concept-processing abilities may be able to handle.

On the other hand, Vendelmans was dying right now,

allowing us a dramatic opportunity to convey the concept of human mortality. We had at best a week or two to make use of that opportunity; then it might be years before the next chance.

"What are you worried about?" Vendelmans demanded.

Yost said, "Do you fear dying, Hal?"

"Dying makes me angry. I don't fear it; but I still have things to do, and I won't be able to do them. Why do you ask?"

"Because so far as we know the chimps see death—chimp death—as simply part of the great cycle of events, like the darkness that comes after the daylight. But human death is going to come as a revelation to them, a shock. And if they pick up from you any sense of fear or even anger over your dying, who knows what impact that will have on their way of thought?"

"Exactly. *Who knows?* I offer you a chance to find out!"

By a narrow margin, finally, we voted to let Hal Vendelmans share his death with the chimpanzees. Nearly all of us had reservations about that. But plainly Vendelmans was determined to have a useful death, a meaningful death; the only way he could face his fate at all was by contributing it like this to the project. And in the end I think most of us cast our votes his way purely out of our love for him.

We rearranged the schedules to give Vendelmans more contact with the animals. There are ten of us, fifty of them; each of us has a special field of inquiry—number theory, syntactical innovation, metaphysical exploration, semiotics, tool use, and so on—and we work with chimps of our own choice, subject, naturally, to the shifting patterns of subtribal bonding within the chimp community. But we agreed that Vendelmans would have to offer his revelations to the alpha intelligences—Leo, Ramona, Grimsky, Alice and Atila—regardless of the current structure of the chimp-human dialogues. Leo, for instance, was involved in an ongoing interchange with Beth Rankin on the notion of the change of seasons. Beth more or less willingly gave up her time with Leo to Vendelmans, for Leo was essential in this. We learned long ago that anything important had to be imparted to the alphas first, and they will impart it to the others. A bright chimp knows more about teaching things to his duller cousins than the brightest human being.

The next morning Hal and Judy Vendelmans took Leo, Ramona, and Attila aside and held a long conversation with them. I was busy in a different part of the compound with Gonzo, Mimsy, Muffin and Chump, but I glanced over occasionally to see what was going on. Hal looked radiant—like Moses just down from the mountain after talking with God. Judy was trying to look radiant too, working at it, but her grief kept breaking through: once I saw her turn away from the chimps and press her knuckles to her teeth to hold it back.

Afterward Leo and Grimsky had a conference out by the oak grove. Yost and Charley Damiano watched it with binoculars, but they couldn't make much sense out of it. The chimps, when they sign to each other, use modified gestures much less precise than the ones they use with us; whether this marks the evolution of a special chimp-to-chimp argot designed not to be understood by us, or is simply a factor of chimp reliance on supplementary nonverbal ways of communicating, is something we still don't know, but the fact remains that we have trouble comprehending the sign language they use with each other, particularly the form the alphas use. Then, too, Leo and Grimsky kept wandering in and out of the trees, as if perhaps they knew we were watching them and didn't want us to eavesdrop. A little later in the day Ramona and Alice had the same sort of meeting. Now all five of our alphas must have been in on the revelation.

Somehow the news began to filter down to the rest of them.

We weren't able to observe actual concept transmission. We did notice that Vendelmans, the next day, began to get rather more attention than normal. Little troops of chimpanzees formed about him as he moved—slowly, and in obvious difficulty—about the compound. Gonzo and Chump, who had been bickering for months, suddenly were standing side by side staring intently at Vendelmans. Chicory, normally shy, went out of her way to engage him in a conversation—about the ripeness of the apples on the tree, Vendemans reported. Anna Livia's young twins Shem and Shaun climbed up and sat on Vendelmans' shoulders.

"They want to find out what a dying god is really like," Yost said quietly.

"But look there," Jan Morton said.

Judy Vendelmans had an entourage too: Mimsy, Muffin, Claudius, Buster, and Kong. Staring in fascination, eyes wide, lips extended, some of them blowing little bubbles of saliva.

"Do they think she's dying too?" Beth wondered.

Yost shook his head. "Probably not. They can see there's nothing physically wrong with her. But they're picking up the sorrow-vibes, the death-vibes."

"Is there any reason to think they're aware that Hal is Judy's mate?" Christensen asked.

"It doesn't matter," Yost said. "They can see that she's upset. That interests them, even if they have no way of knowing why Judy would be more upset than any of the rest of us."

"More mysteries out yonder," I said, pointing into the meadow.

Grimsky was standing by himself out there, contemplating something. He is the oldest of the chimps, gray haired, going bald, a deep thinker. He has been here almost from the beginning, more than thirty years, and very little has escaped his attention in that time.

Far off to the left, in the shade of the big beech tree, Leo stood similarly in solitary meditation. He is twenty, the alpha male of the community, the strongest and by far the most intelligent. It was eerie to see the two of them in their individual zones of isolation, like distant sentinels, like Easter Island statues, lost in private reveries.

"Philosophers," Yost murmured.

Yesterday Vendelmans returned to the hospital for good. Before he went, he made his farewells to each of the fifty chimpanzees, even the infants. In the past week he has altered markedly: he is only a shadow of himself, feeble, wasted. Judy says he'll live only another few weeks.

She has gone on leave and probably won't come back until after Hal's death. I wonder what the chimps will make of her "going away," and of her eventual return.

She said that Leo had asked her if she was dying too.

Perhaps things will get back to normal here now.

Christensen asked me this morning, "Have you noticed the way they seem to drag the notion of death into whatever conversation you're having with them these days?"

I nodded. "Mimsy asked me the other day if the moon dies when the sun comes up and the sun dies when the moon is out. It seemed like such a standard primitive metaphor that I didn't pick up on it at first. But Mimsy's too young for using metaphor that easily and she isn't particularly clever. The older ones must be talking about dying a lot, and it's filtering down."

"Chicory was doing subtraction with me," Christensen said. "She signed, *'You take five, two die, you have three.'* Later she turned it into a verb: *'Three die one equals two.'*"

Others reported similar things. Yet none of the animals were talking about Vendelmans and what was about to happen to him, nor were they asking any overt questions about death or dying. So far as we were able to perceive, they had displaced the whole thing into metaphorical diversions. That in itself indicated a powerful obsession. Like most obsessives, they were trying to hide the thing that most concerned them, and they probably thought they were doing a good job of it. It isn't their fault that we're able to guess what's going on in their minds. They are, after all—and we sometimes have to keep reminding ourselves of this—only chimpanzees.

They are holding meetings on the far side of the oak grove, where the little stream runs. Leo and Grimsky seem to do most of the talking, and the others gather around and sit very quietly as the speeches are made. The groups run from ten to thirty chimps at a time. We are unable to discover what they're discussing, though of course we have an idea. Whenever one of us approaches such a gathering, the chimps very casually drift off into three or four separate groups and look exceedingly innocent—"We just out for some fresh air, boss."

Charley Damiano wants to plant a bug in the grove. But how do you spy on a group that converses only in sign language? Cameras aren't as easily hidden as microphones.

We do our best with binoculars. But what little we've been able to observe has been mystifying. The chimp-to-chimp signs they use at these meetings are even more oblique and confusing than the ones we had seen earlier. It's as if they're holding their meetings in pig-latin, or doubletalk, or in some entirely new and private language.

Two technicians will come tomorrow to help us mount cameras in the grove.

Hal Vendelmans died last night. According to Judy, who phoned Dave Yost, it was very peaceful right at the end, an easy release. Yost and I broke the news to the alpha chimps just after breakfast. No euphemisms, just the straight news. Ramona made a few hooting sounds and looked as if she might cry, but she was the only one who seemed emotionally upset. Leo gave me a long deep look of what was almost certainly compassion, and then he hugged me very hard. Grimsky wandered away and seemed to be signing to himself in the new system. Now a meeting seems to be assembling in the oak grove, the first one in more than a week.

The cameras are in place. Even if we can't decipher the new signs, we can at least tape them and subject them to computer analysis until we begin to understand.

Now we've watched the first tapes of a grove meeting, but I can't say we know a lot more than we did before.

For one thing, they disabled two of the cameras right at the outset. Attila spotted them and sent Gonzo and Claudius up into the trees to yank them out. I suppose the remaining cameras went unnoticed; but by accident or deliberate diabolical craftiness, the chimps positioned themselves in such a way that none of the cameras had a clear angle. We did record a few statements from Leo and some give-and-take between Alice and Anna Livia. They spoke in a mixture of standard signs and the new ones, but, without a sense of the context, we've found it impossible to generate any sequence of meanings. Stray signs such as "shirt," "hat," "human," "change" and "banana fly," interspersed with undecipherable stuff, *seem* to be adding up to something, but no one is sure what. We observed no mention of Hal Vendelmans nor any direct references to death. We may be misleading ourselves entirely about the significance of all this.

Or perhaps not. We codified some of the new signs and this afternoon I asked Ramona what one of them meant. She fidgeted and hooted and looked uncomfortable—and not simply because I was asking her to do a tough abstract thing like giving a definition. She was worried. She looked around for Leo, and when she saw him she made that sign at him. He came bounding over and shoved Ramona away. Then he began to tell me how wise and good and gentle I am. He may be a genius, but even a genius chimp is still a chimp, and I told him I wasn't fooled by all his flattery. Then I asked *him* what the new sign meant.

"Jump high come again," Leo signed.

A simple chimpy phrase referring to fun and frolic? So I thought at first, and so did many of my colleagues. But Dave Yost said, "Then why was Ramona so evasive about defining it?"

"Defining isn't easy for them," Beth Rankin said.

"Ramona's one of the five brightest. She's capable of it. Especially since the sign can be defined by use of four other established signs, as Leo proceeded to do."

"What are you getting at, Dave?" I asked.

Yost said, "'*Jump high come again*' might be about a game they like to play, but it could also be an eschatological reference, sacred talk, a concise metaphorical way to speak of death and resurrection, no?"

Mick Falkenburg snorted. "Jesus, Dave, of all the nutty Jesuitical bullshit—"

"Is it?"

"It's possible sometimes to be too subtle in your analysis," Falkenburg said. "You're suggesting that these chimpanzees have a theology?"

"I'm suggesting that they may be in the process of evolving a religion," Yost replied.

Can it be?

Sometimes we lose our perspective with these animals, as Mick indicated, and we overestimate their intelligence; but just as often, I think, we underestimate them.

Jump high come again.

I wonder. Secret sacred talk? A chimpanzee theology? Belief in life after death? A religion?

They know that human beings have a body of ritual and belief that they call religion, though how much they really comprehend about it is hard to tell. Dave Yost, in his metaphysical discussions with Leo and some of the other alphas, introduced the concept long ago. He drew a hierarchy that began with God and ran downward through human beings and chimpanzees to dogs and cats and onward to insects and frogs, by way of giving the chimps some sense of the great chain of life. They had seen bugs and frogs and cats and dogs, but they wanted Dave to show them God, and he was forced to tell them that God is not actually tangible and accessible, but lives high overhead although His essence penetrates all things. I doubt that they grasped much of that. Leo, whose nimble and probing intelligence is a constant illumination to us, wanted Yost to explain how we talked to God and how God talked to us, if He wasn't around to make signs, and Yost said that we had a thing called religion, which was a system of communicating with God. And that was where he left it, a long while back.

Now we are on guard for any indications of a developing religious consciousness among our troop. Even the scoffers—Mick Falkenburg, Beth, to some degree, Charley Damiano—are paying close heed. After all, one of the underlying purposes of this project is to reach an understanding of how the first hominids managed to cross the intellectual boundary that we like to think separates the animals from humanity. We can't reconstruct a bunch of Australopithecines and study them; but we *can* watch chimpanzees who have been given the gift of language build a quasi-protohuman society, and it is the closest thing to traveling back in time that we are apt to achieve. Yost thinks, I think, Burt Christensen is beginning to think, that we have inadvertently kindled an awareness of the divine, of the numinous force that must be worshipped, by allowing them to see that their gods—us—can be struck down and slain by an even higher power.

The evidence so far is slim. The attention given Vendelmans and Judy; the solitary meditations of Leo and Grimsky; the large gatherings in the grove; the greatly accelerated use of modified sign language in chimp-to-chimp talk at those gatherings; the potentially eschatological reference we think we see in the sign that Leo translated as *jump high come again.* That's it. To those of us who want to interpret that as the foundations of religion, it seems indicative of what we want to see; to the rest, it all looks like coincidence and fantasy. The problem is that we are dealing with non-human intelligence and we must take care not to impose our own thought-constructs. We can never be certain if we are operating from a value system anything like that of the chimps. The built-in ambiguities of the sign-language grammar we must use with them complicate the issue. Consider the phrase "banana fly" that Leo used in a speech—a sermon?—in the oak grove, and remember Ramona's reference to the sick Vendelmans as "rotten banana." If we take *fly* to be a verb, "banana fly" might be considered a metaphorical description of Vendelmans' ascent to heaven. If we take it to be a noun, Leo might have been talking about the Drosophila flies that feed on decaying fruit, a metaphor for the corruption of the flesh after death. On the other hand, he may simply have been making a comment about the current state of our garbage dump.

We have agreed for the moment not to engage the chimpanzees in any direct interrogation about any of this. The Heisenberg principle is eternally our rule here: the observer can too easily perturb the thing observed, so we must make only the most delicate of measurements. Even so, of course, our presence among the chimps is bound to have its impact, but we do what we can to minimize it by avoiding leading questions and watching in silence.

Two unusual things today. Taken each by each, they would be interesting without being significant; but if we use each to illuminate the other, we begin to see things in a strange new light, perhaps.

One thing is an increase in vocalizing, noticed by nearly everyone, among the chimps. We know that chimpanzees in the wild have a kind of rudimentary spoken language—a greeting-call, a defiance-call, the grunts that mean "I like the taste of this," the male chimp's territorial hoot, and such: nothing very complex, really not qualitatively much beyond the language of birds or dogs. They also have a fairly rich nonverbal language, a vocabulary of gestures and facial expressions; but it was not until the first experiments decades ago in teaching chimpanzees human sign language that any important linguistic capacity became apparent in them. Here at the research station the chimps communicate almost wholly in signs, as they have been trained to do for generations and as they have taught their young ones to do; they revert to hoots and grunts only in the most elemental situations. We ourselves communicate mainly in signs when we are talking to each other while working with the chimps, and even in our humans-only conferences we use signs as much as speech, from long habit. But suddenly the chimps are making sounds at each other. Odd sounds, unfamiliar sounds, weird clumsy imitations, one might say, of human speech. Nothing that we can understand, naturally: the chimpanzee larynx is simply incapable of duplicating the phonemes humans use. But these new grunts, these tortured blurts of sound, seem intended to mimic our speech. It was Damiano who showed us, as we were watching a tape of a grove session, how Attila was twisting his lips with his hands in what appeared unmistakably to be an attempt to make human sounds come out.

Why?

The second thing is that Leo has started wearing a shirt and a hat. There is nothing remarkable about a chimp in clothing; although we have never encouraged such anthropomorphization here, various animals have taken a fancy from time to time to some item of clothing, have begged it from its owner, and have worn it for a few days or even weeks. The novelty here is that the shirt and the hat belonged to Hal Vendelmans, and that Leo wears them only when the chimps are gathered in the oak grove, which Dave Yost has lately begun calling the "holy grove." Leo found them in the toolshed beyond the vegetable garden. The shirt is ten sizes too big, Vendelmans having been so brawny, but Leo ties the sleeves across his chest and lets the rest dangle down over his back almost like a cloak.

What shall we make of this?

Jan is the specialist in chimp verbal processes. At the meeting tonight she said, "It sounds to me as if they're trying to duplicate the rhythms of human speech even though they can't reproduce the actual sounds. They're playing at being human."

"Talking the god-talk," said Dave Yost.

"What do you mean?" Jan asked.

"Chimps talk with their hands. Humans do too, when speaking with chimps, but when humans talk to humans they use their voices. Humans are gods to chimps, remember. Talking in the way the gods talk is one way of remaking yourself in the image of the gods, of putting on divine attributes."

"But that's nonsense," Jan said. "I can't possibly—"

"Wearing human clothing," I broke in excitedly, "would also be a kind of putting on divine attributes, in the most literal sense of the phrase. Especially if the clothes—"

"—had belonged to Hal Vendelmans," said Christensen.

"The dead god," Yost said.

We looked at each other in amazement.

Charley Damiano said, not in his usual skeptical way but in a kind of wonder, "Dave, are you hypothesizing that Leo functions as some sort of priest, that those are his sacred garments?"

"More than just a priest," Yost said. "A high priest, I think. A Pope. The Pope of the chimps."

Grimsky is suddenly looking very feeble. Yesterday we saw him moving slowly through the meadow by himself, making a long circuit of the grounds as far out as the pond and the little waterfall, then solemnly and ponderously staggering back to the meeting-place at the far side of the grove. Today he has been sitting quietly by the stream, occasionally rocking slowly back and forth, now and then dipping his feet in. I checked the records: he is 43 years old, well along for a chimp, although some have been known to live fifty years and more. Mick wanted to take him to the infirmary but we decided against it; if he is dying, and by all appearances he is, we ought to let him do it with dignity in his own way. Jan went down to the grove to visit him and reported that he shows no apparent signs of disease. His eyes are clear, his face feels cool. Age has withered him and his time is at hand. I feel an enormous sense of loss, for he has a keen intelligence, a long memory, a shrewd and thoughtful nature. He was the alpha male of the troop for many years, but a decade ago, when Leo came of age, Grimsky abdicated in his favor with no sign of a struggle. Behind Grimsky's grizzled forehead there must lie a wealth of subtle and mysterious perceptions, concepts, and insights about which we know practically nothing, and very soon all that will be lost. Let us hope he's managed to teach his wisdom to Leo and Attila and Alice and Ramona.

Today's oddity: a ritual distribution of meat.

Meat is not very important in the diet of chimps, but they do like to have some, and as far back as I can remember Wednesday has been meat day here, when we give them a side of beef or some slabs of mutton or something of that sort. The procedure for dividing up the meat betrays the chimps' wild heritage, for the alpha males eat their fill first, while the others watch, and then the weaker males beg for a share and are allowed to move in to grab, and finally the females and young ones get the scraps. Today was meat day. Leo, as usual, helped himself first, but what happened after that was astounding. He let Attila feed, and then told Attila to offer some meat to Grimsky, who is even weaker today and brushed it aside. *Then Leo put on Vendelmans' hat* and began to parcel out scraps of meat to the others. One by one they came up to him in the current order of ranking and went through the standard begging maneuver, hand beneath chin, palm upward, and Leo gave each one a strip of meat.

"Like taking communion," Charley Damiano muttered. "With Leo the celebrant at the Mass."

Unless our assumptions are totally off base, there is a real religion going on here, perhaps created by Grimsky and under Leo's governance. And Hal Vendelmans' faded old blue work-hat is the tiara of the Pope.

Beth Rankin woke me at dawn and said, "Come fast. They're doing something strange with old Grimsky."

I was up and dressed and awake in a hurry. We have a closed-circuit system now that pipes the events in the grove back to us, and we paused at the screen so that I could see what was going on. Grimsky sat on his knees at the edge of the stream, eyes closed, barely moving. Leo, wearing the hat, was beside him elaborately tying Vendelmans' shirt over Grimsky's shoulders. A dozen or more of the other adult chimps were squatting in a semicircle in front of them.

Burt Christensen said, "What's going on? Is Leo making Grimsky the assistant Pope?"

"I think Leo is giving Grimsky the last rites," I said.

What else could it have been? Leo wore the sacred headdress. He spoke at length using the new signs—the ecclesiastical language, the chimpanzee equivalent of Latin or Hebrew or Sanskrit—and as his oration went on and on, the congregation replied periodically with outbursts of—I suppose—response and approval, some in signs, some with the grunting garbled pseudo-human sounds that Dave Yost thought was their version of god-talk. Throughout it all Grimsky was silent and remote, though occasionally he nodded or murmured or tapped both his shoulders in a gesture whose meaning was unknown to us. The ceremony went on for more than an hour. Then Grimsky leaned forward, and Kong and Chump took him by the arms eased him down until he was lying with his cheek against the ground.

For two, three, five minutes all the chimpanzees were still. At last Leo came forward and removed his hat, setting it on the ground beside Grimsky, and with great delicacy he untied the shirt Grimsky wore. Grimsky did not move. Leo draped the shirt over his own shoulders and donned the hat again.

He turned to the watching chimps and signed, using the old signs that were completely intelligible to us, "Grimsky now be human being."

We stared at each other in awe and astonishment. A couple of us were sobbing. No one could speak.

The funeral ceremony seemed to be over. The chimps were dispersing. We saw Leo sauntering away, hat casually dangling from one hand, the shirt, in the other, trailing over the ground. Grimsky alone remained by the stream. We waited ten minutes and went down to the grove. Grimsky seemed to be sleeping very peacefully, but he was dead, and we gathered him up—Burt and I carried him; he seemed to weigh almost nothing—and took him back to the lab for the autopsy.

In mid-morning the sky darkened and lightning leaped across the hills to the north. There was a tremendous crack of thunder almost instantly and sudden tempestuous rain. Jan pointed to the meadow. The male chimps were doing a bizarre dance, roaring, swaying, slapping their feet against the ground, hammering their hands against the trunks of the trees, ripping off branches and flailing the earth with them. Grief? Terror? Joy at the translation of Grimsky to a divine state? Who could tell? I had never been frightened by our animals before—I knew them too well, I regarded them as little hairy cousins—but now they were terrifying creatures and this was a scene out of time's dawn, as Gonzo and Kong and Attila and Chump and Buster and Claudius and even Pope Leo himself went thrashing about in that horrendous rain, pounding out the steps of some unfathomable rite.

The lightning ceased and the rain moved southward as quickly as it had come, and the dancers went slinking away, each to his favorite tree. By noon the day was bright and warm and it was as though nothing out of the ordinary had happened.

Two days after Grimsky's death I was awakened again at dawn, this time by Mick Falkenburg. He shook my shoulder and yelled at me to wake up, and as I sat there blinking he said, "Chicory's dead! I was out for an early walk and I found her near the place where Grimsky died."

"Chicory? But she's only—"

"Eleven, twelve, something like that. I know."

I put my clothes on while Mick woke the others, and we went down to the stream. Chicory was sprawled out, but not peacefully—there was a dribble of blood at the corner of her mouth, her eyes were wide and horrified, her hands were curled into frozen talons. All about her in the moist soil of the streambank were footprints. I searched my memory for an instance of murder in the chimp community and could find nothing remotely like it—quarrels, yes, and lengthy feuds, and some ugly ambushes and battles, fairly violent, serious injuries now and then. But this had no precedent.

"Ritual murder," Yost murmured.

"Or a sacrifice, perhaps?" suggested Beth Rankin.

"Whatever it is," I said, "they're learning too fast. Recapitulating the whole evolution of religion, including the worst parts of it. We'll have to talk to Leo."

"Is that wise?" Yost asked.

"Why not?"

"We've kept hands off so far. If we want to see how this thing unfolds—"

"During the night," I said, "the Pope and the College of Cardinals ganged up on a gentle young female chimp and killed her. Right now they may be off somewhere sending Alice or Ramona or Anna Livia's twins to chimp heaven. I think we have to weigh the value of observing the evolution of chimp religion against the cost of losing irreplaceable members of a unique community. I say we call in Leo and tell him that it's wrong to kill."

"He knows that," said Yost. "He must. Chimps aren't murderous animals."

"Chicory's dead."

"And if they see it as a holy deed?" Yost demanded.

"Then one by one we'll lose our animals, and at the end we'll just have a couple of very saintly survivors. Do you want that?"

We spoke to Leo. Chimps can be sly and they can be manipulative, but even the best of them, and Leo is the Einstein of chimpanzees, does not seem to know how to lie. We asked him where Chicory was and Leo told us that Chicory was now a human being. I felt a chill at that. Grimsky was also a human being, said Leo. We asked him how he knew that they had become human and he said, "They go where Vendelmans go. When human go away, he become god. When chimpanzee go away, he become human. Right?"

"No," we said.

The logic of the ape is not easy to refute. We told him that death comes to all living creatures, that it is natural and holy, but that only God could decide when it was going to happen. God, we said, calls His creatures to Himself one at a time. God had called Hal Vendelmans, God had called Grimsky, God would someday call Leo and all the rest here. But God had not yet called Chicory. Leo wanted to know what was wrong with sending Chicory to Him ahead of time. Did that not improve Chicory's condition? No, we replied. No, it only did harm to Chicory. Chicory would have been much happier living here with us than going to God so soon. Leo did not seem convinced. Chicory, he said, now could talk words with her mouth and wore shoes on her feet. He envied Chicory very much.

We told him that God would be angry if any more chimpanzees died. We told him that *we* would be angry. Killing chimpanzees was wrong, we said. It was not what God wanted Leo to be doing.

"Me talk to God, find out what God wants," Leo said.

We found Buster dead by the edge of the pond this morning, with indications of another ritual murder. Leo coolly stared us down and explained that God had given orders that all chimpanzees were to become human beings as quickly as possible, and this could only be achieved by the means employed on Chicory and Buster.

Leo is confined now in the punishment tank and we have suspended this week's meat distribution. Yost voted against both of those decisions, saying we ran the risk of giving Leo the aura of a religious martyr, which would enhance his already considerable power. But these killings have to stop. Leo knows, of course, that we are upset about them. But if he believes his path is the path of righteousness, nothing we say or do is going to change his mind.

Judy Vendelmans called today. She has put Hal's death fairly well behind her, misses the project, misses the chimps. As gently as I could, I told her what has been going on here. She was silent a very long time—Chicory was one of her favorites, and Judy has had enough grief already to handle for one summer—but finally she said, "I think I know what can be done. I'll be on the noon flight tomorrow."

We found Mimsy dead in the usual way late this afternoon. Leo is still in the punishment tank—the third day. The congregation has found a way to carry out its rites without its leader. Mimsy's death has left me stunned, but we are all deeply affected, virtually unable to proceed with our work. It may be necessary to break up the community entirely to save the animals. Perhaps we can send them to other research centers for a few months, three of them here, five there, until this thing subsides. But what if it doesn't subside? What if the dispersed animals convert others elsewhere to the creed of Leo?

The first thing Judy said when she arrived was, "Let Leo out. I want to talk with him."

We opened the tank. Leo stepped forth, uneasy, abashed, shading his eyes against the strong light. He glanced at me, at Yost, at Jan, as if wondering which one of us was going to scold him; and then he saw Judy and it was as though he had seen a ghost. He made a hollow rasping sound deep in his throat and backed away. Judy signed hello and stretched out her arms to him. Leo trembled. He was terrified. There was nothing unusual about one of us going on leave and returning after a month or two, but Leo must not have expected Judy ever to return, must in fact have imagined her gone to the same place her husband had gone, and the sight of her shook him. Judy understood all that, obviously, for she quickly made powerful use of it, signing to Leo, "I bring you message from Vendelmans."

"Tell tell tell!"

"Come walk with me," said Judy.

She took him by the hand and led him gently out of the punishment area and into the compound, and down the hill toward the meadow. I watched from the top of the hill, the tall slender woman and the compact, muscular chimpanzee close together, side by side, hand in hand, pausing now to talk, Judy signing and Leo replying in a flurry of gestures, then Judy again for a long time, a brief response from Leo, another cascade of signs from Judy, then Leo squatting, tugging at blades of grass, shaking his head, clapping hand to elbow in his expression of confusion, then to his chin, then taking Judy's hand. They were gone for nearly an hour. The other chimps did not dare approach them. Finally Judy and Leo, hand in hand, came quietly up the hill to headquarters again. Leo's eyes were shining and so were Judy's.

She said, "Everything will be all right now. That's so, isn't it, Leo?"

Leo said, "God is always right."

She made a dismissal sign and Leo went slowly down the hill. The moment he was out of sight, Judy turned away from us and cried a little, just a little; then she asked for a drink; and then she said, "It isn't easy, being God's messenger."

"What did you tell him?" I asked.

"That I had been in heaven visiting Hal. That Hal was looking down all the time and he was very proud of Leo, except for one thing, that Leo was sending too many chimpanzees to God too soon. I told him that God was not yet ready to receive Chicory and Buster and Mimsy, that they would have to be kept in storage cells for a long time, until their true time came, and that that was not good for them. I told him that Hal wanted Leo to know that God hoped he would stop sending him chimpanzees. Then I gave Leo Hal's old wristwatch to wear when he conducts services, and Leo promised he would obey Hal's wishes. That was all. I suspect I've added a whole new layer of mythology to what's developing here, and I trust you won't be angry with me for doing it. I don't believe any more chimps will be killed. And I think I'd like another drink."

Later in the day we saw the chimps assembled by the stream. Leo held his arm aloft and sunlight blazed from the band of gold on his slim hairy wrist, and a great outcry of grunts in god-talk went up from the congregation and they danced before him, and then he donned the sacred hat and the sacred shirt and moved his arms eloquently in the secret sacred gestures of the holy sign language.

There have been no more killings. I think no more will occur. Perhaps after a time our chimps will lose interest in being religious, and go on to other pastimes. But not yet, not yet. The ceremonies continue, and grow ever more elaborate, and we are compiling volumes of extraordinary observations, and God looks down and is pleased. And Leo proudly wears the emblems of his papacy as he bestows his blessing on the worshippers in the holy grove.

Burning Chrome

by William Gibson

William Gibson is a young Canada-based writer whose stories in Omni and other magazines have been attracting attention—and awards nominations—for the past few years. "Burning Chrome" manifests what we are coming to recognize as typical Gibson characteristics: strong narrative drive, a crackling high-tech prose style and a deep familiarity with the texture of twenty-first century life.

IT was hot the night we burned Chrome. Out in the malls and plazas moths were batting themselves to death against the neon, but in Bobby's loft the only light came from a monitor screen and the green and red LEDs on the face of the matrix simulator. I knew every chip in Bobby's simulator by heart; it looked like your workaday Ono-Sendai VII, the "Cyberspace Seven," but I'd rebuilt it so many times that you'd have had a hard time finding a square millimeter of factory circuitry in all that silicon.

We waited side by side in front of the simulator console, watching the time-display in the screen's lower left corner.

"Go for it," I said, when it was time, but Bobby was already there, leaning forward to drive the Russian program into its slot with the heel of his hand. He did it with the tight grace of a kid slamming change into an arcade game, sure of winning and ready to pull down a string of free games.

A silver tide of phosphenes boiled across my field of vision as the matrix began to unfold in my head, a 3-D chessboard, infinite and perfectly transparent. The Russian program seemed to lurch as we entered the grid. If anyone else had been jacked into that part of the matrix, he might have seen a surf of flickering shadow roll out of the little yellow pyramid that represented our computer. The program was a mimetic weapon, designed to absorb local color and present itself as a crash-priority override in whatever context it encountered.

"Congratulations," I heard Bobby say. "We just became an Eastern Seaboard Fission Authority inspection probe..." That meant we were clearing fiberoptic lines with the cybernetic equivalent of a fire siren, but in the simulation matrix we seemed to rush straight for Chrome's data base. I couldn't see it yet, but I already knew those walls were waiting. Walls of shadow, walls of ice.

Chrome: her pretty childface smooth as steel, with eyes that would have been at home on the bottom of some deep Atlantic trench, cold gray eyes that lived under terrible pressure. They said she cooked her own cancers for people who crossed her, rococo custom variations that took years to kill you. They said a lot of things about Chrome, none of them at all reassuring.

So I blotted her out with a picture of Rikki. Rikki kneeling in a shaft of dusty sunlight that slanted into the loft through a grid of steel and glass: her faded camouflage fatigues, her translucent rose sandals, the good line of her bare back as she rummaged through a nylon gear bag. She looks up, and a half-blond curl falls to tickle her nose. Smiling, buttoning an old shirt of Bobby's, frayed khaki cotton drawn across her breasts.

She smiles.

"Son of a bitch," said Bobby, "we just told Chrome we're an IRS audit and three Supreme Court subpoenas... Hang on to your ass, Jack..."

So long, Rikki. Maybe now I see you never.

And so dark, in the halls of Chrome's ice.

Bobby was a cowboy and ice was the nature of his game, *ice* from ICE, Intrusion Countermeasures Electronics. The matrix is an abstract representation of the relationships between data systems. Legitimate programmers jack into their employers' sector of the matrix and find themselves surrounded by bright geometries representing the corporate data.

Towers and fields of it ranged in the colorless nonspace of the simulation matrix, the electronic consensus hallucination that facilitates the handling and exchange of massive quantities of data. Legitimate programmers never see the walls of ice they work behind, the walls of shadow that screen their operations from others, from industrial espionage artists and hustlers like Bobby Quine.

Bobby was a cowboy. Bobby was a cracksman, a burglar, casing mankind's extended electronic nervous system, rustling data and credit in the crowded matrix, monochrome nonspace where the only stars are dense concentrations of information, and high above it all burn corporate galaxies and the cold spiral arms of military systems.

Bobby was another one of those young-old faces you see drinking in the Gentleman Loser, the chic bar for computer cowboys, rustlers, cybernetic second-story men. We were partners.

Bobby Quine and Automatic Jack. Bobby's the thin pale dude with the dark glasses, and Jack's the mean-looking guy with the myoelectric arm. Bobby's software and Jack's hard; Bobby punches console and Jack runs down all the little things that can give you an edge. Or, anyway, that's what the scene watchers in the Gentleman Loser would've told you, before Bobby decided to burn Chrome. But they also might've told you that Bobby was losing his edge, slowing down. He was twenty-eight, Bobby, and that's old for a console cowboy.

Both of us were good at what we did, but somehow that one big score just wouldn't come down for us. I knew where to go for the right gear, and Bobby had all his licks down pat. He'd sit back with a white terry sweatband across his forehead and whip moves on those keyboards faster than you could follow, punching his way through some of the fanciest ice in the business, but that was when something happened that managed to get him totally wired, and that didn't happen often. Not highly motivated, Bobby, and I was the kind of guy who's happy to have the rent covered and a clean shirt to wear.

But Bobby had this thing for girls, like they were his private Tarot or something, the way he'd get himself moving. We never talked about it, but when it started to look like he was losing his touch that summer, he started to spend more time in the Gentleman Loser. He'd sit at a table by the open doors and watch the crowd slide by, nights when the bugs were at the neon and the air smelled of perfume and fast food. You could see his sunglasses scanning those faces as they passed, and he must have decided that Rikki's was the one he was waiting for, the wild card and the luck changer. The new one.

I went to New York to check out the market, to see what was available in hot software.

The Finn's place has a detective hologram in the window, METRO HOLOGRAFIX, over a display of dead flies wearing fur coats of gray dust. The scrap's waist-high, inside, drifts of it rising to meet walls that are barely visible behind nameless junk, behind sagging pressboard shelves stacked with old skin magazines and yellow-spined years of *National Geographics*.

"You need a gun," said the Finn. He looks like a recombo DNA project aimed at tailoring people for high-speed burrowing. "You're in luck. I got the new Smith and Wesson, the four-oh-eight Tactical. Got this xenon projector slung under the barrel, see, batteries in the grip, throw you a twelve-inch high-noon circle in the pitch dark at fifty yards. The light source is so narrow, it's almost impossible to spot. It's just like voodoo in a nightfight."

I let my arm clunk down on the table and started the fingers drumming; the servos in the hand began whining like overworked mosquitoes. I knew that the Finn really hated the sound.

"You looking to pawn that?" He prodded the duralumin wrist joint with the chewed shaft of a felt-tip pen. "Maybe get yourself something a little quieter?"

I kept it up. "I don't need any guns, Finn."

"Okay," he said, "okay," and I quit drumming. "I only got this one item, and I don't even know what it is." He looked unhappy. "I got it off these bridge-and-tunnel kids from Jersey last week."

"So when'd you ever buy anything you didn't know what it was, Finn?"

"Wise ass." And he passed me a transparent mailer with something in it that looked like an audio cassette through the bubble padding. "They had a passport," he said. "They had credit cards and a watch. And that."

"They had the contents of somebody's pockets, you mean."

He nodded. "The passport was Belgian. It was also bogus, looked to me, so I put it in the furnace. Put the cards in with it. The watch was okay, a Porsche, nice watch."

It was obviously some kind of plug-in military program. Out of the mailer, it looked like the magazine of a small assault rifle, coated with nonreflective black plastic. The edges and corners showed bright metal; it had been knocking around for a while.

"I'll give you a bargain on it, Jack. For old times' sake."

I had to smile at that. Getting a bargain from the Finn was like God repealing the law of gravity when you have to carry a heavy suitcase down ten blocks of airport corridor.

"Looks Russian to me," I said. "Probably the emergency sewage controls for some Leningrad suburb. Just what I need."

"You know," said the Finn, "I got a pair of shoes older than you are. Sometimes I think you got about as much class as those yahoos from Jersey. What do you want me to tell you, it's the keys to the Kremlin? You figure out what the goddamn thing is. Me, I just sell the stuff."

I bought it.

Bodiless, we swerve into Chrome's castle of ice. And we're fast, fast. It feels like we're surfing the crest of the invading program, hanging ten above the seething glitch systems as they mutate. We're sentient patches of oil swept along down corridors of shadow.

Somewhere we have bodies, very far away, in a crowded loft roofed with steel and glass. Somewhere we have microseconds, maybe time left to pull out.

We've crashed her gates disguised as an audit and three subpoenas, but her defenses are specifically geared to cope with that kind of official intrusion. Her most sophisticated ice is structured to fend off warrants, writs, subpoenas. When we breached the first gate, the bulk of her data vanished behind core-command ice, these walls we see as leagues of corridor, mazes of shadow. Five separate landlines spurted May Day signals to law firms, but the virus had already taken over the parameter ice. The glitch systems gobble the distress calls as our mimetic subprograms scan anything that hasn't been blanked by core command.

The Russian program lifts a Tokyo number from the unscreened data, choosing it for frequency of calls, average length of calls, the speed with which Chrome returned those calls.

"Okay," says Bobby, "we're an incoming scrambler call from a pal of hers in Japan. That should help."

Ride 'em cowboy.

Bobby read his future in women; his girls were omens, changes in the weather, and he'd sit all night in the Gentleman Loser, waiting for the season to lay a new face down in front of him like a card.

I was working late in the loft one night, shaving down a chip, my arm off and the little waldo jacked straight into the stump.

Bobby came in with a girl I hadn't seen before, and usually I feel a little funny if a stranger sees me working that way, with those leads clipped to the hard carbon studs that stick out of my stump. She came right over and looked at the magnified image on the screen, then saw the waldo moving under its vacuum-sealed dustcover. She didn't say anything, just watched. Right away I had a good feeling about her; it's like that sometimes.

"Automatic Jack, Rikki. My associate."

He laughed, put his arm around her waist, something in his tone letting me know that I'd be spending the night in a dingy room in a hotel.

"Hi," she said. Tall, nineteen or maybe twenty, and she definitely had the goods. With just those few freckles across the bridge of her nose, and eyes somewhere between dark amber and French coffee. Tight black jeans rolled to mid-calf and a narrow plastic belt that matched the rose-colored sandals.

But now when I see her sometimes when I'm trying to sleep, I see her somewhere out on the edge of all this sprawl of cities and smoke, and it's like she's a hologram stuck behind my eyes, in a bright dress she must've worn once, when I knew her, something that doesn't quite reach her knees. Bare legs long and straight. Brown hair, streaked with blond, hoods her face, blown in a wind from somewhere, and I see her wave good-bye.

Bobby was making a show of rooting through a stack of audio cassettes. "I'm on my way, cowboy," I said, unclipping the waldo. She watched attentively as I put my arm back on.

"Can you fix things?" she asked.

"Anything, anything you want, Automatic Jack'll fix it." I snapped my duralumin fingers for her.

She took a little simstim deck from her belt and showed me the broken hinge on the cassette cover.

"Tomorrow," I said, "no problem."

And my oh my, I said to myself, sleep pulling me down the six flights to the street, *what'll Bobby's luck be like with a fortune cookie like that? If his system worked, we'd be striking it rich any night now.* In the street I grinned and yawned and waved for a cab.

Chrome's castle is dissolving, sheets of ice shadow flickering and fading, eaten by the glitch systems that spin out from the Russian program, tumbling away from our central logic thrust and infecting the fabric of the ice itself. The glitch systems are cybernetic virus analogs, self-replicating and voracious. They mutate constantly, in unison, subverting and absorbing Chrome's defenses.

Have we already paralyzed her, or is a bell ringing somewhere, a red light blinking? Does she know?

Rikki Wildside, Bobby called her, and for those first few weeks it must have seemed to her that she had it all, the whole teeming show spread out for her, sharp and bright under the neon. She was new to the scene, and she had all the miles of malls and plazas to prowl, all the shops and clubs, and Bobby to explain the wild side, the tricky wiring on the dark underside of things, all the players and their names and their games. He made her feel at home.

"What happened to your arm?" she asked me one night in the Gentleman Loser, the three of us drinking at a small table in a corner.

"Hang-gliding," I said, "accident."

"Hang-gliding over a wheatfield," said Bobby, "place called Kiev. Our Jack's just hanging there in the dark, under a Nightwing parafoil, with fifty kilos of radar jammer between his legs, and some Russian asshole accidentally burns his arm off with a laser."

I don't remember how I changed the subject, but I did.

I was still telling myself that it wasn't Rikki who was getting to me, but what Bobby was doing with her. I'd known him for a long time, since the end of the war, and I knew he used women as counters in a game, Bobby Quine versus fortune, versus time and the night of cities. And Rikki had turned up just when he needed something to get him going, something to aim for. So he'd set her up as a symbol for everything he wanted and couldn't have, everything he'd had and couldn't keep.

I didn't like having to listen to him tell me how much he loved her, and knowing he believed it only made it worse. He was a past master at the hard fall and the rapid recovery, and I'd seen it happen a dozen times before. He might as well have had NEXT printed across his sunglasses in green dayglo capitals, ready to flash out at the first interesting face that flowed past the tables in the Gentleman Loser.

I knew what he did to them. He turned them into emblems, sigils on the map of his hustler's life, navigation beacons he could follow through a sea of bars and neon. What else did he have to steer by? He didn't love money, in and of itself, not enough to follow its lights. He wouldn't work for power over other people; he hated the responsibility it brings. He had some basic pride in his skill, but that was never enough to keep him pushing.

So he made do with women.

When Rikki showed up, he needed one in the worst way. He was fading fast, and smart money was already whispering that the edge was off his game. He needed that one big score, and soon, because he didn't know any other kind of life, and all his clocks were set for hustler's time, calibrated in risk and adrenaline and that supernal dawn calm that comes when every move's proved right and a sweet lump of someone else's credit clicks into your own account.

It was time for him to make his bundle and get out; so Rikki got set up higher and farther away than any of the others ever had, even though—and I felt like screaming it at him—she was right there, alive, totally real, human, hungry, resilient, bored, beautiful, excited, all the things she was...

Then he went out one afternoon, about a week before I made the trip to New York to see the Finn. Went out and left us there in the loft, waiting for a thunderstorm. Half the skylight was shadowed by a dome they'd never finished, and the other half showed sky, black and blue with clouds. I was standing by the bench, looking up at that sky, stupid with the hot afternoon, the humidity, and she touched me, touched my shoulder, the half-inch border of taut pink scar that the arm doesn't cover. Anybody else ever touched me there, they went on to the shoulder, the neck...

But she didn't do that. Her nails were lacquered black, not pointed, but tapered oblongs, the lacquer only a shade darker than the carbon-fiber laminate that sheathes my arm. And her hand went down the arm, black nails tracing a weld in the laminate, down to the black anodized elbow joint, out to the wrist, her hand soft-knuckled as a child's, fingers spreading to lock over mine, her palm against the perforated duralumin.

Her other palm came up to brush across the feedback

pads, and it rained all afternoon, raindrops drumming on the steel and soot-stained glass above Bobby's bed.

Ice walls flick away like supersonic butterflies made of shade. Beyond them, the matrix's illusion of infinite space. It's like watching a tape of a prefab building going up; only the tape's reversed and run at high speed, and these walls are torn wings.

Trying to remind myself that this place and the gulfs beyond are only representations, that we aren't "in" Chrome's computer, but interfaced with it, while the matrix simulator in Bobby's loft generates this illusion... The core data begin to emerge, exposed, vulnerable... This is the far side of ice, the view of the matrix I've never seen before, the view that fifteen million legitimate console operators see daily and take for granted.

The core data tower around us like vertical freight trains, color-coded for access. Bright primaries, impossibly bright in that transparent void, linked by countless horizontals in nursery blues and pinks.

But ice still shadows something at the center of it all: the heart of all Chrome's expensive darkness, the very heart...

It was late afternoon when I got back from my shopping expedition to New York. Not much sun through the skylight, but an ice pattern glowed on Bobby's monitor screen, a 2-D graphic representation of someone's computer defenses, lines of neon woven like an Art Deco prayer rug. I turned the console off, and the screen went completely dark.

Rikki's things were spread across my workbench, nylon bags spilling clothes and makeup, a pair of bright red cowboy boots, audio cassettes, glossy Japanese magazines about simstim stars. I stacked it all under the bench and then took my arm off, forgetting that the program I'd bought from the Finn was in the righthand pocket of my jacket, so that I had to fumble it out lefthanded and then get it into the padded jaws of the jeweler's vise.

The waldo looks like an old audio turntable, the kind that played disc records, with the vise set up under a transparent dustcover. The arm itself is just over a centimeter long, swinging out on what would've been the tone arm on one of those turntables. But I don't look at that when I've clipped the leads to my stump; I look at the scope, because that's my arm there in black and white, magnification 40×.

I ran a tool check and picked up the laser. It felt a little heavy; so I scaled my weight-sensor input down to a quarter kilo per gram and got to work. At 40× the side of the program looked like a trailer-truck.

It took eight hours to crack; three hours with the waldo and the laser and four dozen taps, two hours on the phone to a contact in Colorado, and three hours to run down a lexicon disc that could translate eight-year-old technical Russian.

Then Cyrillic alphanumerics started reeling down the monitor, twisting themselves into English halfway down. There were a lot of gaps, where the lexicon ran up against specialized military acronyms in the readout I'd bought from my man in Colorado, but it did give me some idea of what I'd bought from the Finn.

I felt like a punk who'd gone out to buy a switchblade and come home with a small neutron bomb.

Screwed again, I thought. *What good's a neutron bomb in a streetfight?* The thing under the dustcover was right out of my league. I didn't even know where to unload it, where to look for a buyer. Someone had, but he was dead, someone with a Porsche watch and a fake Belgian passport, but I'd never tried to move in those circles. The Finn's muggers from the 'burbs had knocked over someone who had some highly arcane connections.

The program in the jeweler's vise was a Russian military icebreaker, a killer-virus program.

It was dawn when Bobby came in alone. I'd fallen asleep with a bag of take-out sandwiches in my lap.

"You want to eat?" I asked him, not really awake, holding out my sandwiches. I'd been dreaming of the program, of its waves of hungry glitch systems and mimetic subprograms; in the dream it was an animal of some kind, shapeless and flowing.

He brushed the bag aside on his way to the console, punched a function key. The screen lit with the intricate pattern I'd seen there that afternoon. I rubbed sleep from my eyes with my left hand, one thing I can't do with my right. I'd fallen asleep trying to decide whether to tell him about the program. Maybe I should try to sell it alone, keep the money, go somewhere new, ask Rikki to go with me.

"Whose is it?" I asked.

He stood there in a black cotton jumpsuit, an old leather jacket thrown over his shoulders like a cape. He hadn't shaved for a few days, and his face looked thinner than usual.

"It's Chrome's," he said.

My arm convulsed, started clicking, fear translated to the myoelectrics through the carbon studs. I spilled the sandwiches, limp sprouts, and bright yellow dairy-produce slices on the unswept wooden floor.

"You're stone-crazy," I said.

"No," he said, "you think she rumbled it? No way. We'd be dead already. I locked onto her through a triple-blind rental system in Mombasa and an Algerian commsat. She knew somebody was having a look-see, but she couldn't trace it."

If Chrome had traced the pass Bobby had made at her ice, we were good as dead. But he was probably right, or she'd have had me blown away on my way back from New

York. "Why her, Bobby? Just give me one reason..."

Chrome: I'd seen her maybe half a dozen times in the Gentleman Loser. Maybe she was slumming, or checking out the human condition, a condition she didn't exactly aspire to. A sweet little heartshaped face framing the nastiest pair of eyes you ever saw. She'd looked fourteen for as long as anyone could remember, hyped out of anything like a normal metabolism on some massive program of serums and hormones. She was as ugly a customer as the street ever produced, but she didn't belong to the street anymore. She was one of the Boys, Chrome, a member in good standing of the local Mob subsidiary. Word was, she'd gotten started as a dealer, back when synthetic pituitary hormones were still proscribed. But she hadn't had to move hormones for a long time. Now she owned the House of Blue Lights.

"You're flat-out crazy, Quine. You give me one sane reason for having that stuff on your screen. You ought to dump it, and I mean *now*..."

"Talk in the Loser," he said, shrugging out of the leather jacket. "Black Myron and Crow Jane. Jane, she's up on all the sex lines, claims she knows where the money goes. So she's arguing with Myron that Chrome's the controlling interest in the Blue Lights, not just some figurehead for the Boys."

"'The Boys,' Bobby," I said. "That's the operative word there. You still capable of seeing that? We don't mess with the Boys, remember? That's why we're still walking around."

"That's why we're still poor, partner." He settled back into the swivel chair in front of the console, unzipped his jumpsuit, and scratched his skinny white chest. "But maybe not for much longer."

"I think maybe this partnership just got itself permanently dissolved."

Then he grinned at me. That grin was truly crazy, feral

and focused, and I knew that right then he really didn't give a shit about dying.

"Look," I said, "I've got some money left, you know? Why don't you take it and get the tube to Miami, catch a hopper to Montego Bay. You need a rest, man. You've got to get your act together."

"My act, Jack," he said, punching something on the keyboard, "never has been this together before." The neon prayer rug on the screen shivered and woke as an animation program cut in, ice lines weaving with hypnotic frequency, a living mandala. Bobby kept punching, and the movement slowed; the pattern resolved itself, grew slightly less complex, became an alternation between two distant configurations. A first-class piece of work, and I hadn't thought he was still that good. "Now," he said, "there, see it? Wait. There. There again. And there. Easy to miss. That's it. Cuts in every hour and twenty minutes with a squirt transmission to their commsat. We could live for a year on what she pays them weekly in negative interest."

"Whose commsat?"

"Zurich. Her bankers. That's her bankbook, Jack. That's where the money goes. Crow Jane was right."

I stood there. My arm forgot to click.

"So how'd you do in New York, partner? You get anything that'll help me cut ice? We're going to need whatever we can get."

I kept my eyes on his, forced myself not to look in the direction of the waldo, the jeweler's vise. The Russian program was there, under the dustcover.

Wild cards, luck changers.

"Where's Rikki?" I asked him, crossing to the console, pretending to study the alternating patterns on the screen.

"Friends of hers," he shrugged, "kids, they're all into simstim." He smiled absently. "I'm going to do it for her, man."

"I'm going out to think about this, Bobby. You want me to come back, you keep your hands off the board."

"I'm doing it for her," he said as the door closed behind me. "You know I am."

And down now, down, the program a roller coaster through this fraying maze of shadow walls, gray cathedral spaces between the bright towers. Headlong speed.

Black ice. Don't think about it. Black ice.

Too many stories in the Gentleman Loser; black ice is a part of the mythology. Ice that kills. Illegal, but then aren't we all? Some kind of neural-feedback weapon, and you connect with it only once. Like some hideous Word that eats the mind from the inside out. Like an epileptic spasm that goes on and on until there's nothing left at all...

And we're diving for the floor of Chrome's shadow castle.

Trying to brace myself for the sudden stopping of breath, a sickness and final slackening of the nerves. Fear of that cold Word waiting, down there in the dark.

I went out and looked for Rikki, found her in a café with a boy with Sendai eyes, half-healed suture lines radiating from his bruised sockets. She had a glossy brochure spread open on the table, Tally Isham smiling up from a dozen photographs, the Girl with the Zeiss Ikon Eyes.

Her little simstim deck was one of the things I'd stacked under my bench the night before, the one I'd fixed for her the day after I'd first seen her. She spent hours jacked into that unit, the contact band across her forehead like a gray plastic tiara. Tally Isham was her favorite, and with the contact band on, she was gone, off somewhere in the recorded sensorium of simstim's biggest star. Simulated stimuli: the world—all the interesting parts, anyway—as perceived by Tally Isham. Tally raced a black Fokker ground-effect plane across Arizona mesa tops. Tally dived the Truk Island preserves. Tally partied with the superrich on private Greek islands, heartbreaking purity of those tiny white seaports at dawn.

Actually she looked a lot like Tally, same coloring and cheekbones. I thought Rikki's mouth was stronger. More sass. She didn't want to *be* Tally Isham, but she coveted the job. That was her ambition, to be in simstim. Bobby just laughed it off. She talked to me about it, though. "How'd I look with a pair of these?" she'd ask, holding a full-page headshot, Tally Isham's blue Zeiss Ikons lined up with her own amber-brown. She'd had her corneas done twice, but she still wasn't twenty-twenty; so she wanted Ikons. Brand of the stars. Very expensive.

"You still window-shopping for eyes?" I asked as I sat down.

"Tiger just got some," she said. She looked tired, I thought.

Tiger was so pleased with his Sendais that he couldn't help smiling, but I doubted whether he'd have smiled otherwise. He had the kind of uniform good looks you get after your seventh trip to the surgical boutique; he'd probably spent the rest of his life looking vaguely like each new season's media frontrunner; not too obvious a copy, but nothing too original, either.

"Sendai, right?" I smiled back.

He nodded. I watched as he tried to take me in with his idea of a professional simstim glance. He was pretending that he was recording. I thought he spent too long on my arm. "They'll be great on peripherals when the muscles heal," he said, and I saw how carefully he reached for his double espresso. Sendai eyes are notorious for depth-perception defects and warranty hassles, among other things.

"Tiger's leaving for Hollywood tomorrow."

"Then maybe Chiba City, right?" I smiled at him. He didn't smile back. "Got an offer, Tiger? Know an agent?"

"Just checking it out," he said quietly. Then he got up and left. He said a quick good-bye to Rikki, but not to me.

"That kid's optic nerves may start to deteriorate inside

six months. You know that, Rikki? Those Sendais are illegal in England, Denmark, lots of places. You can't replace nerves."

"Hey, Jack, no lectures." She stole one of my croissants and nibbled at the tip of one of its horns.

"I thought I was your adviser, kid."

"Yeah. Well, Tiger's not too swift, but everybody knows about Sendais. They're all he can afford. So he's taking a chance. If he gets work, he can replace them."

"With these?" I tapped the Zeiss Ikon brochure. "Lot of money, Rikki. You know better than to take a gamble like that?"

She nodded. "I want Ikons."

"If you're going up to Bobby's, tell him to sit tight until he hears from me."

"Sure. It's business?"

"Business," I said. But it was craziness.

I drank my coffee, and she ate both my croissants. Then I walked her down to Bobby's. I made fifteen calls, each one from a different pay phone.

Business. Bad craziness.

All in all, it took us six weeks to set the burn up, six weeks of Bobby telling me how much he loved her. I worked even harder, trying to get away from that.

Most of it was phone calls. My fifteen initial and very oblique inquiries each seemed to breed fifteen more. I was looking for a certain service Bobby and I both imagined as a requisite part of the world's clandestine economy, but which probably never had more than five customers at a time. It would be one that never advertised.

We were looking for the world's heaviest fence, for a nonaligned money laundry capable of drycleaning a mega-buck on-line cash transfer and then forgetting about it.

All those calls were a waste, finally, because it was the Finn who put me on to what we needed. I'd gone up to New York to buy a new blackbox rig, because we were going broke paying for all those calls.

I put the problem to him as hypothetically as possible.

"Macao," he said.

"Macao?"

"The Long Hum family. Stockbrokers."

He even had the number. You want a fence, ask another fence.

The Long Hum people were so oblique that they made my idea of a subtle approach look like a tactical nuke-out. Bobby had to make two shuttle runs to Hong Kong to get the deal straight. We were running out of capital, and fast. I still don't know why I decided to go along with it in the first place; I was scared of Chrome, and I'd never been all that hot to get rich.

I tried telling myself that it was a good idea to burn the House of Blue Lights because the place was a creep joint, but I just couldn't buy it. I didn't like the Blue Lights, because I'd spent a supremely depressing evening there once, but that was no excuse for going after Chrome. Actually I halfway assumed we were going to die in the attempt. Even with that killer program, the odds weren't exactly in our favor.

Bobby was lost in writing the set of commands we were going to plug into the dead center of Chrome's computer. That was going to be my job, because Bobby was going to have his hands full, trying to keep the Russian program from going straight for the kill. It was too complex for us to rewrite, and so he was going to try to hold it back for the two seconds I needed.

I made a deal with a streetfighter named Miles. He was going to follow Rikki, the night of the burn, keep her in sight, and phone me at a certain time. If I wasn' there, or didn't answer in just a certain way, I'd told him to grab her and put her on the first tube out. I gave him an envelope to give her, money and a note.

Bobby really hadn't thought about that, much, how things would go for her if we blew it. He just kept telling me he loved her, where they were going to go together, how they'd spend the money.

"Buy her a pair of Ikons first, man. That's what she wants. She's serious about that simstim scene."

"Hey," he said, looking up from the keyboard, "she won't need to work. We're going to make it, Jack. She's my luck. She won't ever have to work again."

"Your luck," I said. I wasn't happy. I couldn't remember when I had been happy. "You seen your luck around lately?"

He hadn't, but neither had I. We'd both been too busy.

I missed her. Missing her reminded me of my one night in the House of Blue Lights, because I'd gone there out of missing someone else. I'd gotten drunk to begin with, then I'd started hitting vasopressin inhalers. If your main squeeze has just decided to walk out on you, booze and vasopressin are the ultimate in masochistic pharmacology; the juice makes you maudlin and the vasopressin makes you remember, I mean really remember. Clinically they use the stuff to counter senile amnesia, but the street finds its own uses for things. So I'd bought myself an ultra-intense replay of a bad affair; trouble is, you get the bad with the good. Go gunning for transports of animal ecstasy and you get what you said, too, and what she said to that, how she walked away and never looked back.

I don't remember deciding to go to the Blue Lights, or how I got there, hushed corridors and this really tacky decorative waterfall trickling somewhere, or maybe just a hologram of one. I had a lot of money that night; somebody had given Bobby a big roll for opening a three-second window in someone else's ice.

I don't think the crew on the door liked my looks, but I guess my money was okay.

I had more to drink there when I'd done what I went there for. Then I made some crack to the barman about closet necrophiliacs, and that didn't go down too well. Then this very large character insisted on calling me War Hero, which I didn't like. I think I showed him some tricks with the arm, before the lights went out, and I woke up two days later in a basic sleeping module somewhere else. A cheap place, not even room to hang yourself. And I sat there on that narrow foam slab and cried.

Some things are worse than being alone. But the thing they sell in the House of Blue Lights is so popular that it's almost legal.

At the heart of darkness, the still center, the glitch systems shred the dark with whirlwinds of light, translucent razors spinning away from us; we hang in the center of a silent slow-motion explosion, ice fragments falling away forever, and Bobby's voice comes in across light-years of electronic void illusion—

"Burn the bitch down. I can't hold the thing back—"

The Russian program, rising through towers of data, blotting out the playroom colors. And I plug Bobby's homemade command package into the center of Chrome's cold heart. The squirt transmission cuts in, a pulse of condensed information that shoots straight up, past the thickening tower of darkness, the Russian program, while Bobby struggles to control that crucial second. An unformed arm of shadow twitches from the towering dark, too late.

We've done it.

The matrix folds itself around me like an origami trick.

And the loft smells of sweat and burning circuitry.

I thought I heard Chrome scream, a raw metal sound, but I couldn't have.

Bobby was laughing, tears in his eyes. The elapsed-time figure in the corner of the monitor read 07:24:05. The burn had taken a little under eight minutes.

And I saw that the Russian program had melted in its slot.

We'd given the bulk of Chrome's Zurich account to a

dozen world charities. There was too much there to move, and we knew we had to break her, burn her straight down, or she might come after us. We took less than ten percent for ourselves and shot it through the Long Hum setup in Macao. They took sixty percent of that for themselves and kicked what was left back to us through the most convoluted sector of the Hong Kong exchange. It took an hour before our money started to reach the two accounts we'd opened in Zurich.

I watched zeros pile up behind a meaningless figure on the monitor. I was rich.

Then the phone rang. It was Miles. I almost blew the code phrase.

"Hey, Jack, man, I dunno—What's it all about, with this girl of yours? Kinda funny thing here..."

"What? Tell me."

"I been on her, like you said, tight but out of sight. She goes to the Loser, hangs out, then she gets a tube. Goes to the House of Blue Lights—"

"She what?"

"Side door. *Employees* only. No way I could get past their security."

"Is she there now?"

"No, man, I just lost her. It's insane down here, like the Blue Lights just shut down, looks like for good, seven kinds of alarms going off, everybody running, the heat out in riot gear...Now there's all this stuff going on, insurance guys, real estate types, vans with municipal plates..."

"Miles, where'd she go?"

"Lost her, Jack."

"Look, Miles, you keep the money in the envelope, right?"

"You serious? Hey, I'm real sorry. I—"

I hung up.

"Wait'll we tell her," Bobby was saying, rubbing a towel across his bare chest.

"You tell her yourself, cowboy. I'm going for a walk."

So I went out into the night and the neon and let the

crowd pull me along, walking blind, willing myself to be just a segment of that mass organism, just one more drifting chip of consciousness under the geodesics. I didn't think, just put one foot in front of another, but after a while I did think, and it all made sense. She'd needed the money.

I thought about Chrome, too. That we'd killed her, murdered her, as surely as if we'd slit her throat. The night that carried me along through the malls and plazas would be hunting her now, and she had nowhere to go. How many enemies would she have in this crowd alone? How many would move, now they weren't held back by fear of her money? We'd taken her for everything she had. She was back on the street again. I doubted she'd live till dawn.

Finally I remembered the café, the one where I'd met Tiger.

Her sunglasses told the whole story, huge black shades with a telltale smudge of fleshtone paintstick in the corner of one lens. "Hi, Rikki," I said, and I was ready when she took them off.

Blue. Tally Isham blue. The clear trademark blue they're famous for, ZEISS IKON ringing each iris in tiny capitals, the letters suspended there like flecks of gold.

"They're beautiful," I said. Paintstick covered the bruising. No scars with work that good. "You made some money."

"Yeah, I did." Then she shivered. "But I won't make any more, not that way."

"I think that place is out of business."

"Oh." Nothing moved in her face then. The new blue eyes were still and very deep.

"It doesn't matter. Bobby's waiting for you. We just pulled down a big score."

"No. I've got to go. I guess he won't understand, but I've got to go."

I nodded, watching the arm swing up to take her hand; it didn't seem to be part of me at all, but she held on to it like it was.

"I've got a one-way ticket to Hollywood. Tiger knows some people I can stay with. Maybe I'll even get to Chiba City."

She was right about Bobby. I went back with her. He didn't understand. But she'd already served her purpose, for Bobby, and I wanted to tell her not to hurt for him, because I could see that she did. He wouldn't even come out into the hallway after she had packed her bags. I put the bags down and kissed her and messed up the paintstick, and something came up inside me the way the killer program had risen above Chrome's data. A sudden stopping of the breath, in a place where no word is. But she had a plane to catch.

Bobby was slumped in the swivel chair in front of his monitor, looking at his string of zeros. He had his shades on, and I knew he'd be in the Gentleman Loser by nightfall, checking out the weather, anxious for a sign, someone to tell him what his new life would be like. I couldn't see it being very different. More comfortable, but he'd always be waiting for that next card to fall.

I tried not to imagine her in the House of Blue Lights, working three-hour shifts in an approximation of REM sleep, while her body and bundle of conditioned reflexes took care of business. The customers never got to complain that she was faking it, because those were real orgasms. But she felt them, if she felt them at all, as faint silver flares somewhere out on the edge of sleep. Yeah, it's so popular, it's almost legal. The customers are torn between needing someone and wanting to be alone at the same time, which has probably always been the name of that particular game, even before we had the neuroelectronics to enable them to have it both ways.

I picked up the phone and punched the number for her airline. I gave them her real name, her flight number. "She's changing that," I said, "to Chiba City. That's right. Japan." I thumbed my credit card into the slot and punched my ID code. "First class." Distant hum as they scanned my credit records. "Make that a return ticket."

But I guess she cashed the return fare, or else she didn't need it, because she hasn't come back. And sometimes late at night I'll pass a window with posters of simstim stars, all those beautiful, identical eyes staring back at me out of faces that are nearly as identical, and sometimes the eyes are hers, but none of the faces are, none of them ever are, and I see her far out on the edge of all this sprawl of night and cities, and then she waves good-bye.

Fire Watch

by Connie Willis

Connie Willis is one of the least known writers ever to win a Nebula, and quite certainly the least known writer ever to win two in the same year. But that this swiftly rising Colorado-based writer should be winning awards is not exactly surprising to those who watch these things closely: her brilliant doomsday story "Daisy, in the Sun" was a Hugo nominee in 1980 and has been widely anthologized since.

History hath triumphed over time,
which besides it nothing but eternity hath triumphed over.
—Sir Walter Raleigh

September 20—Of course the first thing I looked for was the firewatch stone. And of course it wasn't there yet. It wasn't dedicated until 1951, accompanying speech by the Very Reverend Dean Walter Matthews. and this is only 1940. I knew that. I went to see the firewatch stone only yesterday, with some kind of misplaced notion that seeing the scene of the crime would somehow help. It didn't.

The only things that would have helped were a crash

Winner, Nebula for Best Novellete of 1982.

course in London during the Blitz and a little more time. I had not gotten either.

"Travelling in time is not like taking the tube, Mr. Bartholomew," the esteemed Dunworthy had said, blinking at me through those antique spectacles of his. "Either you report on the twentieth or you don't go at all."

"But I'm not ready," I'd said. "Look, it took me four years to get ready to travel with St. Paul. *St. Paul.* Not St. Paul's. You can't expect me to get ready for London in the Blitz in two days."

"Yes," Dunworthy had said. "We can." End of conversation.

"Two days!" I had shouted at my roommate Kivrin. "All because some computer adds an apostrophe **s.** And the esteemed Dunworthy doesn't even bat an eye when I tell him. 'Time travel is not like taking the tube, young man,' he says. 'I'd suggest you get ready. You're leaving day after tomorrow.' The man's a total incompetent."

"No," she said. "He isn't. He's the best there is. He wrote the book on St. Paul's. Maybe you should listen to what he says."

I had expected Kivrin to be at least a little sympathetic. She had been practically hysterical when she got her practicum changed from fifteenth to fourteenth century England, and how did either century qualify as a practicum? Even counting infectious diseases they couldn't have been more than a five. The Blitz is an eight, and St. Paul's itself is, with luck, a ten.

"You think I should go see Dunworthy again?" I said.

"Yes."

"And then what? I've got two days. I don't know the money, the language, the history. Nothing."

"He's a good man," Kivrin said. "I think you'd better listen to him while you can." Good old Kivrin. Always the sympathetic ear.

The good man was responsible for my standing just inside the propped-open west doors, gawking like the country boy I was supposed to be, looking for a stone that wasn't there. Thanks to the good man, I was about as unprepared for my practicum as it was possible for him to make me.

I couldn't see more than a few feet into the church. I could see a candle gleaming feebly a long way off and a closer blur of white moving toward me. A verger, or possibly the Very Reverend Dean himself. I pulled out the letter from my clergyman uncle in Wales that was supposed to gain me access to the Dean, and patted my back pocket to make sure I hadn't lost the microfiche *Oxford English Dictionary, Revised, with Historical Supplements,* I'd smuggled out of the Bodleian. I couldn't pull it out in the middle of the conversation, but with luck I could muddle through the first encounter by context and look up the words I didn't know later.

"Are you from the ayarpee?" he said. He was no older than I am, a head shorter and much thinner. Almost ascetic looking. He reminded me of Kivrin. He was not wearing white, but clutching it to his chest. In other circumstances I would have thought it was a pillow. In other circumstances I would know what was being said to me, but there had been no time to unlearn sub-Mediterranean Latin and Jewish law and learn Cockney and air-raid procedures. Two days, and the esteemed Dunworthy, who wanted to talk about the sacred burdens of the historian instead of telling me what the ayarpee was.

"Are you?" he demanded again.

I considered shipping out the *OED* after all on the grounds that Wales was a foreign country, but I didn't think they had microfilm in 1940. Ayarpee. It could be anything, including a nickname for the fire watch, in which case the impulse to say no was not safe at all. "No," I said.

He lunged suddenly toward and past me and peered out the open doors. "Damn," he said, coming back to me. "Where are they then? Bunch of lazy bourgeois tarts!" And so much for getting by on context.

He looked at me closely, suspiciously, as if he thought I was only pretending not to be with the ayarpee. "The church is closed," he said finally.

I held up the envelope and said, "My name's Bartholomew. Is Dean Matthews in?"

He looked out the door a moment longer, as if he expected the lazy bourgeois tarts at any moment and intended to attack them with the white bundle, then he turned and said, as if he were guiding a tour, "This way, please," and took off into the gloom.

He led me to the right and down the south aisle of the nave. Thank God I had memorized the floor plan or at that moment, heading into total darkness, led by a raving verger, the whole bizarre metaphor of my situation would have been enough to send me out the west doors and back to St. John's Wood. It helped a little to know where I was. We should have been passing number twenty-six: Hunt's painting of "The Light of the World"—Jesus with his lantern—but it was too dark to see it. We could have used the lantern ourselves.

He stopped abruptly ahead of me, still raving. "We weren't asking for the bloody Savoy, just a few cots. Nelson's better off than we are—at least he's got a pillow provided." He brandished the white bundle like a torch in the darkness. It was a pillow after all. "We asked for them over a fortnight ago, and here we still are, sleeping on the bleeding generals from Trafalgar because those bitches want to play tea and crumpets with the tommies at Victoria and the Hell with us!"

He didn't seem to expect me to answer his outburst, which was good, because I had understood perhaps one key word in three. He stomped on ahead, moving out of sight of the one pathetic altar candle and stopping again at a black hole. Number twenty-five: stairs to the Whispering Gallery, the Dome, the library (not open to the public). Up the stairs, down a hall, stop again at a medieval door and knock. "I've got to wait for them," he said. "If

I'm not there they'll likely take them over to the Abbey. Tell the Dean to ring them up again, will you?" and he took off down the stone steps, still holding his pillow like a shield against him.

He had knocked, but the door was at least a foot of solid oak, and it was obvious the Very Reverend Dean had not heard. I was going to have to knock again. Yes, well, and the man holding the pinpoint had to let go of it, too, but even knowing it will all be over in a moment and you won't feel a thing doesn't make it any easier to say, "Now!" So I stood in front of the door, cursing the history department and the esteemed Dunworthy and the computer that had made the mistake and brought me here to this dark door with only a letter from a fictitious uncle that I trusted no more than I trusted the rest of them.

Even the old reliable Bodleian had let me down. The batch of research stuff I cross-ordered through Balliol and the main terminal is probably sitting in my room right now, a century out of reach. And Kivrin, who had already done her practicum and should have been bursting with advice, walked around as silent as a saint until I begged her to help me.

"Did you go to see Dunworthy?" she said.

"Yes. You want to know what priceless bit of information he had for me? 'Silence and humility are the sacred burdens of the historian.' He also told me I would love St. Paul's. Golden gems from the master. Unfortunately, what I need to know are the times and places of the bombs so one doesn't fall on me." I flopped down on the bed. "Any suggestions?"

"How good are you at memory retrieval?" she said.

I sat up. "I'm pretty good. You think I should assimilate?"

"There isn't time for that," she said. "I think you should put everything you can directly into long-term."

"You mean endorphins?" I said.

The biggest problem with using memory-assistance drugs

to put information into your long-term memory is that it never sits, even for a micro-second, in your short-term memory, and that makes retrieval complicated, not to mention unnerving. It gives you the most unsettling sense of *déjà vu* to suddenly know something you're positive you've never seen or heard before.

The main problem, though, is not eerie sensations but retrieval. Nobody knows exactly how the brain gets what it wants out of storage, but short-term is definitely involved. That brief, sometimes microscopic, time information spends in short-term is apparently used for something besides tip-of-the-tongue availability. The whole complex sort-and-file process of retrieval is apparently centered in short-term; and without it, and without help of the drugs that put it there or artificial substitutes, information can be impossible to retrieve. I'd used endorphins for examinations and never had any difficulty with retrieval, and it looked like it was the only way to store all the information I needed in anything approaching the time I had left, but it also meant that I would *never* have known any of the things I needed to know, even for long enough to have forgotten them. If and when I could retrieve the information, I would know it. Till then I was as ignorant of it as if it were not stored in some cobwebbed corner of my mind at all.

"You can retrieve without artificials, can't you?" Kivrin said, looking skeptical.

"I guess I'll have to."

"Under stress? Without sleep? Low body endorphin levels?" What exactly had her practicum been? She had never said a word about it, and undergraduates are not supposed to ask. Stress factors in the Middle Ages? I thought everybody slept through them.

"I hope so," I said. "Anyway, I'm willing to try this idea if you think it will help."

She looked at me with that martyred expression and said, "Nothing will help." Thank you, St. Kivrin of Balliol.

But I tried it anyway. It was better than sitting in Dunworthy's rooms having him blink at me through his historically accurate eyeglasses and tell me I was going to love St. Paul's. When my Bodleian requests didn't come, I overloaded my credit and bought out Blackwell's. Tapes on World War II, Celtic literature, history of mass transit, tourist guidebooks, everything I could think of. Then I rented a high-speed recorder and shot up. When I came out of it, I was so panicked by the feeling of not knowing any more than I had when I started that I took the tube to London and raced up Ludgate Hill to see if the firewatch stone would trigger any memories. It didn't.

"Your endorphin levels aren't back to normal yet," I told myself and tried to relax, but that was impossible with the prospect of the practicum looming up before me. And those are real bullets, kid. Just because you're a history major doing his practicum doesn't mean you can't get killed. I read history books all the way home on the tube and right up until Dunworthy's flunkies came to take me to St. John's Wood this morning.

Then I jammed the microfiche *OED* in my back pocket and went off feeling as if I would have to survive by my native wit and hoping I could get hold of artificials in 1940. Surely I could get through the first day without mishap, I thought; and now here I was, stopped cold by almost the first word that was spoken to me.

Well, not quite. In spite of Kivrin's advice that I not put anything in short-term, I'd memorized the British money, a map of the tube system, a map of my own Oxford. It had gotten me this far. Surely I would be able to deal with the Dean.

Just as I had almost gotten up the courage to knock, he opened the door, and as with the pinpoint, it really was over quickly and without pain. I handed him my letter, and he shook my hand and said something understandable like, "Glad to have another man, Bartholomew." He looked strained and tired and as if he might collapse if I told him the Blitz had just started. I know, I know: Keep your mouth shut. The sacred silence, etc.

He said, "We'll get Langby to show you round, shall we?" I assumed that was my Verger of the Pillow, and I was right. He met us at the foot of the stairs, puffing a little but jubilant.

"The cots came," he said to Dean Matthews. "You'd have thought they were doing us a favor. All high heels and hoity-toity. 'You made us miss our tea, luv,' one of them said to me. 'Yes, well, and a good thing, too,' I said. 'You look as if you could stand to lose a stone or two.'"

Even Dean Matthews looked as though he did not completely understand him. He said, "Did you set them up in the crypt?" and then introduced us. "Mr. Bartholomew's just got in from Wales," he said. "He's come to join our volunteers." Volunteers, not fire watch.

Langby showed me around, pointing out various dimnesses in the general gloom and then dragged me down to see the ten folding canvas cots set up among the tombs in the crypt, also in passing Lord Nelson's black marble sarcophagus. He told me I didn't have to stand a watch the first night and suggested I go to bed, since sleep is the most precious commodity in the raids. I could well believe it. He was clutching that silly pillow to his breast like his beloved.

"Do you hear the sirens down here?" I asked, wondering if he buried his head in it.

He looked round at the low stone ceilings. "Some do, some don't. Brinton has to have his Horlich's. Bence-Jones would sleep if the roof fell in on him. I have to have a pillow. The important thing is to get your eight in no matter what. If you don't, you turn into one of the walking dead. And then you get killed."

On that cheering note he went off to post the watches for tonight, leaving his pillow on one of the cots with orders for me to let nobody touch it. So here I sit, waiting for my first air-raid siren and trying to get all this down before I turn into one of the walking or nonwalking dead.

I've used the stolen *OED* to decipher a little Langby. Middling success. A tart is either a pastry or a prostitute (I assume the latter, although I was wrong about the pillow). Bourgeois is a catchall term for all the faults of the middle class. A Tommy's a soldier. Ayarpee I could not find under any spelling and I had nearly given up when something in long-term about the use of acronyms and abbreviations in wartime popped forward (bless you, St. Kivrin) and I realized it must be an abbreviation. ARP. Air Raid Precautions. Of course. Where else would you get the bleeding cots from?

September 21—Now I'm past the first shock of being here, I realize that the history department neglected to tell me what I'm supposed to do in the three-odd months of this practicum. They handed me this journal, the letter from my uncle, and a ten-pound note, and sent me packing into the past. The ten pounds (already depleted by train and tube fares) is supposed to last me until the end of December and get me back to St. John's Wood for pickup when the second letter calling me back to Wales to sick uncle's bedside comes. Till then I live here in the crypt with Nelson, who Langby tells me, is pickled in alcohol inside his coffin. If we take a direct hit, will he burn like a torch or simply trickle out in a decaying stream onto the crypt floor, I wonder. Board is provided by a gas ring, over which are cooked wretched tea and indescribable kippers. To pay for all this luxury I am to stand on the roofs of St. Paul's and put out incendiaries.

I must also accomplish the purpose of this practicum, whatever it may be. Right now the only purpose I care about is staying alive until the second letter from uncle arrives and I can go home.

I am doing makework until Langby has time to "show me the ropes." I've cleaned the skillet they cook the foul little fishes in, stacked wooden folding chairs at the altar end of the crypt (flat instead of standing because they tend to collapse like bombs in the middle of the night), and tried to sleep.

I am apparently not one of the lucky ones who can sleep through the raids. I spent most of the night wondering what St. Paul's risk rating is. Practica have to be at least a six. Last night I was convinced this was a ten, with the crypt as ground zero, and that I might as well have applied for Denver.

The most interesting thing that's happened so far is that I've seen a cat. I am fascinated; but trying not to appear so since they seem commonplace here.

September 22—Still in the crypt. Langby comes dashing through periodically cursing various government agencies (all abbreviated) and promising to take me up on the roofs. In the meantime, I've run out of makework and taught myself to work a stirrup pump. Kivrin was overly concerned about my memory retrieval abilities. I have not had any trouble so far. Quite the opposite. I called up fire-fighting information and got the whole manual with pictures, including instructions on the use of the stirrup pump. If the kippers set Lord Nelson on fire, I shall be a hero.

Excitement last night. The sirens went early and some of the chars who clean offices in the City sheltered in the crypt with us. One of them woke me out of a sound sleep, going like an air raid siren. Seems she'd seen a mouse. We had to go whacking at tombs and under the cots with a rubber boot to persuade her it was gone. Obviously what the history department had in mind: murdering mice.

September 24—Langby took me on rounds. Into the choir, where I had to learn the stirrup pump all over again, assigned rubber boots and a tin helmet. Langby says Commander Allen is getting us asbestos firemen's coats, but hasn't yet, so it's my own wool coat and muffler and very cold on the roofs even in September. It feels like November and looks it, too, bleak and cheerless with no sun. Up to the dome and onto the roofs which should be flat, but in fact are littered with towers, pinnacles, gutters, and statues, all designed expressly to catch and hold incendiaries out of reach. Shown how to smother an incendiary with sand before it burns through the roof and sets the church on fire. Shown the ropes (literally) lying in a heap at the base ofthe dome in case somebody has to go up one of the west towers or over the top of the dome. Back inside and down to the Whispering Gallery.

Langby kept up a running commentary through the whole tour, part practical instruction, part church history. Before we went up into the Gallery he dragged me over to the south door to tell me how Christopher Wren stood in the smoking rubble of Old St. Paul's and asked a workman to bring him a stone from the graveyard to mark the cornerstone. On the stone was written in Latin, "I shall rise again," and Wren was so impressed by the irony that he had the words inscribed above the door. Langby looked as smug as if he had not told me a story every first-year history student knows, but I suppose without the impact of the firewatch stone, the other is just a nice story.

Langby raced me up the steps and onto the narrow balcony circling the Whispering Gallery. He was already halfway round to the other side, shouting dimensions and acoustics at me. He stopped facing the wall opposite and said softly, "You can hear me whispering because of the shape of the dome. The sound waves are reinforced around the perimeter of the dome. It sounds like the very crack of doom up here during a raid. The dome is one hundred and seven feet across. It is eighty feet above the nave."

I looked down. The railing went out from under me and the black-and-white marble floor came up with dizzying speed. I hung onto something in front of me and dropped to my knees, staggered and sick at heart. The sun had come out, and all of St. Paul's seemed drenched in gold. Even the carved wood of the choir, the white stone pillars, the leaden pipes of the organ, all of it golden, golden.

Langby was beside me, trying to pull me free. "Bartholomew," he shouted. "What's wrong? For God's sake, man."

I knew I must tell him that if I let go, St. Paul's and all the past would fall in on me, and that I must not let that happen because I was an historian. I said something, but it was not what I intended because Langby merely tightened his grip. He hauled me violently free of the railing and back onto the stairway, then let me collapse limply on the steps and stood back from me, not speaking.

"I don't know what happened in there," I said. "I've never been afraid of heights before."

"You're shaking," he said sharply. "You'd better lie down." He led me back to the crypt.

September 25—Memory retrieval: ARP manual. Symptoms of bombing victims: Stage one—shock; stupefaction; unawareness of injuries; words may not make sense except to victim. Stage two—shivering; nausea; injuries, losses felt; return to reality. Stage three—talkativeness that cannot be controlled; desire to explain shock behavior to rescuers.

Langby must surely recognize the symptoms, but how does he account for the fact there was no bomb? I can hardly explain my shock behavior to him, and it isn't just the sacred silence of the historian that stops me.

He has not said anything, in fact assigned me my first watches for tomorrow night as if nothing had happened, and he seems no more preoccupied than anyone else. Everyone I've met so far is jittery (one thing I had in short-term was how calm everyone was during the raids) and the raids have not come near us since I got here. They've been mostly over the East End and the docks.

There was a reference tonight to a UXB, and I have been thinking about the Dean's manner and the church being closed when I'm almost sure I remember reading it was open through the entire Blitz. As soon as I get a chance, I'll try to retrieve the events of September. As to retrieving anything else, I don't see how I can hope to remember the right information until I know what it is I am supposed to do here, if anything.

There are no guidelines for historians, and no restrictions either. I could tell everyone I'm from the future if I thought they would believe me. I could murder Hitler if I could get to Germany. Or could I? Time paradox talk abounds in the history department, and the graduate students back from their practica don't say a word one way or the other. Is there a tough, immutable past? Or is there a new past every day and do we, the historians, make it? And what are the consequences of what we do, if there are consequences? And how do we dare do anything without knowing them? Must we interfere boldly, hoping we do not bring about all our downfalls? Or must we do nothing at all, not interfere, stand by and watch St. Paul's burn to the ground if need be so that we don't change the future?

All those are fine questions for a late-night study session. They do not matter here. I could no more let St. Paul's burn down than I could kill Hitler. No, that is not true. I found that out yesterday in the Whispering Gallery. I could kill Hitler if I caught him setting fire to St. Paul's.

September 26—I met a young woman today. Dean Matthews has opened the church, so the watch have been doing duties as chars and people have started coming in again. The young woman reminded me of Kivrin, though Kivrin is a good deal taller and would never frizz her hair like that. She looked as if she had been crying. Kivrin has looked like that since she got back from her practicum. The Middle Ages were too much for her. I wonder how she would have coped with this. By pouring out her fears to the local priest, no doubt, as I sincerely hoped her look-alike was not going to do.

"May I help you?" I said, not wanting in the least to help. "I'm a volunteer."

She looked distressed. "You're not paid?" she said, and wiped at her reddened nose with a handkerchief. "I read about St. Paul's and the fire watch and all and I thought, perhaps there's a position there for me. In the canteen, like, or something. A paying position." There were tears in her red-rimmed eyes.

"I'm afraid we don't have a canteen," I said as kindly as I could, considering how impatient Kivrin always makes me, "and it's not actually a real shelter. Some of the watch sleep in the crypt. I'm afraid we'll all volunteers, though."

"That won't do, then," she said. She dabbed at her eyes with the handkerchief. "I love St. Paul's, but I can't take on volunteer work, not with my little brother Tom back from the country." I was not reading this situation properly. For all the outward signs of distress, she sounded quite cheerful and no closer to tears than when she had come in. "I've got to get us a proper place to stay. With Tom back, we can't go on sleeping in the tubes."

A sudden feeling of dread, the kind of sharp pain you get sometimes from involuntary retrieval, went over me. "The tubes?" I said, trying to get at the memory.

"Marble Arch, usually," she went on. "My brother Tom saves us a place early and I go—" She stopped, held the handkerchief close to her nose, and exploded into it. "I'm sorry," she said, "this awful cold!"

Red nose, watering eyes, sneezing. Respiratory infection. It was a wonder I hadn't told her not to cry. It's only by luck that I haven't made some unforgivable mistake so far, and this is not because I can't get at the long-term memory. I don't have half the information I need even stored: cats and colds and the way St. Paul's looks in full sun. It's only a matter of time before I am stopped cold by something I do not know. Nevertheless, I am going to try for retrieval tonight after I come off watch. At least I can find out whether and when something is going to fall on me.

I have seen the cat once or twice. He is coal-black with a white patch on his throat that looks as if it were painted on for the blackout.

September 27—I have just come down from the roofs. I am still shaking.

Early in the raid the bombing was mostly over the East End. The view was incredible. Searchlights everywhere, the sky pink from the fires and reflecting the Thames, the exploding shells sparkling like fireworks. There was a constant, deafening thunder broken by the occasional droning of the planes high overhead, then the repeating stutter of the ack-ack guns.

About midnight the bombs began falling quite near with a horrible sound like a train running over me. It took every bit of will I had to keep from flinging myself flat on the roof, but Langby was watching. I didn't want to give him the satisfaction of watching a repeat performance of my behavior in the dome. I kept my head up and my sandbucket firmly in hand and felt quite proud of myself.

The bombs stopped roaring past about three, and there was a lull of about half an hour, and then a clatter like hail on the roofs. Everybody except Langby dived for shovels and stirrup pumps. He was watching me. And I was watching the incendiary.

It had fallen only a few meters from me, behind the clock tower. It was much smaller than I had imagined, only about thirty centimeters long. It was sputtering violently, throwing greenish-white fire almost to where I was standing. In a minute it would simmer down into a molten mass and begin to burn through the roof. Flames and the frantic shouts of firemen, and then the white rubble stretching for miles, and nothing, nothing left, not even the firewatch stone.

It was the Whispering Gallery all over again. I felt that I had said something, and when I looked at Langby's face he was smiling crookedly.

"St. Paul's will burn down," I said. "There won't be anything left."

"Yes," Langby said. "That's the idea, isn't it? Burn St. Paul's to the ground? Isn't that the plan?"

"Whose plan?" I said stupidly.

"Hitler's, of course," Langby said. "Who do you think I meant?" and, almost casually, picked up his stirrup pump.

The page of the ARP manual flashed suddenly before me. I poured the bucket of sand around the still sputtering bomb, snatched up another bucket and dumped that on top of it. Black smoke billowed up in such a cloud that I could hardly find my shovel. I felt for the smothered bomb with the tip of it and scooped it into the empty bucket, then shovelled the sand in on top of it. Tears were streaming down my face from the acrid smoke. I turned to wipe them on my sleeve and saw Langby.

He had not made a move to help me. He smiled. "It's not a bad plan, actually. But of course we won't let it happen. That's what the fire watch is here for. To see that it doesn't happen. Right, Bartholomew?"

I know now what the purpose of my practicum is. I must stop Langby from burning down St. Paul's.

September 28—I try to tell myself I was mistaken about Langby last night, that I misunderstood what he said. Why should he want to burn down St. Paul's unless he is a Nazi spy? How can a Nazi spy have gotten on the fire watch? I think about my faked letter of introduction and shudder.

How can I find out? If I set him some test, some fatal thing that only a loyal Englishman in 1940 would know, I fear I am the one who would be caught out. I *must* get my retrieval working properly.

Until then, I shall watch Langby. For the time being at least that should be easy. Langby has just posted the watches for the next two weeks. We stand every one together.

September 30—I know what happened in September. Langby told me.

Last night in the choir, putting on our coats and boots, he said, "They've already tried once, you know."

I had no idea what he meant. I felt as helpless as that first day when he asked me if I was from the ayarpee.

"The plan to destroy St. Paul's. They've already tried once. The tenth of September. A high explosive bomb. But of course you didn't know about that. You were in Wales."

I was not even listening. The minute he had said, "high explosive bomb," I had remembered it all. It had burrowed in under the road and lodged on the foundations. The bomb squad had tried to defuse it, but there was a leaking gas main. They decided to evacuate St. Paul's, but Dean Matthews refused to leave, and they got it out after all and exploded it in Barking Marshes. Instant and complete retrieval.

"The bomb squad saved her that time," Langby was saying. "It seems there's always somebody about."

"Yes," I said. "There is," and walked away from him.

October 1—I thought last night's retrieval of the events of September tenth meant some sort of breakthrough, but I have been lying here on my cot most of the night trying for Nazi spies in St. Paul's and getting nothing. Do I have to know exactly what I'm looking for before I can remember it? What good does that do me?

Maybe Langby is not a Nazi spy. Then what is he? An arsonist? A madman? The crypt is hardly conducive to thought, being not at all as silent as a tomb. The chars talk most of the night and the sound of the bombs is muffled, which somehow makes it worse. I find myself straining to hear them. When I did get to sleep this morning, I dreamed about one of the tube shelters being hit, broken mains, drowning people.

October 4—I tried to catch the cat today. I had some idea of persuading it to dispatch the mouse that had been terrifying the chars. I also wanted to see one up close. I took the water bucket I has used with the stirrup pump last night to put out some burning shrapnel from one of the anti-aircraft guns. It still had a bit of water in it, but not enough to drown the cat, and my plan was to clamp the bucket over him, reach under, and pick him up, then carry him down to the crypt and point him at the mouse. I did not even come close to him.

I swung the bucket, and as I did so, perhaps an inch of water splashed out. I thought I remembered that the cat was a domesticated animal, but I must have been wrong about that. The cat's wide complacent face pulled back into a skull-like mask that was absolutely terrifying, vicious claws extended from what I had thought were harmless paws, and the cat let out a sound to top the chars.

In my surprise I dropped the bucket and it rolled against one of the pillars. The cat disappeared. Behind me, Langby said, "That's no way to catch a cat."

"Obviously," I said, and bent to retrieve the bucket.

"Cats hate water," he said, still in that expressionless voice.

"Oh," I said, and started in front of him to take the bucket back to the choir. "I didn't know that."

"Everybody knows it. Even the stupid Welsh."

October 8—We have been standing double watches for a week—bomber's moon. Langby didn't show up on the roofs, so I went looking for him in the church. I found him standing by the west doors talking to an old man. The man had a newspaper tucked under his arm and he handed it to Langby, but Langby gave it back to him. When the man saw me, he ducked out. Langby said, "Tourist. Wanted to know where the Windmill Theatre is. Read in the paper the girls are starkers."

I know I looked as if I didn't believe him because he said, "You look rotten, old man. Not getting enough sleep, are you? I'll get somebody to take the first watch for you tonight."

"No," I said coldly. "I'll stand my watch. I like being on the roofs," and added silently, *where I can watch you.*

He shrugged and said, "I suppose it's better than being down in the crypt. At least on the roofs you can hear the one that gets you."

October 10—I thought the double watches might be good for me, take my mind off my inability to retrieve. The watched pot idea. Actually, it sometimes works. A few hours of thinking about something else, or a good night's sleep, and the fact pops forward without any prompting, without any artificials.

The good night's sleep is out of the question. Not only do the chars talk constantly, but the cat has moved into the crypt and sidles up to everyone, making siren noises and begging for kippers. I am moving my cot out of the transept and over by Nelson before I go on watch. He may be pickled, but he keeps his mouth shut.

October 11—I dreamed Trafalgar, ships' guns and smoke and falling plaster and Langby shouting my name. My first waking thought was that the folding chairs had gone off. I could not see for all the smoke.

"I'm coming," I said, limping toward Langby and pulling on my boots. There was a heap of plaster and tangled folding chairs in the transept. Langby was digging in it. "Bartholomew!" he shouted, flinging a chunk of plaster aside. "Bartholomew!"

I still had the idea it was smoke. I ran back for the stirrup pump and then knelt beside him and began pulling on a splintered chair back. It resisted, and it came to me suddenly, There is a body under here. I will reach for a piece of the ceiling and find it is a hand. I leaned back on my heels, determined not be sick, then went at the pile again.

Langby was going far too fast, jabbing with a chair leg. I grabbed his hand to stop him, and he struggled against me as if I were a piece of rubble to be thrown aside. He picked up a large flat square of plaster, and under it was the floor. I turned and looked behind me. Both chars huddled in the recess by the altar. "Who are you looking for?" I said, keeping hold of Langby's arm.

"Bartholomew," he said, and swept the rubble aside, his hands bleeding through the coating of smoky dust.

"I'm here," I said. "I'm all right." I choked on the white dust. "I moved my cot out of the transept."

He turned sharply to the chars and then said quite calmly, "What's under here?"

"Only the gas ring," one of them said timidly from the shadowed recess, "and Mrs. Galbraith's pocketbook." He dug through the mess until he found them both. The gas ring was leaking at a merry rate, though the flame had gone out.

"You've saved St. Paul's and me after all," I said, standing there in my underwear and boots, holding the useless stirrup pump. "We might all have been asphyxiated."

He stood up. "I shouldn't have saved you," he said.

Stage one: shock, stupefaction, unawareness of injuries, words may not make sense except to victim. He would not know his hand was bleeding yet. He would not remember what he had said. He had said he shouldn't have saved my life.

"I shouldn't have saved you," he repeated. "I have my duty to think of."

"You're bleeding," I said sharply. "You'd better lie down." I sounded just like Langby in the Gallery.

October 13—It was a high explosive bomb. It blew a hole in the choir roof; and some of the marble statuary is broken; but the ceiling of the crypt did not collapse, which is what I thought at first. It only jarred some plaster loose.

I do not think Langby has any idea what he said. That should give me some sort of advantage, now that I am sure where the danger lies, now that I am sure it will not come crashing down from some other direction. But what good is all this knowing, when I do not know what he will do? Or when?

Surely I have the facts of yesterday's bomb in long-term, but even falling plaster did not jar them loose this time. I am not even trying for retrieval now. I lie in the darkness waiting for the roof to fall in on me. And remembering how Langby saved my life.

October 15—The girl came in again today. She still has the cold, but she has gotten her paying position. It was a joy to see her. She was wearing a smart uniform and open-toed shoes, and her hair was in an elaborate frizz around her face. We are still cleaning up the mess from the bomb, and Langby was out with Allen getting wood to board up the choir, so I let the girl chatter at me while I swept. The dust made her sneeze, but at least this time I knew what she was doing.

She told me her name is Enola and that she's working for the WVS, running one of the mobile canteens that are sent to the fires. She came, of all things, to thank me for the job. She said that after she told the WVS that there was no proper shelter with a canteen for St. Paul's, they gave her a run in the City. "So I'll just pop in when I'm close and let you know how I'm making out, won't I just?"

She and her brother Tom are still sleeping in the tubes. I asked her if that was safe and she said probably not, but at least down there you couldn't hear the one that got you and that was a blessing.

October 18—I am so tired I can hardly write this. Nine incendiaries tonight and a land mine that looked as though it was going to catch on the dome till the wind drifted its parachute away from the church. I put out two of the incendiaries. I have done that at least twenty times since I got here and helped with dozens of others, and still it is not enough. One incendiary, one moment of not watching Langby, could undo it all.

I know that is partly why I feel so tired. I wear myself out every night trying to do my job and watch Langby, making sure none of the incendiaries falls without my seeing it. Then I go back to the crypt and wear myself out trying to retrieve something, anything, about spies, fires, St. Paul's in the fall of 1940, anything. It haunts me that I am not doing enough, but I do not know what else to do. Without the retrieval, I am as helpless as these poor people here, with no idea what will happen tomorrow.

If I have to, I will go on doing this till I am called home. He cannot burn down St. Paul's so long as I am here to put out the incendiaries. "I have my duty," Langby said in the crypt.

And I have mine.

October 21—It's been nearly two weeks since the blast and I just now realized we haven't seen the cat since. He wasn't in the mess in the crypt. Even after Langby and I were sure there was no one in there, we sifted through the stuff twice more. He could have been in the choir, though.

Old Bence-Jones says not to worry. "He's all right," he said. "The jerries could bomb London right down to the ground and the cats would waltz out to greet them. You know why? They don't love anybody. That's what gets half of us killed. Old lady out in Stepney got killed the other night trying to save her cat. Bloody cat was in the Anderson."

"Then where is he?"

"Someplace safe, you can bet on that. If he's not around St. Paul's, it means we're for it. That old saw about the rats deserting a sinking ship, that's a mistake, that is. It's cats, not rats."

October 25—Langby's tourist showed up again. He cannot still be looking for the Windmill Theatre. He had a newspaper under his arm again today, and he asked for Langby, but Langby was across town with Allen, trying to get the asbestos firemen's coats. I saw the name of the paper. It was *The Worker*. A Nazi newspaper?

November 2—I've been up on the roofs for a week straight, helping some incompetent workmen patch the hole the bomb made. They're doing a terrible job. There's still a great gap on one side a man could fall into, but they insist it'll be all right because, after all, you wouldn't fall clear through but only as far as the ceiling, and "the fall can't kill you." They don't seem to understand it's a perfect hiding place for an incendiary.

And that is all Langby needs. He does not even have to set a fire to destroy St. Paul's. All he needs to do is let one burn uncaught until it is too late.

I could not get anywhere with the workmen. I went down into the church to complain to Matthews, and saw Langby and his tourist behind a pillar, close to one of the windows. Langby was holding a newspaper and talking to the man. When I came down from the library an hour later, they were still there. So is the gap. Matthews says we'll put planks across it and hope for the best.

November 5—I have given up trying to retrieve. I am so far behind on my sleep I can't even retrieve information on a newspaper whose name I already know. Double watches the permanent thing now. Our chars have abandoned us altogether (like the cat), so the crypt is quiet, but I cannot sleep.

If I do manage to doze off, I dream. Yesterday I dreamed Kivrin was on the roofs, dressed like a saint. "What was the secret of your practicum?" I said. "What were you supposed to find out?"

She wiped her nose with a handkerchief and said, "Two things. One, that silence and humility are the sacred burdens of the historian. Two," she stopped and sneezed into the handkerchief. "Don't sleep in the tubes."

My only hope is to get hold of an artificial and induce a trance. That's a problem. I'm positive it's too early for chemical endorphins, and probably hallucinogens. Alcohol is definitely available, but I need something more concentrated than ale, the only alcohol I know by name. I do not dare ask the watch. Langby is suspicious enough of me already. It's back to the *OED,* to look up a word I don't know.

November 11—The cat's back. Langby was out with Allen again, still trying for the asbestos coats, so I thought it was safe to leave St. Paul's. I went to the grocer's for supplies and hopefully, an artificial. It was late, and the sirens sounded before I had even gotten to Cheapside, but the raids do not usually start until after dark. It took awhile to get all the groceries and to get up my courage to ask whether he had any alcohol—he told me to go to a pub—and when I came out of the shop, it was as if I had pitched suddenly into a hole.

I had no idea where St. Paul's lay, or the street, or the shop I had just come from. I stood on what was no longer the sidewalk, clutching my brown-paper parcel of kippers and bread with a hand I could not have seen if I held it up before my face. I reached up to wrap my muffler closer about my neck and prayed for my eyes to adjust, but there was no reduced light to adjust to. I would have been glad of the moon, for all St. Paul's watch curses it and calls it a fifth columnist. Or a bus, with its shuttered headlights giving just enough light to orient myself by. Or a searchlight. Or the kickback flare of an ack-ack gun. Anything.

Just then I did see a bus, two narrow yellow slits a long way off. I started toward it and nearly pitched off the curb. Which meant the bus was sideways in the street, which meant it was not a bus. A cat meowed, quite near, and rubbed against my leg. I looked down into the yellow lights I had thought belonged to the bus. His eyes were picking up light from somewhere, though I would have sworn there was not a light for miles, and reflecting it flatly up at me.

"A warden'll get you for those lights, old tom," I said, and then as a plane droned overhead, "Or a jerry."

The world exploded suddenly into light, the searchlights and a glow along the Thames seeming to happen almost simultaneously, lighting my way home.

"Come to fetch me, did you, old tom?" I said gaily. "Where've you been? Knew we were out of kippers, didn't you? I call that loyalty." I talked to him all the way home and gave him half a tin of the kippers for saving my life. Bence-Jones said he smelled the milk at the grocer's.

November 13—I dreamed I was lost in the blackout. I could not see my hands in front of my face, and Dunworthy came and shone a pocket torch at me, but I could only see where I had come from and not where I was going.

"What good is that to them?" I said. "They need a light to show them where they're going."

"Even the light from the Thames? Even the light from the fires and the ack-ack guns?" Dunworthy said.

"Yes. Anything is better than this awful darkness." So he came closer to give me the pocket torch. It was not a pocket torch, after all, but Christ's lantern from the Hunt picture in the south nave. I shone it on the curb before me so I could find my way home, but it shone instead on the firewatch stone and I hastily put the light out.

November 20—I tried to talk to Langby today. "I've seen you talking to the old gentleman," I said. It sounded like an accusation. I meant it to. I wanted him to think it was and stop whatever he was planning.

"Reading," he said. "Not talking." He was putting things in order in the choir, piling up sandbags.

"I've seen you reading then," I said belligerently, and he dropped a sandbag and straightened.

"What of it?" he said. "It's a free country. I can read to an old man if I want, same as you can talk to that little WVS tart."

"What do you read?" I said.

"Whatever he wants. He's an old man. He used to come home from his job, have a bit of brandy and listen to his wife read the papers to him. She got killed in one of the raids. Now I read to him. I don't see what business it is of yours."

It sounded true. It didn't have the careful casualness of a lie, and I almost believed him, except that I had heard the tone of truth from him before. In the crypt. After the bomb.

"I thought he was a tourist looking for the Windmill," I said.

He looked blank only a second, and then he said, "Oh, yes, that. He came in with the paper and asked me to tell him where it was. I looked it up to find the address. Clever, that. I didn't guess he couldn't read it for himself." But it was enough. I knew that he was lying.

He heaved a sandbag almost at my feet. "Of course you

wouldn't understand a thing like that, would you? A simple act of human kindness?"

"No," I said coldly. "I wouldn't."

None of this proves anything. He gave away nothing, except perhaps the name of an artificial, and I can hardly go to Dean Matthews and accuse Langby of reading aloud.

I waited till he had finished in the choir and gone down to the crypt. Then I lugged one of the sandbags up to the roof and over to the chasm. The planking has held so far, but everyone walks gingerly around it, as if it were a grave. I cut the sandbag open and spilled the loose sand into the bottom. If it has occurred to Langby that this is the perfect spot for an incendiary, perhaps the sand will smother it.

November 21—I gave Enola some of "uncle's" money today and asked her to get me the brandy. She was more reluctant than I thought she'd be so there must be societal complications I am not aware of, but she agreed.

I don't know what she came for. She started to tell me about her brother and some prank he'd pulled in the tubes that got him in trouble with the guard, but after I asked her about the brandy, she left without finishing the story.

November 25—Enola came today, but without bringing the brandy. She is going to Bath for the holidays to see her aunt. At least she will be away from the raids for awhile. I will not have to worry about her. She finished the story of her brother and told me she hopes to persuade this aunt to take Tom for the duration of the Blitz but is not at all sure the aunt will be willing.

Young Tom is apparently not so much an engaging scapegrace as a near-criminal. He has been caught twice picking pockets in the Bank tube shelter, and they have had to go back to Marble Arch. I comforted her as best I could, told her all boys were bad at one time or another. What I really wanted to say was that she needn't worry at all, that young Tom strikes me as a true survivor type, like my own tom, like Langby, totally unconcerned with anybody but himself, well-equipped to survive the Blitz and rise to prominence in the future.

Then I asked her whether she had gotten the brandy.

She looked down at her open-toed shoes and muttered unhappily, "I thought you'd forgotten all about that."

I made up some story about the watch taking turns buying a bottle, and she seemed less unhappy, but I am not convinced she will not use this trip to Bath as an excuse to do nothing. I will have to leave St. Paul's and buy it myself, and I don't dare leave Langby alone in the church. I made her promise to bring the brandy today before she leaves. But she is still not back, and the sirens have already gone.

November 26—No Enola, and she said their train left at noon. I suppose I should be grateful that at least she is safely out of London. Maybe in Bath she will be able to get over her cold.

Tonight one of the ARP girls breezed in to borrow half our cots and tell us about a mess over in the East End where a surface shelter was hit. Four dead, twelve wounded. "At least it wasn't one of the tube shelters!" she said. "Then you'd see a real mess, wouldn't you?"

November 30—I dreamed I took the cat to St. John's Wood.

"Is this a rescue mission?" Dunworthy said.

"No, sir," I said proudly. "I know what I was supposed to find in my practicum. The perfect survivor. Tough and resourceful and selfish. This is the only one I could find. I had to kill Langby, you know, to keep him from burning down St. Paul's. Enola's brother has gone to Bath, and the others will never make it. Enola wears open-toed shoes in the winter and sleeps in the tubes and puts her hair up on metal pins so it will curl. She cannot possibly survive the Blitz."

Dunworthy said, "Perhaps you should have rescued her instead. What did you say her name was?"

"Kivrin," I said, and woke up cold and shivering.

December 5—I dreamed Langby had the pinpoint bomb. He carried it under his arm like a brown-paper parcel, coming out of St. Paul's Station and up Ludgate Hill to the west doors.

"This is not fair," I said, barring his way with my arm. "There is no fire watch on duty."

He clutched the bomb to his chest like a pillow. "That is your fault," he said, and before I could get to my stirrup pump and bucket, he tossed it in the door.

The pinpoint was not even invented until the end of the twentieth century, and it was another ten years before the dispossessed Communists got hold of it and turned it into something that could be carried under your arm. A parcel that could blow a quarter-mile of the City into oblivion. Thank God that is one dream that cannot come true.

It was a sunlit morning in the dream, and this morning when I came off watch the sun was shining for the first time in weeks. I went down to the crypt and then came up again, making the rounds of the roofs twice more, then the steps and the grounds and all the treacherous alleyways between where an incendiary could be missed. I felt better after that, but when I got to sleep I dreamed again, this time of fire and Langby watching it, smiling.

December 15—I found the cat this morning. Heavy raids last night, but most of them over towards Canning Town and nothing on the roofs to speak of. Nevertheless the cat was quite dead. I found him lying on the steps this morning when I made my own, private rounds. Concussion. There was not a mark on him anywhere except the white blackout patch on his throat, but when I picked him up, he was all jelly under the skin.

I could not think what to do with him. I thought for one mad moment of asking Matthews if I could bury him in the crypt. Honorable death in war or something. Trafalgar, Waterloo, London, died in battle. I ended by wrapping him in my muffler and taking him down Ludgate Hill to a building that had been bombed out and burying him in the rubble. It will do no good. The rubble will be no protection from dogs or rats, and I shall never get another muffler. I have gone through nearly all of uncle's money.

I should not be sitting here. I haven't checked the alleyways or the rest of the steps, and there might be a dud or delayed incendiary or something that I missed.

When I came here, I thought of myself as the noble rescuer, the savior of the past. I am not doing very well at the job. At least Enola is out of it. I wish there were some way I could send St. Paul's to Bath for safekeeping. There were hardly any raids last night. Bence-Jones said cats can survive anything. What if he was coming to get me, to show me the way home? All the bombs were over Canning Town.

December 16—Enola has been back a week. Seeing her, standing on the west steps where I found the cat, sleeping in Marble Arch and not safe at all, was more than I could absorb. "I thought you were in Bath," I said stupidly.

"My aunt said she'd take Tom but not me as well. She's got a houseful of evacuation children, and what a noisy lot. Where is your muffler?" she said. "It's dreadful cold up here on the hill."

"I..." I said, unable to answer, "I lost it."

"You'll never get another one," she said. "They're going to start rationing clothes. And wool, too. You'll never get another one like that."

"I know," I said, blinking at her.

"Good things just thrown away," she said. "It's absolutely criminal, that's what it is."

I don't think I said anything to that, just turned and walked away with my head down, looking for bombs and dead animals.

December 20—Langby isn't a Nazi. He's a Communist I can hardly write this. A Communist.

One of the chars found *The Worker* wedged behind a pillar and brought it down to the crypt as we were coming off the first watch.

"Bloody Communists," Bence-Jones said. "Helping Hitler, they are. Talking against the king, stirring up trouble in the shelters. Traitors, that's what they are."

"They love England same as you," the char said.

"They don't love nobody but themselves, bloody selfish lot. I wouldn't be surprised to hear they were ringing Hitler up on the telephone," Bence-Jones said. "''Ello, Adolf, here's where to drop the bombs.'"

The kettle on the gas ring whistled. The char stood up and poured the hot water into a chipped tea pot, then sat back down. "Just because they speak their minds don't mean they'd burn down old St. Paul's, does it now?"

"Of course not," Langby said, coming down the stairs. He sat down and pulled off his boots, stretching his feet in their wool socks. "Who wouldn't burn down St. Paul's?"

"The Communists," Bence-Jones said, looking straight at him, and I wondered if he suspected Langby, too.

Langby never batted an eye. "I wouldn't worry about them if I were you," he said. "It's the jerries that are doing their bloody best to burn her down tonight. Six incendiaries so far, and one almost went into that great hole over the choir." He held out his cup to the char, and she poured him a cup of tea.

I wanted to kill him, smashing him to dust and rubble on the floor of the crypt while Bence-Jones and the char looked on in helpless surprise, shouting warnings to them and the rest of the watch. "Do you know what the Communists did?" I wanted to shout. "Do you? We have to stop him." I even stood up and started toward him as he sat with his feet stretched out before him and his asbestos coat still over his shoulders.

And then the thought of the Gallery drenched in gold, the Communist coming out of the tube station with the package so casually under his arm, made me sick with the same staggering vertigo of guilt and helplessness, and I sat back down on the edge of my cot and tried to think what to do.

They do not realize the danger. Even Bence-Jones, for all his talk of traitors, thinks they are capable only of talking against the king. They do not know, cannot know, what the Communists will become. Stalin is an ally. Communists mean Russia. They have never heard of Karinsky or the New Russia or any of the things that will make "Communist" into a synonym for "monster." They will never know it. By the time the Communists become what they became, there will be no fire watch. Only I know what it means to hear the name "Communist" uttered here, so carelessly, in St. Paul's.

A Communist. I should have known. I should have known.

December 22—Double watches again. I have not had any sleep, and I am getting very unsteady on my feet. I nearly pitched into the chasm this morning, only saved myself by dropping to my knees. My endorphin levels are fluctuating wildly, and I know I must get some sleep soon or I will become one of Langby's walking dead; but I am afraid to leave him alone on the roofs, alone in the church with his Communist party leader, alone anywhere. I have taken to watching him when he sleeps.

If I could just get hold of an artificial, I think I could

induce a trance, in spite of my poor condition. But I cannot even go out to a pub. Langby is on the roofs constantly, waiting for his chance. When Enola comes again, I must convince her to get the brandy for me. There are only a few days left.

December 28—Enola came this morning while I was on the west porch, picking up the Christmas tree. It has been knocked over three nights running by concussion. I righted the tree and was bending down to pick up the scattered tinsel when Enola appeared suddenly out of the fog like some cheerful saint. She stooped quickly and kissed me on the cheek. Then she straightened up, her nose red from her perennial cold, and handed me a box wrapped in colored paper.

"Merry Christmas," she said. "Go on then, open it. It's a gift."

My reflexes are almost totally gone. I knew the box was far too shallow for a bottle of brandy. Nevertheless, I believed she had remembered, had brought me my salvation. "You darling," I said, and tore it open.

It was a muffler. Gray wool. I stared at it for fully half a minute without realizing what it was. "Where's the brandy?" I said.

She looked shocked. Her nose got redder and her eyes started to blur. "You need this more. You haven't any clothing coupons and you have to be outside all the time. It's been so dreadful cold."

"I *needed* the brandy," I said angrily.

"I was only trying to be kind," she started, and I cut her off.

"Kind?" I said. "I asked you for brandy. I don't recall ever saying I needed a muffler." I shoved it back at her and began untangling a string of colored lights that had shattered when the tree fell.

She got that same holy martyr look Kivrin is so wonderful at. "I worry about you all the time up here," she said in a rush. "They're *trying* for St. Paul's, you know. And it's so close to the river. I didn't think you should be drinking. I...it's a crime when they're trying so hard to kill us all that you won't take care of yourself. It's like you're in it with them. I worry someday I'll come up to St. Paul's and you won't be here."

"Well, and what exactly am I supposed to do with a muffler? Hold it over my head when they drop the bombs?"

She turned and ran, disappearing into the gray fog before she had gone down two steps. I started after her, still holding the string of broken lights, tripped over it, and fell almost all the way to the bottom of the steps.

Langby picked me up. "You're off watches," he said grimly.

"You can't do that," I said.

"Oh, yes, I can. I don't want any walking dead on the roofs with me."

I let him lead me down here to the crypt, make me a cup of tea, and put me to bed, all very solicitous. No indication that this is what he has been waiting for. I will lie here till the sirens go. Once I am on the roofs he will not be able to send me back without seeming suspicious. Do you know what he said before he left, asbestos coat and rubber boots, the dedicated fire watcher? "I want you to get some sleep." As if I could sleep with Langby on the roofs. I would be burned alive.

December 30—The sirens woke me, and old Bence-Jones said, "That should have done you some good. You've slept the clock round."

"What day is it?" I said, going for my boots.

"The twenty-ninth," he said, and as I dived for the door, "No need to hurry. They're late tonight. Maybe they won't come at all. That'd be a blessing, that would. The tide's out."

I stopped by the door to the stairs, holding onto the cool stone. "Is St. Paul's all right?"

"She's still standing," he said. "Have a bad dream?"

"Yes," I said, remembering the bad dreams of all the past weeks—the dead cat in my arms in St. John's Wood, Langby with his parcel and his *Worker* under his arm, the firewatch stone garishly lit by Christ's lantern. Then I remembered I had not dreamed at all. I had slept the kind of sleep I had prayed for, the kind of sleep that would help me remember.

Then I remembered. Not St. Paul's, burned to the ground by the Communists. A headline from the dailies. "Marble Arch hit. Eighteen killed by blast." The date was not clear except for the year. 1940. There were exactly two more days left in 1940. I grabbed my coat and muffler and ran up the stairs and across the marble floor.

"Where the hell do you think you're going?" Langby shouted to me. I couldn't see him.

"I have to save Enola," I said, and my voice echoed in the dark sanctuary. "They're going to bomb Marble Arch."

"You can't leave now," he shouted after me, standing where the firewatch stone would be. "The tide's out. You dirty..."

I didn't hear the rest of it. I had already flung myself down the steps and into a taxi. It took almost all the money I had, the money I had so carefully hoarded for the trip back to St. John's Wood. Shelling started while we were still in Oxford Street, and the driver refused to go any farther. He let me out into pitch blackness, and I saw I would never make it in time.

Blast. Enola crumpled on the stairway down to the tube, her open-toed shoes still on her feet, not a mark on her. And when I try to lift her, jelly under the skin. I would have to wrap her in the muffler she gave me, because I was too late. I had gone back a hundred years to be too late to save her.

I ran the last blocks guided by the gun emplacement that had to be in Hyde Park, and skidded down the steps into Marble Arch. The woman in the ticket booth took my last shilling for a ticket to St. Paul's Station. I stuck it in my pocket and raced toward the stairs.

"No running," she said placidly. "To your left, please." The door to the right was blocked off by wooden barricades, the metal gates beyond pulled to and chained. The board with names on it for the stations was X-ed with tape, and a new sign that read, "All trains," was nailed to the barricade, pointing left.

Enola was not on the stopped escalators or sitting against the wall in the hallway. I came to the first stairway and could not get through. A family had set out, just where I wanted to step, a communal tea of bread and butter, a little pot of jam sealed with waxed paper, and a kettle on a ring like the one Langby and I had rescued out of the rubble, all of it spread on a cloth embroidered at the corners with flowers. I stood staring down at the layered tea, spread like a waterfall down the steps.

"I... Marble Arch..." I said. Another twenty killed by flying tiles. "You shouldn't be here."

"We've as much right as anyone," the man said belligerently, "and who are you to tell us to move on?"

A woman lifting saucers out of a cardboard box looked up at me, frightened. The kettle began to whistle.

"It's you that should move on," the man said. "Go on then." He stood off to one side so I could pass. I edged past the embroidered cloth apologetically.

"I'm sorry," I said. "I'm looking for someone. On the platform."

"You'll never find her in there, mate," the man said, thumbing in that direction. I hurried past him, nearly stepping on the teacloth, and rounded the corner into hell.

It was not hell. Shopgirls folded coats and leaned back against them, cheerful or sullen or disagreeable, but certainly not damned. Two boys scuffled for a shilling and lost it on the tracks. They bent over the edge, debating whether to go after it, and the station guard yelled to them to back away. A train rumbled through, full of people. A mosquito landed on the guard's hand and he reached out to slap it and missed. The boys laughed. And behind and before them, stretching in all directions down the deadly tile curves of the tunnel like casualties, backed into the entrance-ways and onto the stairs, were people. Hundreds and hundreds of people.

I stumbled back into the hall, knocking over a teacup. It spilled like a flood across the cloth.

"I told you, mate," the man said cheerfully. "It's Hell in there, ain't it? And worse below."

"Hell," I said. "Yes." I would never find her. I would never save her. I looked at the woman mopping up the tea, and it came to me that I could not save her either. Enola or the cat or any of them, lost here in the endless stairways and cul-de-sacs of time. They were already dead a hundred years, past saving. The past is beyond saving. Surely that was the lesson the history department sent me all this way to learn. Well, fine, I've learned it. Can I go home now?

Of course not, dear boy. You have foolishly spent all your money on taxicabs and brandy, and tonight is the night the Germans burn the City. (Now it is too late, I remember it all. Twenty-eight incendiaries on the roofs.) Langby must have his chance, and you must learn the hardest lesson of all and the one you should have known from the beginning. You cannot save St. Paul's.

I went back out onto the platform and stood behind the yellow line until a train pulled up. I took my ticket out and held it in my hand all the way to St. Paul's Station. When I got there, smoke billowed toward me like an easy spray of water. I could not see St. Paul's.

"The tide's out," a woman said in a voice devoid of hope,

and I went down in a snake pit of limp cloth hoses. My hands came up covered with rank-smelling mud, and I understood finally (and too late) the significance of the tide. There was no water to fight the fires.

A policeman barred my way and I stood helplessly before him with no idea what to say. "No civilians allowed up there," he said. "St. Paul's is for it." The smoke billowed like a thundercloud, alive with sparks, and the dome rose golden above it.

"I'm fire watch," I said, and his arm fell away, and then I was on the roofs.

My endorphin levels must have been going up and down like an air raid siren. I do not have any short-term from then on, just moments that do not fit together: the people in the church when we brought Langby down, huddled in a corner playing cards, the whirling wind of burning scraps of wood in the dome, the ambulance driver who wore open-toed shoes like Enola and smeared salve on my burned hands. And in the center, the one clear moment when I went after Langby on a rope and saved his life.

I stood by the dome, blinking against the smoke. The City was on fire and it seemed as if St. Paul's would ignite from the heat, would crumble from the noise alone. Bence-Jones was by the northwest tower, hitting at an incendiary with a spade. Langby was too close to the patched place where the bomb had gone through, looking toward me. An incendiary clattered behind him. I turned to grab a shovel, and when I turned back, he was gone.

"Langby!" I shouted, and could not hear my own voice. He had fallen into the chasm and nobody saw him or the incendiary. Except me. I do not remember how I got across the roof. I think I called for a rope. I got a rope. I tied it around my waist, gave the ends of it into the hands of the fire watch, and went over the side. The fires lit the walls of the hole almost all the way to the bottom. Below me I could see a pile of whitish rubble. He's under there, I thought, and jumped free of the wall. The space was so narrow there was nowhere to throw the rubble. I was afraid I would inadvertently stone him, and I tried to toss the pieces of planking and plaster over my shoulder, but there was barely room to turn. For one awful moment I thought he might not be there at all, that the pieces of splintered wood would brush away to reveal empty pavement, as they had in the crypt.

I was numbed by the indignity of crawling over him. If he was dead I did not think I could bear the shame of stepping on his helpless body. Then his hand came up like a ghost's and grabbed my ankle, and within seconds I had whirled and had his head free.

He was the ghastly white that no longer frightens me. "I put the bomb out," he said. I stared at him, so overwhelmed with relief I could not speak. For one hysterical moment I thought I would even laugh, I was so glad to see him. I finally realized what it was I was supposed to say.

"Are you all right?" I said.

"Yes," he said, and tried to raise himself on one elbow. "So much the worse for you."

He could not get up. He grunted with pain when he tried to shift his weight to his right side and lay back, the uneven rubble crunching sickeningly under him. I tried to lift him gently so I could see where he was hurt. He must have fallen on something.

"It's no use," he said, breathing hard. "I put it out."

I spared him a startled glance, afraid that he was delirious, and went back to rolling him onto his side.

"I know you were counting on this one," he went on, not resisting me at all. "It was bound to happen sooner or later with all these roofs. Only I went after it. What'll you tell your friends?"

His asbestos coat was torn down the back in a long gash. Under it his back was charred and smoking. He had fallen on the incendiary. "Oh, my God," I said, trying frantically to see how badly he was burned without touching him. I had no way of knowing how deep the burns went, but they seemed to extend only in the narrow space where the coat had torn. I tried to pull the bomb out from under him, but the casing was as hot as a stove. It was not melting, though. My sand and Langby's body had smothered it. I had no idea if it would start up again when it was exposed to the air. I looked around, a little wildly, for the bucket and stirrup pump Langby must have dropped when he fell.

"Looking for a weapon?" Langby said, so clearly it was hard to believe he was hurt at all. "Why not just leave me here? A bit of overexposure and I'd be done for by morning. Or would you rather do your dirty work in private?"

I stood up and yelled to the men on the roof above us. One of them shone a pocket torch down at us, but its light didn't reach.

"Is he dead?" somebody shouted down at me.

"Send for an ambulance," I said. "He's been burned."

I helped Langby up, trying to support his back without touching the burn. He staggered a little and then leaned against the wall, watching me as I tried to bury the incendiary, using a piece of the planking as a scoop. The rope came down and I tied Langby to it. He had not spoken since I helped him up. He let me tie the rope around his waist, still looking steadily at me. "I should have let you smother in the crypt," he said.

He stood leaning easily, almost relaxed against the wood supports, his hands holding him up. I put his hands on the slack rope and wrapped it once around them for the grip I knew he didn't have. "I've been onto you since that day in the Gallery. I knew you weren't afraid of heights. You came down here without any fear of heights when you thought I'd ruined your precious plans. What was it? An attack of conscience? Kneeling there like a baby, whining, 'What have we done? What have we done?' You made me sick. But you know what gave you away first? The cat. Everybody knows cats hate water. Everybody but a dirty Nazi spy."

There was a tug on the rope. "Come ahead," I said, and the rope tauntened.

"That WVS tart? Was she a spy, too? Supposed to meet you in Marble Arch? Telling me it was going to be bombed. You're a rotten spy, Bartholomew. Your friends already blew it up in September. It's open again."

The rope jerked suddenly and began to lift Langby. He twisted his hands to get a better grip. His right shoulder scraped the wall. I put up my hands and pushed him gently so that his left side was to the wall. "You're making a big mistake, you know," he said. "You should have killed me. I'll tell."

I stood in the darkness, waiting for the rope. Langby was unconscious when he reached the roof. I walked past the fire watch to the dome and down to the crypt.

This morning the letter from my uncle came and with it a ten-pound note.

December 31—Two of Dunworthy's flunkies met me in St. John's Wood to tell me I was late for my exams. I did not even protest. I shuffled obediently after them without even considering how unfair it was to give an exam to one of the walking dead. I had not slept in—how long? Since yesterday when I went to find Enola. I had not slept in a hundred years.

Dunworthy was at his desk, blinking at me. One of the flunkies handed me a test paper and the other one called time. I turned the paper over and left an oily smudge from the ointment on my burns. I stared uncomprehendingly at them. I had grabbed at the incendiary when I turned Langby over, but these burns were on the backs of my hands. The answer came to me suddenly in Langby's unyielding voice. "They're rope burns, you fool. Don't they teach you Nazi spies the proper way to come up a rope?"

I looked down at the test. It read, "Number of incendiaries that fell on St. Paul's. Number of land mines. Number of high explosive bombs. Method most commonly used for extinguishing incendiaries. Land mines. High explosive bombs. Number of volunteers on first watch. Second watch. Casualties. Fatalities." The questions made no sense. There was only a short space, long enough for the writing of a number, after any of the questions. Method most commonly used for extinguishing incendiaries. How would I ever fit what I knew into that narrow space? Where were the questions about Enola and Langby and the cat?

I went up to Dunworthy's desk. "St. Paul's almost burned down last night," I said. "What kind of questions are these?"

"You should be answering questions, Mr. Bartholomew, not asking them."

"There aren't any questions about the people," I said. The outer casing of my anger began to melt.

"Of course there are," Dunworthy said, flipping to the second page of the test. "Number of casualties, 1940. Blast, shrapnel, other."

"Other?" I said. At any moment the roof would collapse on me in a shower of plaster dust and fury. "Other? Langby put out a fire with his own body. Enola has a cold that keeps getting worse. The cat..." I snatched the paper back from him and scrawled "one cat" in the narrow space next to "blast." "Don't you care about them at all?"

"They're important from a statistical point of view," he said, "but as individuals, they are hardly relevant to the course of history."

My reflexes were shot. It was amazing to me that Dunworthy's were almost as slow. I grazed the side of his jaw and knocked his glasses off. "Of course they're relevant!" I shouted. "They *are* the history, not all these bloody numbers!"

The reflexes of the flunkies were very fast. They did not let me start another swing at him before they had me by both arms and were hauling me out of the room.

"They're back there in the past with nobody to save them. They can't see their hands in front of their faces and there are bombs falling down on them and you tell me they aren't important? You call that being an historian?"

The flunkies dragged me out the door and down the hall. "Langby saved St. Paul's. How much more important can a person get? You're no historian! You're nothing but a..." I wanted to call him a terrible name, but the only curses I could summon up were Langby's. "You're nothing but a dirty Nazi spy!" I bellowed. "You're nothing but a lazy bourgeois tart!"

They dumped me on my hands and knees outside the door and slammed it in my face. "I wouldn't be an historian if you paid me!" I shouted, and went to see the firewatch stone.

December 31—I am having to write this in bits and pieces. My hands are in pretty bad shape, and Dunworthy's boys didn't help matters much. Kivrin comes in periodically, wearing her St. Joan look, and smears so much salve on my hands that I can't hold a pencil.

St. Paul's Station is not there, of course, so I got out at Holborn and walked, thinking about my last meeting with Dean Matthews on the morning after the burning of the City. This morning.

"I understand you saved Langby's life," he said. "I also understand that between you, you saved St. Paul's last night."

I showed him the letter from my uncle and he stared at it as if he could not think what it was. "Nothing stays saved forever," he said, and for a terrible moment I thought he was going to tell me Langby had died. "We shall have to keep on saving St. Paul's until Hitler decides to bomb the countryside."

The raids on London are almost over, I wanted to tell him. He'll start bombing the countryside in a matter of weeks. Canterbury, Bath, aiming always at the cathedrals. You and St. Paul's will both outlast the war and live to dedicate the firewatch stone.

"I am hopeful, though," he said. "I think the worst is over."

"Yes, sir." I thought of the stone, its letters still readable after all this time. No, sir, the worst is not over.

I managed to keep my bearings almost to the top of Ludgate Hill. Then I lost my way completely, wandering about like a man in a graveyard. I had not remembered that the rubble looked so much like the white plaster dust Langby had tried to dig me out of. I could not find the stone anywhere. In the end I nearly fell over it, jumping back as if I had stepped on a grave.

It is all that's left. Hiroshima is supposed to have had a handful of untouched trees at ground zero, Denver the capitol steps. Neither of them says, "Remember the men and women of St. Paul's Watch who by the grace of God saved this cathedral." The grace of God.

Part of the stone is sheared off. Historians argue there was another line that said, "for all time", but I do not believe that, not if Dean Matthews had anything to do with it. And none of the watch it was dedicated to would have believed it for a minute. We saved St. Paul's every time we put out an incendiary, and only until the next one fell. Keeping watch on the danger spots, putting out the little fires with sand and stirrup pumps, the big ones with our bodies, in order to keep the whole vast complex structure from burning down. Which sounds to me like a course description for History Practicum 401. What a fine time to discover what historians are for when I have tossed my chance for being one out the window as easily as they tossed the pinpoint bomb in! No, sir, the worst is not over.

There are flash burns on the stone, where legend says the Dean of St. Paul's was kneeling when the bomb went off. Totally apocryphal, of course, since the front door is hardly an appropriate place for prayers. It is more likely the shadow of a tourist who wandered in to ask the whereabouts of the Windmill Theatre, or the imprint of a girl bringing a volunteer his muffler. Or a cat.

Nothing is saved forever, Dean Matthews; and I knew that when I walked in the west doors that first day, blinking into the gloom, but it is pretty bad nevertheless. Standing here knee-deep in rubble out of which I will not be able to dig any folding chairs or friends, knowing that Langby died thinking I was a Nazi spy, knowing that Enola came one day and I wasn't there. It's pretty bad.

But it is not as bad as it could be. They are both dead, and Dean Matthews too; but they died without knowing what I knew all along, what sent me to my knees in the Whispering Gallery, sick with grief and guilt: that in the end none of us saved St. Paul's. And Langby cannot turn to me, stunned and sick at heart, and say, "Who did this? Your friends the Nazis?" And I would have to say, "No. The Communists." That would be the worst.

I have come back to the room and let Kivrin smear more salve on my hands. She wants me to get some sleep. I know I should pack and get gone. It will be humiliating to have them come and throw me out, but I do not have the strength to fight her. She looks so much like Enola.

January 1—I have apparently slept not only through the night, but through the morning mail drop as well. When I woke up just now, I found Kivrin sitting on the end of the bed holding an envelope. "Your grades came," she said.

I put my arm over my eyes. "They can be marvelously efficient when they want to, can't they?"

"Yes," Kivrin said.

"Well, let's see it," I said, sitting up. "How long do I have before they come and throw me out?"

She handed the flimsy computer envelope to me. I tore it along the perforation. "Wait," she said. "Before you open it, I want to say something." She put her hand gently on my burns. "You're wrong about the history department. They're very good."

It was not exactly what I expected her to say. "Good is not the word I'd use to describe Dunworthy," I said and yanked the inside slip free.

Kivrin's look did not change, not even when I sat there with the printout on my knees where she could surely see it.

"Well," I said.

The slip was hand-signed by the esteemed Dunworthy. I have taken a first. With honors.

January 2—Two things came in the mail today. One was Kivrin's assignment. The history department thinks of everything—even to keeping her here long enough to nursemaid me, even to coming up with a prefabricated trial by fire to send their history majors through.

I think I wanted to believe that was what they had done, Enola and Langby only hired actors, the cat a clever android with its clockwork innards taken out for the final effect, not so much because I wanted to believe Dunworthy was not good at all, but because then I would not have this nagging pain at not knowing what had happened to them.

"You said your practicum was England in 1300?" I said, watching her as suspiciously as I had watched Langby.

"1349," she said, and her face went slack with memory. "The plague year."

"My God," I said. "How could they do that? The plague's a ten."

"I have a natural immunity," she said, and looked at her hands.

Because I could not think of anything to say, I opened the other piece of mail. It was a report on Enola. Computer-printed, facts and dates and statistics, all the numbers the history department so dearly loves, but it told me what I thought I would have to go without knowing: that she had gotten over her cold and survived the Blitz. Young Tom had been killed in the Baedaker raids on Bath, but Enola had lived until 2006, the year before they blew up St. Paul's.

I don't know whether I believe the report or not, but it does not matter. It is, like Langby's reading aloud to the old man, a simple act of human kindness. They think of everything.

Not quite. They did not tell me what happened to Langby. But I find as I write this that I already know: I saved his life. It does not seem to matter that he might have died in hospital next day; and I find, in spite of all the hard lessons the history department has tried to teach me, I do not quite believe this one: that nothing is saved forever. It seems to me that perhaps Langby is.

January 3—I went to see Dunworthy today. I don't know what I intended to say—some pompous drivel about my willingness to serve in the firewatch of history, standing guard against the falling incendiaries of the human heart, silent and saintly.

But he blinked at me nearsightedly across his desk, and it seemed to me that he was blinking at that last bright image of St. Paul's in sunlight before it was gone forever and that he knew better than anyone that the past cannot be saved, and I said instead, "I'm sorry that I broke your glasses, sir."

"How did you like St. Paul's?" he said, and like my first meeting with Enola, I felt I must be somehow reading the signals all wrong, that he was not feeling loss, but something quite different.

"I loved it, sir," I said.

"Yes," he said. "So do I."

Dean Matthews is wrong. I have fought with memory my whole practicum only to find that it is not the enemy at all, and being an historian is not some saintly burden after all. Because Dunworthy is not blinking against the fatal sunlight of the last morning, but into the gloom of that first afternoon, looking in the great west doors of St. Paul's at what is, like Langby, like all of it, every moment, in us, saved forever.

Corridors

by Barry N. Malzberg

This dark, bitter, powerful story is not science fiction at all so far as I'm concerned. It's an out-and-out mainstream piece about a man who happens to be a science fiction writer, written by one who knows whereof he speaks.

If it is not science fiction, why is it in this anthology? The simplest explanation is that it was nominated by the members of the Science Fiction Writers of America for the Nebula in the category of best short story, and ipso facto is eligible for inclusion. That answer is something of a copout, I know, but it happens to be in concurrence with the rules under which I have assembled this book.

Aside from that, I offer the point that it has been the custom in some years to include documentary nonfiction material in the Nebula awards anthologies. Perhaps we can say that this Malzberg story, which is *fiction, not a documentary at all, nor the representation of any one particular writer's life, is serving in lieu of such material in this year's volume. Again, "Ruthven" is not a thinly disguised version of X or Y or Z whom we all know. But there, say the members of SFWA, but for the grace of God go I— and that is why it is in this book.*

RUTHVEN used to have plans. Big plans: turn the category around, arrest the decline of science fiction into stereotype and cant, open up the category to new vistas and so on. So forth. Now, however, he is at fifty-four merely trying to hold on; he takes this retraction of ambition, understanding of his condition as the only significant change in his inner life over two decades. The rest of it—inner and outer too—has been replication, disaster, pain, recrimination, self-pity and the like: Ruthven thinks of these old partners of the law firm of his life as brothers. At least, thanks to Replication & Disaster, he has a brief for the game. He knows what he is and what has to be done, and most of the time he can sleep through the night, unlike that period during his forties when 4 A.M. more often than not would see him awake and drinking whiskey, staring at his out-of-print editions in many languages.

The series has helped. Ruthven has at last achieved a modicum of fame in science fiction and for the first time—he would not have believed this ever possible—some financial security. Based originally upon a short novel written for *Astounding* in late 1963, which he padded for quick paperback the next year, *The Sorcerer* has proven the capstone of his career. Five or six novels written subsequently at low advances for the same firm went nowhere but: the editor was fired, the firm collapsed, releasing all rights, the editor got divorced, married a subsidiary rights director, got a consultant job with her firm, divorced her, went to a major paperback house as science fiction chief and through a continuing series of coincidences known to those who (unlike Ruthven) always seemed to come out a little ahead commissioned three new Sorcerers from Ruthven on fast deadline to build up cachet with the salesmen. They all had hung out at the Hydra Club together, anyway. Contracts were signed, the first of the three new Sorcerers (written, all of them in ten weeks) sold 150,000 copies, the second was picked up as an alternate by a demented Literary Guild and the third was leased to hardcover. Ruthven's new, high-priced agent negotiated a contract for five more Sorcerers for $100,000.

Within the recent half decade, Ruthven has at last made money from science fiction. One of the novels was a Hugo finalist, another was filmed. He has been twice final balloted for a *Gandalf*. Some of his older novels have been reprinted. Ruthven is now one of the ten most successful science fiction writers: he paid taxes on $79,000 last year. In his first two decades in this field, writing frantically and passing through a succession of dead-end jobs, Ruthven did not make $79,000.

It would be easier for him, he thinks, if he could take his success seriously or at least obtain some peace, but of this he has none. Part of it has to do with his recent insight that he is merely hanging on, that the ultimate outcome of ultimate struggle for any writer in America not hopelessly self-deluded is to hang on; another part has to do with what Ruthven likes to think of as the accumulated damages and injuries sustained by the writing of seventy-three novels. Like a fighter long gone from the ring, the forgotten left hooks taken under the lights in all of the quick-money bouts have caught up with him and stunned his brain. Ruthven hears the music of combat as he never did when it was going on. He has lost the contents of most of these books and even some of their titles but the pain lingers. This is self-dramatization, of course, and Ruthven has enough ironic distance to know it. No writer was ever killed by a book.

Nonetheless, he hears the music, feels the dull knives in his kidneys and occipital regions at night; Ruthven also knows that he has done nothing of worth in a long time. The Sorcerer is a fraud; he is far below the aspirations and intent of his earlier work, no matter how flawed that was. Most of these new books have been written reflexively under the purposeful influence of scotch and none of them possesses real quality. Even literacy. He has never been interested in these books. Ruthven is too far beyond self-delusion to think that the decline of his artistic gifts, the collapse of his promise, means anything *either*. Nothing means anything except holding on as he now knows. Nonetheless, he *used* to feel that the quality of work made some difference. Didn't he? Like the old damages of the forgotten books he feels the pain at odd hours.

He is not disgraced, of this he is fairly sure, but he is disappointed. If he had known that it would end this way, perhaps he would not have expended quite so much on those earlier books. The Sorcerer might have had a little more energy; at least he could have put some color in the backgrounds.

Ruthven is married to Sandra, his first and only wife. The marriage has lasted through thirty-one years and two daughters, one divorced, one divorced and remarried, both far from his home in the Southeast. At times Ruthven considers his marriage with astonishment: he does not quite know how he has been able to stay married so long granted the damages of his career, the distractions, the deadening, the slow and terrible resentment which has built within him over almost three decades of commercial writing. At other times, however, he feels that his marriage is the only aspect of his life (aside from science fiction itself) which has a unifying consistency. And only death will end it.

He accepts that now. Ruthven is aware of the lives of all his colleagues: the divorces, multiple marriages, disastrous affairs, two- and three-timing, bed-hopping at conventions; the few continuing marriages seem to be cover or mausoleum...but after considering his few alternatives Ruthven has nonetheless stayed married and the more active outrage of the earlier decades has receded. It all comes back to his insight: nothing matters. Hang on. If nothing makes any difference then it is easier to stay with Sandra by far. Also, she has a position of her own; it cannot have been marriage to a science fiction writer which enticed her when they met so long ago. She has taken that and its outcome with moderate good cheer and has given him less trouble, he supposes, than she might. He has not shoved the adulteries and recrimination in her face but surely she knows of them; she is not stupid. And she is now married to $79,000 a year, which is not inconsiderable. At least this is all Ruthven's way of rationalizing the fact that he has had (he knows now) so much less from this marriage than he might have, the fact that being a writer has done irreparable damage to both of them. And the children. He dwells on this less than previously. His marriage, Ruthven thinks, is like science fiction writing itself: if there was a time to get out that time is past and now he would be worse off anywhere else. Who would read him? Where would he sell? What else could he do?

Unlike many of his colleagues, Ruthven had never had ambitions outside the field. Most of them had had literary pretensions, at least had wanted to reach wider audiences, but Ruthven had never wanted anything else. To reproduce, first for his own pleasure and then for money, the stories of the forties *Astounding* which moved him seemed to be a sensible ambition. Later of course he did get serious about the category, wanting to make it anew and etc.... but that was later. Much later. It seemed a noble thing in the fifties to want to be a science fiction writer and his career has given him all that he could have hoped for at fourteen. Or twenty-four.

He has seen what their larger hopes have done to so many of his peers who started out with him in the fifties, men of large gifts who in many cases had been blocked in every way in their attempts to leave science fiction, some becoming quite embittered, even dying for grief or spite, others accepting their condition at last only at the cost of self-hatred. Ruthven knows their despair, their self-loathing. The effects of his own seventy-three novels have set in, and of course there was a time when he took science fiction almost as seriously as the most serious... but that was *later,* he keeps on reminding himself, *after* breaking in, after publication in the better magazines, after dealing with the audience directly and learning (as he should have always known) that they were mostly a bunch of kids. His problems had come later but his colleagues, so many of them, had been ambitious from the start, which made matters more difficult for them.

But then, of course, others had come in without any designs at all and had stayed that way. And they too—those who were still checking into *Analog* or the Westercon—were just as miserable and filled with self-hatred as the ambitious, or as Ruthven himself had been a few years back. So perhaps it was the medium of science fiction itself that did this to you. He is not sure.

He thinks about things like this still...the manner in which the field seems to break down almost all of its writers. At one time he had started a book about this, called it *The Lies of Science Fiction,* and in that bad period around his fiftieth birthday had done three or four chapters, but he was more than enough of a professional to know that he could not sell it, was more than ready to put it away when *The Sorcerer* was revived. That had been a bad time to be sure; ten thousand words on *The Lies of Science Fiction* had been his output for almost two full years. If it had not been for a little residual income on his novels, a few anthology sales, the free-lance work he had picked up at the correspondence school and Sandra's occasional substitute teaching, things might have bottomed. At that it was a near thing, and his daughters' lives, although they were already out of the house, gave Sandra anguish.

Ruthven still shudders, thinking of the images of flight which overcame him, images so palpable that often they would put him in his old Ford Galaxie, which he would drive sometimes almost a hundred miles to the state border before taking the U-turn and heading back. He had, after all, absolutely nowhere to go. He did not think that anyone who had ever known him except Sandra would put him up for more than two nights (Felicia and Carole lived with men in odd arrangements), and he had never lived alone in his life. His parents were dead.

Now, however, things are better. He is able to produce a steady two thousand words a day almost without alcohol, his drinking is now a ritualized half a pint of scotch before dinner and there are rumors of a larger movie deal pending if the purchaser of the first movie can be bought off a clause stupidly left in his contract giving him series rights. Ruthven will be guest of honor at the Cincinnati convention three years hence if the committee putting together the bid is successful. That would be a nice crown to his career at fifty-seven, he thinks, and if there is some bitterness in this—Ruthven is hardly self-deluded—there is satisfaction as well. He has survived three decades as a writer in this country, and a science fiction writer at that, and when he thinks of his colleagues and the condition of so many with whom he started he can find at least a little self-respect. He is writing badly, *The Sorcerer* is hackwork, but he *is* still producing and making pretty big money and (the litany with which he gets up in the morning and goes to bed at night) nothing matters. Nothing matters at all. Survival is the coin of the realm. Time is a river with banks.

Now and then, usually during the late afternoon naps which are his custom (to pass the time quicker before the drinking, which is the center of his day), Ruthven is assaulted by old possibilities, old ambitions, old dread, visions of what he wanted to be and what science fiction did to him, but these are, as he reminds himself when he takes his first heavy one at five, only characteristic of middle age. Everyone feels this way. Architects shake with regret, doctors flee the reservation, men's hearts could break with desire and the mockery of circumstance. What has happened is not symptomatic of science fiction but of his age, his country. His condition. Ruthven tells that to himself, and on six ounces of scotch he is convinced, *convinced* that it is so, but as Sandra comes into the room to tell him that dinner is seven minutes away he thinks that someday he will have to get *The Lies of Science Fiction* out of his desk and look at it again. Maybe there was something in these pages beyond climacteric. Maybe he had better reconsider.

But for now the smells of roast fill the house, he must drink quickly to get down the half-pint in seven minutes, the fumes of scotch fill his breath, the scents and sounds of home fill all of the corridors and no introspection is worth it. None of it is worth the trouble. Because, Ruthven tells himself for the thirty-second time that day (although it is not he who is doing the counting) that nothing nothing nothing nothing nothing nothing nothing matters.

Back in the period of his depression when he was attempting to write *The Lies of Science Fiction* but mostly trying to space out his days around alcohol, enraged (and unanswerable) letters to his publishers about his out-of-print books and drives in his bald-tired Galaxie... back in that gray period as he drove furiously from supermarket to the state border to the liquor store, Ruthven surmised that he had hit upon some of the central deceptions which had wrecked him and reduced him and so many of his colleagues to this condition. To surmise was not to conquer, of course; he was as helpless as ever but there was a dim liberation in seeing how he had been lied to, and he felt that at least he could take one thing from the terrible years through which he had come: he was free of self-delusion.

Ruthven thought often of the decay of his colleagues, of the psychic and emotional fraying which seemed to set in between their fifth and fifteenth years of professional writing and reduced their personal lives and minds to rubble. Most were drunks, many lived in chaos, all of them in their work and persona seemed to show distress close to panic. One did not have to meet them at the conventions or hang out with them at the SFWA parties in New York to see that these were people whose lives were askew; the work showed it. Those who were not simply reconstructing or revising their old stories were working in new areas in which the old control had gone, the characters were merely filters for events or possessed of a central obsession, the plots lacked motivation or causality and seemed to deal with an ever more elaborate and less comprehended technology. Whether the ideas were old or new, they were half-baked, the novels were padded with irrelevant events and syntax, characters internalized purposelessly, false leads were pursued for thousands of words. The decay seemed to cut across all of the writers and their work; those that had been good seemed to suffer no less than the mediocre or worse, and there was hardly a science fiction writer of experience who was not—at least to Ruthven's antennae—displaying signs of mental illness.

That decay, Ruthven came to think, had to do with the very nature of the genre: the megalomaniacal, expansive visions being generated by writers who increasingly saw the disparity between Spaceways and their own hopeless condition. While the characters flourished and the science gleamed the writers themselves were exposed to all the abuses known to the litterateurs in America and—intelligent, even the dumbest of them, to a fault—they were no longer able to reconcile their personal lives with their vision: the vision became pale or demented. At a particularly bleak time, Ruthven even came to speculate that science fiction writing was a form of illness which, like syphilis, might swim undetected in the blood for years but would eventually, untreated, strike to kill. The only treatment would be retirement, but most science fiction writers were incapable of writing anything else after a while and the form itself was addictive: it was as if every potential sexual partner carried venereal disease. You could stop fucking but only at enormous psychic or emotional course, and *then* what? Regardless, that virus killed.

Later, as he began to emerge from this, Ruthven felt a little more sanguine about the genre. It might not *necessarily* destroy you to write it if you could find a little personal dignity and, more importantly, satisfactions outside of the field. But the counsel of depression seemed to be the real truth: science fiction was aberrant and dangerous, seductive but particularly ill-suited to the maladjusted who were drawn to it, and if you stayed with it long enough, the warpage was permanent.

After all, wasn't science fiction for most of its audience an aspect of childhood they would outgrow?

This disparity between megalomania and anonymity had been one of the causes of the decay in his colleagues, he decided. Another was the factor of truncation. Science fiction dealt with the sweep of time and space, the enormity of technological consequence in all eras, but as a practical necessity and for the sake of their editors all science fiction writers had to limit the genre and themselves as they wrote it. *True* science fiction as the intelligent editors knew (and the rest followed the smart ones) would not only be dangerous and threatening, it would be incomprehensible. How could twenty-fourth century life in the Antares system be depicted? How could the readership for an escape genre be led to understand what a black hole would be?

The *writers* could not understand any of this, let alone a young and gullible readership interested in marvels that were to be made accessible. (Malzberg had been into aspects of this in his work but Ruthven felt that the man had missed the point: lurking behind Malzberg's schematics was the conviction that science fiction *should* be able to find a language for its design, but any penny-a-word stable hack for *Amazing* in the fifties knew better and Malzberg would have known better too if he had written science fiction before he went out to smash it.) So twenty-fourth century aliens in the Antares system would speak a colloquial Brooklynese, commanders of the Black Hole Explorer would long for their Ganymede Lady. The terrific would be made manageable, the awesome shaped by the exigencies of pulp fiction into the nearby. The universe would become Brooklyn with remote dangerous sections out in

Bushwick or Greenpoint but plenty of familiar stops and safer neighborhoods.

The writers, awash in the market and struggling to live by their skills, would follow the editors and map out a universe to scale... but Ruthven speculated that the knowledge that they had drained their vision, grayed it for the sake of publication, had filled them first with disappointment and finally self-hatred: like Ruthven they had been caught early by the *idea* of science fiction; transcendence and complexity and however far they had gone from there, they still felt at the base that this was a wondrous and expensive genre. Deliberately setting themselves against all for which the field had once stood could not have been easy for them. Rationalization would take the form of self-abuse: drink, divorce, obesity, sadism, in extreme cases penury, drugs or the outright cultivation of death. (Only H. Beam Piper had actually pulled the trigger on himself but that made him an honest man and a gun collector.) That was your science fiction writer, then, an ecclesiastic who had been first summoned from the high places and then dumped in the mud of Calvary to cast lots with the soldiers. All for a small advance.

That had been some of Ruthven's thinking, but then he had been very depressed. He had done a lot of reading and thinking about the male mid-life crisis. Sandra and he were barely dealing with one another; they lived within the form of marriage but not its substance (didn't everyone long married end that way?). His sexual panic, drinking, terror of death and sense of futility were more characteristic, perhaps, of the climacteric than of science fiction. The poor old field had taken a lot of blame over its lifetime (a lifetime, incidentally, exactly as long as Ruthven's: he had been born on April 12, 1926) for matters not of its own making, and once again was being blamed for pain it had not created. Maybe.

It wasn't science fiction alone which had put him in the ditch at late mid-life, Ruthven thought, any more than science fiction had been responsible for Hiroshima, Sputnik, the collapse of Apollo or the rotten movies of the nineteen-fifties which had first enticed and then driven the public away. The field had been innocent witness to much of these and the target of some but it was unfair to blame the genre for what seemed (at least according to the books he read) an inevitability in middle class, middle aged, male America.

It was this ambivalence—the inability to fuse his more recondite perspective with the visceral, hateful feeling that science fiction had destroyed all of their lives—which stopped *The Lies of Science Fiction.* Ruthven does not kid himself: even if the contracts for *The Sorcerer* had not come in and his career turned around, he probably would have walked away from the book. Its unsaleability was a problem but he knew that he might have sold it *somewhere,* an amateur press, and he had enough cachet in the field to place sections here and there in the fan magazines. It wouldn't have been much but it would have been more per diem than what Sandra was making or he from the correspondence school.

But he had not wanted to go on. His commitment, if anything, had been to stop. Ruthven from the modest perspective of almost four years, can now admit that he was afraid to continue. He could not bear to follow it through to the places it might have taken him. At the worst, it might have demonstrated that his life, that all of their lives in science fiction, had been as the title said: a lie . . . a lie which would lead to nothing but its replications by younger writers, who in turn would learn the truth. The book might have done more than that: it could have made his personal life impossible. Under no circumstance would he have been able to write that book and live with Sandra . . . but the drives on the Interstate had made it coldly evident that he had nowhere else to go. If he were not a middle-aged, married science fiction writer, then what was he?

Oh, it was a good thing that *The Sorcerer* had come

through and that he had gotten back to fiction. The novels were rotten but that was no problem: he didn't *want* to be good any more, he just wanted to survive. Now and then Ruthven still drives the Interstate in his new Impala; now and then he is still driven from sleep to stare at the foreign editions...but he no longer stares in anguish or drives in fury; everything seems to have bottomed out. Science fiction can still do many things to him but it no longer has the capacity to deliver exquisite pain, and for this he is grateful.

Eventually someone else, perhaps one of the younger writers, *will* do *The Lies of Science Fiction* or something similar, but of this in his heart is Henry Martin Ruthven convinced: he will never read it. He may be dead. If not he will stay clear. Science fiction now is only that means by which he is trying to hang on in the pointless universe and that which asks that he make anything more of it (what is there to make of it?) will have to check the next bar because Henry Martin Ruthven is finished. He knows the lies of science fiction, all right. But above all and just in time, he knows the truths of it too.

Ruthven attends the Cincinnati World Convention as guest of honor. At a party the first night in the aseptic and terrifying hotel he is surrounded by fans and committee, editors and colleagues, and it occurs to him that most of the people in these crowded rooms were not born when he sold his first story, "The Hawker," the *Worlds of If* on August 18, 1952. This realization fills him with terror: it is one thing to apprehend in isolation how long he has been around in this field and how far the field in its mad branching and expansion has gone from all of them who started in the fifties, but it is quite another to be confronted in terms that he cannot evade. Because his career has turned around in the decade, most of these people have a good knowledge of his work, he is guest of honor, he is hardly ignored, but still—

Here and there in the packed three-room suite he sees people he knows, editors and writers and fans with whom he has been at conventions for years, but he cannot break out of his curious sense of isolation and his conversations are distracted. Gossip about the business, congratulations on having survived to be a guest of honor, that sort of thing. Ruthven would almost prefer to be alone in his room or drinking quietly at the bar but that is obviously impossible. How can a guest of honor be alone on the first night of his convention? It would be, among other things, a commentary on science fiction itself and no one, least of all he, wants to face it.

None of his family are here. Felicia is no surprise: she is starting her second year of law school in Virginia and could not possibly miss the important early classes; besides, they have had no relationship for years. Maybe never. Carole had said that she might be in from Oakland, would do what she could, but he has heard that kind of thing from Carole before and does not expect her. The second marriage is falling apart, he knows, Sandra will tell him that much, and Carole is hanging on desperately (he surmises) much as Ruthven himself hung on years ago when, however bad it might be, there was nothing else. He wishes that he could share this with Carole but of course it would be the finish of him. There are hundreds of sentences which said to the wrong people would end his marriage on the spot and that is another of them.

Sandra did want to be here but she is not. She has been feeling weak all year and now at last they have a diagnosis: she will have a hysterectomy soon. Knowing what being guest of honor meant to him Sandra had offered to go regardless, stay in the room if she could not socialize, but Ruthven had told her not to. He knew that she did not want to come, was afraid of the crowds and the hysteric pulse and was for the first time in her life truly afraid of dying. She is an innocent. She considers her own death only when she feels very ill.

Not so many years ago, being alone at a large convention, let alone as guest of honor, would have inflamed Ruthven. He would have manipulated his life desperately to get even a night away alone, a Labor Day weekend would have been redemption... but now he feels depressed. He can take no pleasure from the situation and how it occurred. He is afraid for Sandra and misses her a little too, wishes that his daughters, who have never understood him or his work, could have seen him just this once celebrated. But he is alone and he is beginning to feel that it is simply too late for adultery. He has had his opportunities now and then, made his luck, but well past fifty and into what he thinks of as leveling out, Ruthven has become resigned to feeling that what he should have done can be done no more—take the losses, the time is gone. There are women of all ages, appearance and potential here, many are alone, others in casual attachments, many—even more than he might imagine he suspects—available. But he will probably sleep alone all the nights of this convention, either sleep alone or end up standing in the hotel bar past four with old friends drinking and remembering the fifties. The desperation and necessity are gone: Sandra is not much, he accepts this, but she has given him all of which she is capable, which makes her flaws in this marriage less serious than Ruthven's because he could have given more. His failure comes from the decision, consciously, to deny. Perhaps it was the science fiction that shut him down. He just does not know.

Ruthven stands in the center of the large welcoming party, sipping scotch and conversing. He feels detached from the situation and from his own condition; he feels that if he were to close his eyes other voices would overwhelm him... the voices of all the other conventions. Increasingly he finds that he has more to hear from—and more to say to—the dead than to the living. Now with his eyes closed, rocking, it is as if Mark Clifton, Edmond Hamilton, Kuttner and Kornbluth are standing by him glasses in hand, looking at one another in commiseration and silence. There is really no need for any of them to speak. For a while none of them do.

Finally, Ruthven says as he has before, "It hurts, doesn't it? It hurts." Kuttner nods, Kornbluth raises a sardonic eyebrow. Mark Clifton shrugs. "It hurts," Clifton says, "oh it hurts all right, Henry. Look at the record." There seems nothing more to say. A woman in red who looks vaguely like Felicia touches his arm. Her eyes are solemn and intense. She has always wanted to meet him, she says; she loves his work. She tells Ruthven her name and that she is a high school English teacher in Boston.

"Thank you," he says, "I'm glad you like the books." Everybody nods. Hamilton smiles. "You might as well," Kornbluth says with a shrug, "I can't any more and there's really nothing else." Ruthven shrugs. He tells the woman that the next scotch is on him or more properly the committee. He walks her over to the bar. Her hand is in his. Quickly, oh so quickly, her hand is in his.

At eight-fifteen the next morning Ruthven delivers his guest-of-honor speech. There are about three thousand in the large auditorium; convention attendance is just over ten thousand but 30 percent is not bad. Most attendees of modern world conventions are not serious readers now; they are movie fans or television fans or looking for a good time. Ruthven has thought for months about this speech and has worked on it painfully.

Once he thought—this was, of course, years ago—that if he were ever guest of honor at a major convention he would deliver a speech denunciatory of science fiction and what it did to its writers. Later, when he began to feel as implicated as anyone, the speech became less an attack than an elegy for the power and mystery that had been drained by bad writing and editing, debased by a juvenile audience. But after *The Lies of Science Fiction* had been put away and the edge of terror blunted, the very idea of the speech seemed childish. He was never going to be guest of honor and if he were, what right did he have to tell anyone anything? Science fiction was a private circumstance, individually perceived.

Nonetheless he had, when the time came to plan, considered the speech at length. What he decided to do, finally, was review his career in nostalgic terms, dropping in just enough humor to distract the audience from the thrust of his intention because after bringing his career up to date he wanted to share with them his conviction that it did not matter. Nothing mattered except that it had kept him around until the coincidence of *The Sorcerer,* and *The Sorcerer* meant nothing except that Ruthven would not worry about money until he was dead. "Can't you see the overwhelming futility of it?" he would ask. "The Lies of Science Fiction" seemed a good title except that it would be printed in the convention book and be taken as a slap at the committee and indeed the very field which was doing him honor. Better to memorialize his book through the speech itself. Anyway, the title would have alerted the audience to the bitterness of his conclusion. He wanted to spring it on them.

So he had called it "Me and the Cosmos and Science Fiction," harmless enough, and Ruthven delivers the first thirty-two minutes of his thirty-five minute address from the text and pretty much as he had imagined. Laughter is frequent; his anecdotes of Campbell, Gold and Roger Elwood are much appreciated. There is applause when he speaks of the small triumph of the science fiction writer the day Apollo landed. "*We* did that," he remembers telling a friend, "at three cents a word." The audience applauds. They probably understand. This much, anyway.

Then, to his astonishment and disgust, Ruthven comes off the text and loses control. He has never hated himself so. Just as he is about to lift his head and explain coldly that none of it matters his voice falters and breaks. It has happened in the terrible arguments with Sandra in the old days and in the dreams with Kornbluth, Hamilton, Kuttner and Clifton, but never before in public, and Ruthven delivers the last paragraphs of his speech in a voice and from a mood he has never before known:

"We tried," he says. "I want you to know that, that even the worst of us, the most debased hack, the one-shot writer, the fifty-book series, all the hundreds and thousands of us who ever wrote a line of this stuff for publication: we tried. We tried desperately to say something because we were the only ones who could, and however halting our language, tuneless the song, it was ours.

"We wanted to celebrate, don't you see? We wanted to celebrate the insistent, circumstantial fact of the spirit itself, that wherever and in whatever form the spirit could yet sing amidst the engines of the night, that the engines could extinguish our lives but never our light, and that in the spaces between we could still thread our colors of substantiation. In childhood nights we felt it, later we lost it, but retrieval was always the goal, to get back there, to make it work, to justify ourselves to ourselves, to give the light against the light. We tried and failed; in a billion words we failed and failed again, but throughout was our prayer and somewhere in its center lived something else, the mystery and power of what might have been flickering.

"In these spaces, in all the partitions, hear our song. Let it be known that while given breath we sang until it drew the very breath from us and extinguished our light forever."

And then, in hopeless and helpless fury, Ruthven pushes aside the microphone and cries.

Another Orphan

by John Kessel

The long-legged Mr. Kessel is a one-time New Yorker with degrees in physics and English who did his graduate work with James Gunn at the University of Kansas and is now a member of the English department of North Carolina State University. His science fiction stories have been appearing with increasing frequency since the late 1970s. This tale of a strange voyage of the mind is his first award-winner.

"And I am only escaped alone to tell thee."
—Job

HE woke to darkness and swaying and the stink of many bodies. He tried to to lift his head and reach across the bed and found he was not in his bed at all. He was in a canvas hammock that rocked back and forth in a room of other hammocks.

"Carol?" Still half-asleep, he looked around, then lay back, hoping that he might wake and find this just a dream. He felt the distance from himself he often felt in dreams. But the room did not go away, and the smell of sweat and salt water and some overwhelming stink of oil became more

Winner, Nebula for Best Novella of 1982.

real. The light slanting down through a latticed grating above became brighter; he heard the sound of water and the creak of canvas, and the swaying did not stop, and the men about him began to stir. It came to him, in that same dream-like calm, that he was on a ship.

A bell sounded twice, then twice again. Most of the other men were up, grumbling, and stowing away the hammocks.

"What ails you, Fallon?" someone called. "Up, now."

TWO

His name was Patrick Fallon. He was 32 years old, a broker for a commission house at the Chicago Board of Trade. He played squash at an athletic club every Tuesday and Thursday night. He lived with a woman named Carol Bukaty.

The night before, he and Carol had gone to a party thrown by one of the other brokers and his wife. As sometimes happened with these parties, this one had degenerated into an exchange of sexual innuendo, none of it apparently serious, but with undertones of suspicions and the desire to hurt. Fallon had had too much wine and had said a few things to the hostess and about Carol that he had immediately wanted to retract. They'd driven back from the party in silence, but the minute they'd closed the door it had been a fight. Neither of them shouted, but his quiet statement that he did not respect her at all and hers that she was sickened by his excess, managed quite well. They had become adept in three years at getting at each other. They had, in the end, made up, and had made love.

As Fallon had lain there on the edge of sleep, he had had the idle thought that what had happened that evening was silly, but not funny. That something was wrong.

Fallon had the headache that was the residue of the wine; he could still smell Carol. He was very hungry and dazed as he stumbled into the bright sunlight on the deck of the ship. It was there. It was real. He was awake. The ocean stretched flat and empty in all directions. The ship rolled slightly as it made way with the help of a light wind, and despite the early morning it was already hot. He did not hear the sound or feel the vibration of an engine. Fallon stared, unable to collect the scattered impressions into coherence; they were all consistent with the picture of an antiquated sailing ship on a very real ocean, all insane when compared with where his mind told him he ought to be.

The men had gone to their work as soon as they'd stretched into the morning light. They wore drab shirts and canvas trousers; most were barefoot. Fallon walked unsteadily along the deck, trying to keep out of their way as they set to scrubbing the deck. The ship was unlike anything he had ever seen on Lake Michigan; he tried to ignore the salt smell that threatened to make it impossible for him to convince himself this was Lake Michigan. Yet it seemed absurd for such a small vessel to be in the middle of an ocean. He knew that the Coast Guard kept sailing ships for training its cadets, but these were no cadets.

The deck was worn, scarred and greasy with a kind of oily, clear lard-like grease. The rail around the deck was varnished black and weather-beaten, but the pins set through it to which the rigging was secured were ivory. Fallon touched one—it was some kind of tooth. More ivory was used for rigging-blocks and on the capstan around which the anchor chain was wound. The ship was a thing of black wood fading to white under the assault of water and sun, and of white ivory corroding to black under the effect of dirt and hard use. Three long boats, pointed at both ends, hung from arms of wood and metal on the left—the port—side; another such boat was slung at the rear of the deck on the starboard side, and on the raised part of the deck behind the mainmast two other boats were turned turtle and secured. Add to this the large hatch on the main deck and a massive brick structure that looked like some old-fashioned oven just behind the front mast, and there hardly seemed room for the fifteen or twenty men on deck to go about their business. There was certainly no place to hide.

"Fallon! Set your elbows to that deck or I shall have to set your nose to it!" A short, sandy-haired man accosted him. Stocky and muscular, he was some authority; there was insolence in his grin, and some seriousness. The other men looked up.

Fallon got out of the man's way. He went over to one of the groups washing down the deck with salt water, large scrub brushes, and what looked like push brooms with leather flaps instead of bristles, like large versions of the squeegees used to clean windows. The sandy-haired man watched him as he got down on his hands and knees and grabbed one of the brushes.

"There's a good lad, now. Ain't he, fellows?"

A couple of them laughed. Fallon started scrubbing, concentrating on the grain of the wood, at first fastidious about not wetting the already damp trousers he had apparently slept in, soon realizing that that was a lost cause. The warm water was sloshed over them, the men leaned on the brushes, and the oil slowly flaked up and away through the spaces in the rail into the sea. The sun rose and it became even hotter. Now and then one of the men tried to say a word or two to him, but he did not answer.

"Fallon here's got the hypos," someone said.

"Or the cholera," another said. "He does look a bit bleary about the eye. Are you thirsty, Fallon? D' your legs ache? Are your bowels knotted?"

"My bowels are fine," he said.

That brought a good laugh. "Fine, he says! Manxman!" The sailor called to a decrepit old man leaning on his squeegee. "Tell the King-Post that Fallon's bowels are fine, now! The scrubbing does seem to have eased them."

"Don't ease them here, man!" the old man said seriously. The men roared again, and the next bucket of water was sloshed up between Fallon's legs.

THREE

In the movies men had faced similar situations. The amnesiac soldier came to on a farm in Wales. But invariably the soldier would give evidence of his confusion, challenging the farm owner, pestering his fellow workers with questions about where he was and how he got there, telling them of his persistent memory of a woman in white with golden hair. Strangely—strangely even to Fallon—he did not feel that way. Confusion, yes, dread, curiosity—but no desire to call attention to himself, to try to make the obvious reality of his situation give way to the apparent reality of his memories. He did not think this was because of any strength of character or remarkable powers of adaptation. In fact, everything he did that first day revealed his ignorance of what he was supposed to know and do on the ship. He did not feel any great presence of mind; for minutes at a time he would stop working, stunned with awe and fear at the simple alienness of what was happening. If it was a dream, it was a vivid dream. If anything was a dream, it was Carol and the Chicago Board of Trade.

The soldier in the movie always managed, despite the impediments of his amnesia and the ignorance of those around him, to find the rational answer to his mystery. That shell fragment which had grazed his forehead in Normandy had sent him back to Wessex sanitorium, from which he had wandered during an air raid, to be picked up by a local handyman driving his lorry to Llanelly, who in the course of the journey decided to turn a few quid by leasing the poor soldier to a farmer as his half-wit cousin laborer. So it had to be that some physicist at the University of Chicago, working on the modern equivalent of the Manhattan Project, had accidentally created a field of gravitational energy so intense that a vagrant vortex had broken free from it, and, in its lightning progress through the city on its way to extinction, had plucked Fallon from his bed in the suburbs, sucked him through a puncture in the fabric of space and time, to deposit him in a hammock on a mid-nineteenth-century sailing ship. Of course.

Fallon made a fool of himself ten times over during the day. Despite his small experience with fresh-water sailing, he knew next to nothing about the work he was meant to do on this ship. Besides cleaning the deck and equipment, the men scrubbed a hard, black soot from the rigging and spars. Fallon would not go up into the rigging. He was afraid, and tried to find work enough on the deck. He did not ask where the oil and soot had come from; it was obvious the source had been the brick furnace that was now topped by a tight-fitting wooden cover. Some of the cracks in the deck were filled with what looked like dried blood, but it was only the casual remark of one of the other men that caused him to realize, shocked at his own slowness, that this was a whaling ship.

The crew was an odd mixture of types and races; there were white and black, a group of six Orientals who sat apart on the rear deck and took no part in the work, men with British and German accents, and an eclectic collection of others—Polynesians, an Indian, a huge, shaven-headed black African, and a mostly naked man covered from head to toe with purple tattoos, whorls and swirls and vortexes, images and symbols, none of them quite decipherable as a familiar object or person. After the decks had been scrubbed to a remarkable whiteness, the mate named Flask set Fallon to tarring some heavy ropes in the fore part of the ship, by himself, where he would be out of the others' way. The men seemed to realize that something was wrong with him, but said nothing and apparently did not take it amiss that one of their number should begin acting strangely.

Which brought him, hands and wrists smeared with warm tar, to the next question: how did they know who he was? He was Fallon to all of them. He had obviously been there before he awakened; he had been a regular member of the crew with a personality and role to fill. He knew nothing of that. He had the overwhelming desire to get hold of a mirror to see whether the face he wore was indeed the face he had worn in Chicago the night before. The body was the same, down to the appendix scar he'd carried since he was nine years old. His arms and hands were the same; the fatigue he felt and the rawness of his skin told him he had not been doing this type of work long. So assume he was there in his own person, his Chicago person, the *real* Fallon. Was there now some confused nineteenth-century sailor wandering around a brokerage house on Van Buren? The thought made him smile. The sailor at the Board of Trade would probably get the worst of it.

So they knew who he was, even if he didn't remember ever having been here before. There was a Patrick Fallon on the ship, and *he* had somehow been brought here to fill that role. Reasons unknown. Method unknown. Way out....

Think of it as an adventure. How many times as a boy had he dreamed of similar escapes from the mundane? Here he was, the answer to a dream, twenty-five years later. It would make a tremendous story when he got back, if he could find someone he could trust enough to tell it to—if he could get back.

There was a possibility that he tried to keep himself from dwelling on. He had come here while asleep, and though this reality gave no evidence of being a dream, if there was a symmetry to insanity, then on waking the next morning, might he not be back in his familiar bed? Logic presented the possibility. He tried not to put too much faith in logic. Logic had not helped him when he was on the wrong side of the soybeans market in December, 1980.

The long tropic day declined; the sunset was a travel

agent's dream. They were traveling east, by the signpost of that light. Fallon waited, sitting by a coil of rope, watching the helmsman at the far end of the ship lean, dozing, on the long ivory tiller that served this ship in place of the wheel with handspikes he was familiar with from Errol Flynn movies. It had to be a bone from some long-dispatched whale, another example of the savage Yankee practicality of whoever had made this whaler. It was a queerly innocent, gruesome artistry. Fallon had watched several idle sailors in the afternoon carving pieces of bone while they ate their scrap of salt pork and hard bread.

"Fallon, you can't sleep out here tonight, unless you want the Old Man to find you lying about." It was a tall sailor of about Fallon's age. He had come down from aloft shortly after Fallon's assignment to the tar bucket, had watched him quietly for some minutes before giving him a few pointers on how the work was done. In the falling darkness, Fallon could not make out his expression, but the voice held a quiet distance that might mask just a trace of kindness. Fallon tried to get up and found his legs had grown so stiff he failed on the first try. The sailor caught his arm and helped him to his feet. "You're all right?"

"Yes." Fallon was embarrassed.

"Let's get below, then," They stepped toward the latticed hatch near the bow.

"And there he is," the sailor said, pausing, lifting his chin aft.

"Who?" Fallon looked back with him and saw the black figure there, heavily bearded, tall, in a long coat, steadying himself by a hand in the rigging. The oil lamp above the compass slightly illuminated the dark face—and gleamed deathly white along with the ivory leg that projected from beneath his black coat. Fixed, immovable, the man leaned heavily on it.

"Ahab," the sailor said.

FOUR

Lying in the hammock, trying to sleep, Fallon was assaulted by the feverish reality of where he was. The ship rocked him like a gentle parent in its progress through the calm sea; he heard the rush of water breaking against the hull as the *Pequod* made headway, the sighing of the breeze above, heard the steps of the nightwatch on deck, the occasional snap of canvas, the creaking of braces; he sweated in the oppressive heat below-decks; he drew heavy breaths, trying to calm himself, of air laden with the smell of mildewed canvas and what he knew to be whale oil. He held his hands before his face and in the profound darkness knew them to be his own. He touched his neck and felt the slickness of sweat beneath the beard. He ran his tongue over his lips and tasted salt. Through the open hatch he could make out stars that were unchallenged by any other light. Would the stars be the same in a book as they were in reality?

In a book. Any chance he had to sleep flew from him whenever he ran up against that thought. Any logic he brought to bear on his situation crumbled under the weight of that absurdity. A time machine he could accept, some chance cosmic displacement that sucked him into the past. But not into a book. That was insanity; that was hallucination. He knew that if he could sleep now, he would wake once more in the real world. But he had nothing to grab hold of. He lay in the darkness listening to the ship and could not sleep at all.

They had been compelled to read *Moby Dick* in the junior-year American Renaissance class he'd taken to fulfill the last of his Humanities requirements. Fallon remembered being bored to tears by most of Melville's book, struggling with his interminable sentences, his wooly speculations that had no bearing on the story; he remembered being caught up by parts of that story. He had seen the movie with Gregory Peck. Richard Basehart, king of the sci-fi flicks, had played Ishmael. Fallon had not seen anyone who looked like Richard Basehart on this ship. The mate, Flask—he remembered that name now. He remembered that all the harpooners were savages. Queequeg.

He remembered that in the end, everyone but Ishmael died.

He had to get back. Sleep, sleep, you idiot, he told himself. He could not keep from laughing; it welled up in his chest and burst through his tightly closed lips. Fallon's laugh sounded more like a man gasping for breath than one overwhelmed by humor: he barked, he chuckled, he sucked in sudden draughts of air as he tried to control the spasms. Tears were in his eyes, and he twisted his head from side to side as if he were strapped to a bed in some ward. Some of the others stirred and cursed him, but Fallon, a character in a book where everyone died on the last page, shook with helpless laughter, crying, knowing he would not sleep.

FIVE

With a preternatural clarity born of the sleepless night, Fallon saw the deck of the *Pequod* the next morning. He was a little stunned yet, but if he kept his mind in tight check the fatigue would keep him from thinking, and he would not feel the distress that was waiting to burst out again. Like a man carrying a balloon filled with acid, Fallon carried his knowledge tenderly.

He observed with scientific detachment, knowing that sleep would ultimately come, and with it perhaps escape. The day was bright and fair, a duplicate of the previous one. The whaler was clean and prepared for her work; all sails were set to take advantage of the light breeze, and the mastheads were manned with lookouts. Men loitered on deck. On the rear deck—the quarter-deck, they called it—Ahab paced, with remarkable steadiness for a man wearing an ivory leg, between the compass in its box and the mainmast, stopping for seconds to stare pointedly at each end of his path. Fallon could not take his eyes off the man. He was much older than Fallon had imagined him from his memories of the book. Ahab's hair and beard were still black, except for the streak of white which ran through them as the old scar ran top to bottom across his face, but the face itself was deeply worn, and the man's eyes were sunken in wrinkles, hollow. Fallon remembered Tigue who had traded in the gold pit, who had once been the best boy on the floor—the burn-out, they called him now, talking a very good game about shorting the market. Tigue's eyes had the same hollow expectation of disaster waiting inevitably for him—just him—that Ahab's held. Yet when Fallon had decided Ahab had to be the same empty nonentity, the man would pause at the end of his pathway and stare at the compass, or the gold coin that was nailed to the mast, and his figure would tighten in the grip of some stiffening passion, as if he were shot through with lightning. As if he were at the focal point of some cosmic lens that concentrated all the power of the sun on him, so that he might momentarily burst into spontaneous flame.

Ahab talked to himself, staring at the coin. His voice was conversational, and higher pitched than Fallon had imagined it would be. Fallon was not the only man who watched him in wonder and fear.

"There's something ever egotistical in mountain-tops and towers, and all other grand and lofty things; look here—three peaks as proud as Lucifer. The firm tower, that is Ahab; the volcano, that is Ahab; the courageous, the undaunted, and victorious fowl, that, too, is Ahab; all are Ahab; and this round globe is but the image of the rounder globe, which, like a magician's glass, to each and every man in turn but mirrors back his own mysterious self..."

All spoken in the tone of a man describing a minor auto accident (the brown Buick swerved to avoid the boy on the bicycle, crossed over the yellow line and hit the milk truck which was going south on Main Street). As soon as he had stopped, Ahab turned and, instead of continuing his pacing, went quietly below.

One of the ship's officers—the first mate, Fallon thought—who had been talking to the helmsman before Ahab began to speak, now advanced to look at the coin. Fallon began to remember what was going to happen. Theatrically, though there was nobody there to listen to him, the mate began to speak aloud about the Trinity and the sun, hope and despair. Next came another mate, who talked of spending it quickly, then gave a reading comparing the signs of the zodiac to a man's life. Overwritten and silly, Fallon thought.

Flask now came to the doubloon and figured out how many cigars he could buy with it. Then came the old man who had sloshed the water all over Fallon the previous morning, who gave a reading of the ship's doom under the sign of the lion. Then Queequeg, then one of the Orientals, then a black boy—the cabin boy.

The boy danced around the mast twice, crouching low, rising on his toes, and each time around stared at the doubloon with comically bugged eyes. He stopped. "I look, you look, he looks, we look, ye look, they look."

I look, you look, he looks, we look, ye look, they look.

They all looked at it; they all spouted their interpretations. That was what Melville had wanted them to do to prove his point. Fallon did not feel like trying to figure out what that point was. After the dramatics, the *Pequod* went back to dull routine, and he to clean up work on the deck, to tarring more ropes. They had a lot of ropes.

He took a break and walked up to the mast to look at the coin himself. Its surface was stamped with the image of three mountains, with a flame, a tower, and a rooster at their peaks. Above were the sun and the signs of the zodiac. REPUBLICA DEL EQUADOR: QUITO, it said. A couple of ounces, worth maybe $1,300 on the current gold market, according to the London fix Fallon last remembered. It wouldn't be worth as much to these men, of course; this was pre-inflation money. He remembered that the doubloon had been nailed there by Ahab as a reward to whoever spotted Moby Dick first.

I look, you look, he looks, we look, ye look, they look.

Fallon looked, and nothing changed. His tiredness grew as the day wore through a brutally hot afternoon. When evening at last came and the grumbling of his belly had been at least partially assauged by the meager meal served the men, Fallon fell exhausted into the hammock. He did not worry about not sleeping this time; consciousness fell away as if he had been drugged. He had a vivid dream. He was trying, under cover of darkness, to pry the doubloon away from the mast so that he might throw it into the sea. Anxiously trying not to let the helmsman at the tiller spot him, he heard the step, tap, step, tap of Ahab's pacing a deck below. It was one of those dreams where one struggles in unfocused terror to accomplish some simple task. He was afraid he might be found any second by Ahab. If he were caught, then he would be exposed and vilified before the crew's indifferent gaze.

He couldn't do it. He couldn't get his fingers under the edge of the coin, though he bruised them bloody. He heard the knocking of Ahab's whalebone step ascending the deck; the world contracted to the coin welded to the mast, his broken nails, the terrible fear. He heard the footsteps drawing nearer behind him as he frantically tried to free the doubloon, yet he could not run, and he would not turn around. At the last, after an eternity of anxiety, a hand fell on his shoulder and spun him around, his head leaping into his throat. It was not Ahab, but Carol.

He woke breathing hard, pulse pounding. He was still in the hammock, in the forecastle of the *Pequod.* He closed his eyes again, dozed fretfully through the rest of the night. Morning came: he was still there.

The next day several of the other men prodded him about not having taken a turn at the masthead for a long time. He stuck to mumbled answers and hoped they would not go to any of the officers. He wanted to disappear. He wanted it to be over. The men treated him more scornfully as the days passed. And the days passed, and still nothing happened to free him. The doubloon glinted in the sun each morning, the center of the ship, and Fallon could not get away. I look, you look, he looks, we look, ye look, they look.

SIX

Fallon had assumed his sullen station by the tar bucket. There he felt at least some defense from his confusion. He could concentrate on the smell and feel of the tar; he remembered the summers on the tarred road in front of his grandparents' house in Elmira, how the sun would raise shining bubbles of tar at the edges of the re-surfaced country road, how the tar would stick to your sneakers and get you a licking if you tracked it into grandmother's immaculate kitchen. He and his cousin Seth had broken the bubbles with sticks and watched them slowly subside into themselves. The tar bucket on the *Pequod* was something Fallon could focus on. The tar was real; the air he breathed was real—Fallon himself was real.

Stubb, the second mate, stood in front of him, arms akimbo. He stared at Fallon; Fallon lifted his head and saw the man's small smile. There was no charity in it.

"Time to go aloft, Fallon. You've been missing your turn, and we won't have any slackers aboard."

Fallon couldn't think of anything to say. He stumbled to his feet, wiping his hands on a piece of burlap. A couple of the other sailors were watching, waiting for Fallon to shy off or for Stubb to take him.

"Up with ye!" Stubb shoved Fallon's shoulder, and he

turned, fumbling for the rigging. Fallon looked momentarily over the side of the ship to the sea that slid calmly by them; the gentle rolling of the deck that he had in so short a time become accustomed to now returned to him with frightening force. Stubb was still behind him. Taking a good breath, he pulled himself up and stepped barefoot onto the rail. Facing inward now, he tried to climb the rigging. Stubb watched him with dispassion, waiting, it seemed, for his failure. Expecting it. It was like trying to climb one of those rope ladders at the county fair: each rung he took twisted the ladder in the direction of his weight, and the rocking of the ship, magnified as he went higher, made it hard for his feet to find the next step. He had never been a particularly self-conscious man, but felt he was being watched by them all now, and was acutely conscious of how strange he must seem. How touched with idiocy and fear.

Nausea rose, the deck seemed farther below than it had any reason to be, the air was stifling, the wind was without freshness and did not cool the sweat from his brow and neck. He clutched the ropes desperately; he tried to take another step, but the strength seemed drained from his legs. Humiliated, burning with shame yet at the same time mortally afraid of falling—and of more than that, of the whole thing, of the fact that here he was where he ought not to be, cheated, abused, mystified—he wrapped his arms around the rigging, knees wobbly, sickness in his gut, bile threatening to heave itself up the back of his throat. Crying, eyes clenched tight, he wished it would all go away.

"Fallon! Fallon, ye dog, ye dog-*fish,* why don't ye climb! You had better climb, weak-liver, for I don't want you down on my deck again if ye won't!" Stubb roared his rage. Fallon opened his eyes, saw the red-faced man staring furiously up at him. Perhaps he'll have a stroke, Fallon thought.

He hung there, half-up, half-down, unable to move. I want to go home, he thought. Let me go home. Stubb raged and ridiculed him; others gathered to laugh and watch. Fallon closed his eyes and tried to go away. He heard a sound like the wooden mallet of the carpenter.

"What is the problem here, Mr. Stubb?" A calm voice. Fallon looked down again. Ahab stood with his hand on the mainmast to steady himself, looking up. His thumb was touching the doubloon.

Stubb was taken by surprise, as if Ahab were some apparition that had been called up by an entirely inappropriate spell. He jerked his head upward to indicate Fallon.

Squinting against the sun, Ahab studied Fallon for some time. His face was unnaturally pale in comparison to the tanned faces of the others turned up to look at him. Yet against the pallor, the white scar ran, a death-like sign, down the side of his face. His dark hair was disarrayed in the hot breeze. He was an old man; he swayed in the attempt to steady himself.

"Why don't ye go up?" Ahab called to Fallon.

Fallon shook his head. He tried to step up another rung, but though his foot found the rope, he didn't seem to have the strength he needed to pull himself up.

Ahab continued to look at him. He did not seem impatient or angry, only curious, as if Fallon were an animal sitting frozen on a traffic mall, afraid of the cars that passed. He seemed content to stand watching Fallon indefinitely. Stubb shifted nervously from foot to foot, his anger displaced and negated. The crewmen simply watched. Some of them looked above Fallon in the rigging; the ropes he clung to jerked, and he looked up himself to see that the man who had been standing at the masthead was coming down to help him.

"Bulkington!" Ahab cried, waving to the man to stop, "Let him be!" The sailor retreated upward and swung himself onto the yardarm above the mainsail. The *Pequod* waited. If there were whales to be hunted, they waited too.

Very distinctly, so that Fallon heard every word, Ahab said, "You must go up. Ye have taken the vow with the rest, and I will not have you go back on it. Would you go back on it? You must go up, or else you must come down, and show yourself for the coward and weakling you would then be."

Fallon clung to the rigging. He had taken no vow. It was all a story. What difference did it make what he did in a story? If he was to be a character in a book, why couldn't he defy it, do what he wanted instead of following the path they indicated? By coming down he could show himself as himself.

"Have faith!" Ahab called.

Above him, Bulkington hawked and spat, timing it so that with the wind and the rocking of the *Pequod,* he hit the sea and not the deck. Fallon bent his head back and looked up at him. It was the kind sailor who had helped him below on that first night. He hung suspended. He looked down and watched Ahab sway with the rolling of the deck, his eyes still fixed on Fallon. The man was crazy. Melville was crazy for inventing him.

Fallon clenched his teeth, pulled on the ropes and pushed himself up another step toward the masthead. He was midway up the mainsail, thirty feet above the deck. He concentrated on one rung at a time, breathing steadily, and pulled himself up. When he reached the level of the mainyard, Bulkington swung himself below Fallon and helped him along. The complicated motion that came when the sailor stepped onto the ropes had Fallon clinging once again, but this time he was out of it fairly quickly. They ascended, step by dizzying step, to the masthead. The sailor got onto the port masthead hoop, helping Fallon into the starboard. The *Pequod's* flag snapped in the wind a couple of feet above their heads.

"And here we are, Fallon," Bulkington said. Immediately he dropped himself down into the rigging again, so nimbly and suddenly that Fallon's breath was stopped in fear for the man's fall.

Way below, the men were once more stirring. Ahab exchanged some words with Stubb; then, moving out to the rail and steadying himself by a hand on one of the stays, a foreshortened black puppet far below, he turned his white face up to Fallon once again. Cupping his hand to his mouth, he shouted, "Keep a steady eye, now! If ye see fin or flank of him, call away!"

Call away. Fallon was far avove it all now, alone. He had made it. He had taken no vow and was not obligated to do anything he did not wish to. He had ascended to the masthead of his own free will, but, if he was to become a whaler, then what harm would there be in calling out whales—normal whales? Not literary ones. Not white ones.

He looked out to the horizon. The sea stretched out to the utmost ends of the world, covering it all, every secret, clear and blue and a little choppy under the innocent sky.

SEVEN

Fallon became used to the smell of the *Pequod.* He became accustomed to feeling sweaty and dirty, to the musty smell of mildew and the tang of brine trying to push away the stench of the packing plant.

He had not always been fastidious in his other life. In the late sixties, after he had dropped out of Northwestern, he had lived in an old house in a rundown neighborhood with three other men and a women. They had called it "The Big House," and to the outside observer they must have been hippies. "Hair men." "Freaks." "Dropouts." It was a vocabulary that seemed quaint now. The perpetual pile of dirty dishes in the sink, the Fillmore West posters, the black light, the hot and cold running roaches, the early-fifties furniture with corners shredded to tatters by the three cats. Fallon realized that that life had been as different from his world at the Board of Trade as the deck of the *Pequod* was now.

Fallon had dropped out because, he'd told himself, there was nothing he wanted from the university that he couldn't get from its library, or by hanging around the student union. It was hard for him to believe how much he had read then: Skinner's behaviorism, Spengler's history, pop physics and Thomas Kuhn, Friedman and Galbraith, Shaw, Conrad, Nabokov, and all he could find of Hammett, Chandler, Macdonald and their imitators. Later he had not been able to figure out just why he had forsaken a degree so easily; he didn't know if he was too irresponsible to do the work, or too slow, or above it all and following his own path. Certainly he had not seen himself as a rebel, and the revolutionary fervor his peers affected (it had seemed affectation ninety percent of the time) never took hold of Fallon completely. He had observed, but not taken part in, the melee at the Democratic Convention. But he put in his time in the back bedroom listening to the Doors and blowing dope until the world seemed no more than a slightly bigger version of the Big House and his circle of friends. He read *The Way of Zen*. He knew Hesse and Kerouac. He hated Richard Nixon and laughed at Spiro Agnew. Aloft in the rigging of the *Pequod,* those years came back to Fallon as they never had in his last five years at the CBT. What a different person he had been at twenty. What a strange person, he realized, he had become at twenty-eight. What a marvelous—and frightening—metamorphosis.

He had gotten sick of stagnating, he told himself. He had seen one or another of his friends smoke himself into passivity. He had seen through the self-delusions of the other cripples in the Big House: cripples was what he had called them when he'd had the argument with Marty Solokov and had stalked out. Because he broke from that way of living did not mean he was selling out, he'd told them. He could work any kind of job; he didn't want money or a house in the suburbs. He had wanted to give himself the feeling of getting started again, of moving, of putting meaning to each day. He had quit washing dishes for the university, moved into a dingy flat closer to the center of the city, and scanned the help-wanted columns. He still saw his friends often and got stoned maybe not quite so often, and listened to music and read. But he had had enough of "finding himself," and he recognized in the others how finding yourself became an excuse for doing nothing.

Marty's cousin was a runner for Pearson Joel Chones on the Chicago Mercantile Exchange who had occasionally come by the house, gotten high and gone to concerts. Fallon had slept with her once. He called her up, and she asked around, and eventually he cut his hair short—not too short—and became a runner for Pearson, too. He became marginally better groomed. He took a shower and changed his underwear every day. He bought three ties and wore one of them on the trading floor because that was one of the rules of the exchange.

It occurred to Fallon to find Ishmael, if only to see the man who would live while he died. He listened and watched; he learned the name of every man on the ship—he knew Flask and Stubb and Starbuck and Bulkington, Tashtego, Dagoo and Queequeg, identified Fedallah, the lead Philippine boatsman. There *was* no Ishmael. At first Fallon was puzzled, then came the beginnings of hope. If the reality he was living in could be found to differ from the reality of Melville's book in such an important particular, then could it not differ in some other way—some way that would at least lead to his survival? Maybe this Ahab caught his white whale. Maybe Starbuck would steel himself to the point where he could defy the madman and take over the ship. Perhaps they would never sight Moby Dick.

Then an unsettling realization smothered the hope before it could come fully to bloom: there was not necessarily an Ishmael in the book. "*Call* me Ishmael," it started. Ishmael was a pseudonym for some other man, and there would be no one by that name on the *Pequod.* Fallon congratulated himself on a clever bit of literary detective work.

Yet the hope refused to remain dead. Yes, there was no Ishmael on the *Pequod;* or anyone on the ship not specifically named in the book might be Ishmael, any one of the anonymous sailors, within certain broad parameters of age and character—and Fallon wracked his brain trying to remember what the narrator said of himself—might be Ishmael. He grabbed at that; he breathed in the possibility and tried on the suit for size. Why not? If absurdity were to rule to the extent that he had to be there in the first place, then why couldn't he be the one who lived? More than that, why couldn't he make himself that man? No one else knew what Fallon knew. He had the advantage over them. Do the things that Ishmael did, and you may be him. If you have to be a character in a book, why not be the hero?

Fallon's first contact with the heart of capitalism at the CME had been frightening and amusing. Frightening when he screwed up and delivered a May buy-order to a July trader and cost the company 10,000 dollars. It was only through the grace of God and his own guts in facing it out that he had made it through the disaster. He had, he discovered, the ability to hide himself behind a facade which, to the self-interested observer, would appear to be whatever that observer wished it to be. If his superior expected him to be respectful and curious, then Fallon was respectfully curious. He did it without having to compromise his inner self. He was not a hypocrite.

The amusing part came after he had it all down and he began to watch the market like an observer at a very complex monopoly game. Or, more accurately, like a baseball fan during a pennant race. There were at least as many statistics as in a good baseball season, enough personalities, strategies, great plays, blunders, risk and luck. Fallon would walk onto the floor at the beginning of the day—the huge room with its concert-hall atmosphere, the banks of price boards around the walls, the twilight, the conditioned air, the hundreds of bright-coated traders and agents—and think of half time at homecoming. The floor at the end of the day, as he walked across the hardwood scattered with mounds of paper scraps like so much confetti, was a basketball court after the NCAA finals. Topping it all off, giving it that last significant twist that was necessary to all good jokes, was the fact that this was all supposed to mean something; it was real money they were playing with, and one tick of the board in Treasury Bills cost somebody eleven-hundred dollars. This was serious stuff, kid. The lifeblood of the nation—of the free world. Fallon could hardly hold in his laughter, could not stop his fascination.

Fallon's first contact with the whale—his first lowering—was in Stubb's boat. The man at the forward masthead cried out, "There she blows! Three points off starboard! There she blows! Three—no, four of 'em!"

The men sprang to the longboats and swung them away over the side. Fallon did his best to look as if he was helping. Stubb's crew leapt into the boat as it was dropped into the swelling sea, heedless to the possibility of broken bones or sprained ankles. Fallon hesitated a second at the rail, then threw himself off with the feeling of a man leaping off the World Trade Center. He landed clumsily and half-bowled over one of the men. He took his place at a center oar and pulled away. Like the man falling off the building, counting off the stories as they flew past him, Fallon thought, "So far, so good." And waited for the crash.

"Stop snoring, ye sleepers, and pull!" Stubb called, halfway between jest and anger. "Pull, Fallon! Why don't you pull? Have you never seen an oar before? Don't look over your shoulder, lad, *pull!* That's better. Don't be in a hurry, men—softly, softly now—but damn ye, pull until you break something! Tashtego! Can't you harpoon me some men with backs to them? *Pull!*"

Fallon pulled until he thought the muscles in his arms would snap, until the small of his back spasmed as if he were indeed being harpooned by the black-haired Indian behind him in the bow. The sea was rough, and they were soon soaked with spray. After a few minutes Fallon forgot the whales they pursued, merged into the rhythm of the work, fell in with the cunning flow of Stubb's curses and pleas, the crazy sermon, now whispered, now shouted. He concentrated on the oar in his hands, the bite of the blade into the water, the simple mechanism his body had become, the working of his lungs, the dry rawness of the breath dragged in and out in time to their rocking, back-breaking work. Fallon closed his eyes, heard the pulse in his ears, felt the cool spray and the hot sun, saw the rose fog of the blood in his eyelids as he faced into the bright and brutal day.

At twenty-five, Fallon was offered a position in the office upstairs. At twenty-seven, he had an offer from DCB International to become a broker. By that time he was living with Carol. Why not? He was still outside it all, still safe within. Let them think what they would of him; he was protected, in the final analysis, by that great indifference he held to his breast the way he held Carol close at night. He was not a hypocrite. He said nothing he did not believe in. Let them project upon him whatever fantasies they might hold dear to themselves. He was outside and above it all, analyzing futures for DCB International. Clearly, in every contract that crossed his desk, it was stated that DCB and its brokers were not responsible for reverses that might be suffered as a result of suggestions they made.

So he had spent the next four years, apart from it, pursuing his interests, which, with the money he was making, he found were many. Fallon saw very little of the old friends now. Solokov's cousin told him he was now in New York, cadging money from strangers in Times Square. Solokov, she said, claimed it was a pretty good living. He claimed he was still beating the system. Fallon had grown up enough to realize that no one really beat any system—as if there were a system. There was only buying and selling, subject to the forces of the market and the infirmities of the players. Fallon was on the edges of it, could watch quietly, taking part as necessary (he had to eat), but still stay safe. He was no hypocrite.

"To the devil with ye, boys, will ye be outdone by Ahab's heathens? Pull, spring it, my children, my fine hearts-alive, smoothly, smoothly, bend it hard starboard! Aye, Fallon, let me see you sweat, lad, can you sweat for me?"

They rose on the swell, and it was like rowing uphill; they slid down the other side, still rowing, whooping like children on a toboggan ride, all the time Stubb calling on them. Fallon saw Starbuck's boat off to his right; he heard the rush of water beneath them, and the rush of something faster and greater than their boat.

Tashtego grunted behind him.

"A hit, a hit!" Stubb shouted, and beside Fallon the whaleline was running out with such speed that it sang and hummed and smoked. One of the men sloshed water over the place where it sled taut as a wire over the gunnel. Then the boat jerked forward so suddenly that Fallon was nearly knocked overboard when his oar, still trailing in the water, slammed into his chest. Gasping at the pain, he managed to get the oar up into the air. Stubb had half-risen from his seat in the stern.

They flew through the water. The whaleboat bucked as it slapped the surface of every swell the whale pulled them through. Fallon held on for dear life, not sure whether he ought to be grateful he hadn't been pitched out when the ride began. He tried to twist around to see the monster that was towing them, but able to turn only half way, all he could see for the spray and the violent motion was the swell and rush of white water ahead of them. Tashtego, crouched in the bow, grinned wickedly as he tossed out wooden blocks tied to the whaleline in order to tire the whale with their drag. You might as well try to tire a road grader.

Yet he could not help but feel exhilarated, and he saw that the others in the boat, hanging on or trying to draw the line in, were flushed and breathing as hard as he.

He turned again and saw the whale.

Fallon had been a good swimmer in high school. He met Carol Bukaty at a swimming pool about a year after he had gone to work at the CME. Fallon first noticed her in the pool, swimming laps. She was the best swimmer there, better than he, though he might have been stronger than she in the short run. She gave herself over to the water and did not fight it; the kick of her long legs was steady and strong. She breathed easily and her strokes were relaxed, yet powerful. She did not swim for speed, but she looked as if she could swim for days, so comfortable did she seem in the water. Fallon sat on the steps at the pool's edge and watched her for half an hour without once getting bored. He found her grace in the water arousing. He knew he had to speak to her. He slid into the pool and swam laps behind her.

At last she stopped. Holding onto the trough at the end of the pool, she pushed her goggles up onto her forehead and brushed the wet brown hair away from her eyes. He drew up beside her.

"You swim very well," he said.

She was out of breath. "Thank you."

"You look as if you wouldn't ever need to come out of the water. Like anything else might be a comedown after swimming." It was a strange thing for him to say, it was not what he wanted to say, but he did not know what he wanted, besides her.

She looked puzzled, smiled briefly, and pulled herself onto the side of the pool, letting her legs dangle in the water. "Sometimes I feel that way," she said. "I'm Carol Bukaty." She stuck out her hand, very businesslike.

"Pat Fallon."

She wore a grey tank suit; she was slender and small-breasted, tall, with a pointed chin and brown eyes. Fallon later discovered that she was an excellent dancer, that she purchased women's clothing for one of the major Chicago department stores, that she traveled a great deal, wrote lousy poetry, disliked cooking, liked children, and liked him. At first he was merely interested in her sexually, though the first few times they slept together it was not very good at all. Gradually the sex got better, and in the meantime Fallon fell in love.

She would meet him at the athletic club after work; they would play racquet ball in the late afternoon, go out to dinner and take in a movie, then spend the night at his or her apartment. He met her alcoholic father, a retired policeman who told endless stories about ward politics and the Daley machine, and Carol spent a Christmas with him at his parents'. After they moved in together, they settled into a comfortable routine. He felt secure in her affection for him. He did not want her, after a while, as much as he had that first day, those first months, but he still needed her. It still mattered to him what she was doing and what she thought of him. Sometimes it mattered to him too much, he thought. Sometimes he wanted to be without her at all, not because he had anything he could only do without her, but only because he wanted to *be* without her.

He would watch her getting dressed in the morning and wonder what creature she might be, and what that creature was doing in the same room with him. He would lie beside her as she slept, stroking the short brown hair at her temple with his fingertips, and be overwhlemed with the desire to possess her, to hold her head between his hands and know everything that she was; he would shake with the sudden frustration of its impossibility until it was all he could do to keep from striking her. Something was wrong with him, or with her. He had fantasies of how much she would miss him if he died, of what clothes she would wear to the funeral, of what stories she would tell her lovers in the future after he was gone.

If Carol felt any of the same things about him, she did not tell him. For Fallon's part, he did not try to explain what he felt in any but the most oblique ways. She should know how he felt, but of course she did not. So when things went badly, and they began to do so more and more, it was not possible for him to explain to her what was wrong, because he could not say it himself, and the pieces of his discontent were things that he was too embarrassed to admit. Yet he could not deny that sometimes he felt as if it was all over between them, that he felt nothing—and at others he would smile just to have her walk into the room.

Remarkable creature though the whale was, it was not so hard to kill one after all. It tired, just as a man would tire under the attack of a group of strangers. It slowed in the water, no longer able so effortlessly to drag them after it. They pulled close, and Stubb drove home the iron, jerked it back and forth, drew it out and drove it home again, fist over fist on the hilt, booted foot over the gunnel braced against the creature's flesh, sweating, searching for the whale's hidden life. At last he found it, and the whale shuddered and thrashed a last time, spouting pink mist, then dark blood, where once it spouted feathery white spray. Like a man, helpless in the end, it rolled over and died. Stubb was jolly, and the men were methodical; they tied their lines around the great tail and, as shadows grew long and the sun fell perpendicularly toward the horizon, drew the dead whale to the *Pequod.*

EIGHT

During the cutting up and boiling down of the whale that night, Fallon, perhaps in recognition of his return to normality as indicated by his return to the masthead, was given a real job: slicing the chunks of blubber that a couple of other sailors were hewing out of the great strips that were hauled over the side into "bible leaves." Fallon got the hang of it pretty quickly, though he was not fast, and Staley, the British sailor who was cutting beside him, kept poking at him to do more. "I'm doing all the work, Fallon," he said, as if his ambition in life were to make sure that he did no more than his own share of the work.

Using a sharp blade like a long cleaver, Fallon would position the chunk of blubber, skin side down on the cutting table, and imitating Staley, cut the piece into slices like the pages of a book, with the skin as its spine. The blubber leaves flopped outward or stuck to each other, and the table became slick with grease. Fallon was at first careful about avoiding his hands, but the blubber would slide around the table as he tried to cut it if he didn't hold it still. Staley pushed him on, working with dexterity, though Fallon noted that the man's hands were scarred, with the top joint of the middle finger of his left hand missing.

His back and shoulders ached with fatigue, and the smoke from the try-works stung his eyes. When he tried to wipe the tears away, he only smeared his face with grease. But he did a creditable job, cursing all the time. The cursing helped, and the other men seemed to accept him more for it. When finally they were done, and the deck was clean the next day, they were issued a tot of grog and allowed to swim within the lee of the stationary ship. The men were more real to him than when he had sat and watched from the outcast's station of the tar bucket. He was able to speak to them more naturally than he had ever done. But he did not forget his predicament.

"Ye are too serious, Fallon," Staley told him, offering Fallon some of his grog. "I can see you brooding there, and look how it set you into a funk. Ye are better now, perhaps, but mind you stick to your work and ye may survive this voyage."

"I won't survive it. Neither will you—unless we can do something about Captain Ahab."

Bulkington, who had been watching them, came by. "What of Captain Ahab?"

Fallon saw a chance in this. "Does his seeking after this white whale seem right to you?"

"The whale took his leg," Staley said.

"Some say it unmanned him," the other said, lower. "That's two legs you'd not like to lose yourself, I'll daresay."

Fallon drew them aside, more earnest now. "We will lose more than our balls if we do nothing about this situation. The man is out of his mind. He will drag us all down with him, and this ship with all of us, if we can't convince Starbuck to do something. Believe me, I know."

Friendly Bulkington did not look so friendly. "You do talk strange, Fallon. We took an oath, and we signed the papers before we even sailed a cable from shore. A captain is a captain. You are talking mutiny."

He had to go carefully.

"No, wait. Listen to me. Why are we sent on this trip? Think of the—the stockholders, or whatever you call them. The owners. They sent us out to hunt whales."

"The white whale is a whale." Staley looked petulant.

"Yes, of course, it's a whale. But there are hundreds of whales to be caught and killed. We don't need to hunt that one. Hasn't he set his sights on just Moby Dick? What about that oath? That gold piece on the mast? That says he's just out for vengeance. There was nothing about vengeance in the papers we signed. What do you think the owners would say if they knew about what he plans? Do you think they would approve of this wild goose chase?"

Staley was lost. "Goose chase?"

Bulkington was interested. "Go on."

Fallon had his foot in the door; he marshaled the arguments he had rehearsed over and over again. "There's no more oil in Moby Dick than in another whale...."

"They say he's monstrous big," Staley interjected.

Fallon looked pained. "Not so big as any two whales, then. Ahab is not after any oil you can boil out of the whale's flesh. If the owners knew what he intended, the way I do, if they knew how sick he was the week before he came out of that hole of a cabin he lives in, if they saw that light in his eye and the charts he keeps in his cabinet...."

"Charts? What charts? Have you been in his cabin?"

"No, not exactly," Fallon said. "Look, I know some things, but that's just because I keep my eyes open and I have some sources."

"Fallon, where do you hail from? I swear that I cannot half the time make out what you are saying. Sources? What do you mean by that?"

"Oh, Jesus!" He had hoped for better from Bulkington.

Staley darkened. "Don't blaspheme, man! I'll not take the word of a blasphemer."

Fallon saw another opening. "You're right! I'm sorry. But look, didn't the old man himself blaspheme more seriously than I ever could the night of that oath? If you are a god-fearing man, Staley, you'll know that that is true. Would you give your obedience to such a man? Moby Dick is just another of God's creatures, a dumb animal. Is it right to seek vengeance on an animal? Do you want to be responsible for that? God would not approve."

Staley looked troubled, but stubborn. "Do not tell me what the Almighty approves. That is not for the likes of you to know. And Ahab is the captain." With that he walked to the opposite side of the deck and stood there watching them as if he wanted to separate himself as much as possible from the conversation, yet still know what was going on.

Fallon was exasperated and tired.

"Why don't you go with Staley, Bulkington? You don't have to stick around with me, you know. I'm not going to do your reputation any good."

Bulkington eyed him steadily. "You are a strange one, Fallon. I did not think anything of you when I first saw you on the *Pequod.* But you may be talking some sense."

"Staley doesn't think so."

Bulkington took a pull on his grog. "Why did you try to persuade Staley of Ahab's madness? You should have known that you couldn't convince such a man that the sky is blue, if it were written in the articles he signed that it was green. Starbuck perhaps, or me. Not Staley. Don't you listen to the man you are talking to?"

Fallon looked at Bulkington; the tall sailor looked calmly back at him, patient, waiting.

"Okay, you're right," Fallon said. "I have the feeling I would not have a hard time convincing you, anyway. You know Ahab's insane, don't you?"

"It's not for me to say. Ahab has better reasons than those you give to him." He drew a deep breath, looked up at the sky, down at the men who swam in the shadow of the ship. He smiled. "They should be more wary of sharks," he said.

"The world does look a garden today, Fallon. But it may be that the old man's eyes are better than ours."

"You know he's mad, and you won't do anything?"

"The matter will not bear too deep a looking into." Bulkington was silent for a moment. "You know the story about the man born with a silver screw in his navel? How it tasked him, until one day he unscrewed it to divine its purpose?"

Fallon had heard the joke in grade school on the South Side. "His ass fell off."

"You and Ahab are too much like that man."

They both laughed. "I don't have to unscrew my navel," Fallon said. "We're all going to lose our asses anyway."

They laughed again. Bulkington put his arm around his shoulders, and they toasted Moby Dick.

NINE

There came a morning when, on pumping out the bilge, someone noticed that considerable whale oil was coming up with the water. Starbuck was summoned and, after descending into the hold himself, emerged and went aft and below to speak with Ahab. Fallon asked one of the others what was going on.

"The casks are leaking. We're going to have to lay up and break them out. If we don't, we stand to lose a lot of oil."

Some time later Starbuck reappeared. His face was red to the point of apoplexy, and he paced around the quarter-deck with his hands knotted behind his back. They waited for him to tell them what to do; he stared at the crewmen, stopped, and told them to be about their business. "Keep pumping," he told the others. "Maintain the look-out." He then spoke briefly to the helmsman leaning on the whale-bone tiller, and retreated to the corner of the quarter-deck to watch the wake of the ship. After a while Ahab himself staggered up onto the deck, found Starbuck, and spoke to him. He then turned to the men on deck.

"Furl the t'gallantsails," he called, "and close reef the topsails, fore and aft; back the main-yard; up Burtons, and break out in the main hold."

Fallon joined the others around the hold. Once the work had commenced, he concentrated on lifting, hauling, and not straining his back. The Manxman told them that he had been outside Ahab's cabin during the conference and that Ahab had threatened to shoot Starbuck dead on the spot when the mate demanded they stop chasing the whale to break out the hold. Fallon thought about the anger in Starbuck's face when he'd come up again. It struck him that the Starbuck of Melville's book was pretty ineffectual; he had to be to let that madman go on with the chase. But this Starbuck—whether like the one in the book or not—did not like the way things were going. There was no reason why Fallon had to sit around and wait for things to happen. It was worth a shot.

But not that afternoon.

Racism assured that the hardest work in the dank hold was done by the colored men—Dagoo, Tashtego, and Queequeg. They did not complain. Up to their knees in the bilge, clambering awkwardly over and about the barrels of oil in the murderous heat and unbreathable air of the hold, they did their jobs.

It was evening before the three harpooneers were told they could halt for the day and they emerged, sweaty, covered with slime, and bruised. Fallon collapsed against the side of the try-works; others sat beside him. Tall Queequeg was taken by a coughing fit, then went below to his hammock. Fallon gathered his strength, felt the sweat drying stickily on his arms and neck. There were few clouds, and the moon was waxing full. He saw Starbuck then, standing at the rear of the quarter-deck, face toward the mast. Was he looking at the doubloon?

Fallon got shakily to his feet; his legs were rubbery. The first mate did not notice him until he was close. He looked up.

"Yes?"

"Mr. Starbuck, I need to speak to you."

Starbuck looked at him as if he saw him for the first time. Fallon tried to look self-confident, serious. He'd gotten that one down well at DCB.

"Yes?"

Fallon turned so that he was facing inward toward the deck and Starbuck had his back to it to face him. He could see what was happening away from them and would know if anyone came near.

"I could not help but see that you were angry this morning after speaking to Captain Ahab."

Starbuck looked puzzled.

"I assume that you must have told Ahab about the leaking oil, and he didn't want to stop his hunt of the whale long enough to break out the hold. Am I right?"

The mate watched him guardedly. "What passed between Captain Ahab and me was none of your affair, or of the crew's. Is that what you've come to trouble me with?"

"It is a matter that concerns me," Fallon said. "It concerns the rest of the crew, and it ought to concern you. We are being bound by his orders, and what kind of orders is he giving? I know what you've been thinking; I know that this personal vengeance he seeks frightens and repulses you. I *know* what you're thinking. I could see what was in your mind when you stood at this rail this afternoon. He is not going to stop until he kills us all."

Starbuck seemed to draw back within himself. Fallon saw how beaten the man's eyes were; he did not think the mate was a drinker, but he looked like someone who had just surfaced after a long weekend. He could almost see the clockwork turning within Starbuck, a beat too slow, with the belligerence of the drunk being told the truth about himself that he did not want to admit. Fallon's last fight with Stein Jr. at the brokerage had started that way.

"Get back to your work," Starbuck said. He started to turn away.

Fallon put his hand on his shoulder. "You have to—"

Starbuck whirled with surprising violence and pushed Fallon away so that he nearly stumbled and fell. The man at the tiller was watching them.

"To work! You do not know what I am thinking! I'll have you flogged if you say anything more! A man with a three-hundreth lay has nothing to tell me. Go on, now."

Fallon was hot. "God damn you. You stupid—"

"Enough!" Starbuck slapped him with the back of his hand, the way Stein had tried to slap Fallon. Stein had missed. It appeared that Mr. Starbuck was more effectual than Stein Jr. Fallon felt his bruised cheek. The thing that hurt the most was the way he must have looked, like a hangdog insubordinate who had been shown his place. As Fallon stumbled away, Starbuck said, in a steadier voice, "Tend to your own conscience, man. Let me tend to mine."

TEN

Lightning flashed again.

"I now know that thy right worship is defiance. To neither love nor reverence wilt thou be kind; and even for hate thou canst but kill, and all are killed!"

Ahab had sailed them into the heart of a typhoon. The sails were in tatters, and the men ran across the deck shouting against the wind and trying to lash the boats down tighter before they were washed away or smashed. Stubb had gotten his left hand caught between one of the boats and the rail; he now held it with his right and grimaced. The mastheads were touched with St. Elmo's fire. Ahab stood with the lightning rod in his right hand and his right foot planted on the neck of Fedallah, declaiming at the lightning. Fallon held tightly to a shroud to keep from being thrown off his feet. The scene was ludicrous; it was horrible.

"No fearless fool now fronts thee!" Ahab shouted at the

storm. "I own thy speechless, placeless power; but to the last gasp of my earthquake life will dispute its unconditional, unintegral mastery in me! In the midst of the personified impersonal, a personality stands here!"

Terrific, Fallon thought. Psychobabble. Melville writes in a storm so Ahab can have a backdrop against which to define himself. They must not have gone in for realism much in Melville's day. He turned and tried to lash the rear quarter boat tighter; its stern had already been smashed in by a wave that had just about swept three men, including Fallon, overboard. Lightning flashed, followed a split-second later by the rolling thunder. Fallon recalled that five-seconds' count meant the lightning was a mile away; by that measure the last bolt must have hit them in the ass. Most of the crew were staring open-mouthed at Ahab and the glowing, eerie flames that touched the masts. The light had the bluish tinge of mercury vapor lamps in a parking lot. It sucked the color out of things; the faces of the frightened men were the sickly hue of fish bellies.

"Thou canst blind, but I can then grope. Thou canst consume, but I can then be ashes!" You bet. "Take the homage of these poor eyes, and shutter-hands. I would not take it...." Ahab ranted on. Fallon hardly gave a damn anymore. The book was too much. Ahab talked to the storm and the God behind it; the storm answered him back, lighting flash for curse. It was dramatic, stagy; it was real: Melville's universe was created so that such dialogues could take place; the howling gale and the tons of water, the crashing waves, flapping canvas, the sweating, frightened men, the blood and seawater—all were created to have a particular effect, to be sure, but it was the real universe, and it would work that way because that was the way it was set up to work by a frustrated, mystified man chasing his own obsessions, creating the world as a warped mirror of his distorted vision.

"There is some unsuffusing thing beyond thee, thou

clear spirit, to whom all thy eternity is but time, all thy creativeness mechanical...."

There is an ex-sailor on a farm in Massachusetts trying to make ends meet while his puzzled wife tries to explain him to the relatives.

"The boat! The boat!" cried Starbuck. "Look at thy boat, old man!"

Fallon looked, and backed away. A couple of feet from him the harpoon that was lashed into the bow was tipped with the same fire that illuminated the masts. Silently within the howling storm, from its barbed end twin streamers of electricity writhed. Fallon backed away to the rail, heart beating quickly, and clutched the slick whalebone.

Ahab staggered toward the boat; Starbuck grabbed his arm. "God! God is against thee, old man! Forbear! It's an ill voyage! Ill begun, ill continued; let me square the yards while we may, old man, and make a fair wind of it homewards, to go on a better voyage than this."

Yes, yes, at last Starbuck had said it! Fallon grabbed one of the braces; he saw others of the crew move to the rigging as if to follow Starbuck's order before it was given. They cried, some of them in relief, others in fear, others as if ready at last to mutiny. Yes!

Ahab threw down the last links of the lightning rod. He grabbed the harpoon from the boat and waved it like a torch about his head; he lurched toward Fallon.

"You!" he shouted, staggering to maintain his balance under the tossing deck, hoisting the flaming harpoon to his shoulder as if he meant to impale Fallon on the spot. "But cast loose that rope's end and you will be transfixed—by this clear spirit!" The electricity at the barb hummed inches before him; Fallon could feel his skin prickling and smelled ozone. He felt the rail at the small of his back, cold. The other sailors fell away from the ropes; Starbuck looked momentarily sick. Fallon let go of the brace.

Ahab grinned at him. He turned and held the glowing

steel before him with both hands like a priest holding a candle at mass on a feast day.

"All your oaths to hunt the white whale are as binding as mine; and heart, soul, and body, lung and life, old Ahab is bound. And that you may know to what tune this heart beats; look ye here! Thus I blow out the last fear!"

He blew out the flame.

They ran out the night without letting the anchors over the side, heading due into the gale instead of riding with the wind at their backs, with tarpaulins and deck truck blown or washed overboard, with the lightning rod shipped instead of trailing in the sea as it ought to, with the man at the tiller beaten raw about the ribs trying to keep the ship straight, with the compass spinning round like a top, with the torn remains of the sails not cut away until long after midnight.

By morning the storm had much abated, the wind had come around, and they ran before it in heavy seas. Fallon and most of the other common sailors, exhausted, were allowed to sleep.

ELEVEN

The argument with Starbuck and his attempts to rouse others to defy Ahab had made Fallon something of a pariah. He was now as isolated as he had been when he'd first come to himself aboard the *Pequod.* Only Bulkington did not treat him with contempt or fear, but Bulkington would do nothing about the situation. He would rather talk, and they often discussed what a sane man would do in their situation, given the conflicting demands of reason and duty. Fallon's ability to remain detached always failed him somewhere in the middle of these talks.

So Fallon came to look upon his stints at the masthead as escape of a sort. It was there that he had first realized that he could rise above the deck of the *Pequod,* both literally and figuratively, for some moments; it was there that he had first asserted his will after days of stunned debility. He would not sing out for the white whale, if it should be his fortune to sight it, but he did sing out more than once for lesser whales. The leap of his heart at the sight of them was not feigned.

They were sailing the calm Pacific east and south of Japan. They had met the *Rachel,* and a thrill had run through the crew at the news that she had encountered Moby Dick and had failed to get him, losing several boats, and the captain's son, in the process. Fallon's memory was jogged. The *Rachel* would pick up Ishmael at the end of the book, when all the others were dead.

They met the *Delight,* on which a funeral was in process. From the mainmast lookout, Fallon heard the shouted talk between Ahab and her captain about another failed attempt at the white whale. He watched as the dead man, sewn up in his hammock, was dropped into the sea.

It was a clear, steel-blue day. The sea rolled in long, quiet swells; the *Pequod* moved briskly ahead before a fair breeze, until the *Delight* was lost in the distance astern. The air was fresh and clear out to the rim of the world, where it seemed to merge with the darker sea. It was as fair a day as they had seen since Fallon had first stood a watch at thc masthead.

Up above the ship, almost out of the world of men entirely, rolling at the tip of the mast in rhythm to the rolling of the sea swells, which moved in time with his own easy breathing, Fallon lost his fear. He seemed to lose even himself. Who was he? Patrick Fallon, analyst for a commodities firm. Perhaps that had been some delusion; perhaps that world had been created somewhere inside of him, pressed upon him in a vision. He was a sailor on the *Pequod.* He thought that this was part of some book, but he had not been a reader for many years.

Memories of his other life persisted. He remembered

the first time he had ever made love to a woman—to Sally Torrance, in the living room of her parents' house while they were away skiing in Minnesota. He remembered cutting his palm playing baseball when the bat had shattered in his hand. The scar in the middle of his hand could not be denied.

Who denied it? He watched an albatross swoop down from above him to skim a few feet above the water, trying to snag some high-leaping fish. It turned away, unsuccessful, beating its wings slowly as it climbed the air. There was rhythm to its unconscious dance. Fallon had never seen anything more beautiful. He hung his arms over the hoop that surrounded him, felt the hot sun beating on his back, the band of metal supporting him.

This was the real world; he accepted it. He accepted the memories that contradicted it. I look, you look, he looks. Could his mind and heart hold two contradictory things? What would happen to him then? He accepted the albatross, the fish, the sharks he could see below the water's surface from his high vantage point. He accepted the grace of the sea, its embrace on this gentlest of days, and he accepted the storm that had tried to kill them only days before. The *Delight,* reason told him—let reason be; he could strain reason no further than he had—the *Delight* might perhaps have been a ship from a story he had read, but he had no doubt that the man who had been dropped to his watery grave as Fallon watched had been a real man.

The blue of sky and sea, the sound of the flag snapping above him, the taste of the salt air, the motion of the sea and earth itself as they swung Fallon at the tip of the mast, the memories and speculations, the feel of warm sun and warm iron—all the sensual world flowed together for Fallon then. He could not say what he felt. Joy that he could hardly contain swelled in his chest. He was at one with all his perceptions, with all he knew and remembered, with Carol, wherever or whatever she might be, with Bulkington and Dagoo and Starbuck and Stein Jr. and the Big House and Queequeg and the CBT and Ahab. Ahab.

Why had Fallon struggled so long against it? He was alive. What thing had driven him to fight so hard? What had happened to him was absurd, but what thing was not absurd? What thing had made him change from the student to the dropout to the analyst to the sailor? Who might Patrick Fallon be? He stretched out his right arm and turned his hand in the sun.

"Is it I, or God, or who, that lifts this arm?" Fallon heard the words quite distinctly, as if they were spoken only for him, as if they were not spoken at all but were only thoughts. God perhaps did lift Fallon's arm, and if that were so, then who was Fallon to question the wisdom or purpose of the motion? It was his only to move.

A disturbance in the blue of the day.

Why should he not have a choice? Why should that God give him the feeling of freedom if in fact He was directing Fallon's every breath? Did the Fates weave this trance-like calm blue day to lead Fallon to these particular conclusions, so that not even his thoughts in the end were his own, but only the promptings of some force beyond him? And what force could that be if not the force that created this world, and who created this world but Herman Melville, a man who had been dead for a very long time, a man who had no possible connection with Fallon? And what could be the reason for the motion? If this was the real world, then why had Fallon been given the life he had lived before, tangled himself in, felt trapped within, only to be snatched away and clumsily inserted into a different fantasy? What purpose did it serve? Whose satisfaction was being sought?

The moment of wholeness died; the world dissolved into its disparate elements. The sea rolled on. The ship fought it. The wind was opposed by straining canvas. The albatross dove once again, and skimming over the surface so fast it was a white blur, snatched a gleam of silver—a flying fish—from midflight. It settled to the ocean's surface, tearing at its prey.

The day was not so bright as it had been. Fallon tried to accept it still. He did not know if there was a malign force behind the motion of the earth in its long journey, or a beneficent one whose purpose was merely veiled to men such as himself—or no force at all. Such knowledge would not be his. He was a sailor on the *Pequod.*

Upon descending, Fallon heard from Bulkington that Starbuck and Ahab had had a conversation about turning back to Nantucket, that the mate had seemed almost to persuade the captain to give up the hunt, but that he had failed.

Fallon knew then that they must be coming to the end of the story. It would not be long before they spotted the white whale, and three days after that the *Pequod* would go down with all hands not previously killed in the encounter with the whale—save one. But Fallon had given up the idea that he might be that one. He did not, despite his problems, qualify as an Ishmael. That would be overstating his importance, he thought.

TWELVE

He woke suddenly to the imperative buzzing of his alarm clock. His heart beat very fast. He tried to slow it by breathing deeply. Carol stirred beside him, then slept again.

He felt disoriented. He walked into the bathroom, staring, as if he had never seen it before. He slid open the mirrored door of the medicine chest and looked inside at the almost-empty tube of toothpaste, the old safety razor, the pack of double-edged blades, the darvon and tetracycline capsules, the foundation make-up. When he slid the door shut again, his tanned face looked back at him.

He was slow getting started that morning; when Carol got up, he was still drinking his coffee, with the radio playing an old Doors song in the background. Carol leaned over him, kissed the top of his head. It appeared that she loved him.

"You'd better get going," she said. "You'll be late."

He hadn't worried about being late, and it hit him for the first time what he had to do. He had to get to the Board of Trade. He'd have to talk to Stein Jr., and there would be a sheaf of notes on his desk asking him to return calls to various clients who would have rung him up while he was gone. He pulled on the jacket of his pinstriped suit, brushed back his hair, and left.

Waiting for the train, he realized that he hadn't gone anywhere to return from.

He had missed his normal train and arrived late. The streets were nowhere near as crowded as they would have been an hour earlier. He walked north on LaSalle Avenue between the staid, dark old buildings. The sky that showed between them was bright, and already the temperature was rising; it would be a hot one. He wished it were the weekend. Was it Thursday? It couldn't still be Wednesday. He was embarrassed to realize he wasn't sure what day it was.

He saw a very pretty girl in the lobby of the Board of Trade as he entered through the revolving doors. She was much prettier than Carol, and had that unself-conscious way of walking. But she was around the corner before he had taken more than a few steps inside. He ran into Joe Wendelstadt in the elevator, and Joe began to tell him a story about Raoul Lark from Brazil who worked for Cacex in Chicago, and how Lark had tried to pick up some feminist the other night. And succeeded. Those Brazilians.

Fallon got off before Joe could reach the climax. In his office Molly, the receptionist, said Stein wanted to see him. Stein smelled of cigarettes, and Fallon suddenly became self-conscious. He had not brushed his own teeth. When did he ever forget that? Stein had an incipient zit on the end of his nose. He didn't really have anything to talk to Fallon about; he was just wasting time as usual.

Tigue was sick or on vacation.

Fallon worked through the morning on various customer accounts. He had trouble remembering where the market had closed the day before. He had always had a trick memory for such figures, and it had given him the ability to impress a lot of people who knew just as much about the markets as he did. He spent what was left of the morning on the phone to his clients, with a quick trip down to the trading floor to talk to Parsons in the soybean pit.

Carol called and asked him if he could join her for lunch. He remembered he had a date with Kim, a woman from the CME he had met just a week before. He made his excuses to Carol and took off for the Merc.

Walking briskly west on Jackson, coming up on the bridge across the river, he realized he had been rushing around all day and yet could hardly remember what he'd done since he had woken up. He still couldn't remember whether it was Wednesday or Thursday.

As he crossed the bridge with the crowds of lunch-hour office workers, the noontime sun glared brightly for a second from the oily water of the river. Fallon's eyes did not immediately recover. He stopped walking and somebody bumped into him.

"Excuse me," he said unconsciously.

There was a moment of silence, then the noise of the city resumed, and he could see again. He stood at the side of the bridge and looked down at the water. The oil on the surface made rainbow-colored black swirls. Fallon shook his head and went on.

Kim stood him up at the restaurant. She did not arrive to meet him, and he waited a long time by the cashier. Finally he made the woman seat him at a table for two. He looked at his watch but had some trouble reading the time. Was he due back at the office?

Just then someone sat down opposite him. It was an old man in a dark suit who had obviously undergone some great ordeal. His face held a look of great pain or sorrow—with hate burning just beneath it. Though his hair was black (and quite unforgivably unkempt for midtown Chicago, as was his rough suit), a shock of white fell across his forehead, and a scar ran from the roots of that white hair straight down the man's face, leaping the brow and eye to continue across the left cheek, sinewing down the jaw and neck to disappear beneath his shirt collar.

He looked strangely familiar.

"It won't work," the man said. "You cannot get away. You have signed the articles, like the rest, and are in for a three-hundreth lay."

"Three-hundreth lay?" Fallon was bewildered.

"A three-hundreth part of the general catastrophe is yours. Don't thank me. It isn't necessary." The old man looked even more sorrowful and more wild, if it were possible to combine those seemingly incompatible emotions.

"To tell you the truth," he said, "wouldn't hold you to the contract if it were strictly up to me." He shrugged his shoulders and opened his palms before him. "But it isn't."

Fallon's heart was beating fast again. "I don't remember any contract. You're not one of my clients. I don't trade for you. I've been in this business for a long time, mister, and I know better than to sign. . . ."

The wildness swelled in the man. There was something burning in him, and he looked about to scream, or cry.

"*I* have been in the business longer than *you!*" He swung his leg out from beneath the table and rapped it loudly with his knuckle. Fallon saw that the leg was of white bone. "And *I* can tell *you* that you signed the contract when you signed aboard this ship—there's no other way to get aboard—and you must serve until you strike land again or it sinks beneath you!"

The diners in the restaurant dined on, oblivious. Fallon looked toward the plate glass at the front of the room and saw the water rising rapidly up it, sea-green and turbid, as the restaurant and the city fell to the bottom of the sea.

THIRTEEN

Once again he was jerked awake, this time by the din of someone beating the deck of the forecastle above them with a club. The other sleepers were as startled as Fallon. He rolled out of the hammock with the mists of his dream still clinging to him, pulled on his shirt and scrambled up to the deck.

Ahab was stalking the quarter-deck in a frenzy of impatience. "Man the mastheads!" he shouted.

The men who had risen with Fallon did just that, some of them only half-dressed. Fallon was one of the first up and gained one of the hoops at the main masthead. Three others stood on the mainyard below him. Fallon scanned the horizon and saw off to starboard and about a mile ahead of them the jet of mist that indicated a whale. As it rose and fell in its course through the rolling seas, Fallon saw that it was white.

"What do you see?" Ahab called from far below. Had he noticed Fallon's gaze fixed on the spot in front of them?

"Nothing! Nothing, sir!" Fallon called. Ahab and the men on deck looked helpless so far below him. Fallon did not know if his lying would work, but there was the chance that the other men in the rigging, not being as high as he, would not be able to make out Moby Dick from their lower vantage points. He turned away from the whale and made a good show of scanning the empty horizon.

"Top gallant sails!—stunsails! Alow and aloft, and on both sides!" Ahab ordered. The men fixed a line from the mainmast to the deck, looped its lower end around Ahab's rigid leg. Ahab wound the rope around his shoulders and arm, and they hoisted him aloft, twisting with the pressure of the hemp, toward the masthead. He twirled slowly as they raised him up, and his line of sight was obscured by the rigging and sails he had to peer through.

Before they had lifted him two-thirds of the way up, he began to shout.

"There she blows!—there she blows! A hump like a snow-hill! It is Moby Dick!"

Fallon knew enough to begin shouting and pointing immediately, and the men at the other two masts did the same. Within a minute everyone who had remained on the deck was in the rigging trying to catch a glimpse of the creature they had sought, half of them doubting his existence, for so many months.

Fallon looked down toward the helmsman, who stood on his toes, the whalebone tiller under his arm, arching his neck trying to see the whale.

The others in the rigging were now arguing about who had spotted Moby Dick first, with Ahab the eventual victor. It was his fate, he said, to be the one to first spot the whale. Fallon couldn't argue with that.

Ahab was lowered to the deck, giving orders all the way, and three boats were swung outboard in preparation for the chase. Starbuck was ordered to stay behind and keep the ship.

As they chased the whale, the sea became calmer, so the rowing became easier—though just as back-breaking—and they knifed through the water, here as placid as a farm pond, faster than ever. Accompanying the sound of their own wake, Fallon heard the wake of the whale they must be approaching. He strained arms, back, and legs, pulling harder in time to Stubb's cajoling chant, and the rushing grew. He snatched a glance over his shoulder, turned to the rowing, then looked again.

The white whale glided through the sea smoothly, giving the impression of immeasurable strength. The wake he left was as steady as that of a schooner; the bow waves created by the progress of his broad, blank brow through the water fanned away in precise lines whose angle with respect to the massive body did not change. The three whaleboats rocked gently as they broke closer through these successive waves; the foam of Moby Dick's wake was abreast of them now, and Fallon saw how quickly it subsided into itself, giving the sea back its calm face, innocent of knowledge of the creature that had passed. Attendant white birds circled above their heads, now and then falling to or rising from the surface in busy flutterings of wings and awkward beaks. One of them had landed on the broken shaft of a harpoon that protruded from the snow-white whale's humped back; it bobbed up and down with the slight rocking of the whale in its long, muscular surging through the sea. Oblivious. Strangely quiet. Fallon felt as if they had entered a magic circle.

He knew Ahab's boat, manned by the absurd Filipinos, was ahead of them and no doubt preparing to strike first. Fallon closed his eyes, pulled on his oar, and wished for it not to happen. For it to stop now, or just continue without any change. He felt as if he could row a very long time; he was no longer tired or afraid. He just wanted to keep rowing, feeling the rhythm of the work, hearing the low and insistent voice of Stubb telling them to break their backs. Fallon wanted to listen to the rushing white sound of the whale's wake in the water, to know that they were perhaps keeping pace with it, to know that, if he should tire, he could look for a second over his shoulder and find Moby Dick there still. Let the monomaniac stand in the bow of his boat—if he was meant to stand there, if it was an unavoidable necessity—let him stand there with the raised lance and concentrate his hate into one purified moment of will. Let him send that will into the tip of that lance so that it might physically glow with the frustrated obtuseness of it. Let him stand there until he froze from the suspended desire, and let the whale swim on.

Fallon heard a sudden increase in the rushing of the

water, several inarticulate cries. He stopped pulling, as did the others, and turned to look in time to see the whale lift itself out of the water, exposing flanks and flukes the bluish white of cemetery marble, and flip its huge tail upward to dive perpendicularly into the sea. Spray drenched them, and sound returned with the crash of the waves coming together to fill the vacuum left by the departure of the creature that had seconds before given weight and direction, place, to the placeless expanse of level waters. The birds circled above the subsiding foam.

They lifted their oars. They waited.

"An hour," Ahab said.

They waited. It was another beautiful day. The sky was hard and blue as the floor of the swimming pool where he had met Carol. Fallon wondered again if she missed him, if he had indeed disappeared from that other life when he had taken up residence in this one—but he thrust those thoughts away. They were meaningless. There was no time in that world after his leaving it; that world did not exist, or if it existed, the order of its existence was not of the order of the existence of the rough wood he sat on, the raw flesh of his hands and the air he breathed. Time was the time between the breaths he drew. Time was the duration of the dream he had had about being back in Chicago, and he could not say how long that had been, even if it had begun or ended. He might be dreaming still. The word "dream" was meaningless, and "awake." And "real," and "insane," and "known," and all those other interesting words he had once known. Time was waiting for Moby Dick to surface again.

The breeze freshened. The sea began to swell.

"The birds!—the birds!" Tashtego shouted, so close behind Fallon's ear that he winced. The Indian half-stood, rocking the whaleboat as he pointed to the sea birds, which had risen and were flying toward Ahab's boat twenty yards away.

"The whale will breach there," Stubb said.

Ahab was up immediately. Peering into the water, he leaned on the steering oar and reversed the orientation of his boat. He then exchanged places with Fedallah, the other men reaching up to help him through the rocking boat. He picked up the harpoon, and the oarsmen stood ready to row.

Fallon looked down into the sea, trying to make out what Ahab saw. Nothing, until a sudden explosion of white as the whale, rocketing upward, turned over as it finally hit the surface. In a moment Ahab's boat was in the whale's jaws, Ahab in the bows almost between them. Stubb was shouting and gesturing, and Fallon's fellows fell to the oars in a disorganized rush. The Filipinos in the lead boat crowded into the stern while Ahab, like a man trying to open a recalcitrant garage door, tugged and shoved at Moby Dick's jaw, trying insanely to dislodge the whale's grip. Within seconds filled with crashing water, cries and confusion, Moby Dick had bitten the boat in two, and Ahab had belly-flopped over the side like a swimming-class novice.

Moby Dick then began to swim tight circles around the smashed boat and its crew. Ahab struggled to keep his head above water. Neither Stubb nor Flask could bring his boat close enough to pick him up. The *Pequod* was drawing nearer, and finally Ahab was able to shout loudly enough to be heard, "Sail on the whale—drive him off!"

It worked. The *Pequod* picked up the remnants of the whaleboat while Fallon and the others dragged its crew and Ahab into their own boat.

The old man collapsed in the bottom of the boat, gasping for breath, broken and exhausted. He moaned and shook. Fallon was sure he was finished whale chasing, that Stubb and the others would see the man was used up, that Starbuck would take over and sail them home. But in a minute or two Ahab was leaning on his elbow asking after his boat's crew, and a few minutes after that they had resumed the chase with double oarsmen in Stubb's boat.

Moby Dick drew steadily away as exhaustion wore them down. Fallon did not feel he could row any more after all. The *Pequod* picked them up and they gave chase in vain under all sail until dark.

FOURTEEN

On the second day's chase all three boats were smashed in. Many suffered sprains and contusions, and one was bitten by a shark. Ahab's whale-bone leg was shattered, with a splinter driven into his own flesh. Fedallah, who had been the captain's second shadow, was tangled in the line Ahab had shot into the white whale, dragged out of the boat, and drowned. Moby Dick escaped.

FIFTEEN

It came down to what Fallon had known it would come down to eventually.

In the middle of that night he went to talk to Ahab, who slept in one of the hatchways as he had the night before. The carpenter was making him another leg, wooden this time, and Ahab was curled sullenly in the dark lee of the after scuttle. Fallon did not know whether he was waiting or asleep.

He started down the stairs, hesitated on the second step. Ahab lifted his head. "What do you need?" he asked.

Fallon wondered what he wanted to say. He looked at the man huddled in the darkness and tried to imagine what moved him, tried to see him as a man instead of a thing. Was it possible he was only a man, or had Fallon himself become stylized and distorted by living in the book of Melville's imagination?

"You said—talking to Starbuck today—you said that everything that happens is fixed, decreed. You said it was rehearsed a billion years before any of it took place. Is it true?"

Ahab straightened and leaned toward Fallon, bringing his face into the dim light thrown by the lamps on deck. He looked at him for a moment in silence.

"I don't know. So it seemed as the words left my lips. The Parsee is dead before me, as he foretold. I don't know."

"That is why you're hunting the whale."

"That is why I'm hunting the whale."

"How can this hunt, how can killing an animal tell you anything? How can it justify your life? What satisfaction can it give you in the end, even if you boil it all down to oil, even if you cut Moby Dick into bible-leaves and eat him? I don't understand it."

The captain looked at him earnestly. He seemed to be listening, and leaping ahead of the questions. It was very dark in the scuttle, and they could hardly see each other. Fallon kept his hands folded tightly behind him. The blade of the cleaver he had shoved into his belt lay cool against the skin at the small of his back; it was the same knife he used to butcher the whale.

"If it is immutably fixed, then it does not matter what I do. The purpose and meaning are out of my hands, and thine. We have only to take our parts, to be the thing that it is written for us to be. Better to live that role given us than to struggle against it or play the coward, when the actions must be the same nonetheless. Some say I am mad to chase the whale. Perhaps I am mad. But if it is my destiny to seek him, to tear, to burn and kill those things that stand in my path—then the matter of my madness is not relevant, do you see?"

He was not speaking in character.

"If these things are not fixed, and it was not my destiny to have my leg taken by the whale, to have my hopes blasted in this chase, then how cruel a world it is. No mercy, no power but its own controls it; it blights our lives out of merest whim. No, not whim, for there would then be no will behind it, no builder of this Bedlam hospital, and in the madhouse, when the keeper is gone, what is to stop the inmates from doing as they please? In a universe of cannibals, where all creatures have preyed upon each other, carrying on an eternal war since the world began, why should I not exert my will in whatever direction I choose? Why should I not bend others to my will?" The voice was reasonable, and tired. "Have I answered your question?"

Fallon felt the time drawing near. He felt light, as if the next breeze might lift him from the deck and carry him away. "I have an idea," he said. "My idea is—and it is an idea I have had for some time now, and despite everything that has happened, and what you say, I can't give it up—my idea is that all that is happening..." Fallon waved his hand at the world, "...is a story. It is a book written by a man named Herman Melville and told by a character named Ishmael. You are the main character in the book. All the things that have happened are events in the book.

"My idea also is that I am not from the book, or at least I wasn't originally. Originally I lived a different life in another time and place, a life in the real world and not in a book. It was not ordered and plotted like a book, and...."

Ahab interrupted in a quiet voice: "You call this an ordered book? I see no order. If it were so orderly, why would the whale task mc so?"

Fallon knotted his fingers still tighter behind him. Ahab was going to make him do it. He felt the threads of the situation weaving together to create only that bloody alternative, of all the alternatives that might be. In the open market, the price for the future and price for the physical reality converged on delivery day.

"The order's not an easy thing to see, I'll admit," Fallon said. He laughed nervously.

Ahab laughed louder. "It certainly is not. And how do you know this other life you speak of was not a play? A different kind of play. How do you know your thoughts are your own? How do you know that this dark little scene was not prepared just for us, or perhaps for someone who is reading about us at this very moment and wondering about the point of the drama just as much as we wonder at the pointlessness of our lives?" Ahab's voice rose gaining an edge of compulsion. "How do we know anything?" He grabbed his left wrist, pinched the flesh and shook it.

"How do we know what lies behind this matter? This flesh is a wall, the painting over the canvas, the mask drawn over the player's face, the snow fallen over the fertile field, or perhaps the scorched earth. I know there is something there; there must be something, but it cannot be touched because we are smothered in this flesh, this life. How do we know—"

"Stop it! Stop it!" Fallon shouted. "Please stop asking things! You should not be able to say things like that to me! Ahab does not talk to me!"

"Isn't this what I am supposed to say?"

Fallon shuddered.

"Isn't this scene in your book?"

He was dizzy, sick. "No! Of course not!"

"Then why does that disturb you? Doesn't this prove that we are not pieces of a larger dream, that this is a real world, that the blood that flows within our veins is real blood, that the pain we feel has meaning, that the things we do have consequence? We break the mold of existence by existing. Isn't that reassurance enough?" Ahab was shouting now, and the men awake on deck trying to get the boats in shape for that last day's chase and the *Pequod's* ultimate destruction put aside their hammers and rope and listened now to Ahab's justification.

It was time. Fallon, shaking with anger and fear, drew the knife from behind him and leapt at the old man. In bringing up the blade for the attack he hit it against the side of the narrow hatchway. His grip loosened. Ahab threw up his hands, and despite the difference in age and mobility between them, managed to grab Fallon's wrist before he could strike the killing blow. Instead, the deflected cleaver struck the beam beside Ahab's head and stuck there. As Fallon tried to free it, Ahab brought his forearm up and smashed him beneath the jaw. Fallon fell backward, striking his head with stunning force against the opposite side of the scuttle. He momentarily lost consciousness.

When he came to himself again, Ahab was sitting before him with his strong hands on Fallon's shoulders, supporting him, not allowing him to move.

"Good, Fallon, good," he said. "You've done well. But now, no more games, no more dramas, no easy way out. Admit that this is not the tale you think it is! Admit that you do not know what will happen to you in the next second, let alone the next day or year! Admit that we are both free and unfree, alone and crowded in by circumstance in this world that we indeed did not make, but indeed have the power to affect! Put aside those notions that there is another life somehow more real than the life you live now, another air to breathe somehow more pure, another love or hate somehow more vital than the love or hate you bear me. Put aside your fantasy and admit that you are alive, and thus may momentarily die. Do you hear me, Fallon?"

Fallon heard, and saw, and felt and touched, but he did not know. The *Pequod,* freighted with savages and isolatoes, sailed into the night, and the great shroud of the sea rolled on as it rolled five thousand years ago.

A Letter from the Clearys

by Connie Willis

Connie Willis for the second time this year—with a hard little tale of the day after doomsday.

THERE was a letter from the Clearys at the post office,. I put it in my back pack along with Mrs. Talbot's magazine and went outside to untie Stitch.

He had pulled his leash out as far as it would go and was sitting around the corner, half-strangled, watching a robin. Stitch never barks, not even at birds. He didn't even yip when Dad stitched up his paw. He just sat there the way we found him on the front porch, shivering a little and holding his paw up for Dad to look at. Mrs. Talbot says he's a terrible watchdog, but I'm glad he doesn't bark. Rusty barked all the time and look where it got him.

I had to pull Stitch back around the corner to where I could get enough slack to untie him. That took some doing,

Winner, Nebula for Best Short Story, 1982.

because he really liked that robin. "It's a sign of spring, isn't it, fella?" I said, trying to get at the knot with my fingernails. I didn't loosen the knot, but I managed to break one of my fingernails off to the quick. Great. Mom will demand to know if I've noticed any other fingernails breaking.

My hands are a real mess. This winter I've gotten about a hundred burns on the back of my hands from that stupid wood stove of ours. One spot, just above my wrist, I keep burning over and over so it never has a chance to heal. The stove isn't big enough, and when I try to jam a log in that's too long, that same spot hits the inside of the stove every time. My stupid brother David won't saw them off to the right length. I've asked him and asked him to please cut them shorter, but he doesn't pay any attention to me.

I asked Mom if she would please tell him not to saw the logs so long, but she didn't. She never criticizes David. As far as she's concerned he can't do anything wrong just because he's twenty-three and was married.

"He does it on purpose," I told her. "He's hoping I'll burn to death."

"Paranoia is the number-one killer of fourteen-year-old girls," Mom said. She always says that. It makes me so mad I feel like killing her. "He doesn't do it on purpose. You need to be more careful with the stove, that's all." But all the time she was holding my hand and looking at the big burn that won't heal like it was a time bomb set to go off.

"We need a bigger stove," I said, and yanked my hand away. We do need a bigger one. Dad closed up the fireplace and put the woodstove in when the gas bill was getting out of sight, but it's just a little one, because Mom didn't want one that would stick way out in the living room. Anyway, we were only going to use it in the evenings.

We won't get a new one. They are all too busy working on the stupid greenhouse. Maybe spring will come early, and my hand will have a half a chance to heal. I know better. Last winter the snow kept up till the middle of June, and this is only March. Stitch's robin is going to freeze his little tail if he doesn't head back south. Dad says that last year was unusual, that the weather will be back to normal this year, but he doesn't believe it either or he wouldn't be building the greenhouse.

As soon as I let go of Stitch's leash, he backed around the corner like a good boy and sat there waiting for me to stop sucking my finger and untie him. "We'd better get a move on," I told him. "Mom'll have a fit." I was supposed to go by the general store to try and get some tomato seeds, but the sun was already pretty far west, and I had at least a half-hour's walk home. If I got home after dark, I'd get sent to bed without supper, and then I wouldn't get to read the letter. Besides, if I didn't go to the general store today they'd have to let me go tomorrow, and I wouldn't have to work on the stupid greenhouse.

Sometimes I feel like blowing it up. There's sawdust and mud on everything, and David dropped one of the pieces of plastic on the stove while they were cutting it and it melted onto the stove and stank to high heaven. But nobody else even notices the mess; they're too busy talking about how wonderful it's going to be to have home-grown watermelon and corn and tomatoes next summer.

I don't see how it's going to be any different from last summer. The only things that came up at all were the lettuce and the potatoes. The lettuce was about as tall as my broken fingernail and the potatoes were as hard as rocks. Mrs. Talbot said it was the altitude, but Dad said it was the funny weather and this crummy Pike's Peak granite that passes for soil around here. He went up to the little library in the back of the general store and got a do-it-yourself book on greenhouses and started tearing everything up, and now even Mrs. Talbot is crazy about the idea.

The other day I told them, "Paranoia is the number-one killer of people at this *altitude,*" but they were too busy cutting slats and stapling plastic to pay any attention to me.

Stitch walked along ahead of me, straining at his leash, and as soon as we were across the highway, I took it off. He never runs away like Rusty used to. Anyway, it's impossible to keep him out of the road, and the times I've tried keeping him on his leash, he dragged me out into the middle and I got in trouble with Dad over leaving footprints. So I keep to the frozen edges of the road, and he moseys along, stopping to sniff at potholes; when he gets behind, I whistle at him and he comes running right up.

I walked pretty fast. It was getting chilly out, and I'd only worn my sweater. I stopped at the top of the hill and whistled at Stitch. We still had a mile to go. I could see the Peak from where I was standing. Maybe Dad is right about spring coming. There was hardly any snow on the Peak, and the burned part didn't look quite as dark as it did last fall, like maybe the trees are coming back.

Last year at this time the whole peak was solid white. I remember because that was when Dad and David and Mr. Talbot went hunting and it snowed every day and they didn't get back for almost a month. Mom just about went crazy before they got back. She kept going up to the road to watch for them even though the snow was five feet deep and she was leaving footprints as big as the Abominable Snowman's. She took Rusty with her even though he hated the snow about as much as Stitch hates the dark. And she took a gun. One time she tripped over a branch and fell down in the snow. She sprained her ankle and was almost frozen stiff by the time she made it back to the house. I felt like saying, "Paranoia is the number-one killer of mothers," but Mrs Talbot butted in and said the next time I had to go with her and how this was what happened when people were allowed to go places by themselves, which meant me going to the post office. I said I could take care of myself, and Mom told me not to be rude to Mrs. Talbot and Mrs. Talbot was right, I should go with her the next time.

She wouldn't wait till her ankle was better. She bandaged it up and we went the very next day. She didn't say a word the whole trip, just limped through the snow. She never even looked up till we got to the road. The snow had stopped for a little while, and the clouds had lifted enough so you could see the Peak. It was like a black-and-white photograph, the gray sky and the black trees and the white mountain. The Peak was completely covered with snow. You couldn't make out the toll road at all.

We were supposed to hike up the Peak with the Clearys.

When we got back to the house, I said, "The summer before last the Clearys never came."

Mom took off her mittens and stood by the stove, pulling off chunks of frozen snow. "Of course they didn't come, Lynn," she said.

Snow from my coat was dripping onto the stove and sizzling. "I didn't mean *that,*" I said. "They were supposed to come the first week in June. Right after Rick graduated. So what happened? Did they just decide not to come or what?"

"I don't know," she said, pulling off her hat and shaking her hair out. Her bangs were all wet.

"Maybe they wrote to tell you they'd changed their plans," Mrs. Talbot said. "Maybe the post office lost the letter."

"It doesn't matter," Mom said.

"You'd think they'd have written or something," I said.

"Maybe the post office put the letter in somebody else's box," Mrs. Talbot said.

"It doesn't matter," Mom said, and went to hang her coat over the line in the kitchen. She wouldn't say another word about them. When Dad got home I asked him too about the Clearys, but he was too busy telling about the trip to pay any attention to me.

Stitch didn't come. I whistled again and then started

back after him. He was all the way at the bottom of the hill, his nose buried in something. "Come *on,*" I said, and he turned around and then I could see why he hadn't come. He'd gotten himself tangled up in one of the electric wires that was down. He'd managed to get the cable wound around his legs like he does his leash sometimes, and the harder he tried to get out, the more he got tangled up.

He was right in the middle of the road. I stood on the edge of the road trying to figure out a way to get to him without leaving footprints. The road was pretty much frozen at the top of the hill, but down here snow was still melting and running across the road in big rivers. I put my toe out into the mud, and my sneaker sank in a good half-inch, so I backed up, rubbed out the toe print with my hand, and wiped my hand on my jeans. I tried to think what to do. Dad is as paranoic about footprints as Mom is about my hands, but he is even worse about my being out after dark. If I didn't make it back in time, he might even tell me I couldn't go to the post office anymore.

Stitch was coming as close as he ever would to barking. He'd gotten the wire around his neck and was choking himself. "All right," I said. "I'm coming." I jumped out as far as I could into one of the rivers and then waded the rest of the way to Stitch, looking back a couple of times to make sure the water was washing away the footprints.

I unwound Stitch and threw the loose end of the wire over to the side of the road where it dangled from the pole, all ready to hang Stitch next time he comes along.

"You stupid dog," I said. "Now hurry!" and I sprinted back to the side of the road and up the hill in my sopping wet sneakers. He ran about five steps and stopped to sniff at a tree. "Come on!" I said. "It's getting dark. Dark!"

He was past me like a shot and halfway down the hill. Stitch is afraid of the dark. I know, there's no such thing in dogs. But Stitch really is. Usually I tell him, "Paranoia is the number-one killer of dogs," but right now I wanted him to hurry before my feet started to freeze. I started running, and we got to the bottom of the hill about the same time.

Stitch stopped at the driveway of the Talbot's house. Our house wasn't more than a few hundred feet from where I was standing, on the other side of the hill. Our house is down in kind of a well formed by hills on all sides. It's so deep and hidden you'd never even know it's there. You can't even see the smoke from our wood stove over the top of the Talbot's hill. There's a shortcut through the Talbot's property and down through the woods to our back door, but I don't take it anymore. "Dark, Stitch," I said sharply, and started running again. Stitch kept right at my heels.

The Peak was turning pink by the time I got to our driveway. Stitch peed on the spruce tree about a hundred times before I got it dragged back across the dirt driveway. It's a real big tree. Last summer Dad and David chopped it down and then made it look like it had fallen across the road, but the trunk is full of splinters, and I scraped my hand right in the same place as always. Great.

I made sure Stitch and I hadn't left any marks on the road (except for the marks he always leaves—another dog could find us in a minute, that's probably how Stitch showed up on our front porch, he smelled Rusty) and then got under cover of the hill as fast as I could. Stitch isn't the only one who gets nervous after dark. And besides, my feet were starting to hurt. Stitch was really paranoic tonight. He didn't even quit running after we were in sight of the house.

David was outside, bringing in a load of wood. I could tell just by looking at it that they were all the wrong length. "Cutting it kind of close, aren't you?" he said. "Did you get the tomato seeds?"

"No," I said. "I brought you something else, though. I brought everybody something."

I went on in. Dad was rolling out plastic on the living-room floor. Mrs. Talbot was holding one end for him. Mom was holding the card table, still folded up, waiting for them to finish so she could set it up in front of the stove for supper. Nobody even looked up. I unslung my backpack and took out Mrs. Talbot's magazine and the letter.

"There was a letter at the post office," I said. "From the Clearys."

They all looked up.

"Where did you find it?" Dad said.

"On the floor, mixed in with all the third-class stuff. I was looking for a magazine for Mrs. Talbot."

Mom leaned the card table against the couch and sat down. Mrs. Talbot looked blank.

"The Clearys were our best friends," I explained to her. "From Illinois. They were supposed to come see us the summer before last. We were going to hike up Pike's Peak and everything."

David banged in the door. He looked at Mom sitting on the couch and Dad and Mrs. Talbot still standing there holding the plastic like a couple of statues. "What's wrong?" he said.

"Lynn says she found a letter from the Clearys today," Dad said.

David dumped the logs on the hearth. One of them rolled onto the carpet and stopped at Mom's feet. Neither of them bent over to pick it up.

"Shall I read it out loud?" I said, looking at Mrs. Talbot. I was still holding her magazine. I opened up the envelope and took out the letter.

"'Dear Janice and Todd and everybody,'" I read. "'How are things in the glorious West? We're raring to come out and see you, though we may not make it quite as soon as we hoped. How are Carla and David and the baby? I can't wait to see little David. Is he walking yet? I bet Grandma Janice is so proud she's busting her britches. Is that right?

Do you westerners wear britches, or have you all gone to designer jeans.'"

David was standing by the fireplace. He put his head down across his arms on the mantelpiece.

"'I'm sorry I haven't written, but we were very busy with Rick's graduation, and anyway I thought we would beat the letter out to Colorado. But now it looks like there's going to be a slight change in plans. Rick has definitely decided to join the Army. Richard and I have talked ourselves blue in the face, but I guess we've just made matters worse. We can't even get him to wait to join until after the trip to Colorado. He says we'd spend the whole trip trying to talk him out of it, which is true, I guess. I'm just so worried about him. The Army! Rick says I worry too much, which is true too, I guess, but what if there was a war?'"

Mom bent over and picked up the log that David had dropped and laid it on the couch beside her.

"'If it's okay with you out there in the Golden West, we'll wait until Rick is done with basic the first week in July and then all come out. Please write and let us know if this is okay. I'm sorry to switch plans on you like this at the last minute, but look at it this way: you have a whole extra month to get into shape for hiking up Pike's Peak. I don't know about you, but I sure can use it.'"

Mrs. Talbot had dropped her end of the plastic. It didn't land on the stove this time, but it was so close to it, it was curling from the heat. Dad just stood there watching it. He didn't even try to pick it up.

"'How are the girls? Sonja is growing like a weed. She's out for track this year and bringing home lots of medals and dirty sweat socks. And you should see her knees! They're so banged up I almost took her to the doctor. She says she scrapes them on the hurdles, and her coach says there's nothing to worry about, but it does worry me a little. They just don't seem to heal. Do you ever have problems like that with Lynn and Melissa?

"'I know, I know. I worry too much. Sonja's fine. Rick's fine. Nothing awful's going to happen between now and the first week in July, and we'll see you then. Love, the Clearys. P.S. Has anybody ever fallen off Pike's Peak?'"

Nobody said anything. I folded up the letter and put it back in the envelope.

"I should have written them," Mom said. "I should have told them, 'Come now.' Then they would have been here."

"And we would probably have climbed up Pike's Peak that day and gotten to see it all go blooey and us with it," David said, lifting his head up. He laughed and his voice caught on the laugh and cracked. "I guess we should be glad they didn't come."

"Glad?" Mom said. She was rubbing her hands on the legs of her jeans. "I suppose we should be glad Carla took Melissa and the baby to Colorado Springs that day so we didn't have so many mouths to feed." She was rubbing her jeans so hard she was going to rub a hole right through them. "I suppose we should be glad those looters shot Mr. Talbot."

"No," Dad said. "But we should be glad the looters didn't shoot the rest of us. We should be glad they only took the canned goods and not the seeds. We should be glad the fires didn't get this far. We should be glad..."

"That we still have mail delivery?" David said. "Should we be glad about that too?" He went outside and shut the door behind him.

"When I didn't hear from them, I should have called or something," Mom said.

Dad was still looking at the ruined plastic. I took the letter over to him. "Do you want to keep it or what?" I said.

"I think it's served its purpose," he said. He wadded it up, tossed it in the stove, and slammed the door shut. He didn't even get burned. "Come help me on the greenhouse, Lynn," he said.

It was pitch dark outside and really getting cold. My sneakers were starting to get stiff. Dad held the flashlight and pulled the plastic tight over the wooden slats. I stapled the plastic every two inches all the way around the frame and my finger about every other time. After we finished one frame, I asked Dad if I could go back in and put on my boots.

"Did you get the seeds for the tomatoes?" he said, as if he hadn't even heard me. "Or were you too busy looking for the letter?"

"I didn't look for it," I said. "I found it. I thought you'd be glad to get the letter and know what happened to the Clearys."

Dad was pulling the plastic across the next frame, so hard it was getting little puckers in it. "We already knew," he said.

He handed me the flashlight and took the staple gun out of my hand. "You want me to say it?" he said. "You want me to tell you exactly what happened to them? All right. I would imagine they were close enough to Chicago to have been vaporized when the bombs hit. If they were, they were lucky. Because there aren't any mountains like ours around Chicago. So they got caught in the fire storm or they died of flashburns or radiation sickness or else some looter shot them."

"Or their own family," I said.

"Or their own family." He put the staple gun against the wood and pulled the trigger. "I have a theory about what happened the summer before last," he said. He moved the gun down and shot another staple into the wood. "I don't think the Russians started it or the United States either. I think it was some little terrorist group somewhere or maybe just one person. I don't think they had any idea what would happen when they dropped their bomb. I think they were just so hurt and angry and frightened by the way things were that they lashed out. With a bomb." He stapled the frame clear to the bottom and straightened up to start on the other side. "What do you think of that theory, Lynn?"

"I told you," I said. "I found the letter while I was looking for Mrs. Talbot's magazine."

He turned and pointed the staple gun at me. "But whatever reason they did it for, they brought the whole world crashing down on their heads. Whether they meant it or not, they had to live with the consequences."

"If they lived," I said. "If somebody didn't shoot them."

"I can't let you go to the post office anymore," he said. "It's too dangerous."

"What about Mrs. Talbot's magazines?"

"Go check on the fire," he said.

I went back inside. David had come back and was standing by the fireplace again, looking at the wall. Mom had set up the card table and the folding chairs in front of the fireplace. Mrs. Talbot was in the kitchen cutting up potatoes, only it looked like it was onions from the way she was crying.

The fire had practically gone out. I stuck a couple of wadded-up magazine pages in to get it going again. The fire flared up with a brilliant blue and green. I tossed a couple of pine cones and some sticks onto the burner paper. One of the pine cones rolled off to the side and lay there in the ashes. I grabbed for it and hit my hand on the door of the stove.

Right in the same place. Great. The blister would pull the old scab off and we could start all over again. And of course Mom was standing right there, holding the pan of potato soup. She put it on top of the stove and grabbed up my hand like it was evidence in a crime or something. She didn't say anything. She just stood there holding it and blinking.

"I burned it," I said. "I just burned it."

She touched the edges of the old scab, as if she was afraid of catching something.

"It's a burn!" I shouted, snatching my hand back and

cramming David's stupid logs into the stove. "It isn't radiation sickness. It's a *burn!*"

"Do you know where your father is, Lynn?" she asked.

"He's out on the back porch," I said, "building his stupid greenhouse."

"He's gone," she said. "He took Stitch with him."

"He can't have taken Stitch," I said. "Stitch is afraid of the dark." She didn't say anything. "Do you *know* how dark it is out there?"

"Yes," she said, and looked out the window. "I know how dark it is."

I got my parka off the hook by the fireplace and started out the door.

David grabbed my arm. "Where the hell do you think you're going?"

I wrenched away from him. "To find Stitch. He's afraid of the dark."

"It's too dark," he said. "You'll get lost."

"So what? It's safer than hanging around this place," I said and slammed the door shut on his hand.

I made it halfway to the woodpile before he grabbed me.

"Let me go," I said. "I'm leaving. I'm going to go find some other people to live with."

"There aren't any other people! For Christ's sake, we went all the way to South Park last winter. There wasn't anybody. We didn't even see those looters. And what if you run into them, the looters who shot Mr. Talbot?"

"What if I do? The worst they could do is shoot me. I've been shot at before."

"You're acting crazy. You know that, don't you?" he said. "Coming in here out of the clear blue, taking potshots at everybody with that crazy letter!"

"Potshots!" I said, so mad I was afraid I was going to start crying. "Potshots. What about last summer? Who was taking potshots then?"

"You didn't have any business taking the shortcut," David said. "Dad told you never to come that way."

"Was that any reason to try and *shoot* me? Was that any reason to *kill* Rusty?"

David was squeezing my arm so hard I thought he was going to snap it right in two. "The looters had a dog with them. We found its tracks all around Mr. Talbot. When you took the shortcut and we heard Rusty barking, we thought you were the looters." He looked at me. "Mom's right. Paranoia's the number-one killer. We were all a little crazy last summer. We're all a little crazy all the time, I guess. And then you pull a stunt like bringing that letter home, reminding everybody of everything that's happened, of everybody we've lost...." He let go of my arm and looked down at his hand.

"I told you," I said. "I found it while I was looking for a magazine. I thought you'd all be glad I found it."

"Yeah," he said. "I'll bet."

He went inside and I stayed out a long time, waiting for Dad and Stitch. When I came in, nobody even looked up. Mom was still standing at the window. I could see a star over her head. Mrs. Talbot had stopped crying and was setting the table. Mom dished up the soup and we all sat down. While we were eating, Dad came in.

He had Stitch with him. And all the magazines. "I'm sorry, Mrs. Talbot," he said. "If you'd like, I'll put them under the house and you can send Lynn for them one at a time."

"It doesn't matter," she said. "I don't feel like reading them any more."

Dad put the magazines on the couch and sat down at the card table. Mom dished him up a bowl of soup. "I got the seeds," he said. "The tomato seeds had gotten water-soaked, but the corn and squash were okay." He looked at me. "I had to board up the post office, Lynn," he said. "You understand that, don't you? You understand that I can't let you go there anymore? It's just too dangerous."

"I told you," I said. "I found it. While I was looking for a magazine."

"The fire's going out," he said.

After they shot Rusty, I wasn't allowed to go anywhere for a month for fear they'd shoot me when I came home, not even when I promised to take the long way around. But then Stitch showed up and nothing happened and they let me start going again. I went every day till the end of summer and after that whenever they'd let me. I must have looked through every pile of mail a hundred times before I found the letter from the Clearys. Mrs. Talbot was right about the post office. The letter was in somebody else's box.

Swarm

by Bruce Sterling

Texas-born Bruce Sterling made a startling fictional debut in 1977, when he was 23 years old, with the ingenious and audacious novel Involution Ocean. *He followed it with another in 1980—* The Artificial Kid— *and has published a number of short stories as well. So far he does not seem to have achieved the reputation he deserves, as one of the most inventive and keen-minded science fiction writers to come along in the past decade or two. But I think that that will begin to change in short order: major writers do not long remain in obscurity in the science fiction field, and I suspect Sterling is finally on the verge of some—much overdue—attention.*

I will miss your conversation during the rest of the voyage," the alien said.

Captain-doctor Simon Afriel folded his jeweled hands over his gold-embroidered waistcoat. "I regret it also, ensign," he said in the alien's own hissing language. "Our talks together have been very useful to me. I would have paid to learn so much, but you gave it freely."

"But that was only information," the alien said. He shrouded his bead-bright eyes behind thick nictitating membranes. "We Investors deal in energy, and precious metals. To prize and pursue mere knowledge is an immature racial trait." The alien lifted the long ribbed frill behind his pinhole-sized ears.

"No doubt you are right," Afriel said, despising him. "We humans are as children to other races, however; so a certain immaturity seems natural to us." Afriel pulled off his sunglasses to rub the bridge of his nose. The starship cabin was drenched in searing blue light, heavily ultraviolet. It was the light the Investors preferred, and they were not about to change it for one human passenger.

"You have not done badly," the alien said magnanimously. "You are the kind of race we like to do business with: young, eager, plastic, ready for a wide variety of goods and experiences. We would have contacted you much earlier, but your technology was still too feeble to afford us a profit."

"Things are different now," Afriel said. "We'll make you rich."

"Indeed," the Investor said. The frill behind his scaly head flickered rapidly, a sign of amusement. "Within two hundred years you will be wealthy enough to buy from us the secret of our star-flight. Or perhaps your Mechanist faction will discover the secret through research."

Afriel was annoyed. As a member of the Reshaped faction, he did not appreciate the reference to the rival Mechanists. "Don't put too much stock in mere technical expertise," he said. "Consider the aptitude for languages we Shapers have. It makes our faction a much better trading partner. To a Mechanist, all Investors look alike."

The alien hesitated. Afriel smiled. He had made an appeal to the alien's personal ambition with his last statement, and the hint had been taken. That was where the Mechanists always erred. They tried to treat all Investors equally, using the same programmed routines each time. They lacked imagination.

Something would have to be done about the Mechanists, Afriel thought. Something more permanent than the small but deadly confrontations between isolated ships in the Asteroid Belt and the ice-rich rings of Saturn. Both factions maneuvered constantly looking for a decisive stroke, bribing away each other's best talent, practicing ambush, assassination, and industrial espionage.

Captain-doctor Simon Afriel was a past master of these pursuits. That was why the Reshaped faction had paid the millions of kilowatts necessary to buy his passage. Afriel held doctorates in biochemistry and alien linguistics, and a master's degree in magnetic weapons engineering. He was thirty-eight years old and had been Reshaped according to the state of the art at the time of his conception. His hormonal balance had been altered slightly to compensate for long periods spent in free-fall. He had no appendix. The structure of his heart had been redesigned for greater efficiency, and his large intestine had been altered to produce the vitamins normally made by intestinal bacteria. Genetic engineering and rigorous training in childhood had given him an intelligence quotient of one hundred and eighty. He was not the brightest of the agents of the Ring Council, but he was one of the most mentally stable and the best trusted.

"It seems a shame," the alien said, "that a human of your accomplishments should have to rot for two years in this miserable, profitless outpost."

"The years won't be wasted," Afriel said.

"But why have you chosen to study the Swarm? They can teach you nothing, since they cannot speak. They have no wish to trade, having no tools or technology. They are the only spacefaring race to be essentially without intelligence."

"That alone should make them worthy of study."

"Do you seek to imitate them, then? You would make monsters of yourselves." Again the ensign hesitated. "Perhaps you could do it. It would be bad for business, however."

There came a fluting burst of alien music over the ship's speakers, then a screeching fragment of Investor language. Most of it was too high-pitched for Afriel's ears to follow.

The alien stood, his jeweled skirt brushing the tips of his clawed, bird-like feet. "The Swarm's symbiote has arrived," he said.

"Thank you," Afriel said. When the ensign opened the cabin door, Afriel could smell the Swarm's representative; the creature's warm, yeasty scent had spread rapidly through the starship's recycled air.

Afriel quickly checked his appearance in a pocket mirror. He touched powder to his face and straightened the round velvet hat on his shoulder-length reddish-blond hair. His earlobes glittered with red impact-rubies, thick as his thumbs' ends, mined from the Asteroid Belt. His knee-length coat and waistcoat were of gold brocade; the shirt beneath was of dazzling fineness, woven with red-gold thread. He had dressed to impress the Investors, who expected and appreciated a prosperous look from their customers. How could he impress this new alien? Smell, perhaps. He freshened his perfume.

Beside the starship's secondary air-lock, the Swarm's symbiote was chittering rapidly at the ship's commander. The commander was an old and sleepy Investor, twice the size of most of her crewmen. Her massive head was encrusted in a jeweled helmet. From within the helmet her clouded eyes glittered like cameras.

The symbiote lifted on its six posterior legs and gestured feebly with its four clawed forelimbs. The ship's artificial gravity, a third again as strong as Earth's, seemed to bother it. Its rudimentary eyes, dangling on stalks, were shut tight against the glare. It must be used to darkness, Afriel thought.

The commander answered the creature in its own language. Afriel grimaced, for he had hoped that the creature spoke Investor. Now he would have to learn another language, a language designed for a being without a tongue.

After another brief interchange the commander turned to Afriel. "The symbiote is not pleased with your arrival," she told Afriel in the Investor language. "There has apparently been some disturbance here involving humans, in the recent past. However, I have prevailed upon it to admit you to the Nest. The episode has been recorded. Payment for my diplomatic services will be arranged with your faction when I return to your native star system."

"I thank Your Authority," Afriel said. "Please convey to the symbiote my best personal wishes, and the harmlessness and humility of my intentions. . . ." He broke off short as the symbiote lunged toward him, biting him savagely in the calf of his left leg. Afriel jerked free and leapt backward in the heavy artificial gravity, going into a defensive position. The symbiote had ripped away a long shred of his pants leg; it now crouched quietly, eating it.

"It will convey your scent and composition to its nestmates," said the commander. "This is necessary. Otherwise you would be classed as an invader, and the Swarm's warrior caste would kill you at once."

Afriel relaxed quickly and pressed his hand against the puncture wound to stop the bleeding. He hoped that none of the Investors had noticed his reflexive action. It would not mesh well with his story of being a harmless researcher.

"We will reopen the airlock soon," the commander said phlegmatically, leaning back on her thick reptilian tail. The symbiote continued to munch the shred of cloth. Afriel studied the creature's neckless segmented head. It had a mouth and nostrils; it had bulbous atrophied eyes on stalks; there were hinged slats that might be radio receivers, and two parallel ridges of clumped wriggling antennae, sprouting among three chitinous plates. Their function was unknown to him.

The airlock door opened. A rush of dense, smoky aroma entered the departure cabin. It seemed to bother the half-dozen Investors, who left rapidly. "We will return in six hundred and twelve of your days, as by our agreement," the commander said.

"I thank Your Authority," Afriel said.

"Good luck," the commander said in English. Afriel smiled.

The symbiote, with a sinuous wriggle of its segmented body, crept into the airlock. Afriel followed it. The airlock door shut behind them. The creature said nothing to him but continued munching loudly. The second door opened, and the symbiote sprang through it, into a wide, round, stone tunnel. It vanished at once into the gloom.

Afriel put his sunglasses into a pocket of his jacket and pulled out a pair of infrared goggles. He strapped them to his head and stepped out of the airlock. The artificial gravity vanished, replaced by the almost imperceptible gravity of the Swarm's asteroid nest. Afriel smiled, comfortable for the first time in weeks. Most of his adult life had been spent in free-fall, in the Shaper's colonies in the rings of Saturn.

Squatting in a dark cavity in the side of the tunnel was a disk-headed, furred animal the size of an elephant. It was clearly visible in the infrared of its own body heat. Afriel could hear it breathing. It waited patiently until Afriel had launched himself past it, deeper into the tunnel. Then it took its place in the end of the tunnel, puffing itself up with air until its swollen head securely plugged the end of the corridor. Its multiple legs were firmly planted in sockets in the walls.

The Investor's ship had left. Afriel remained here, inside one of the millions of planetoids that circled the giant star Betelgeuse in a girdling ring with almost five times the mass of Jupiter. As a source of potential wealth it dwarfed the entire solar system, and it belonged, more or less, to the Swarm. At least, no other race had challenged them for it within the memory of the Investors.

Afriel peered up the corridor. It seemed deserted, and without other bodies to cast infrared heat, he could not see very far. Kicking against the wall, he floated hesitantly down the corridor.

He heard a human voice. "Doctor Afriel!"

"Doctor Mirny!" he called out. "This way!"

He first saw a pair of young symbiotes scuttling towards him, the tips of their clawed feet barely touching the walls. Behind them came a woman wearing goggles like his own. She was young, and attractive in the trim, anonymous way of the genetically reshaped.

She screeched something at the symbiotes in their own language, and they stopped, waiting. She coasted forward, and Afriel caught her arm, expertly stopping their momentum.

"You didn't bring any luggage?" she said anxiously.

He shook his head. "We got your warning before I was sent out. I have only the clothes I'm wearing and a few items in my pockets."

She looked at him critically. "Is that what people are wearing in the Rings these days? Things have changed more than I thought."

Afriel looked at his brocaded coat and laughed. "It's a matter of policy. The Investors are always readier to talk to a human who looks ready to do business on a large scale. All the Shapers' representatives dress like this these days. We've stolen a jump on the Mechanists; they still dress in those coveralls." He hesitated, not wanting to offend her. Galina Mirny's intelligence was rated at almost two hundred. Men and women that bright were sometimes flighty and unstable, likely to retreat into private fantasy worlds or become enmeshed in strange and impenetrable webs of plotting and rationalization. High intelligence was the strategy the Shapers had chosen in the struggle for cultural dominance, and they were obliged to stick to it, despite its occasional disadvantages. They had tried breeding the super-bright—those with quotients over two hundred—but so many had defected from the Shapers' colonies that the faction had stopped producing them.

"You wonder about my own clothing," Mirny said.

"It certainly has the appeal of novelty," Afriel said with a smile.

"It was woven from the fibers of a pupa's cocoon," she said. "My original wardrobe was eaten by a scavenger symbiote during the troubles last year. I usually go nude, but I didn't want to offend you by too great a show of intimacy."

Afriel shrugged. "I usually go nude myself in my own environment. If the temperature is constant, then clothes are useless, except for pockets. I have a few tools on my person, but most are of little importance. We're the Reshaped, our tools are here." He tapped his head. "If you can show me a safe place to put my clothes...."

She shook her head. It was impossible to see her eyes for the goggles, which made her expression hard to read. "You've made your first mistake, doctor. There are no places of our own here. It was the same mistake the Mechanist agents made, the same one that almost killed me as well. There is no concept of privacy or property here. This is the Nest. If you seize any part of it for yourself—to store equipment, to sleep in, whatever—then you become an intruder, an enemy. The two Mechanists—a man and a woman—tried to secure an unused chamber for their computer lab. Warriors broke down their door and devoured them. Scavengers ate their equipment, glass, metal, and all."

Afriel smiled coldly. "It must have cost them a fortune to ship all that material here."

Mirny shrugged. "They're wealthier than we are. Their machines, their mining. They meant to kill me, I think.

Surreptitiously, so the warriors wouldn't be upset by a show of violence. They had a computer that was learning the language of the springtails faster than I could."

"But you survived," Afriel pointed out. "And your tapes and reports—especially the early ones, when you still had most of your equipment—were of tremendous interest. The Council is behind you all the way. You've become quite a celebrity in the Rings, during your absence."

"Yes, I expected as much," she said.

Afriel was nonplused. "If I found any deficiency in them," he said carefully, "it was in my own field, alien linguistics." He waved vaguely at the two symbiotes who accompanied her. "I assume you've made great progress in communicating with the symbiotes, since they seem to do all the talking for the Nest."

She looked at him with an unreadable expression and shrugged. "There are at least fifteen different kinds of symbiotes here. Those that accompany me are called the springtails, and they speak only for themselves. They are savages, doctor, who received attention from the Investors only because they can still talk. They were a space-going race at one time, but they've forgotten it. They discovered the Nest and they were absorbed, they became parasites." She tapped one of them on the head. "I tamed these two because I learned to steal and beg food better than they can. They stay with me now and protect me from the larger ones. They are jealous, you know. They have only been with the Nest for perhaps ten thousand years and are still uncertain of their position. They still think, and wonder sometimes. After ten thousand years there is still a little of that left to them."

"Savages," Afriel said. "I can well believe that. One of them bit me while I was still aboard the starship. He left a lot to be desired as an ambassador."

"Yes, I warned him you were coming," said Mirny. "He didn't much like the idea, but I was able to bribe him with food....I hope he didn't hurt you badly."

"A scratch," Afriel said. "I assume there's no chance of infection."

"I doubt it very much. Unless you brought your own bacteria with you."

"Hardly likely," Afriel said, offended. "I have no bacteria. And I wouldn't have brought microorganisms to an alien culture anyway."

Mirny looked away. "I thought you might have some of the special genetically altered ones....I think we can go now. The springtail will have spread your scent by mouth-touching in the subsidiary chamber, ahead of us. It will be spread throughout the Nest in a few hours. Once it reaches the Queen, it will spread very quickly."

Placing her feet against the hard shell of one of the young springtails, she launched herself down the hall. Afriel followed her. The air was warm and he was beginning to sweat under his elaborate clothing, but his antiseptic sweat was odorless.

They exited into a vast chamber dug from the living rock. It was arched and oblong, eighty meters long and about twenty in diameter. It swarmed with members of the Nest.

There were hundreds of them. Most of them were workers, eight-legged and furred, the size of Great Danes. Here and there were members of the warrior caste, horse-sized furry monsters with heavy fanged heads the size and shape of overstuffed chairs.

A few meters away, two workers were carrying a member of the sensor caste, a being whose immense flattened head was attached to an atrophied body that was mostly lungs. The sensor had eyes and its furred chitin sprouted long coiled antennae that twitched feebly as the workers bore it along. The workers clung to the hollowed rock of the chamber walls with hooked and suckered feet.

A paddle-limbed monster with a hairless, faceless head came sculling past them, through the warm reeking air.

The front of its head was a nightmare of sharp grinding jaws and blunt armored acid spouts. "A tunneler," Mirny said. "It can take us deeper into the Nest—come with me." She launched herself toward it and took a handhold on its furry, segmented back. Afriel followed her, joined by the two immature springtails, who clung to the thing's hide with their forelimbs. Afriel shuddered at the warm, greasy feel of its rank, damp fur. It continued to scull through the air, its eight fringed paddle feet catching the air like wings.

"There must be thousands of them," Afriel said.

"I said a hundred thousand in my last report, but that was before I had fully explored the Nest. Even now there are long stretches I haven't seen. They must number close to a quarter of a million. This asteroid is about the size of the Mechanists' biggest base—Ceres. It still has rich veins of carbonaceous material. It's far from mined out."

Afriel closed his eyes. If he were to lose his goggles, he would have to feel his way, blind, through these teeming, twitching, wriggling thousands. "The population's still expanding, then?"

"Definitely," she said. "In fact, the colony will launch a mating swarm soon. There are three dozen male and female alates in the chambers near the Queen. Once they're launched, they'll mate and start new Nests. I'll take you to see them presently." She hesitated. "We're entering one of the fungal gardens now."

One of the young springtails quietly shifted position. Grabbing the tunneler's fur with its forelimbs, it began to gnaw on the cuff of Afriel's pants. Afriel kicked it soundly, and it jerked back, retracting its eyestalks.

When he looked up again, he saw that they had entered a second chamber, much larger than the first. The walls around, overhead and below were buried under an explosive profusion of fungus. The most common types were swollen, barrel-like domes, multi-branched massed thickets, and spaghetti-like tangled extrusions, that moved very slightly in the faint and odorous breeze. Some of the barrels were surrounded by dim mists of exhaled spores.

"You see those caked-up piles beneath the fungus, its growth medium?" Mirny said.

"Yes."

"I'm not sure whether it is a plant form or just some kind of complex biochemical sludge," she said. "The point is that it grows in sunlight, on the outside of the asteroid. A food source that grows in naked space! Imagine what that would be worth, back in the Rings."

"There aren't words for its value," Afriel said.

"It's inedible by itself," she said. "I tried to eat a very small piece of it once. It was like trying to eat plastic."

"Have you eaten well, generally speaking?"

"Yes. Our biochemistry is quite similar to the Swarm's. The fungus itself is perfectly edible. The regurgitate is more nourishing, though. Internal fermentation in the worker hindgut adds to its nutritional value."

Afriel stared. "You grow used to it," Mirny said. "Later I'll teach you how to solicit food from the workers. It's a simple matter of reflex tapping—it's not controlled by pheromones, like most of their behavior." She brushed a long lock of clumped and dirty hair from the side of her face. "I hope the pheromonal samples I sent back were worth the cost of transportation."

"Oh, yes," said Afriel. "The chemistry of them was fascinating. We managed to synthesize most of the compounds. I was part of the research team myself." He hesitated. How far did he dare trust her? She had not been told about the experiment he and his superiors had planned. As far as Mirny knew, he was a simple, peaceful researcher, like herself. The Shapers' scientific community was suspicious of the minority involved in military work and espionage.

As an investment in the future, the Shapers had sent researchers to each of the nineteen alien races described to them by the Investors. This had cost the Shaper economy many gigawatts of precious energy and tons of rare metals and isotopes. In most cases, only two or three researchers could be sent; in seven cases, only one. For the Swarm, Galina Mirny had been chosen. She had gone peacefully, trusting in her intelligence and her good intentions to keep her alive and sane. Those who had sent her had not known whether her findings would be of any use or importance. They had only known that it was imperative that she be sent, even alone, even ill-equipped, before some other faction sent their own people and possibly discovered some technique or fact of overwhelming importance. And Dr. Mirny had indeed discovered such a situation. It had made her mission into a matter of Ring security. That was why Afriel had come.

"You synthesized the compounds?" she said. "Why?"

Afriel smiled disarmingly. "Just to prove to ourselves that we could do it, perhaps."

She shook her head. "No mind-games, Doctor Afriel, please. I came this far partly to escape from such things. Tell me the truth."

Afriel stared at her, regretting that the goggles meant he could not meet her eyes. "Very well," he said. "You should know, then, that I have been ordered by the Ring Council to carry out an experiment that may endanger both our lives."

Mirny was silent for a moment. "You're from Security, then?"

"My rank is captain."

"I knew it.... I knew it when those two Mechanists arrived. They were so polite, and so suspicious—I think they would have killed me at once if they hadn't hoped to bribe or torture some secret out of me. They scared the life out of me, Captain Afriel.... You scare me, too."

"We live in a frightening world, doctor. It's a matter of faction security."

"Everything's a matter of faction security with you lot," she said. "I shouldn't take you any farther, or show you anything more. This Nest, these creatures—they're not *intelligent,* captain. They can't think, they can't learn. They're innocent, primordially innocent. They have no knowledge of good and evil. They have no knowledge of *anything.* The last thing they need is to become pawns in a power struggle within some other race, light-years away."

The tunneler had turned into an exit from the fungal chambers and was paddling slowly along in the warm darkness. A group of creatures like gray, flattened basketballs floated by from the opposite direction. One of them settled on Afriel's sleeve, clinging with frail, whiplike tentacles. Afriel brushed it gently away, and it broke loose, emitting a stream of foul reddish droplets.

"Naturally I agree with you in principle, doctor," Afriel said smoothly. "But consider these Mechanists. Some of their extreme factions are already more than half machine. Do you expect humanitarian motives from them? They're cold, doctor—cold and soulless creatures who can cut a living man or woman to bits and never feel their pain. Most of the other factions hate us. They think we've set ourselves up as racist supermen because we won't interbreed, because we've chosen the freedom to manipulate our own genes. Would you rather that one of these cults do what we must do, and use the results against us?"

"This is double-talk." She looked away. All around them workers laden down with fungus, their jaws full and guts stuffed with it, were spreading out into the Nest, scuttling alongside them or disappearing into branch tunnels departing in every direction, including straight up and straight down. Afriel saw a creature much like a worker, but with only six legs, scuttle past in the opposite direction, overhead. It was a parasite mimic. How long, he wondered, did it take a creature to evolve to look like that?

"It's no wonder that we've had so many defectors, back

in the Rings," she said sadly. "If humanity is so stupid as to work itself into a corner like you describe, then it's better to have nothing to do with them. Better to live alone. Better not to help the madness spread."

"That kind of talk will only get us all killed," Afriel said. "We owe an allegiance to the faction that produced us."

"Tell me truly, captain," she said. "Haven't you ever felt the urge to leave everything—everyone—all your duties and constraints, and just go somewhere to think it all out? Your whole world, and your part in it? We're trained so hard, from childhood, and so much is demanded from us. Don't you think it's made us lose sight of our goals, somehow?"

"We live in space," Afriel said flatly. "Space is an unnatural environment, and it takes an unnatural effort from unnatural people to prosper there. Our minds are our tools, and philosophy has to come second. Naturally I've felt those urges you mention. They're just another threat to guard against. I believe in an ordered society. Technology has unleashed tremendous forces that are ripping society apart. Some one faction must arise from the struggle and integrate things. We who are Reshaped have the wisdom and restraint to do it humanely. That's why I do the work I do." He hesitated. "I don't expect to see our day of triumph. I expect to die in some brushfire conflict, or through assassination. It's enough that I can foresee that day."

"But the arrogance of it, captain!" she said suddenly. The arrogance of your little life and its little sacrifice! Consider the Swarm, if you really want your humane and perfect order. Here it is! Where it's always warm and dark, and it smells good, and food is easy to get, and everything is endlessly and perfectly recycled. The only resources that are ever lost are the bodies of the mating swarms, and a little air from the airlocks when the workers go out to harvest. A Nest like this one could last unchanged for hundreds of thousands of years. Hundreds, of thousands, of years. Who, or what, will remember us and our stupid faction in even a thousand years?"

Afriel shook his head. "That's not a valid comparison. There is no such long view for us. In another thousand years we'll be machines, or gods." He felt the top of his head; his velvet cap was gone. No doubt something was eating it by now.

The tunneler took them even deeper into the honeycombed free-fall maze of the asteroid. They saw the pupal chambers, where pallid larvae twitched in swaddled silk; the main fungal gardens; the graveyard pits, where winged workers beat ceaselessly at the soupy air, feverishly hot from the heat of decomposition. Corrosive black fungus ate the bodies of the dead into coarse black powder, carried off by blackened workers themselves three-quarters dead.

Later they left the tunneler and floated on by themselves. The woman moved with the ease of long habit; Afriel followed her, colliding bruisingly with squeaking workers. There were thousands of them, clinging to ceiling, walls, and floor, clustering and scurrying at every conceivable angle.

Later still they visited the chamber of the winged princes and princesses, and echoing round vault where creatures forty meters long hung crooked-legged in midair. Their bodies were segmented and metallic, with organic rocket nozzles on their thoraxes, where wings might have been. Folded along their sleek backs were radar antennae on long sweeping booms. They looked more like interplanetary probes under construction than anything biological. Workers fed them ceaselessly. Their bulging spiracled abdomens were full of compressed oxygen.

Mirny begged a large chunk of fungus from a passing worker, deftly tapping its antennae and provoking a reflex action. She handed most of the fungus to the two springtails, which devoured it greedily and looked expectantly for more.

Afriel tucked his legs into a lotus position and began chewing with determination on the leathery fungus. It was tough, but tasted good, like smoked meat—a Terran delicacy he had tasted only once. The smell of smoke meant disaster in a Shaper's colony.

Mirny maintained a stony silence. "Food's no problem," Afriel said cheerfully. "Where do we sleep?"

She shrugged. "Anywhere.... there are unused niches and tunnels here and there. I suppose you'll want to see the Queen's chamber next."

"By all means."

"I'll have to get more fungus. The warriors are on guard there and have to be bribed with food."

She gathered an armful of fungus from another worker in the endless stream, and they exited through another tunnel. Afriel, already totally lost, was further confused in the maze of chambers and tunnels. At last they exited into an immense lightless cavern, bright with infrared heat from the Queen's monstrous body. It was the colony's central factory. The fact that it was made of warm and pulpy flesh did not conceal its essentially industrial nature. Tons of predigested fungal pap went into the slick blind jaws at one end. The rounded billows of soft flesh digested and processed it, squirming, sucking, and undulating, with loud, machinelike churnings and gurglings. Out of the other end came an endless conveyorlike blobbed stream of eggs, each one packed in a thick hormonal paste of lubrication. The workers avidly licked the eggs clean and bore them off to nurseries. Each egg was the size of a man's torso.

The process went on and on. There was no day or night here in the lightless center of the asteroid. There was no remnant of a diurnal rhythm in the genes of these creatures. The flow of production was as constant and even as the working of an automated mine.

"This is why I'm here," Afriel murmured in awe. "Just look at this, doctor. The Mechanists have computer-run mining machinery that is generations ahead of ours. But here—in the bowels of this nameless little world, is a genetically run technology that feeds itself, maintains itself, runs itself, efficiently, endlessly, mindlessly. It's the perfect organic tool. The faction that could make use of these tireless workers could make itself an industrial titan. And our knowledge of biochemistry is unsurpassed. We Shapers are just the ones to do it."

"How do you propose to do that?" Mirny asked with open skepticism. "You would have to ship a fertilized queen all the way to the solar system. We could scarcely afford that, even if the Investors would let us, which they wouldn't."

"I don't need an entire colony," Afriel said patiently. "I only need the genetic information from one egg. Our laboratories back in the Rings could clone endless numbers of them."

"But the workers are useless without the rest of the colony to give them orders. They need the pheromones to trigger their behavior modes."

"Exactly," Afriel said. "As it so happens, I possess those pheromones in concentrated form. What I must do now is test them. I must prove that I can use them to make the workers do what I choose. Once I've proven it's possible, I'm authorized to smuggle the genetic information necessary back to the Rings. The Investors won't approve. There are, of course, moral questions involved, and they are not genetically advanced. But we can win their approval back with the profits we make. Best of all, we can beat the Mechanists at their own game."

"You've carried the pheromones here?" Mirny said. "Didn't the Investors suspect something when they found them?"

"Now it's you who has made an error," Afriel said calmly. "You assume that they are infallible. You are wrong. A race without curiosity will never explore every possibility, the way we Shapers did." Afriel pulled up his pants cuff and extended his right leg. "Consider this varicose vein along my shin. Circulatory problems of this sort are common among those who spend a lot of time in free-fall. This vein, however, has been blocked artificially, and its walls biochemically treated to reduce osmosis. Within the vein are ten separate colonies of genetically altered bacteria, each one specially to produce a different Swarm pheromone."

He smiled. "The Investors searched me very thoroughly, including x-rays. They insist, naturally, on knowing about everything transported aboard one of their ships. But the vein appears normal to x-rays, and the bacteria are trapped within compartments in the vein. They are indetectable. I have a small medical kit on my person. It includes a syringe. We can use it to extract the pheromones and test them. When the tests are finished—and I feel sure they will be successful, in fact I've staked my career on it—we can empty the vein and all its compartments. The bacteria will die on contact with air. We can refill the vein with the yolk from a developing embryo. The cells may survive during the trip back, but even if they die, they won't rot. They'll never come in contact with bacteria that can decompose them. Back in the Rings, we can learn to activate and suppress different genes to produce the different castes, just as is done in nature. We'll have millions of workers, armies of warriors if need be, perhaps even organic rocketships, grown from altered alates. If this works, who do you think will remember me then, eh? Me and my arrogant little life and little sacrifice?"

She stared at him; even the bulky goggles could not hide her new respect and even fear. "You really mean to do it, then."

"I made the sacrifice of my time and energy. I expect results, doctor."

"But it's kidnapping. You're talking about breeding a slave race."

Afriel shrugged, with contempt. "You're juggling words, doctor. I'll cause this colony no harm. I may steal some of its workers' labor while they obey my own chemical orders, but that tiny minority won't be missed. I admit to the murder of one egg, but that is no more a crime than a human abortion. Can the theft of one strand of genetic material be called 'kidnapping'? I think not. As for the scandalous idea of a slave race—I reject it out of hand. These creatures are genetic robots. They will no more be slaves than are laser drills or bulldozers. At the very worst, they will be domestic animals."

Mirny considered the issue. It did not take her long. "It's true. It's not as if a common worker will be staring at the stars, pining for its freedom. They're just brainless neuters."

"Exactly, doctor."

"They simply work. Whether they work for us or the Swarm makes no difference to them."

"I see that you've seized on the beauty of the idea."

"And if it worked," Mirny said, "if it worked, our faction would profit astronomically."

Afriel smiled genuinely, unaware of the chilling sarcasm of his expression. "And the personal profit, doctor.... the valuable expertise of the first to exploit the technique." He spoke gently, quietly. "Ever see a nitrogen snowfall on Titan? I think a habitat of one's own there—larger, much larger than anything possible before.... A genuine city, Galina, a place where a man can scrap the rules and discipline that madden him...."

"Now it's you who are talking defection, captain-doctor."

Afriel was silent for a moment, then smiled with an effort. "Now you've ruined my perfect reverie," he said. "Besides, what I was describing was the well-earned retirement of a wealthy man, not some self-indulgent hermitage.... there's a clear but subtle difference." He hesitated. "In any case, I conclude that you're with me in this project?"

She laughed and touched his arm. There was something uncanny about the small sound of her laugh, drowned by a great organic rumble from the Queen's monstrous intestines.... "Do you expect me to resist your arguments for two years? Better that I give in now and save us friction."

"Yes."

"After all, you won't do any harm to the colony. They'll never know anything has happened. And if their genetic line is successfully reproduced back home, there'll never be any reason for humanity to bother them again."

"True enough," said Afriel, though in the back of his mind he instantly thought of the fabulous wealth of Betelguese's asteroid system. A day would come, inevitably, when humanity would move to the stars en masse, in earnest. It would be well to know the ins and outs of every race that might become a rival.

"I'll help you as best I can," she said. There was a moment's silence. "Have you seen enough of this area?"

"Yes." They left the Queen's chamber.

"I didn't think I'd like you at first," she said candidly. "I think I like you better now. You seem to have a sense of humor that most Security people lack."

"It's not a sense of humor," Afriel said sadly. "It's a sense of irony disguised as one."

There were no days in the unending stream of hours that followed. There were only ragged periods of sleep, apart at first, later together, as they held each other in free-fall. The sexual feel of skin and body became an anchor to their common humanity, a divided, frayed humanity so many lightyears away that the concept no longer had any meaning to them. Life in the warm and swarming tunnels was the here and now; the two of them were like germs in a bloodstream, moving ceaselessly with the pulsing ebb and flow. They tested the pheromones, one by one, as the hours stretched into months and time grew meaningless.

The pheromonal workings were complex, but not impossibly difficult. The first of the ten pheromones was a simple grouping stimulus, causing large numbers of workers to gather as the pheromone was spread from palp to palp. The workers then waited for further instructions; if none were forthcoming, they dispersed. To work effectively, the pheromones had to be given in a mix, or series, like computer commands; number one, grouping, for instance, together with the third pheromone, a transferral order, which caused the workers to empty any given chamber and move its effects to another. The ninth pheromone had the best industrial possibilities; it was a building order, causing the workers to gather tunnelers and dredgers and set them to work. Others were annoying; the tenth pheromone provoked grooming behavior, and the workers' furry palps stripped off the remaining rags of Afriel's clothing. The eighth pheromone sent the workers off to harvest material on the asteroid's surface, and in their eagerness to observe its effects the two explorers were almost trapped and swept off into space.

The two of them no longer feared the warrior caste. They knew that a dose of the sixth pheromone would send them scurrying off to defend the eggs, just as it sent the workers to tend them. Mirny and Afriel took advantage of this and secured their own chambers, dug by chemically hijacked workers and defended by a hijacked airlock guardian. They had their own fungal gardens to refresh the air, stocked with the fungus they liked best, and digested by a worker they kept drugged for their own food use. From constant stuffing and lack of exercise the worker had swollen up into its replete form and hung from one wall like a monstrous grape.

Afriel was tired. He had been without sleep recently for a long time; how long, he didn't know. His body rhythms had not adjusted as well as Mirny's, and he was prone to fits of depression and irritability that he had to repress with an effort. "The Investors will be back sometime," he said. "Sometime soon."

Mirny shrugged. "The Investors," she said, and followed the remark with something in the language of the springtails, that he didn't catch. Despite his linguistic training, Afriel had never caught up with her in her use of the springtails' grating jargon. His training was almost a liability; the springtail language had decayed so much that it was a pidgin tongue, without rules or regularity. He knew enough to give them simple orders, and with his partial control of the warriors he had the power to back it up. The springtails were afraid of him, and the two juveniles that Mirny had tamed had grown into fat, overgrown tyrants that freely terrorized their elders. Afriel had been too busy to seriously study the springtails or the other symbiotes. There were too many practical matters at hand.

"If they come too soon, I won't be able to finish my latest study," she said in English.

Afriel pulled off his infrared goggles and knotted them tightly around his neck. "There's a limit, Galina," he said, yawning. "You can only memorize so much data without equipment. We'll just have to wait quietly until we can get back. I hope the Investors aren't shocked when they see me. I lost a fortune with those clothes."

"It's been so dull since the mating swarm was launched. And we've had to stop the experiments to let your vein heal. If it weren't for the new growth in the alates' chamber, I'd be bored to death." She pushed greasy hair from her face with both hands. "Are you going to sleep?"

"Yes, if I can."

"You won't come with me? I keep telling you that this new growth is important. I think it's a new caste. It's definitely not an alate. It has eyes like an alate, but it's clinging to the wall."

"It's probably not a Swarm member at all, then," he said tiredly, humoring her. "It's probably a parasite, an alate mimic. Go on and see it, if you want to. I'll be here waiting for you."

He heard her leave. Without his infrareds on, the darkness was still not quite total; there was a very faint luminosity from the steaming, growing fungus in the chamber beyond. The stuffed worker replete moved slightly on the wall, rustling and gurgling. He fell asleep.

When he awoke, Mirny had not yet returned. He was not alarmed. First, he visited the original airlock tunnel, where the Investors had first left him. It was irrational—the Investors always fulfilled their contracts—but he feared that they would arrive someday, become impatient, and leave without him. The Investors would have to wait, of course. Mirny could keep them occupied in the short time it would take him to hurry to the nursery and rob a developing egg of its living cells. It was best that the egg be as fresh as possible.

Later he ate. He was munching fungus in one of the anterior chambers when Mirny's two tamed springtails found him. "What do you want?" he asked in their language.

"Food-giver no good," the larger one screeched, waving its forelegs in brainless agitation. "Not work, not sleep."

"Not move," the second one said. It added hopefully, "Eat it now?"

Afriel gave them some of his food. They ate it, seemingly more out of habit than real appetite, which alarmed him. "Take me to her," he told them.

The two springtails scurried off; he followed them easily, adroitly dodging and weaving through the crowds of workers. They led him several miles through the network, to the alates' chamber. There they stopped, confused. "Gone," the large one said.

The chamber was empty. Afriel had never seen it empty before, and it was very unusual for the Swarm to waste so much space. He felt dread. "Follow the food-giver," he said. "Follow smell."

The springtails snuffled without much enthusiasm along one wall; they knew he had no food and were reluctant to do anything without an immediate reward. At last one of them picked up the scent, or pretended to, and followed it up across the ceiling and into the mouth of a tunnel.

It was hard for Afriel to see much in the abandoned chamber; there was not enough infrared heat. He leapt upward after the springtail.

He heard the roar of a warrior and the springtail's choked-off screech. It came flying from the tunnel's mouth, a spray of clotted fluid bursting from its ruptured head. It tumbled end over end until it hit the far wall with a flaccid crunch. It was already dead.

The second springtail fled at once, screeching with grief and terror. Afriel landed on the lip of the tunnel, sinking into a crouch as his legs soaked up momentum. He could smell the acrid stench of the warrior's anger, a pheromone so thick that even a human could scent it. Dozens of other warriors would group here within minutes, or seconds. Behind the enraged warrior he could hear workers and tunnelers shifting and cementing rock.

He might be able to control one enraged warrior, but never two, or twenty. He launched himself from the chamber wall and out an exit.

He searched for the other springtail—he felt sure he could recognize it, it was so much bigger than the others—but he could not find it. With its keen sense of smell, it could easily hide from him if it wanted to.

Mirny did not return. Uncountable hours passed. He slept again. He returned to the alates' chambers; there were warriors on guard there, warriors that were not interested in food and opened their immense serrated fangs when he approached. They looked ready to rip him apart; the faint reek of aggressive pheromones hung about the place like a fog. He did not see any symbiotes of any kind on the warriors' bodies. There was one species, a thing like a huge tick, that clung only to warriors, but even the ticks were gone.

He returned to his chambers to wait and think. Mirny's body was not in the garbage pits. Of course, it was possible that something else might have eaten her. Should he extract the remaining pheromone from the spaces in his vein and try to break into the alates' chamber? He suspected that Mirny, or whatever was left of her, was somewhere in the tunnel where the springtail had been killed. He had never explored that tunnel himself. There were thousands of tunnels he had never explored.

He felt paralyzed by indecision and fear. If he were quiet, if he did nothing, the Investors might arrive at any moment. He could tell the Ring Council anything he wanted about Mirny's death; if he had the genetics with him, no one would quibble. He did not love her; he respected her, but not enough to give up his life, or his faction's investment. He had not thought of the Ring Council in a long time, and the thought sobered him. He would have to explain his decision....

He was still in a brown study when he heard a whoosh of air as his living airlock deflated itself. Three warriors had come for him. There was no reek of anger about them. They moved slowly and carefully. He knew better than to try to resist. One of them seized him gently in its massive jaws and carried him off.

It took him to the alates' chamber and into the guarded tunnel. A new, large chamber had been excavated at the end of the tunnel. It was filled almost to bursting by a black-splattered white mass of flesh. In the center of the soft speckled mass were a mouth and two damp, shining eyes, on stalks. Long tendrils like conduits dangled, writhing, from a clumped ridge above the eyes. The tendrils ended in pink, fleshy plug-like clumps.

One of the tendrils had been thrust through Mirny's skull. Her body hung in midair, limp as wax. Her eyes were open, but blind.

Another tendril was plugged into the braincase of a mutated worker. The worker still had the pallid tinge of a larva; it was shrunken and deformed, and its mouth had the wrinkled look of a human mouth. There was a blob like a tongue in the mouth, and white ridges like human teeth. It had no eyes.

It spoke with Mirny's voice. "Captain-doctor Afriel. . . ."

"Galina. . . ."

"I have no such name. You may address me as Swarm."

Afriel vomited. The central mass was an immense head. Its brain almost filled the room.

It waited politely until Afriel had finished.

"I find myself awakened again," Swarm said dreamily. "I am pleased to see that it is no major emergency that concerns me. Instead it is a threat that has become almost routine." It hesitated delicately. Mirny's body moved slightly in midair; her breathing was inhumanly regular. The eyes opened and closed. "Another young race."

"What are you?"

"I am the Swarm. That is, I am one of its castes. I an a tool, an adaptation; my specialty is intelligence. I am not often needed. It is good to be needed again."

"Have you been here all along? Why didn't you greet us? We'd have dealt with you. We meant no harm."

The wet mouth on the end of the plug made laughing sounds. "Like yourself, I enjoy irony," it said. "It is a pretty trap you have found yourself in, captain-doctor. You meant to make the Swarm work for you and your race. You meant to breed us and study us and use us. It is an excellent plan, but one we hit upon long before your race evolved."

Stung by panic, Afriel's mind raced frantically. "You're an intelligent being," he said. "There's no reason to do us any harm. Let us talk together. We can help you."

"Yes," Swarm agreed. "You will be helpful. Your companion's memories tell me that this is one of those uncomfortable periods when galactic intelligence is rife. Intelligence is a great bother. It makes all kinds of trouble for us."

"What do you mean?"

"You are a young race and lay great stock by your own cleverness," Swarm said. "As usual, you fail to see that intelligence is not a survival trait."

Afriel wiped sweat from his face. "We've done well," he

said. "We came to you, and peacefully. You didn't come to us."

"I refer to exactly that," Swarm said urbanely. "This urge to expand, to explore, to develop, is just what will make you extinct. You naively suppose that you can continue to feed your curiosity indefinitely. It is an old story, pursued by countless races before you. Within a thousand years—perhaps a little longer—your species will vanish."

"You intend to destroy us, then? I warn you it will not be an easy task—"

"Again you miss the point. Knowledge is power! Do you suppose that fragile little form of yours—your primitive legs, your ludicrous arms and hands, your tiny, scarcely wrinkled brain—can *contain* all that power? Certainly not! Already your race is flying to pieces under the impact of your own expertise. The original human form is becoming obsolete. Your own genes have been altered, and you, captain-doctor, are a crude experiment. In a hundred years you will be a Neanderthal. In a thousand years you will not even be a memory. Your race will go the same way as a thousand others."

"And what way is that?"

"I do not know." The thing on the end of the Swarm's arm made a chuckling sound. "They have passed beyond my ken. They have all discovered something, learned something, that has caused them to transcend my understanding. It may be that they even transcend *being*. At any rate, I cannot sense their presence anywhere. They seem to do nothing, they seem to interfere in nothing; for all intents and purposes, they seem to be dead. Vanished. They may have become gods, or ghosts. In either case, I have no wish to join them."

"So then—so then you have—"

"Intelligence is very much a two-edged sword, captain-doctor. It is useful only up to a point. It interferes with the business of living. Life, and intelligence, do not mix very well. They are not at all closely related, as you childishly assume."

"But you, then—you are a rational being—"

"I am a tool, as I said." The mutated device on the end of its arm made a sighing noise. "When you began your pheromonal experiments, the chemical imbalance became apparent to the Queen. It triggered certain genetic patterns within her body, and I was reborn. Chemical sabotage is a problem that can best be dealt with by intelligence. I am a brain replete, you see, specially designed to be far more intelligent than any young race. Within three days I was fully self-conscious. Within five days I had deciphered these markings on my body. They are the genetically encoded history of my race... within five days and two hours I recognized the problem at hand and knew what to do. I am now doing it. I am six days old."

"What is it you intend to do?"

"Your race is a very vigorous one. I expect it to be here, competing with us, within five hundred years. Perhaps much sooner. It will be necessary to make a thorough study of such a rival. I invite you to join our community on a permanent basis."

"What do you mean?"

"I invite you to become a symbiote. I have here a male and a female, whose genes are altered and therefore without defects. You make a perfect breeding pair. It will save me a great deal of trouble with cloning."

"You think I'll betray my race and deliver a slave species into your hands?"

"Your choice is simple, captain-doctor. Remain an intelligent, living being, or become a mindless puppet, like your partner. I have taken over all the functions of her nervous system; I can do the same to you."

"I can kill myself."

"That might be troublesome, because it would make me resort to developing a cloning technology. Technology, though I am capable of it, is painful to me. I am a genetic artifact; there are fail-safes within me that prevent me from taking over the Nest for my own uses. That would mean falling into the same trap of progress as other intelligent races. For similar reasons, my lifespan is limited. I will live for only a thousand years, until your race's brief flurry of energy is over and peace resumes once more."

"Only a thousand years?" Afriel laughed bitterly. "What then? You kill off my descendants, I assume, having no further use for them."

"No. We have not killed any of the fifteen other races we have taken for defensive study. It has not been necessary. Consider that small scavenger floating by your head, captain-doctor, that is feeding on your vomit. Five hundred million years ago its ancestors made the galaxy tremble. When they attacked us, we unleashed their own kind upon them. Of course, we altered our side, so that they were smarter, tougher, and, of course, totally loyal to us. Our Nests were the only world they knew, and they fought with a valor and inventiveness we never could have matched. ...Should your race arrive to exploit us, we will naturally do the same."

"We humans are different."

"Of course."

"A thousand years here won't change us. You will die and our descendants will take over this Nest. We'll be running things, despite you, in a few generations. The darkness won't make any difference."

"Of course not. You don't need eyes here. You don't need anything."

"You'll allow me to stay alive? To teach them anything I want?"

"Certainly, captain-doctor. We are doing you a favor, in all truth. In a thousand years your descendants here will be the only remnants of the human race. We are generous with our immortality; we will take it upon ourselves to preserve you."

"You're wrong, Swarm. You're wrong about intelligence, and you're wrong about everything else. Maybe other races would crumble into parasitism, but we humans are different."

"Certainly. You'll do it, then?"

"Yes. I accept your challenge. And I will defeat you."

"Splendid. When the Investors return here, the springtails will say that they have killed you, and will tell them to never return. They will not return. The humans should be the next to arrive."

"If I don't defeat you, they will."

"Perhaps." Again it sighed. "I'm glad I don't have to absorb you. I would have missed your conversation."

The Nebula Winners, 1965-1981

1965

Best Novel: DUNE *by Frank Herbert*

Best Novella: "The Saliva Tree" *by Brian W. Aldiss* "He Who Shapes" *by Roger Zelazny* (tie)

Best Novelette: "The Doors of His Face, the Lamps of His Mouth" *by Roger Zelazny*

Best Short Story: "'Repent, Harlequin!' Said the Ticktockman" *by Harlan Ellison*

1966

Best Novel: FLOWERS FOR ALGERNON *by Daniel Keyes* BABEL-1 *by Samuel R. Delany* (tie)

Best Novella: "The Last Castle" *by Jack Vance*

Best Novelette: "Call Him Lord" *by Gordon R. Dickson*

Best Short Story: "The Secret Place" *by Richard McKenna*

1967

Best Novel: THE EINSTEIN INTERSECTION *by Samuel R. Delany*

Best Novella: "Behold the Man" *by Michael Moorcock*

Best Novelette: "Gonna Roll the Bones" *by Fritz Leiber*

Best Short Story: "Aye, and Gomorrah" *by Samuel R. Delany*

1968

Best Novel: RITE OF PASSAGE *by Alexei Panshin*
Best Novella: "Dragonrider" *by Anne McCaffrey*
Best Novelette: "Mother to the World" *by Richard Wilson*
Best Short Story: "The Planners" *by Kate Wilhelm*

1969

Best Novel: THE LEFT HAND OF DARKNESS *by Ursula K. Le Guin*
Best Novella: "A Boy and His Dog" *by Harlan Ellison*
Best Novelette: "Time Considered as a Helix of Semi-Precious Stones" *by Samuel R. Delany*
Best Short Story: "Passengers" *by Robert Silverberg*

1970

Best Novel: RINGWORLD *by Larry Niven*
Best Novella: "Ill Met in Lankhmar" *by Fritz Leiber*
Best Novelette: "Slow Sculpture" *by Theodore Sturgeon*
Best Short Story: No award

1971

Best Novel: A TIME OF CHANGES *by Robert Silverberg*
Best Novella: "The Missing Men" *by Katherine MacLean*
Best Novelette: "The Queen of Air and Darkness" *by Poul Anderson*
Best Short Story: "Good News from the Vatican" *by Robert Silverberg*

1972

Best Novel: THE GODS THEMSELVES *by Isaac Asimov*
Best Novella: "A Meeting with Medusa" *by Arthur C. Clarke*
Best Novelette: "Goat Song" *by Poul Anderson*
Best Short Story: "When It Changed" *by Joanna Russ*

1973

Best Novel: RENDEZVOUS WITH RAMA *by Arthur C. Clarke*
Best Novella: "The Death of Doctor Island" *by Gene Wolfe*
Best Novelette: "Of Mist, and Grass, and Sand" *by Vonda N. McIntyre*
Best Short Story: "Love Is the Plan the Plan Is Death" *by James Tiptree, Jr.*

1974

Best Novel: THE DISPOSSESSED *by Ursula K. Le Guin*
Best Novella: "Born with the Dead" *by Robert Silverberg*
Best Novelette: "If the Stars Are Gods" *by Gordon Eklund and Gregory Benford*
Best Short Story: "The Day before the Revolution" *by Ursula K. Le Guin*
Grand Master: *Robert A. Heinlein*

1975

Best Novel: THE FOREVER WAR *by Joe Haldeman*
Best Novella: "Home Is the Hangman" *by Roger Zelazny*
Best Novelette: "San Diego Lightfoot Sue" *by Tom Reamy*
Best Short Story: "Catch That Zeppelin!" *by Fritz Leiber*
Grand Master: *Jack Williamson*

1976

Best Novel: MAN PLUS *by Frederik Pohl*
Best Novella: "Houston, Houston, Do You Read?" *by James Tiptree, Jr.*
Best Novelette: "The Bicentennial Man" *by Isaac Asimov*
Best Short Story: "A Crowd of Shadows" *by Charles L. Grant*
Grand Master: *Clifford Simak*

1977

Best Novel: GATEWAY *by Frederik Pohl*
Best Novella: "Stardance" *by Spider and Jeanne Robinson*
Best Novelette: "The Screwfly Solution" *by Raccoona Sheldon*
Best Short Story: "Jeffty Is Five" *by Harlan Ellison*
Grand Master: *Jack Williamson*

1978

Best Novel: DREAMSNAKE *by Vonda N. McIntyre*
Best Novella: "The Persistence of Vision" *by John Varley*
Best Novelette: "A Glow of Candles, A Unicorn's Eye" *by Charles L. Grant*
Best Short Story: "Stone" *by Edward Bryant*
Grand Master: *L. Sprague de Camp*

1979

Best Novel: THE FOUNTAINS OF PARADISE *by Arthur C. Clarke*
Best Novella: "Enemy Mine" *by Barry Longyear*
Best Novelette: "Sandkings" *by George R. R. Martin*
Best Short Story: "giANTS" *by Edward Bryant*

1980

Best Novel: TIMESCAPE *by Gregory Benford*
Best Novella: "The Unicorn Tapestries" *by Suzy McKee Charnas*
Best Novelette: "The Ugly Chickens" *by Howard Waldrop*
Best Short Story: "Grotto of the Dancing Deer" *by Clifford D. Simak*
Grand Master: *Fritz Leiber*

1981

Best Novel: THE CLAW OF THE CONCILIATOR *by Gene Wolfe*
Best Novella: "The Saturn Game" *by Poul Anderson*
Best Novelette: "The Quickening" *by Michael Bishop*